Traci Douglass is a *USA* ̅ ̅ ̅ ̅ ̅
romance author with Mil ̅ ̅ ̅ ̅
Publishing and Tule Publishing, and has an MFA in
Writing Popular Fiction from Seton Hill University.
She writes sometimes funny, usually awkward,
always emotional stories about strong, quirky,
wounded characters overcoming past adversity
to find their for ever person and heartfelt, healing
happily-ever-afters. Connect with her through her
website: tracidouglassbooks.com.

Sue MacKay lives with her husband in
New Zealand's beautiful Marlborough Sounds,
with the water on her doorstep and the birds and
the trees at her back door. It is the perfect setting
to indulge her passions of entertaining friends by
cooking them sumptuous meals, drinking fabulous
wine, going for hill walks or kayaking around the
bay—and, of course, writing stories.

FAMILY OF THREE UNDER THE TREE

TRACI DOUGLASS

BROODING VET FOR THE WALLFLOWER

SUE MacKAY

MILLS & BOON

First published in Great Britain 2024
by Mills & Boon, an imprint of HarperCollins*Publishers* Ltd,
1 London Bridge Street, London, SE1 9GF

www.harpercollins.co.uk

HarperCollins*Publishers* Macken House, 39/40 Mayor Street Upper, Dublin 1, D01 C9W8, Ireland

Family of Three Under the Tree © 2024 Traci Douglass

Brooding Vet for the Wallflower © 2024 Sue MacKay

ISBN: 978-0-263-32178-4

11/24

This book contains FSC™ certified paper and other controlled sources to ensure responsible forest management.

For more information visit www.harpercollins.co.uk/green.

Printed and Bound in the UK using 100% Renewable Electricity at CPI Group (UK) Ltd, Croydon, CR0 4YY

FAMILY OF THREE UNDER THE TREE

TRACI DOUGLASS

MILLS & BOON

To Charlotte,
the editorial steward of my first 17 books
with Mills & Boon.
Thank you for all your guidance and support. <3

And to Annie,
my new editor guide.
Cheers to 17 more together, starting with this one! <3

CHAPTER ONE

Dr. Sam Perkins inhaled the pine-scented air as he walked up the curving sidewalk to his rental place in Wyckford, Massachusetts. For now, this house worked fine, even if it made his latent handyman skills itch to be used again. Renovating things relaxed him, and had helped him work his way through medical school while keeping him sane despite the crazy hours. Kept him going day to day as he worked on one project after another even as he slowly lost his beloved wife to ALS. Something about the smell of sawdust and fixing what was broken calmed and focused him the same way his patients and surgeries did. He'd always been a caretaker, first for his single mother as a kid, and now for his daughter, Ivy. It was what he did, who he was.

The approaching winter was still a novelty though. In San Diego, where he and his daughter had moved from two years ago after his wife passed away, the temperatures stayed consistently around seventy degrees and the skies were reliably clear and blue. Here, in Massachusetts in December, the temperatures fluctuated between cold and colder, and the threat of nor'easters could chill you to the bone. Last year, he'd been caught off guard by the snowfall. This year, even though Thanksgiving had just happened and there were no storms in the forecast, he was prepared with both a heavy-duty shovel and a snowblower, just in case.

He drew in another deep breath, hoping the crisp air would perk him up and dissolve the stress of the day. Since taking over as head of neurosurgery at Wyckford General Hospital this past September, his plate was beyond full, with what seemed like endless rounds office hours, emergency consults in the ER and follow-ups with the patients in his ALS research study. Amyotrophic lateral sclerosis was a progressive neurodegenerative disease that affected nerve cells in the brain and spinal cord. It had claimed his wife, despite Sam's valiant efforts to the contrary, and Sam was determined to find a cure, even if it was too late to save Natalia. He owed her that much for his failure.

Light snowflakes began falling, landing on his cheeks as he stepped up to his door. The neighborhood had a quaint, small-town vibe, with lots of well-kept homes, manicured lawns and even the occasional white picket fence. Very different from the modern, contemporary Mission Hills home they'd had on the West Coast, but still nice.

When Sam walked inside, the first thing that greeted him was the aroma of vinegar from kimchi and the earthy, miso-like scent of doenjang jjigae—a hearty Korean stew with vegetables and beef in broth. The second was their overeager mutt, Spork. He was part shih tzu, part schnauzer, and all energy. Sam toed off his boots and set them by Ivy's near the heating vent on the floor, then scratched the dog behind the ears. They'd adopted Spork from the local rescue shelter and the canine was settling in just fine, at least based on the number of toys scattered all over the house.

"Hi, Daddy," his daughter called from where she sat at the island in the kitchen down the hall. Ivy's backpack rested on the stool beside her and was almost as big as she was. Sam couldn't remember ever having that much homework in first grade, but apparently times had changed.

"Hi, *yeobo*," he called back, using his pet name for his daughter as he tossed his keys onto the side table then walked toward the delicious smells from his childhood, Spork still circling his ankles with his favorite octopus stuffed animal in his mouth. Sam gave Ivy a kiss on the cheek. "How was school?"

"Good. Adi and I got to pet an iguana today."

"Wow." Sam grinned as he turned to greet the nanny. "Hey, Hala."

"Mr. Perkins." The woman bowed slightly, her black hijab covering her gray hair. In her early seventies, she'd emigrated from Jordan to the US with her husband almost thirty years ago and had worked as a nanny ever since. She also did some housekeeping for Sam and picked Ivy up from school when he had to work late. They were lucky to have her, even if Hala had no qualms about giving Sam life advice whether he needed it or not. "Dinner should be ready shortly. I heated up something from the freezer."

"Thank you." Sam turned back to his daughter. "An iguana, huh? That sounds cool."

"It was!" Ivy swiveled slightly, her pink-stockinged feet tapping against the legs of her stool. "His name was Fred."

"Fred the iguana." Sam snorted. "Got it."

He moved the backpack to take a seat on the other stool. At least the kitchen in their rental had been updated. Quartz countertops gleamed under the recessed lighting, and new stainless steel appliances and freshly painted cabinets completed the modern decor. Sam wasn't the best cook ever, but he knew a few good recipes, most learned at the hip of his Korean mother, who'd insisted he learn to fend for himself when he went off to college. The others had been gleaned from Natalia's Italian heritage. An odd culinary mix but a tasty one. Meal prep, which Sam did on the weekends, was a lifesaver for him.

"Anything else interesting happen today?" he asked his daughter. His mom had always led with that question after school, and it felt like a tradition now. Sam's dad had left when he was just a baby, so it had always been the two of them. He'd gotten his first job as a bagger at a grocery store near their home after school when he'd been just thirteen to help pay the bills. "What did you learn?"

Ivy continued coloring the rainbow dinosaur in front of her. "I learned about butterflies and states and pastrami."

Sam glanced at Hala, who appeared to be holding back a laugh, before looking back at Ivy, confused. "Pastrami?"

"Yeah." Ivy nodded. "The stars are cool!"

"Oh. Right." Sam bit back a smile of his own. "You mean astronomy."

"That's what I said, Daddy. Pastrami."

Chuckling, Sam pushed to his feet and ruffled his little girl's hair. He was still wearing his scrubs from the hospital and needed to shower and change before dinner. "Be right back."

"Wait, Daddy," his daughter called before he'd made it out of the room. "I didn't tell you the most exciting part!"

Sam turned back, steeling himself for just about anything. "And what's that?"

"Ice, Ice Baby."

Sam frowned, leaning a shoulder against the door frame, trying to puzzle out what that meant. "The song?"

"No. The town pop-up festival," Hala supplied helpfully. "The town has done it every year that my husband and I have lived in Wyckford. It's put on by the local town council once the weather gets cold enough to support an ice rink. The fire department sets it up in the town square. All proceeds go to support the local food bank."

"Can we go, Daddy? Please?" Ivy said, so excited she was practically bouncing on her stool. "I've never been ice-skating before and Adi's going and there's hot cocoa and Santa and please! I can't miss it!"

He sighed, still processing her stream-of-consciousness chatter. His first instinct was to say no. Standing around in the freezing cold after working at the hospital all day wasn't exactly Sam's idea of an enjoyable time. But Christmas was Ivy's favorite holiday, and they were trying to start a new life and new traditions here in town. And he couldn't let her down, especially when it was obvious from her excitement that she really wanted to go. Plus, he'd promised himself he'd make this year's holiday special for his daughter, so...

"Fine," he said, scrubbing a hand over his face. "When is it?"

"It's a secret," Ivy said, grinning.

"A secret?"

"They don't announce the dates ahead of time," Hala said. "It just pops up one day."

"Great." Sam wasn't a man who enjoyed surprises. In his experience, they were bad news.

"Yay!" Ivy ran over to hug his legs in appreciation before scrabbling back up on her stool to finish her dinosaur before dinner. "This is going to be the best Christmas ever!"

Sam really hoped that was true. They could use a bit of brightness and cheer after all the heartache in California, and he felt obligated to do his part to make that happen, even if he wasn't thrilled about it. He walked down the hall to the master bedroom and closed the door, then stripped before heading into his attached bathroom and stepping into the shower for a quick scrub and rinse. And sure, maybe he'd been told over the years that he could be a bit of a buzzkill because of his penchant for analysis and logic and detail, but those same qualities served him well when it came to his career—and to his skills as a caretaker. Seeing what people needed and fulfilling those needs. In truth, he honestly didn't care what other people thought. Living with a terminally ill person had taught him that. Losing Natalia had taught him the lesson that the important things in his life were his work and his family and protecting and serving those who relied on him. And perhaps he did use those duties as a barrier to keep people who weren't part of that circle away sometimes, especially after losing his wife. Better to avoid getting entangled with others than risk failing anyone else ever again. He had enough to handle with Ivy and his patients.

Letting people in, letting them help you, isn't a weakness, you know.

Those had been some of Natalia's final words to him before her passing. And while they were true, Sam hadn't been ready to listen then. Still wasn't ready to listen now. Relying on other people, allowing them into his life and heart, required a level of trust and vulnerability he never wanted to experience again. So, until further notice, he planned to stick to his status quo. Even if it was lonely sometimes.

He shut off the water and grabbed a towel to dry off, then padded into his bedroom to put on fresh jeans and a dark green sweater before pulling on socks and padding back to the kitchen to eat. Hala had just set dinner on the island and was serving them each up a bowl of stew and kimchi before getting one herself. Her husband wasn't picking her up until later due to a late shift at the hospital that night. He ran the hospital's environmental services department.

They chatted about their days while they ate, and Sam was grateful his daughter seemed to be settling in so well. She even had a best friend now. He took another bite of stew, ignoring the odd pinch of melancholy as memories of eating this same dish with his mother flooded in. He hadn't made many new connections in town himself, being so busy and all. But he was surrounded by people all the time at work, so it wasn't like he was a hermit. Plus, he chatted with his neighbors when he took Spork for walks. Or picked Ivy up from school. And while he often found himself awake at night and staring at the ceiling, wondering if the Natalia-sized hole inside him would ever heal, that was life, wasn't it? His mom used to tell him a bend in the road was not the end of the road. His life was different now than he'd expected, but he would make it work. He always did. Better than getting his heart stomped on and obliterated by grief. He was always the strong one, the dependable one, the person who took care of everyone else. The sooner he got over whatever this momentary bout of melancholy was the better.

Ivy needed him, and Sam didn't want any more complications in his life.

"Can I, Daddy?" Ivy asked, drawing him out of his thoughts.

Sam wiped his mouth with his napkin to hide the fact he hadn't been paying attention. "Can you what, *yeobo*?"

"Spend the night tonight at Adi's house after the meeting?" Ivy said. "Please? She said it was all right with her parents."

"I don't know." Sam frowned. It was a school night, and sleepovers were usually restricted to weekends.

"Remember I have the day off tomorrow, Dr. Perkins," Hala added.

And Sam had a full schedule the next day, which would take him well into the night, so maybe it wasn't such a bad idea after all. "You're sure it's okay with her parents?"

"Yes, Daddy." Ivy gave him a solemn nod. "You can ask them yourself when you drop me off at the meeting."

"What meeting?" Sam had a feeling he'd missed way more of their conversation than he'd thought.

"The town hall meeting. Adi said you can bring me there, and I'll go home after with them."

"Adi said, huh?" Sam shook his head. His daughter's new best friend sounded about as bossy as her aunt. Dr. Riley Turner was a radiologist who often worked with Sam on the scans for his research study. While Sam got along fine with the woman on a professional level, that's where it ended. They exchanged pleasantries at work, discussed results after scans, and that was all. And the only thing he knew about these monthly town halls was that they were basically the small-town equivalent of reality TV, where everyone went to see and be seen.

Not exactly his cup of tea, but Ivy was still watching him, practically brimming with anticipation, so he finally gave in. "Fine. Now hurry up and eat so we can get you downtown."

People said you could never go home again, but in Riley's case, she'd never left.

At first, she'd stayed in Wyckford because she'd been too busy training to be a radiologist and rebelling against the rules her family had always imposed on her. Then later, following the car accident two years ago that had killed her parents and left Riley with a severe spinal cord injury, she'd been too sick. Even now, she was still trying to get back to the way her life had been before, working hard in PT with the hopes she might walk unassisted again someday.

For a long time, she'd imagined the most awful thing that could possibly happen to her would be living in her older brother Brock's shadow forever. But then the accident had shown her a whole new level of awful. Now she knew how precious life and freedom and independence were, and she didn't plan to give up any of them any time soon.

Riley rolled toward the entrance of the Wyckford Municipal Building for the monthly town hall meeting, carefully avoiding eye contact with all the people standing around outside for fear they'd want to help her. "The do-gooders," as she called them. She appreciated the sentiment, she really did, but she didn't need help. She did just fine on her own. Usually, Riley avoided gatherings like this so she wouldn't have to deal with them, but tonight she was meeting her Realtor here to discuss new places for Riley to look for potential residences.

Not that she didn't love and appreciate living at Brock's place, but the lack of privacy left a lot to be desired. Plus, with her brother now so stupidly happy in lurve, it left Riley feeling like a third wheel. Not that she wasn't thrilled for her brother and his new wife, Cassie, or her beloved young niece, Adi. But they'd recently had a baby too, so that made the house even more crowded.

And maybe it was her restless spirit, but Riley longed for space of her own, a new chance at life on her own. A chance to escape her brother's golden boy shadow once and for all after thirty-two years.

Not that she wasn't grateful for all Brock had done for her after the accident. He'd lost his first wife a few years prior and had been dealing with his grief and problems because of that, trying to raise Adi on his own while juggling their father's GP practice alone. Still, being together like that, grieving their respective losses, had brought them closer, healed old wounds and strengthened their sibling bond. But that phase was over and now Riley wanted something all her own, something unique and true and right. Something that would bolster her ability to take care of herself instead of relying on anyone else.

She paused at the threshold to take a deep breath before heading through the double doors into the chaos. The building was an old factory the town had renovated into a new useable space for their local government offices and meetings, thanks to a federal grant. The contractors had also made it fully accessible, so it featured wide halls, ramps everywhere there were stairs and an elevator up to the second floor, though that level was used mainly for storage these days. Riley smiled politely as she passed several townsfolk on her way to find an empty space to park her wheelchair. She'd come straight from her shift at the hospital, so still had on her green scrubs beneath her coat and comfy white sneakers instead of boots, and her long dark hair pulled back into a sensible ponytail.

As she traveled down the center aisle toward the front, she saw familiar faces in the rows lining either side, including Brock and Cassie and Adi. Cassie had mentioned earlier that they were leaving the baby home with a sitter. ER nurse Madi Scott and flight paramedic Tate Griffin were there too, as was Riley's physical therapist Luna Norton and her partner, firefighter Mark Bates. Mark was there in an official capacity as the newly appointed assistant fire chief, according to the agenda posted on the town's Facebook page, to discuss setting up the ice rink for the town's yearly pop-up holiday festival. She waved to each of them as she passed, praying she hadn't made a mistake coming here tonight. These things could last notoriously long as they turned into big spectacles, a chance for everyone to see and be seen, to voice their opinions—sometimes loudly—and catch up on all the local gossip, the town's biggest export—with Wyckford General as its main supplier. Given it was the largest employer in the area, most people either worked there or had family members who did, so it made sense.

Riley finally found a quiet spot near the far wall toward the front of the room and settled in for the show. At the very front of the space was a dais, on top of which was a long table where the town council sat. Lucille Munson spotted her from there and waved, her eye-wateringly bright pink track suit and lime-green headband on brand for the older woman. She was the queen of the busybodies in town and loved her shocking colors almost as much as she loved sticking her nose into other people's business. Riley plastered on a polite smile, the same one she used with difficult patients in the CT room, and waved a hand in response.

"Happy holidays, Doc," said a grinning security guard standing nearby. "Here, let me help you with your chair."

"No," Riley said, her tone sharper than she'd intended. "I got it, thanks."

The guard's grin faltered and he gave her a dubious look. "Might be easier if—"

"If what? If I let you handle things for me? Sorry, not gonna happen. I'm not here to make your life easier, Barry. And don't forget I punched you in the nose in kindergarten, and I'm not above doing it again."

His eyes widened slightly, and he looked like he was going

to argue, but then Lucille called for him to help her with some supplies, so he had no choice but to rush off. Good. All Riley wanted at that point was a hot shower and a year-long nap. And yes, Christmas was coming up, but it was hard getting into the holiday spirit when you were exhausted all the time. Between her crazy schedule and frequent PT visits, Riley had virtually no time to herself these days. She searched the crowd for her Realtor, Lynette, but didn't see her. If she'd ditched Riley in this cheerful hell without telling her, she was going to… She pulled out her phone to check for texts. Yep, there was a message from Lynette. She'd gotten caught at a showing and couldn't make it. Said she'd call Riley tomorrow. Perfect. Grumbling, she shoved her phone back into her pocket.

She hadn't reached Scrooge territory yet this year, but she was close.

Ben Murphy, Cassie's dad, took a seat near Riley, greeting her and Luther Martin, the town curmudgeon who sat on the other side of him. Now more than ever, Riley felt a kinship with Luther and his attitude. Sarcasm kept people at bay, especially the do-gooders. And while their situations were different—Luther was old while Riley was injured—people still tended to see them as less than, as needing assistance when they clearly didn't. It was infuriating. She appreciated their concern, but there were only so many pitying stares and platitudes a person could take. Her spinal cord had been damaged in the accident, not her brain, and Riley was still perfectly capable of taking care of herself.

She bent over to lock her chair wheels and when she straightened, Riley froze. What was Sam Perkins doing over by the entrance? Worse, why did her stomach flutter with invisible butterflies every time she saw him? She

squashed them down fast, not wanting to feel that for anyone, let alone him.

"Everyone quiet down please," Lucille said into the mic on
the table. She commanded the town council like a queen di-
recting her lieges, and tonight was no different. "Thank you
all for coming. On tonight's agenda, of course, is the pop-
up Ice, Ice Baby festival, and we have Assistant Chief Bates
with the fire department here to update us on their plans for
this year's ice rink installation. We're also taking vendor
sign-ups for the festival, so if you have or would like to make
something to sell, please use the sheets at the back of room
to get your name on the list. The exact date, as always, will
be a surprise, but it'll be in December prior to the holidays,
so you can plan accordingly. And finally, we'll discuss the
suggestion of adding a new event to the festival schedule, the
Ho-Ho-Horrorfest, and open the floor to public comments."
A chorus of boos and cheers on the topic rang out before Lucille shushed them down. "Right. Let's get started."

Riley couldn't help watching Sam and his daughter as they
hurried down the center aisle to take seats in the front row
near Brock and Cassie. His little girl was as cute as a button,
with the same dark hair as her dad but with green eyes instead of Sam's brown ones. She was best friends with Riley's
niece, Adi. Other than the fact the man had arrived in town
to assist Cassie with a patient's case and had never left, no
one seemed to know much about him. Which was odd in a
town where everyone knew everyone else's business. She'd
managed to discover from Cassie that he was a widower and
that he and his daughter had moved here from San Diego.
Cassie had known and worked with Sam in California and
had called him in to consult on the neurological aspects of
a reconstructive surgery. Whenever Riley did scans for one

of Sam's patients in Radiology, she and Sam always stuck to discussing the cases, never anything personal, which was fine. She'd had enough of people poking into her personal business a long time ago, even if she was curious about him.

Over the course of the next two hours, Mark walked to the head table and discussed the ice rink, then a myriad of townsfolk argued about the horror movie fest until Riley's eyes had glazed over. Occasionally, she glanced over at Sam to find him either whispering something to his daughter or staring blankly at the stage, probably fighting the same boredom-induced brain fog Riley was. He always seemed quiet and thoughtful and a bit tightly wound, which she found intriguing. And he was handsome, in a Daniel Henney sort of way. Before Riley's accident, he would've been just her type. But the last thing she was looking for now was romance. She didn't need anyone else in her life telling her what to do. Nope.

Then Sam looked over at her and their gazes locked, and for a brief second, a strange awareness passed through her, like warm honey on a summer's night—warm and sweet and comforting and...

Whoops.

The meeting ended and Riley hightailed it toward the nearest exit in record time, her heart racing for some stupid reason. Not fear exactly, but like she'd narrowly escaped a trap. A trap like Sam Perkins. She needed to get home and get some sleep—to get out of here before they did something stupid like start talking to each other socially. *Keep it professional, keep it safe, keep it free.* That was the way.

Bah humbug, indeed.

CHAPTER TWO

SAM WATCHED RILEY TURNER LEAVE, wishing he could do the same, but he still had to drop Ivy off with Brock and Cassie. He recognized lots of people here, both colleagues and patients, and he wasn't sure why she'd suddenly pinged on his radar tonight, but he didn't like it. He also shouldn't care that she'd kept glancing at him throughout the meeting, her gaze making the skin on his neck tingle with awareness. And then when he'd looked over and met her eyes and time had seemed to slow for some reason, it'd almost felt like…

Stop it.

He didn't want to socialize with Riley Turner outside the hospital. That could only lead to more talking and closeness and… No. He'd always appreciated people who were professional, poised and knowledgeable at their jobs. Riley was all those things to a T, and that was probably why she had a way of intriguing him that he hadn't expected and wasn't prepared for. It had nothing to do with her wheelchair. His wife had used one for the last year of her life, and Sam had become so used to it, he barely even registered them anymore. Plus, he saw how people at the hospital treated Riley, acting as though her disability superseded anything else about her. Natalia used to get so angry when people treated her that way. He knew Riley did too. He'd seen her tell several people off already for trying to push unwanted help on her.

A check of his watch said it was nearly 9:00 p.m. now, and people were slowly filing out of the meeting space. Sam took a deep breath, allowing some of the tension that had been building inside him since he'd locked eyes with Riley to dissipate. She was gone, and now he could get back to his comfort zone, his details. He had a penchant for being exacting to a fault with his cases, which frustrated some people, but if he was eventually going to find a cure for ALS, every single detail mattered. Every change in a patient's condition had to be documented and studied. And yes, maybe he insisted on being in control and having input into every decision in his research study. But he had to. It was his name on the reports, his professional reputation on the line. His patients depended on him. On some level, he knew he was using work as a barrier to keep the things that scared him—emotions, heartbreak, vulnerability—at bay, but he was okay with that exchange. What was a little loneliness if it meant peace?

"Daddy! Daddy!" Ivy tugged on his arm to get his attention. "We're ready to leave."

Brock Turner stood and stretched before smiling over at Sam. "I hope it's okay if Ivy stays with us tonight. Adi asked me late in the day, and I didn't have time to call you."

"Are you sure it's okay with you?" Sam asked.

"Fine." They knew each other from working together at the hospital. Brock was the town GP, as well as working in the ER when they needed extra help. He'd called Sam down for neurological consults on patients several times. And from what he'd gathered about the man, Sam knew Brock had been a single father himself—before being reunited with and marrying his old flame, Dr. Cassie Murphy—so they had that in common as well. Brock shrugged into his coat. "I'll make sure the girls get on the bus in the morning."

"And I'll make sure they have a good breakfast first," Cassie added, smiling as she helped Adi into her jacket. Ivy had never taken hers off. "I'm up early anyway with the baby, so..."

"Then I guess I'm good with it too. Thank you," Sam said, pulling his coat back on. "I've got a busy schedule tomorrow and my nanny has the day off."

"In that case, Ivy can come back to our place after school too, if you need," Cassie told Sam. "I'm off, so I can spend time with them after school. You can pick Ivy up at our house after you finish at the hospital."

"Riley told me you worked with her on your research project." Brock chuckled. "Be careful. She can be salty when cornered."

Adi scrunched her nose. "What's 'salty'?"

Cassie ruffled Adi's hair. "Our cue to leave, that's what. Have a good night, Dr. Perkins."

Sam hugged his daughter. "Do you have all your stuff, *yeobo*? If you need anything, call."

Ivy grabbed the handle of her pink overnight bag. "I'm fine, Daddy. Stop worrying so much."

He touched his finger to the tip of her nose. "Worrying about you is my purpose in life. Please be good and don't make a nuisance of yourself. I'll see you tomorrow night."

"What's a *yeobo*?" Adi asked.

Sam laughed. "A Korean word that means 'sweetheart.'"

"Oh." Adi watched him curiously. "You're Korean?"

"Half," Sam said. "Ivy's a quarter."

Adi's eyes widened as she turned to her best friend. "You're money!"

"Come on, girls." Cassie herded them toward the exit. "For real this time."

"Right behind you." Brock gave his wife a quick kiss, and Sam felt a familiar pang in his chest. Despite his determination to remain alone, he still missed a lot of things about being married. It was the easy, casual shows of affection that most often got him in the feels: a lingering glance, a soft touch, a comforting word. All those little things that made a life complete.

"One more thing about my sister." Brock rocked back on his heels. "I know I said she was salty, and she is—especially when it comes to her injuries—but she's been through a lot the past couple of years and is struggling to find her way back to normal again."

Sam knew what that was like: having your future pulled out from under you and being left to search for any safe harbor. He was still processing his own loss himself, but he felt farther along than he had been. Moving across the country to come to Wyckford had helped. "Well, she's done excellent work with my patients, and that's all I care about. I'm sure things will be fine."

"Hmm." Brock seemed to consider that for a second before hurrying after his family. "Well, good luck to you. And whenever you need help with Ivy, just let us know. We're always happy to have her."

Sam couldn't imagine asking for help, especially with his daughter, but he filed the information away just in case. Then he headed home, alone this time. He missed Ivy's constant chatter almost immediately. He pulled into his driveway and saw the lights were still on, which meant that Hala was still there, and felt immensely glad. He still hated coming home to an empty house.

"How was the town hall?" Hala asked when he walked in.

She was knitting in the living room, waiting for her husband to pick her up. "Crazy as ever?"

"Since it was my first one, I don't have anything to compare it to." Sam plonked down on the couch, feeling exhausted. "But it was interesting."

"Interesting how?"

He told her about the meeting and mentioned seeing Riley there. He wasn't sure why.

Hala's knitting needles continued to fly with a speed and skill that could've given Sam's immense surgical skills a run for their money. "Dr. Turner's been through a lot recently. Everyone in town knew about her accident and helped support her and her family through the aftermath. You've been through a lot too."

Sam scowled. That was the second time someone had brought up Riley's past, and he didn't like it. He didn't want to be curious about her, didn't want to know more about her. "I'm sure she's fine. I am too."

"Are you?" A car horn sounded outside, and Hala finally looked up as she put her things into the tote bag near her feet, then walked to the foyer to pull on her coat and gloves. "I'll see you on Thursday. Good night, Dr. Perkins."

"Good night, Hala."

Alone at last, Sam locked up the house and shut off the lights, then went to bed. He stayed awake though, trying to get into the book he'd been reading, but his mind kept circling back to what Hala had said.

Dr. Turner's been through a lot recently. So have you.

Sam didn't want people's worry. He didn't want their interest either. He wasn't a sideshow exhibit. He just wanted to live his life as best he could now, moving forward and taking care of business and those around him just like he always did. Still, he couldn't shake the odd sense of connection he felt now that he'd realized that maybe he and Riley both had painful pasts they were recovering from. He wondered how she dealt with the pain, the memories, the isolation...

Frustrated with the direction his mind had taken, he shut off the light and went to sleep.

"Just a little longer, and we'll be done," Riley said through the speaker in the reading room to the MRI suite. She'd arrived early this morning to start the necessary scans before the patient's follow-up consultation. Daisy Randall was only forty-two, and she'd been diagnosed with ALS the previous December after nearly nine months of testing by various specialists. The patient's whole life and future had been shattered in the blink of an eye.

Riley could relate, which was probably why they'd become good friends.

Daisy's symptoms had started with a strange, sudden weakness in her left leg, which had progressed to a persistent limp. She'd seen GPs and physical therapists and several neurologists and had all kinds of scans and tests and treatments. Nothing had helped. Finally, she'd been referred to Sam Perkins for yet another opinion, and he'd given Daisy her definitive diagnosis of ALS. She'd enrolled in his research study shortly after that. Riley admired the woman's bravery and clear-eyed view of her future more than anything.

While a tech helped Daisy off the table in the other room and into the dressing area, Riley compiled the images from the completed MRI into the patient's digital chart for comparison with the previous set from her last follow-up visit six months prior.

"Sorry I'm late," Sam said as he walked into the dark

reading room to view the images on the screen over Riley's shoulder. Suddenly being surrounded by Sam's scent of soap and spice, along with his warmth brushing her shoulder, had all the oxygen in the room disappearing for Riley. She tried to play off the ache in her chest as a cold. She didn't want to be aware of him. She vehemently did not want to get involved with anyone romantically right now, and Sam was a colleague, which made him strictly off-limits. It was bad enough she'd mooned over him at the town hall last night, where anyone and everyone could've seen. She wasn't sure what it was about him that turned her insides to goo, but she didn't like it. Not at all. Her life was complicated enough. She forced herself to concentrate on the work in front of her and not the muscular male body hovering near her right shoulder.

Get it together, girl.

Riley cleared her tight throat and began to relay the results to Sam in her best flat professional tone. "Objectively, Daisy's MRI results today are relatively stable compared to those from last time, with only slight hyperintensity increases in the CST and hypo-intensity in the motor cortex and brain atrophy consistent with the disease's progression. Subjectively, the patient reports worsening weakness in her legs, and she uses her wheelchair most of the time now for mobility. The tech will put her in the conference room at the end of the hall to go over the results with you."

"Right." Sam straightened. "What about you?"

"What about me?" Riley snapped before catching herself. He put her on edge. Another reason to steer clear. She took a deep breath and tried again. "Sorry. Long morning. Did you have more questions about the patient's scans?"

Sam crossed his arms. "No. I just know that you and Daisy are friends and thought she might appreciate having your support during the consult, since she's here alone today." He checked his watch. "If you're not busy, that is."

"Oh." Riley remembered the first weeks after the accident, all her subsequent surgeries and what a confusing time it had been for her. She'd relied heavily on her family to help her through it. Daisy's mother was moving to Wyckford from Boston to stay with Daisy, but it wouldn't be until after the first of the year. Riley swallowed the lump of guilt in her throat for the way she'd talked to Sam and checked her schedule on her computer. "Uh, actually, it looks like I am free."

"Great. I'll meet you in the consult room in five minutes." He started out then turned back. "Unless you need assistance—"

"I don't," she said, cutting him off.

Once he'd gone, she shifted in her chair, wincing slightly. The initial pain from her injuries as her nerves had slowly grown back together had gradually receded over the first few months until it was tolerable. On the worst days, she was entirely stuck in the chair. On the best days, she could walk at home with the use of a set of Lofstrand forearm crutches. But even now, after all her progress, if she sat too long, or stood too long, or forgot to stretch daily, or made any wrong moves—or basically lived, period—the pain could become debilitating. She used the chair at work and when going out in public because it was easier, though she hadn't given up on her dream of building up to the crutches full-time and doing away with the chair completely.

She rarely talked about what it was like for her these days, unless it was with someone who understood, like her physical therapist Luna, or Daisy. Otherwise, you ran the risk of people constantly telling you how strong and inspirational you were—or Riley's personal favorite, telling you that everything happened for a reason. Seriously? She wanted to scream at them, ask them what possible reason there could be for her parents dying and her being paralyzed. And the worst part of all was it was her fault they'd been out on the icy roads that night. The do-gooders meant well, she knew, meant to be comforting. But sometimes comfort came from just being there.

And she absolutely would be for Daisy now.

She went to lock her computer screen as her mind returned to Dr. Perkins. She hadn't expected him to invite her to the consult, but she'd be there for her friend no matter what. Also, she *really* hadn't expected him to treat her like the do-gooders tended to, and she didn't want him starting now. She had enough do-gooders in her life. It was weird because up until today, he'd never once treated her differently because of the chair. It was like he hadn't even seen it, which had been both odd and nice. Maybe that's why she'd suddenly developed her strange aware-ness of him the other night. Like a cat who always hung around people who ignored them.

Or pathetic losers who need to get a life. Or get laid. Or both.

Riley shook her head and pushed away from her desk. Dating was a whole other issue to navigate after her injuries. She'd been a bit of a hellion before the accident and had na-ively expected things to continue that way afterward. Then the first guy she'd been with after her spinal cord injury had freaked out during sex: getting her out of the chair, getting her back into it, all the stuff in between. A real mood killer. Since then, she'd taken matters into her own hands and used her trusty toys rather than risking humiliation and embar-rassment with a partner again, even though sex was not just possible but enjoyable after spinal cord injuries, if done right.

I bet Sam would get it right.

Her traitorous brain put it out there before she could quash the idea. She had no business thinking about the guy like that, regardless of how he reacted to her chair.

Besides, Sam had never given any indication that he was even interested in her, or anyone else at the hospital for that matter, and it was none of her business anyway. She had enough to think about between her job and her recovery. Based on the latest reports from her specialists, Riley's long-term prognosis was still up in the air. Maybe she'd walk again on her own, maybe she wouldn't.

The funny thing was, despite it all, she still felt whole. Or mostly, anyway. But just because she was okay with her body as it was now didn't mean she could expect anyone else to be. And while her sex drive was as healthy as ever, what she missed most was the intimacy—lying next to someone, sated and sleepy, and falling asleep in their arms.

With a sigh, she started out of the reading room and down the hall for Daisy's consult. There, she found Daisy sitting alone on one side of a round wooden conference table while Sam fiddled with the large flat-screen monitor on the wall where the MRI imaging would be displayed. Riley smiled over at Daisy as she parked her chair at the table then reached down to lock her wheels, doing her best not to notice how Sam's green scrub shirt stretched taut over the rippling muscles of his upper back and shoulders, or how the sinew in his forearms flexed as he pressed buttons on the remote. Then Sam turned quickly and caught Riley's gaze, and something odd quivered in her belly.

Wow. Where had *that* come from?

She focused on the tablet she'd brought with her to see the

scan notes on her screen, her cheeks hot as Sam took a seat a few chairs down from her.

"How are you feeling, Daisy?" he asked.

"Okay, I guess." The patient shrugged, looking defeated, and Riley reached across the table to take her friend's hand. "The past few months have been a lot, you know? I told my mom not to come today because I just need some time to myself. Since she moved back in with me, I don't feel like I have any privacy at all." She shook her head. "It's not her fault that I need so much more help with things now. And I know it's safer to not be alone. But I'm still processing, and I need space to do that. I thought things would get better with time as I adjusted and accepted my diagnosis, but all the stress and anxiety can still be overwhelming sometimes."

"That's perfectly normal," Sam reassured her. "Did you set up an appointment with the therapist I suggested? It can be helpful to talk things out with someone completely outside of the situation."

"I did," Daisy said. "The worst times are late at night, though, when I'm alone with my thoughts. Not knowing how much time I have left. You told me the average life expectancy is three to five years from diagnosis, but I've read about people who get less and some who get more. Stephen Hawking lived more than fifty years with the disease. And how long will I be able to talk and breathe on my own or eat without a feeding tube?" She dropped her head into her hand. "It's all so horrible and awful and incredibly unfair."

Riley squeezed Daisy's fingers. "You're right. It totally sucks. But please know I'm here for you, whatever you need, whenever you need. Call me in the middle of the night to talk, okay?"

Daisy looked up at her with a watery smile. "Okay."

Sam let a moment pass before clearing his throat. "Right. Are you ready to go over today's results and our plans for the next few months, Daisy?"

She nodded, and Sam started going over the MRI results while Riley found herself watching him again. He was good, explaining things in easy-to-understand ways, always with empathy and understanding for Daisy, even when talking in the most clinical terms. He seemed to trust his patients to ask questions as needed, and to know themselves and what they wanted for their care. They'd worked together on cases many times over the past year and a half, but for some reason he'd caught Riley's attention today and made her even more curious about him.

In a purely professional capacity, of course.

Then she looked over and found Daisy watching her watch Sam, and Riley immediately transferred her attention to the screen of her tablet again, but it was too late. Based on the look Daisy had given her, she'd thought Riley was ogling Sam, and now she'd have to explain that too.

Great.

At least Sam seemed oblivious to the situation, even as Riley stifled the urge to fan herself. When had it gotten so hot in the consult room?

"Pending the results of your PET scan next week," Sam continued, as he finished the slideshow of images on the wall monitor then set the remote control on the table, "I believe we can continue to monitor you for another six months with the same protocols in place. Any questions?"

"Not right now, Doc." Daisy squinted at her paperwork as Sam slid it across the table to her. "I'll have to drink more of that yucky contrast for the PET scan, won't I? It's in the separate building across the street?"

"Yes, and yes." Riley grimaced on her behalf. "But at least they keep the contrast cold, so the chalk taste isn't so bad. And I'll read the results with Sam when they come back before your next consult with Dr. Perkins. I can come to that follow-up meeting too if you want."

"Yes, please."

"Excellent." Sam stood and walked over to shut off the monitor, then patted Daisy on the shoulder as he passed behind her on his way to the door. "Let us know if you need anything. We're here for you."

"And I meant what I said about the middle of the night," Riley added. "Call me anytime it gets bad."

"Are you sure?" Daisy asked, sounding skeptical.

"Absolutely," Riley said, then rolled around the table to hug her friend as Sam left.

As she and Daisy embraced, their chairs clanking together, Daisy whispered in her ear, "I saw you eyeing my doc. He's hot, isn't he?"

"What?" Riley pulled back, flustered. "No. I mean yes. I mean, I don't know. I haven't noticed how Sam looks."

"Then you must be blind as well as paralyzed, girl," Daisy teased gently. "It's okay to like him as more than just a co-worker. I know for a fact that he's single."

"Yes. His wife died," Riley said, sitting back in her chair. "And stop trying to set me up. I'm not interested in that right now."

Daisy gave her a flat look as they both headed for the door. "Whatever. I'd tap that if he wasn't my doctor."

Riley sighed as she turned off the lights in the conference room, then followed her friend out into the hall. "We are not talking about this."

Because the last thing Riley wanted to think about the rest

of the day was tapping Sam or anyone else. But especially Sam, because she had a sinking feeling that she'd probably like it, and him, way too much. It was always the quiet, serious ones you had to look out for where your heart was concerned.

CHAPTER THREE

SAM SPENT THE rest of the day split between surgeries and more exams, including of several residents of the Sunny Village Retirement Home who'd come in with everything from neck and back pain to midstage dementia. He'd also performed an anterior cervical laminectomy and several lumbar punctures for testing.

The afternoon's highlight, though, had been an ER consult on a seventy-year-old patient brought in by her husband. She'd barely been conscious upon arrival, complaining of tingling in her extremities and mental fogginess. After all other medical conditions had been ruled out, Sam had been called. The ER had taken an extensive history and determined the patient was in good health for her age, and when asked about her activities that morning, she'd said she'd been cleaning the bar her son owned. Sam had just started examining the patient himself when the woman's son arrived carrying a paper plate covered with foil. Apparently, his mother had eaten several of the "special" treats while at his bar. The lab had confirmed the presence of THC in the woman's bloodstream, and they'd all had a good laugh over her just being stoned and not seriously ill. Sam had been relieved it hadn't been a stroke or worse.

After that, he'd headed back to his office to catch up on his dictation and spent the rest of the day there. Sitting back and yawning, he realized it was time to pick up his daughter at the Turners'.

The Turners.

Thoughts of the family brought back memories of that morning and how Riley had sat in on his consult with Daisy Randall. He'd known the two were friends, but seeing Riley be so supportive of Daisy had been touching. He would have given a lot to have someone like her around during Natalia's last days, when everything had been grim and hopeless. When they'd exhausted all possible avenues to keep her going. When death had been a blessing.

Get it together.

A familiar lump of grief and guilt constricted his throat as he pulled on his coat and packed it in for the night. It was silly to wish for things that would never be. It didn't matter whether Riley would comfort him in his time of need because that would never happen. He couldn't protect his wife. What made him think he could be trusted with anyone new in his life? Still, as he turned off the lights in his office and locked the door, he pictured Riley, with her long dark hair and bright blue eyes. The whole family, it seemed, had that same coloring, Brock and Adi included. Of course, on Brock it looked rugged, while on young Adi it looked innocent and sweet. And on Riley...

Sam sighed and rubbed his eyes. It didn't matter what it looked like on Riley. He tried never to think about his co-workers outside of work in anything more than a passing fashion. But for some reason, she kept creeping back into his head. Must be exhaustion.

Or perhaps it was her professional abilities. He'd always been impressed with people who were excellent at what they did, and Riley was certainly that. Earlier today, before Daisy's appointment, she'd noticed and pointed out things that he hadn't caught himself, a rare occurrence. She was smart and analytical and detail-oriented, a must for any medical professional. But his new fascination with her seemed to go beyond that, because the moments he remembered best about her had nothing to do with her brilliant radiology skills, and instead featured her kindness, compassion and heart shining through.

Sam grumbled to himself as he rode the elevator down to the first floor then walked out to his car in the parking lot. Natalia used to tease him about being a cold fish, claiming she'd melted the ice king's heart. But deep down, Sam felt things as strongly as everyone else. He just kept it hidden because that's what he'd learned to do growing up. His mother had needed him to be strong, to be the man of the house from an early age. He'd grown up young and shut off his emotions to provide for and protect those he loved. It was a sacrifice that had served him well. Those close to him knew he cared. He showed them in all the little things he did for them, in the way he held them and comforted them and did everything in his power to make their lives as easy and happy as possible. Then Natalia had died, and his sense of control had imploded. He'd had to become both provider and nurturer to his daughter while also processing his own grief. It was still a process, even now, but he tried to let his walls down with Ivy as best he could.

The problem he seemed to have now, though, was his emotions were bleeding through anyway these days, and usually at the most inopportune times. That was uncomfortable and unsettling. Sam didn't like to feel things too deeply. Emotions made one messy and vulnerable, two things he avoided being at all costs. And while his daughter needed his heart, she also needed his strength, and his patients needed his cool, calm, collected side. So, he compartmentalized as much as possible. Or at least he had, until these odd new reactions to Riley Turner had seeped in from nowhere.

For whatever reason, she had a way of getting under his skin now, in both good ways and bad.

Like at the town hall when they'd locked eyes. It'd felt like everything had disappeared except for her.

It was inconvenient, inexplicable and incredibly intoxicating.

Then this morning at Daisy's consult, she'd somehow worked her way even deeper into his psyche, with her healing smiles and her gentle hugs. There'd been a point when Sam himself had almost wished for her to hold his hand too, to tell him that he could call her anytime, just to talk or...

Enough. All this was ridiculous.

He stalked to his car. Even though it was only a bit after 6:00 p.m., the sun had set at least an hour before, another casualty of winter in Massachusetts. The days were so much shorter this time of year. Sam slid behind the wheel of his vehicle and started the engine, making another firm vow to forget about Riley Turner as anything more than a colleague, no matter how difficult a challenge that was proving to be.

By the time Riley drove home after work, used the power transfer seat in her specially equipped Chevy Traverse to get from the driver's seat back into her wheelchair, then down the ramp and out of the back of the vehicle, the whole process took a good ten minutes before she reached the front door. Adi and Ivy were there waiting for her, both wearing what looked like stretchy orange lamé balloons with fins and scales on them, and with holes cut out in front for their faces. She had no clue what those were, but it seemed like a Cassie problem, for which Riley was grateful.

As she passed the girls, she caught bits of their chatter, something about the yearly school Christmas play. In the kitchen, Winnie, the family's French bulldog, tried to bite her chair wheels again, but Riley got the dog's attention by tossing her favorite toy into the living room, then followed the canine in there to check her mail. All she wanted was a hot shower and a long nap. Unfortunately, what she got was her brother sitting on the couch watching TV. He didn't look away from his streaming show as she passed by.

"Long day?" Brock asked her, sounding polite but uninterested.

"Always." Riley sorted her letters into piles of bills and junk. "Did my Realtor call? She was supposed to be scouting new places for me to see, but she ditched me the other night at the town hall."

"Not that I know of." He finally glanced her way. "You know, there's no rush moving out. Take your time, find the right place for you."

"I appreciate that, but it's time." After all their losses the past few years, his generosity meant a lot to her. But she needed to get on with things, and while she understood her brother's protective nature, she didn't need a babysitter. Her life felt restricted enough as it was these days. "Where's Cassie?"

Brock sighed and turned his attention back to the screen. "Out."

"Hmm." Riley turned and headed toward the hall, where her bedroom was located on the right. Brock was a good man. But he was also annoyingly perfect, and everyone loved him. And how in the hell did you grow up next to *that*? Unfortunately, even as adults, Riley had sometimes still found herself playing the comparison game with Brock because all his successes had seemed like her failures. Then the accident had happened and given her a different perspective. In some ways, they were closer now than they'd ever been before. She still wanted a place of her own though.

Adi and Ivy followed Riley because the concept of boundaries didn't exist for seven-year-olds, and they stood off to the side while she changed into her pj's then went into her attached bathroom to take off her makeup. The builders had finished construction on Brock's new house shortly after Riley's accident, so he'd had them add all sorts of accessibility features for her knowing she'd be staying there awhile, including a wheelchair-accessible shower with a built-in seat that allowed her to transfer back and forth easily. The kitchen was also fully adapted to wheelchair height, with cabinets and counters that raised and lowered as needed. When she moved out, she'd either build a house on her own or do extensive renovations to retain all these special amenities, and they'd probably cost a fortune, but tonight she didn't have the bandwidth to think about it.

She'd just finished using her last makeup wipe when the doorbell sounded and both girls ran from Riley's bedroom, squealing with joy. From down the hall, she heard Ivy call, "Daddy!"

Which meant Sam was here.

Her pulse tripped without her consent. It made no sense, her reactions to him, because she had no reason to care if he was there or not. He'd come to pick up his daughter, no big deal. Still, she couldn't seem to stop herself from rolling out of the bedroom and down the hall toward the kitchen, her blood pounding through her veins. She rounded the corner just as Sam bent to pick his daughter up.

"Yeobo!" He kissed the little girl's cheek, his handsome face lighting up with joy, such a difference from his normal cool aloofness at work. "How was your day?"

"Good! Adi and I got picked to be goldfish in the holiday festival."

Ah. Goldfish, Riley thought. That's what those costumes were.

"And I told the teacher we'd babysit Fred over the holidays and—"

"Whoa, whoa." Sam frowned. "Who's Fred?"

"The iguana." Ivy gave him a look full of *duh*. "Remember? I told you about him the other day."

Riley bit back a laugh over the mental picture of evenkeeled Sam wrangling an ornery lizard. Or at least she did until Brock turned and saw her in the doorway. Then her stomach sank. "Hey, sis. Can you come here a minute, please?"

She hadn't been expecting to see visitors and smoothed a hand down the front of her pink poodle-print flannel pj's and reluctantly went over to them, giving her brother a stern stare of warning. She wouldn't put it past him to do this on purpose to try and embarrass her. They might be adults, but old sibling tricks never went away, apparently. She glared at her brother, then said to Sam with as much dignity as she could muster, "Good evening, Dr. Perkins."

"Evening, Dr. Turner." Sam's tone held its usual crisp efficiency, though he was eyeing her pj's dubiously. "You look very…relaxed…tonight."

She bit back a snarky response, her face hot, then turned to her brother. "Did you need something?"

"Hey, girls," Brock said, looking completely unruffled in the face of her irritation, darn him. "Why don't you go get Ivy's things together?"

"Okay!" the girls said in unison, before racing off to Adi's room, leaving the adults in peace.

Brock waited until they were gone, then lowered his voice. "Sam asked where to buy presents locally for Ivy for Christmas."

She blinked at her brother like he'd grown a second head. They'd both grown up in this town. He knew as well as she did where to buy gifts for kids. She raised an annoyed brow at him. "And did you tell Sam where to go?"

"I did," Brock said, his hint of a smile setting off warning bells inside her head. Yep, this was a setup on her brother's part. She'd seen that smile before, when they were both in high school and Brock had gotten her a date with a guy who he'd thought would be "appropriate" for her, as in someone who wouldn't embarrass him in front of his friends. The date, with a math nerd who'd spent the evening explaining advanced calculus to her—and, yeah, it had been as exciting as it sounded—had been a total disaster. And now? Well, she had no clue what he was trying to do now, but she was sure she wouldn't like it. Especially if it involved Sam Perkins. The man might be hot, but his personality was as cold as Siberia as far as Riley was concerned. "And I thought it might be nice if you gave him a personal tour of downtown. Showed him where things are, that sort of thing. Be neighborly."

"I don't need a tour," Sam said at the same time Riley said, "Neighborly?"

If there was one thing that ground Riley's corn more than her brother being too perfect all the time, it was her brother trying to play matchmaker. He wasn't good at it. And who did Sam think he was, turning down a tour with her? She knew more about Wyckford than just about anyone. Indignant with both men, Riley glared up at them. "Brock, stop it. And, Sam, if you don't need help, why did you ask?"

"I didn't ask for help." Sam gave her brother a quick, reproachful look. "I asked for store names. I'm behind on my shopping and I like to support local businesses. Your brother came up with the rest himself."

Brock just shrugged before returning to the living room, infuriating Riley even more. What…the…?

Tempted as she was to tell them both where to park their sleighs and how to get there, she decided that poor Ivy shouldn't have to suffer with bad gifts because the men in her life were idiots. So, she took a deep breath and tried to sound as calm as possible. "I'll text you a list of stores if you give me your number."

Sam stared at her. "You want my number?"

Seriously? "Look, I get that you might think you're the town's hottest bachelor or something, but I am not interested, okay? You asked for names, I'm going to give them to you. That's all."

Tiny dots of crimson stained Sam's high cheekbones as he fumbled to pull his phone from his pocket. Good. That would teach him to make assumptions about people. And to think she'd thought he was different. As if she'd want to date him! She didn't want to date anybody. She didn't need a man to make her life complete. She didn't need anyone. She…

He cleared his throat as he frowned down at his screen. "I'll need your number first so I can text you mine. And to be clear, I don't want to date you either. I have more than enough going on in my life without romance."

"Same," Riley agreed, crossing her arms as she rattled off her digits for Sam.

Afterward, they both lingered there awkwardly, looking anywhere but at each other until Sam finally cleared his throat and hazarded another glance at her. "Nice pj's, by the way."

"Thanks." Riley raised her chin and gripped the arms of her chair, feeling oddly flustered and achy now, though she wasn't sure why. It certainly had nothing to do with the man in front of her. "They were a gift."

For a moment, their gazes held, and time grew taut, just as it had the other night at the town hall.

Weird how that kept happening when he was around.

Before Riley could contemplate it too long, though, Ivy called from down the hall, breaking the spell. "Almost ready, Daddy."

Sam snapped out of it, looking as perplexed by the situation as Riley felt. He studied the toes of his boots like they were the most interesting thing in the world. "I'll keep an eye out for that list then.'

"I'll send it as soon as I get back to my phone." She took a deep breath then turned back toward the hallway, calling over her shoulder, "Have a good night, Dr. Perkins."

Sam looked up at her again, this time with a small smile playing at the corners of his lips—one that sent her stupid pulse stumbling again. "Good night, Dr. Turner of the pink poodle pj's."

Riley blinked at him. Was that a joke? Was stoic Sam Perkins trying to be funny? Unsure how to handle that, she continued down the hall toward her bedroom as the girls raced past her on their way to the kitchen, orange fish suits glinting under the overhead lights.

Dr. Turner of the pink poodle pj's...

She couldn't help smiling as she rolled into her bedroom and shut the door behind her. Maybe there was a regular guy under his pristine professional facade after all.

CHAPTER FOUR

RILEY PUSHED HER wheelchair toward the only table left available in the corner of the Wyckford General Hospital cafeteria, her eyes fixed on the steaming tray of mac and cheese balanced on her lap. The last thing she wanted was hot food all down her front. Normally, she went for something healthier, but the rich entrée was the only meal option left at three in the morning, unless you wanted a wilted salad. Of course, the fact it was also her favorite comfort food didn't hurt either. It had been a busy, stressful couple of hours on the night shift, with several emergency cases from the ER due to a car accident, so she needed the break. Her stomach growled in anticipation as she reached her spot amidst a sea of others that were already closed off for the cleaning crew and maneuvered her chair into place.

She glanced around the space, the hum of vacuums and the smell of floor polish from the cleaning crew working in the area comforting, grateful for a bit of solitude. As a radiologist, Riley didn't have a problem being alone. She spent most of her days in a dark room staring at X-rays and scan images on her computer screen. And the night shift was usually quiet and allowed her time to surf the net between patients or read during her downtime. It also allowed her to mostly avoid the dreaded do-gooders, like the lady from behind the register who was making a beeline for Riley now.

"Here, hon," the woman said, the name badge pinned to the front of her white cafeteria uniform proclaiming her name was Madge. She was obviously new because all the others knew better than to approach Riley without her expressly asking for assistance. "Let me help you with that."

"I'm fine," Riley said, flashing the woman a tight smile. "I got it."

The woman scoffed and took the tray from Riley anyway, laying out her plate and silverware like she was four instead of thirty-two. Riley ground her teeth through it all, determined not to snap at the woman, but drew the line when the woman picked up the napkin and started toward Riley's collar like she needed a bib.

"Touch me and die," she growled low, causing the woman to halt midway, the napkin dangling from Madge's fingers like an SOS flag as her startled eyes widened. "I said I'm fine."

Madge slowly straightened, her surprised expression giving way to affront. "Well, I never. I was only trying to make life easier for you."

"You know what would make life easier for me?" Riley asked. "If people like you treated me like a grown, capable adult instead of a child. Now, if you'll excuse me, my dinner is getting cold."

She faced the table as Madge walked away, the woman muttering under her breath about ungrateful people and how rude Riley had been.

Maybe she was right. Maybe Riley had been rude. But then no one was trying to infantilize Madge because she was differently abled than other people. One of the few things Riley still had left from her old life was her independence, and she intended to keep it.

She'd just picked up her fork and was about to dig into her food when the sound of footsteps approached from behind her once more. If that was Madge returning for round two in the Do-Gooder Olympics, Riley might just have to scream. Then the footsteps halted next to her table and a familiar masculine voice asked, "Mind if I join you? I promise to treat you like a big girl."

Oh, man.

Skin prickling with heat, Riley slowly looked up to see Sam standing there with a tray of food in his hands. She'd forgotten he was working the night shift too. They'd seen each other earlier in the ER when she'd run down some stat films for one of Brock's patients. They'd given each other a polite nod in passing and she'd thought that was the end of it. But no, here he was, invading her personal space again. Like he hadn't been doing that anyway since the other night in the kitchen. She'd found herself thinking about him at the most inopportune times, like in the shower or when she was trying to fall asleep, and it was beyond annoying. She didn't want to think about him like that. She didn't want to wonder what he was doing or where he was. And she certainly didn't want to be attracted to the guy, even if he was tall and handsome, with a guarded look in his eyes that made her inquisitive side yearn to know more. But she'd also reached her brusque quotient with Madge, so she had nothing left. She shrugged and kept eating. "Go ahead."

Sam raised a dark brown brow then slid into the seat across from her. "Thank you. And thanks for the list of stores you sent me."

Riley gave a curt nod, feeling a bit grinch-y now. Sam was back in professional mode tonight, thoughtful and logical and exceedingly polite. And while it might work well with his patients, for some reason it was driving her batty now. Maybe because it made her want to ruffle him up. She'd always preferred life a bit more on the spontaneous side. Or at least she had until her wild side nearly cost her everything. She concentrated on what he'd said rather than the way his feet brushed hers under the table. "Hope it helps."

He continued fixing his wilted salad, carefully tossing the dressing with the veggies so none spilled over the side of the plate. "I'm sure it will, once I find out where they're located."

Riley snorted. "Wyckford isn't that big. You can walk through the entire downtown in twenty minutes on a bad traffic day. You'll find them."

Sam harrumphed then dug into his own dinner.

Silence stretched between them, only interrupted by occasional chatter from housekeeping around them. Riley snuck glances at him as she ate, until finally Sam said, "So, about the hit-and-run case from earlier tonight… I just got off the phone with the officers who responded to the scene. It seems they found a piece of fabric caught on a nearby fence that they tracked down to a Tucker Larson. They also found debris from his truck at the scene."

"Doesn't surprise me," Riley said. "The Larson boys have been trouble around Wyckford for years. Tucker, the older and healthier one of the two, is usually the ringleader. Lance, the younger one, has cystic fibrosis. He's smaller and frailer, but still a troublemaker. They caused some trouble out in the forest a few months ago. Mark Bates and the police caught them." She shook her head, stabbing her fork into her mac and cheese. "Up until now, they only posed a danger to themselves. It seems that changed tonight." Thoughts of the woman in the ER who'd been struck by their vehicle then left behind like roadkill infuriated Riley. She hoped this time the police locked them both up for a good long while. "Why do people think they can get away with stuff like that?"

"No clue," Sam said, wiping his mouth with a napkin. "Thankfully, the victim should make a full recovery. And the officers are already searching for the Larson brothers. Good thing too since they sound dangerous."

"They are," Riley said. "And that accident happened near the school too. Imagine if it had been a child instead."

Sam visibly shuddered. "Don't want to. If anything happened to Ivy, I'm not sure what I'd do."

His demeanor shifted then, true emotion breaking through, and it was such a transformation that Riley had to tear her gaze away from him to avoid gawking. His dark eyes took on a mesmerizing heat, and his voice grew husky and deep. She couldn't help imagining other times when he might lose control like that, and whew…when had it gotten so hot in there? She avoided fanning herself by shoveling more food into her mouth.

"What do you know about reptiles?" he asked her out of nowhere.

Stunned out of her unwanted lust, Riley swallowed. "Excuse me?"

"Reptiles," Sam said before taking another bite of his salad. "My daughter has apparently volunteered us to watch the class pet over the holidays, and based on my call to the teacher to try and get out of it, it's apparently too late to change it. So, I need to figure out what to do with an iguana."

"Oh. Right." She'd forgotten about that little snippet from the other night and this time she couldn't hide her grin. "Don't worry. Fred isn't much trouble. We kept him last year and all he did was eat and poop. And sun himself on the branch in his cage for a week."

Sam looked intrigued now. "What did you feed him?"

She used her fork to point toward his salad. "They're herbivores, so greens and some fruit. We gave him collard greens and kale. And a bit of banana and grapes, though that's more of a treat than regular food. You can google it too."

"That was going to be my next step, after talking to someone who knew what they were doing." He gave her a half smile and her heart squeezed a bit. "Ivy's so excited about it."

"She's adorable," Riley said, smiling herself. "I'm glad the girls found each other."

"Me too," he said, finishing up his salad. "Friends are important."

"They are," she agreed. She wasn't sure what she'd do without her friends here in Wyckford, Luna and Cassie and Madi and Daisy. Probably go insane.

"With Fred off my list, now I just have to worry about the gifts for Ivy."

"You're a list kind of guy, aren't you?" Riley said before she thought about it. Whoops. Talking to Sam was easier now than she'd expected since he'd loosened up a bit. Maybe too easy. "Sorry. It's none of my business."

He chuckled and she felt the sound straight to her toes before she could stop it. "No, you're right. I am a list guy. It's what keeps my life running smoothly. Otherwise, total chaos."

"I get it," she agreed as she pushed her empty plate aside. "Though a little chaos can be fun sometimes too."

The minute the words were out, she wanted to take them back. That had come out way more flirty than she'd intended if the look Sam was giving her now was any indication, his dark eyes inscrutable.

Yeah. Time to go.

Riley wheeled away from the table to put her dishes on the conveyor belt nearby, leaving Sam to stare after her while she wished the floor would open and swallow her whole.

She'd hoped for a quick escape, but unfortunately the odds were not in her favor.

"Chaos, huh?" Sam said, placing his things on the conveyor belt after her then following her out into the quiet hall. "That's more your style? Never would've gotten that from your work. You're more anal than me when it comes to documentation."

"Have to be," she said, pushing the up button for the elevator, glad this was where they would part. She'd go back to the third floor, he'd walk to the ER on the other side of the building and her humiliating foray into flirting with the last man she should have would be over. "Keeps the malpractice vultures away."

What the hell was I thinking?

"True." Sam seemed to hesitate before saying, "Thank you."

Riley frowned, even more discombobulated now. The guy had somehow managed to knock her completely off balance without her even noticing. "For what?"

"For letting me eat with you tonight," he said, flashing a smile that would've melted her insides to goo if she'd been that type of woman. Which she absolutely wasn't, but still. "And for the advice on Fred. And for the list, again."

"You're welcome," she said as the elevator finally dinged, thankfully. "I'll see you around."

"Of course," Sam said, and turned away as Riley rolled onto the elevator.

She'd just pressed the button for the third floor and the doors were closing when a hand shoved between them, stopping them. She fumbled for the correct button to open them again and was shocked to see Sam there. He looked flushed and uncomfortable and as awkward as she felt, and her heart went out to him a little bit more.

"Uh, sorry. I just… Well, I don't have much free time, as you know. And with my schedule it would be hard for me to lose more than a day to shopping and I've been considering the offer your brother made the other night and…"

The elevator beeped angrily as he blocked the doors, cutting him off.

Riley shook her head. "What are you trying to ask me, Dr. Perkins?"

"I wondered if you might still consider showing me around downtown?" he said.

Shocked, Riley wasn't sure how to answer at first. The last thing she needed was more private time with Sam, considering how he seemed to do a number on her senses without even trying. She really needed to do something about that. But she also felt kind of sorry for him too.

Friends are important.

She couldn't help thinking that maybe he didn't have many around here, being new to town and all. Looked at that way, showing him around might just be her civic duty. That's the excuse she settled on anyway, against her better judgment. Maybe her impulsive side wasn't dead after all. "Okay."

"Okay?" he repeated, sounding as surprised as she felt by her answer. He coughed then and pulled out his phone, still blocking the whining elevator doors. "Okay. What's your schedule like this weekend?"

"I have Saturday off, but I'm working Sunday."

He nodded, typing on his phone. "Saturday then? I'll have to see if Hala can watch Ivy for a few hours. And I can drive."

"No. I'll drive," Riley said. "Text me your address. And bring Ivy along. I'm sure Adi will be thrilled to have more time with her bestie. And it'll give you an idea of the kinds of things to get for gifts too."

"Right." Sam nodded. "Okay. Saturday it is then."

"Yep." Riley still felt a bit stupefied by it all but smiled anyway. "See you then."

"See you." Sam finally stepped back and the elevator doors shut, leaving Riley alone with her spinning thoughts. What had she just gotten herself into?

Sam walked back to the ER to check on his consults in a bit of a daze. Why had he done that?

The only excuse he had was momentary insanity. What other explanation could there be for him charging back to that elevator to ask her to give him a tour of a town the size of a postage stamp that he was more than capable of exploring himself in just a few hours?

He shook his head as he walked through the automatic sliding doors and back into the controlled chaos of the ER. Didn't matter the size or location of a hospital, there always seemed to be people in need of medical attention, and Wyckford's was no exception. Residents and nurses bustled around, wheeling patients here and there, the smell of disinfectant sharp in the air. Considering his actions with Riley just now, perhaps he should have himself checked out. But beneath his confusion and self-recriminations, a low-level electricity buzzed through his system, an anticipation he hadn't felt in a long time—thought he might not ever feel again. And that was even more unsettling to him than making a fool of himself in front of Riley.

"Hey, Dr. Perkins," Madi Scott said from behind the

nurses' station as he passed. "Got those labs back on the hit-and-run victim."

"Thank you," Sam said, stopping to look, grateful for the distraction. Her levels were improving, which was good. They would keep her overnight for observation, but with luck she could go home tomorrow. "See if you can find a room for her upstairs. I want a twenty-four-hour admit."

"Will do, Doc," Madi said, flashing him a bright smile. She was one of those perpetually perky people that he always marveled at. Natalia had been that way too. Sam didn't get it, but he appreciated it. "Everything okay with you?"

"Fine," he said, eager to get out of her spotlight. "Just tired."

Not a lie. He was currently working on four hours of sleep. He'd stayed up late the night before helping to finish Ivy's science project for school. He'd made enough construction paper germs to last him a lifetime. Now all he really wanted was to find an empty on-call room and curl up on the tiny twin bed there for an hour or two.

Unfortunately, it wasn't to be. A brawl at the local bar, Wicked Wayz, had led to two new arrivals, one with a serious concussion from whacking his head against a pool table following a fall after being punched. Of course, his blood alcohol level complicated matters as well. They had to keep him for observation just to let him dry out before they could reevaluate his condition.

Sam eventually made his way to the small staff break room in the department for a dose of caffeine and quiet, only to find Brock Turner in there as well, scarfing down a bag of chips and an energy drink from the vending machines. They were the only two in the room.

"Hey," Brock said when Sam walked in.

"Hey." He made a beeline for the coffee machine, shoving a pod into the thing before filling it with water and hitting Start. "Busy night."

"Always." Brock tipped his head back, dumping what was left of the chips into his mouth before tossing the empty bag into the trash nearby. "Listen, I'm sorry about what happened the other night at my house."

"What happened?" Sam asked, shooting him a confused scowl over his shoulder.

"You know, about the whole tour thing," Brock clarified, looking a tad guilty. "I wasn't trying to set you two up or anything, I swear. I just thought it would be a good idea is all. Sorry if I made you uncomfortable."

Given that Sam had just finalized that very tour with his sister, he wasn't sure how to answer. He nodded and shrugged. "It's fine."

Next thing Sam knew, Brock walked over and slapped him on the shoulder. "If you ever want to talk, about work or whatever, I'm around. I know what it's like. Raising a kid on your own after losing the person you thought you'd share forever with."

Sam sighed and looked down at his hands. He had always been a private person, and he didn't want to burden anyone with his personal problems. But man, he was tired. And when he got tired, his barriers weakened. That's probably what had happened with Riley in that elevator. He'd been fighting his attraction to her for a while and tonight it just got out of hand. It had just been so nice to have company, someone to talk to who didn't pity him or worry about him or expect anything from him other than conversation. He hadn't realized how much he'd missed that until tonight. It could have been anyone across that table. But then he remembered her gorgeous blue eyes and inquisitive face and knew that wasn't true. He didn't want to talk to just anyone. He wanted to talk to Riley. She was snarky, yes, but she was also a blank slate, with none of his past guilt or sorrow thrown in to muddy things. Being with her felt fresh and new and clean. It made him feel hopeful, and wasn't that something? Another emotion Sam thought he'd never feel again after losing Natalia.

The coffee machine beeped, and he took his cup and turned to find Brock still standing there, waiting for an answer. Treading carefully, he said, "Uh, thanks. I appreciate it. And don't worry about the tour. Riley and I just made plans for Saturday to tour downtown, so no harm done."

"Really?" Brock looked impressed. "Wow."

Sam had figured it would come out sooner or later anyway in this town, so best to be up-front. They weren't doing anything wrong. It was just a tour. He sipped more coffee to dislodge the silly lump of excitement lodged in his throat. It *was* just a tour. Nothing more.

"Oh, nothing," Brock said. "I'm just surprised you got her to agree is all. She's been a bit withdrawn since the accident."

Sam had heard brief accounts of what had happened the night Riley had been injured through the hospital grapevine, but he wasn't one to put much stock in gossip and it felt like an invasion of privacy to learn the details from anyone other than her, so he didn't ask Brock more about that. If Riley wanted him to know, she'd tell him herself. "Well, in my professional experience with her, she seems fine. And it's just a quick tour of downtown. Shouldn't take more than a few hours. And Ivy's coming too. Riley said she'd ask Adi if she wanted to come."

Brock chuckled. "Good luck then, my friend." He clapped

Sam on the shoulder again as he continued out of the break room. "I need to get back to work. And have fun Saturday."

Taking a seat at one of the small round tables, Sam pondered what Brock had said. The times he'd been around Riley during cases, she'd seemed anything but withdrawn—a bit abrasive with him, maybe, but Sam had never minded that. In fact, he liked people with a fighting spirit. He admired Riley's intelligence and gumption. He thought of her sitting across from him in the cafeteria, her long dark hair pulled back to reveal her neck and a small golden heart dangling from a chain dipping into the V-neck of her scrub top. Whenever she'd leaned forward to take a bite of food, that top had gaped open a little more, revealing a hint of the curves beneath, that little gold heart gleaming like a beacon. He wondered what it would be like to hold her, feel those curves pressed against him, kiss her lips, hear her sigh his name as he pleasured her...

Stop it.

Yeah, he was losing it big-time tonight, first running back to ask her to take him on a tour and now fantasizing about her in the break room. He needed sleep and a shower and perhaps a lobotomy. Not necessarily in that order.

"Dr. Perkins?" Madi called from the doorway. "Found the patient a room. Just need you to sign off on it."

"Great, thanks," Sam said. He downed the rest of his coffee then stood, doing a full-body shake like Spork did every night after his walk, trying to get his mind refocused on work and not Riley Turner.

One brought him calm and clarity, the other chaos and confusion—and no small amount of desire, misplaced as it was.

Madi left and Sam started to follow her out, wondering if it was too late to back out of Saturday, but no. He'd look even more foolish changing his mind again. She was already probably wondering what was going on with him. Better to keep the date-that-wasn't-a-date and do the tour then be done with it—and her—once and for all.

As he'd told Brock, it was only a few hours. He could control his inappropriate lust where she was concerned for that long. Of course he could. Knowing the girls would be there as well helped.

He wouldn't do anything crazy in front of Ivy or Adi, like try to hold Riley's hand or put his arm around her or kiss her. Nope. All of that was off the table. He was an adult. A parental figure. A role model for his daughter, not a hormonal teenager.

He'd lost Natalia, the woman he'd thought he'd spend the rest of his life with, the woman he'd failed to save, despite his years of medical training. He'd never been able to do enough to help his mother growing up either. They were always just squeaking by, money-wise. With school and a part-time job and trying to keep his grades up to get a scholarship for college, he hadn't been able to help her around the house like he should have. He hadn't been enough for them, plain and simple.

No reason to think he'd be enough for Riley now either.

Looking at it that way put a quick kibosh on his libido.

Now if he could just remember that on Saturday, he'd be all set.

CHAPTER FIVE

SAM AND IVY were standing on their front porch when Riley arrived to pick them up bright and early on Saturday morning. It had snowed a little the night before, so everything had a fresh coat of white. They climbed into Riley's specially appointed SUV, Sam in the front passenger seat, and Ivy in the back with Adi.

"Daddy, we're going to have so much fun!" Ivy squealed from the back seat.

"Sure," Sam said, with as much excitement as a kid finding coal in their stocking. Despite giving himself another pep talk this morning while he'd gotten ready, seeing Riley pull up had given him serious reservations about spending a few hours with her outside of work. Images of her in those silly flannel pj's kept popping into his head at the most inopportune moments, which then led to thoughts of her taking said pj's off to reveal her naked body, which had kept Sam up most of the night, tossing and turning, hot and bothered and completely baffled.

None of this was Riley's fault. She'd obviously not been expecting to see anyone that night at her brother's house and had just been going about her business. No. If anyone was to blame, it was Sam, for going along with her brother's scheme. He still couldn't quite fathom why he hadn't put a firm end to things, except for that moment—only a few sec-

onds, really—where he'd looked into Riley's eyes and felt…
pain and passion and a profound sense of fate.

Yeah, he had a problem.

If he hadn't been sitting in a car with other people, he
would've smacked himself.

Sam did not believe in fate. Sam believed in logic and
facts and hard work.

So, he concentrated on buckling his seat belt to distract
himself from what could be early-onset dementia or possibly
a stroke inside his head. Something had to be happening in
there for him to be going off the rails like this and waxing
poetic about a woman he'd sworn he wouldn't pursue. He
couldn't trust himself not to fail someone again like he had
Natalia and his mother. He had a hard enough time keeping
up with Ivy these days. He needed to stick with his work and
his quiet little family life at home. That was all. No muss, no
fuss. No chance of losing anyone again.

Right?

Right. Which meant he needed to stay on the straight and
narrow where Riley Turner was concerned. Yes, they'd had
a nice conversation in the cafeteria the other night, and yes,
maybe she'd flirted with him a little bit—he still wasn't sure
about that. But that was no reason to go off the deep end each
time he saw her. He couldn't walk around in a constant state
of…*whatever* this was…for her. They'd have a nice couple
of hours around town, then go their separate ways. It was
for the best all around.

Therefore, as they headed downtown, Sam focused on the
passing scenery, not his inappropriate awareness of Riley
behind the wheel beside him, all pink-cheeked and fresh,
sparkling like a shiny new ornament. People had swapped
out their turkeys and pumpkins post-Thanksgiving for lights

and trees and inflatable snowmen and other assorted creatures, to the point that it looked like the entire town was decorated to within an inch of its life. The new added layer of snow gave the whole town an old-fashioned, Hallmark movie kind of feel.

Eventually, they parked near a large plaza outside the local attorney's office. Barricades were set up around a large flatbed truck with what had to be the world's largest evergreen strapped to the back.

"This is where the town tree lighting takes place during the pop-up festival," Riley said as she maneuvered from the driver's seat back into her wheelchair. "They drain the fountain and set up supports inside it to hold the tree securely."

She then rolled down the ramp that bisected the seats in the vehicle and out the back doors of the SUV, which had automatically opened with the push of a button on Riley's key fob. Sam's wife had had a similar setup in her car back in California.

He got out too, helping the girls from the back before Riley locked everything up again. Someone had shoveled all the sidewalks and plowed the roads earlier, making it easier to get around, which was good. The last thing they needed was someone breaking a limb.

"Hey, girl!" One of the workmen near the flatbed came over to give Riley's shoulders a squeeze. "How you doin'?"

Riley laughed, her pretty smile lighting up the overcast day. Sam found himself wishing he could see that smile more often before he remembered he shouldn't. He wasn't here to admire Riley. He was here to find gifts for his daughter for Christmas. That was all.

"Sam, meet Eric Barnes," Riley said, introducing them. "We went to school together."

Sam shook the man's hand. "Seems like everyone knows everyone else around here."

"Ain't that the truth," Eric chuckled good-naturedly. "Born in Wyckford, stay in Wyckford."

"For better or worse," Riley muttered, rolling her eyes. "How's the tree coming along?"

"Good. The crane operator should be here soon and then we just need to get this puppy upright before we can decorate it in time for the pop-up festival."

"And when is that again?" Riley asked, innocent as could be.

Eric shook his head. "Nice try, Doc. You know I can't tell you that."

"What about Santa?" Ivy interrupted. "Is he coming too?"

"He'll be here for Christmas." Adi nudged her with an elbow. "It's too early, silly."

Sam knew nothing about trees but acted dutifully impressed by the huge conifer until they finally moved on, walking farther down Wyckford's main street. Along the way, Riley pointed out different spots where holiday events might take place during the festival and where Sam might find gifts for Ivy and Hala. The girls walked ahead of them, whispering excitedly about their fish costumes and what they wanted for Christmas and who knew what else. Every so often they'd look back at Sam and Riley, giggle, then go back to whispering again.

Sam was suspicious. "What do you think they're planning?"

"Who knows," Riley said, shrugging. "Let's stop at the hardware store."

"I doubt there's anything in there my daughter would want," Sam said.

"You never know," Riley countered, stopping near an elderly man in a Santa hat on a ladder outside the entrance. He was stringing up twinkle lights around the front windows. Riley frowned up at him. "Be careful, Arthur. I don't want to see you in my department again for X-rays."

Mr. Schmidt, the store's owner, glanced down at Riley. Sam had already met the man on his forays into the place for supplies to fix things around his rental home. "Stop fussing at me, missy," Arthur said. "I'm fine. I've managed to live all ninety-two years of my life without your guidance. I think I can keep doing so just fine." Then the ladder beneath him teetered slightly, and he gripped the ledge at the top of the window for dear life. "Hold on to me, will you?"

Riley steadied the ladder with one hand. "Have you met Dr. Perkins, Arthur?"

"Sure," Schmidt said, grinning down at Sam before returning his focus to his lights. "He's in here almost every weekend. Regular Bob the Builder, this one is on the weekends. How are you, Sam? Where's Ivy?"

"On up ahead." Sam held the other side of Arthur's ladder and glanced to where the girls were peering into the display window of a local candy store called Sweeties. "And I'm good, thanks. Do you want help with those lights, Mr. Schmidt?"

"Nah. I'm done." The older man clipped in the last of the string of lights then returned to the ground, still spry for his age. Arthur dusted off his hands before squinting at them both. "What brings you both downtown today? Going to try your hand at bingo?"

"Nope." Riley hiked her thumb toward Sam. "I'm giving our newest town resident a tour."

"Ah. That's nice of you." Arthur leaned closer to Sam and

dropped his voice to a stage whisper. "But take heed, Dr. Perkins. This one is salty."

"Hey! I heard that." Riley scowled at them before breaking into a grin. "Okay, yes. Maybe I am salty, but there's nothing wrong with having some attitude."

"Personally, I like a firebrand woman," Arthur said, beaming at Riley.

"You like women period, Arthur," she scoffed. "Sam, did you know Mr. Schmidt got the highest bids at the town charity auction last fall? There was a regular catfight to win a date with the town's most eligible bachelor here." Riley winked at the older man, and Arthur's chest puffed up a little.

"That's right," Arthur agreed with obvious pride. "I received the highest bid of the night. Those women at the retirement village are insatiable, I tell you. Watch out for the seasoned crowd!"

Sam smiled politely, going along with the joke but feeling a bit like he was standing outside looking in. These people had lived their whole lives together. They were like a family, albeit a dysfunctional one. And once more, Sam's chest pinched with loneliness. He'd grown up alone, no extended family at all. Then he'd married Natalia and they'd had Ivy and become their own little unit. Now it was just him and his daughter. Hala and her husband were there too, but it wasn't quite the same. He sighed. Deep down, seeing Riley interact with the townsfolk made him secretly wish he could be a part of that too. Maybe as Ivy grew up here and he met more people, he'd relax and feel more comfortable. He tried to picture himself strolling down the street there, laughing and chatting with the person beside him. A person who looked an awful lot like Riley Turner. Afterward, they'd go home, and she'd put on those pink poodle-print pj's, and he could slowly take them off her, kissing every inch of her body slowly and sweetly until they ended up naked and in bed, limbs entwined and hearts racing.

Gah!

Sam's head snapped up, and he hoped his face wasn't as red as it felt, heat prickling up from beneath the collar of his coat. He'd promised himself he wouldn't go there today. This was not supposed to happen. He should be able to control himself around her, but it seemed all it took was one grin or laugh or wink and he was lost. Not good. He checked his watch, floundering for something to do to distract himself. "We, uh, we should keep going, Riley. You still have a lot to show me."

After a quick goodbye to Arthur, they continued walking, the girls a short distance ahead. From somewhere close, the scent of popcorn filled the air, and Wyckford municipal workers were up on cherry pickers, stretching lights across the main street. Other than that, though, the town seemed oddly quiet for a Saturday morning. Yes, it was a small town, and the temps had dropped again last night with the snow, leaving a chilly haze in the air, but he'd still expected more traffic than this.

"Where is everyone?" Sam asked, frowning as they crossed the street.

"Bingo," Riley said. "It's a Saturday-morning hot spot, like Arthur mentioned. They have prizes."

The girls had stopped again, this time in front of a local craft shop to gawk at the beautiful handmade items on display.

"Want to go in and look around?" Riley asked them.

"Yes, please!" the girls squealed in unison.

Riley whispered to Sam once the girls were inside, "Pay

attention in here. See what Ivy likes, then ask the gals to hold it for you. You can come back to get it later."

Sam nodded, following her into the shop. Hardwood floors sparkled beneath a bevy of holiday cheerfulness from the bedecked artificial trees everywhere and the Christmas music playing through the speakers overhead. They were even burning pine-scented incense somewhere, giving the air a sweet scent he associated with cozy childhood dreams.

Riley started talking to the owners about the going-on in town while his daughter and Adi perused the aisles filled with toys. Sam made polite small talk with them for a moment before turning his attention to a display of hand-knit dog hats near the register, some with reindeer antlers. He thought one might look cute on Spork and picked one out for his pooch. When he finally tuned in to the conversation between Riley and the owners again, it was in time to see Riley headed for the dressing rooms near the back of the store with one of the owners by her side and an elf costume draped across her lap.

"Where are you going?" he called after her, confused.

"Be right back," she said. "Just trying this on."

He really should've paid more attention. He could never seem to find the right balance with Riley. Either he was totally locked in, lusting after her, or completely focused elsewhere. Sighing, Sam turned around and found himself face-to-face with one of the owners, Louise Dalton. He'd operated on her brother the year before for an aneurysm. "How's Robbie?" he asked. "Still progressing?"

"Yep. He's doing great, Doc." Louise beamed at him. "You saved his life. Thank you."

Even after all these years as a neurosurgeon, it still humbled him to know he'd helped people. He saw them during the worst days of their lives and was grateful when he could

make things better for them. "Glad to be of service. Tell Robbie I said hello."

"Will do, Doc," Louise said before going to help another
customer.

Sam wandered over to see where Ivy and Adi were and
found them near the back of the store too, admiring a winter
village display complete with a train that blew steam from
its tiny smokestack as it circled the base of a Christmas tree.

"Look, Daddy!" Ivy pointed. "Isn't it cool? Can we get
one? Please? I love trains!"

"We have a *Star Wars* one at our house," Adi said. "My
dad helped me pick it out last year. It has the cantina and all
the action figures. This year he said we could get a new Luke
Skywalker too, since Winnie ate the old one." She looked
up at Sam, squinting. "Did you know droids don't like ice?"

"I did not know," Sam said, struggling to keep up with the
ping-ponging subjects.

"I don't like ice either," Adi continued. "Ice killed my
mommy and my grandparents and hurt Aunt Riley."

Okay. More unsolicited info about Riley's past, which only
made him even more curious about her, which was not helpful
at all in the current situation. Especially when the dressing
room door opened and Riley rolled out in what had to be the
sexiest elf costume known to man, complete with a jaunty cap
and a little green spandex dress that looked shrink-wrapped
to her body. A body he'd only ever seen in scrubs or jeans
and a sweater or those silly pink pj's, but now...

Merry son of a nutcracker...

Riley flashed him a self-deprecating smile and gestured
toward her outfit, as if asking his opinion, while the owner
who'd helped returned to the front counter to ring up customers. Sam wanted to say something, anything, but he found

himself speechless, dumbstruck by the glory that was Riley Turner in that costume. She must've taken his silence as a negative, however, because her bright smile dimmed, and she swiveled her chair back toward the dressing room again. "Never mind. I'll change."

"Wait!" Sam managed to force out before it was too late. He shook his head to clear it of the crazy image of him picking Riley up like Santa's bag of gifts, slinging her over his shoulder, and carrying her away to unwrap that green spandex from her one inch at a time, making sure to worship every inch of her until she begged for more.

She stopped, turning slightly to see him, her expression wary.

Say something, idiot!

"You look…"

Amazing? Adorable? Stunningly hot?

Sam's usually ordered mind tripped over words until what ended up coming out was "Green."

"Green?" She raised one dark brow. "Is that good or bad?"

"Good!" the girls shouted in unison.

Sam swallowed hard and nodded, saying more quietly, "Definitely good."

Riley's grin slowly returned like the sun coming out from behind snow clouds as she rolled back up to him, her other clothes and coat folded neatly in her lap. "All right then. Let's go."

It took Sam's hormone-befuddled brain a few seconds to hoist itself out of the smutty pool it had fallen into and back to reality, then he chased after her, rounding up the girls and following Riley outside. "Go where? And are you sure you don't want to change first? Won't you be cold in that?"

"No. We're just going to the end of this block. Louise said

someone who helps run the bingo game called in sick, and they need extra help until lunch. Since we're already here, I told her I'd do it. Costumes are mandatory for those running the show since the holiday season is upon us. I'll help up front while you play bingo with the girls. Get the whole Wyckford experience. It'll be fun."

"Bingo," Sam parroted before hurrying after her and the girls toward a brick building on the corner. Spending a few hours in a crowded hall with strangers sounded like torture. As did having to keep himself from drooling over Riley in that costume. He tried to remind himself of all the reasons he didn't want to want her. Coworkers. Failure. Grief. Guilt. Right now, none of them were working. Man, he was in danger here. "But I thought we were going to look at more shops."

"I've shown you basically all of them. It's a small town. The selection is limited if you want to buy local. There might be some other vendors at the pop-up festival though. Come on, Sam. Have a little adventure."

Sam and adventure went together about as well as turpentine and Toblerone and he felt completely out of his depth, but with the rest of them already at the entrance to the crowded establishment, and the fact they'd ridden here with Riley, he didn't have much choice.

Before coming to Wyckford, Sam had always considered himself a man who could handle anything, but here, now, he felt out of his league and not ready for any of this. Not for bingo. And certainly not for his sudden, uncontrollable, ever-increasing attraction to Riley. When she opened the door for him, her movements showed off her bust in that costume to dazzling effect, and Sam found his resistance crumbling as he went inside with the girls.

CHAPTER SIX

THE CITIZENS OF Wyckford took their bingo seriously. What Riley hadn't expected, though, was single dad Sam's effect on the women present. Females seemed to come out of the woodwork to bring him drinks or snacks or ask if he needed help or to tell him what a great job he was doing with Ivy. It was like a man with a kid was the world's greatest aphrodisiac. Maybe it was, because even Riley had to admit he looked adorable sandwiched between the girls, showing them how to mark numbers on their cards using the pink sparkly daubers they'd insisted he get for them from the registration table. From his serious expression, he was trying to follow all the rules and proper sportsmanship in the game. Ever logical, by the book and straitlaced, that was Sam.

It would be nice to see Sam ruffled. Sexy too.

Whoops.

No, no, no. Riley refused to melt over him. She didn't melt over men. Never had, never would.

Then he looked up and caught her eye, and the world faded away again until it was just the two of them and no one else and…

What was up with that?

And okay, fine. Maybe there was a little melting taking place inside her.

Still, she shook it off, reminding herself she did not want

a man right now. She'd worked hard for her independence and refused to give it up for anyone. Certainly not a man who hadn't even shown the least bit of interest in her. Sam always appeared cool, confident, competent and in control. Everything you wanted in a neurosurgeon.

Then she remembered how he'd blocked the elevator at the hospital the other day, fumbling his words as he asked her to come with him today. Also, just now, when she'd come out of the dressing room, he'd looked astonished at her appearance. Astonished and appreciative. It had been a while, but she still remembered what masculine interest looked and felt like. Sam had wanted her back in that store, even if he'd quickly denied it. Huh. Both times, he'd given her a peek underneath his normally stoic exterior, and she'd seen a man who was a little awkward in new social situations, who blushed under scrutiny, who obviously cared for his daughter and those around him and wanted to do what he could to support the new town he called home by buying local. It was almost enough to thaw the icy walls she'd built around her heart after the accident.

She glanced over at him again to find Lucille and her blue-haired posse from the retirement home now closing wagons around him at the table. Poor guy. From where Riley sat at the caller's table at the front of the room, she gave Sam a thumbs-up for reassurance. He flashed her a grateful grin that had her insides quivering.

Oh, boy.

Before she could anxiety spiral too much about her reactions to him though, Ben Murphy took the seat beside Riley. He was the bingo committee chair and MC that morning. He grinned and patted her shoulder. "Thanks for filling in. It's a huge help."

"Thanks. And no problem." Riley was glad for something else to focus on besides Sam and his too-attractive face. "What do you need me to do?"

"You'll be our caller this morning," Ben said. "The computer there selects the numbers. When it pops up on the screen, you call it into the mic here. We also flash them on a big screen, but the software handles all that. And don't forget to play to the crowd. The more fun they have, the more cards they buy and the more money we make for charity."

"Got it." She positioned her wheelchair next to the ball machine and proceeded to run the game for the next three hours, during which they gave away five hundred dollars in cash, two microwaves and a weekend trip for two to a casino in Boston. The octogenarian crowd was rowdy, even more than Riley expected and she was well-versed in the escapades of the residents of Sunny Village Retirement Home. At one point, she leaned over to Ben and said, "I thought they'd get tired after a while."

Ben laughed. "Not with cash and prizes up for grabs. They can go all day if it means winning."

Riley understood that all too well. She'd once camped outside the entrance to Gillette Stadium for three days to get tickets to a concert she didn't even want to see just to prove all the people who'd said she couldn't wrong.

Same with her walking again now. She'd do it, no matter what.

By the time the morning game session finally ended, it was lunchtime, and Riley was starving. She'd grabbed a quick piece of toast and coffee at Brock's earlier before picking up Sam and Ivy but nothing since. And while there'd been trays of assorted rolls and cookies passed around the game tables, she'd been too busy calling numbers to grab any. Now, as she made her way over to where Sam and their girls still sat as the rest of the crowd filed out of the building, she grabbed a remaining Danish and shoved it into her mouth to quiet her rumbling stomach. Cherry. Her favorite.

"How did it go?" she asked the girls as they left the bingo hall. It had been stuffy inside, but Riley shivered in the cold breeze, regretting not putting her coat back on. Sam, ever the gentleman, helped her put it on while they waited for the light to change. She didn't even mind his assistance. "Did you win anything?"

"They let me keep my doober!" Ivy shouted, holding up a bright pink bottle of glitter ink.

"Dauber." Adi nudged her friend in the side before showing off her own purple glitter bottle. "Bingo!"

The conversation then descended into chaos as the girls each shouted "bingo" over and over, trying to outdo the other as they walked back toward her SUV.

"You did well," Sam said, shaking his head and smiling at his daughter's antics. "I think you missed your destiny as number caller."

"Yeah?" Riley snorted. "Maybe I'll take it up as a side hustle. Make a little extra bank for my new home nest egg." The light turned green, and they crossed the street with the rest of the group waiting around them. The overcast sky was a little brighter now, but the wind had picked up too. Halfway through the crosswalk, a piece of her hair came loose from her ponytail and blew into her face, covering her eyes. Normally it wouldn't be a problem, but Riley needed both hands for her chair. Great. She stopped, since she couldn't see anything anyway, and reached up to brush the hair away before the light turned yellow, but Sam beat her to it.

"Here," he said, his warm fingertips lingering against her

skin, sending hot tingles of awareness through Riley again and making her breath catch. Time seemed to slow again, and the rest of the world faded. All she could see were his lips, his dark eyes, all she wanted was for him to kiss her, and…

A car horn beeped because they were blocking traffic. Reality snapped back to normal speed again.

Yikes.

Riley hurried toward the opposite sidewalk, Sam at her side. He seemed to take a sudden interest in anything that wasn't her. Which was fine because Riley felt like a mess inside. Why was she acting like this around him? She didn't want to be involved with him, regardless of how attracted to Sam she was. It seemed to take forever to reach the SUV, even though it was only two blocks away. Finally, they got to her vehicle and Sam helped the girls into the back while Riley got herself situated behind the wheel once more. After starting the engine, she fiddled with the radio as he buckled himself into his seat belt in the passenger seat.

They drove away, circling the block to head back toward Sam's place. To fill the awkward void, Riley said, "Thanks for being a good sport about the bingo."

"Thanks for showing me around town," he countered, staring out the window beside him instead of at her. Just as well, because Riley didn't trust herself not to throw herself into his arms at this point. She needed time alone to sort through all this and figure out what was happening here. "We've been in Wyckford over a year now, but I don't think I've ever experienced this place in the same way I did today. I'm grateful to you for showing me that."

Her insides warmed despite the lingering chill inside the car. Sam Perkins seemed to push all her buttons when it came to wanting. Made her feel things she hadn't since the accident. Heady stuff. Scary stuff too, and she wasn't sure what to do with it. It had come out of nowhere. What was also strange, and dangerous, was how she kept forgetting about everything else—the accident, the cold, the girls, her vow to stand on her own two feet, everything—all of it zeroing down to only him whenever their gazes locked, or he touched her. Riley was used to being the person who seduced, not the other way around. They drove back to his house on autopilot, her mind racing as she pulled into his driveway without even realizing they'd arrived.

Ivy and Adi clambered out of the car on their own and entered the house using the security keypad on the front door let themselves in, while Riley and Sam watched from the SUV. Neither of them moved until Riley couldn't stand it anymore. "I guess I'll see you—"

Before she could finish that sentence, however, Sam kissed her, soft and slow. Stunned, Riley froze before relaxing into it. He felt warm and solid and infinitely sweet, and something tightly coiled and stiff inside her unfurled, softened. His warmth, the softness of his lips, the way his hands cupped her cheeks like she was precious and fleeting and infinitely desirable made her want to burrow into him and stay there forever…

Finally, after a long, breathless moment, Sam pulled away, looking as shocked as Riley felt. His dark eyes fathomless and voice low, he muttered, "I'm not sure why I did that. I just…there's something about you…something… I can't seem to…"

Still mumbling, he got out and went inside, sending Adi back to Riley few moments later.

Nonplused, she drove home, silent while her niece continued to chatter about bingo.

* * *

Sam had officially lost his mind. That was the only explanation he could come up with for why he'd kissed Riley. One second, he'd been reminding himself about all the reasons he should leave her alone, and the next, his logical mind had taken a back seat to his libido. All he'd been able to see was Riley's little green dress and her big blue eyes and how he'd like to slide his hand up her thigh, to see if he could make her blush again, and…

Man, he was in trouble here.

Bemused, he hung up their coats then headed for the kitchen to pull something from the freezer to defrost for later while his daughter went upstairs to her room to play. Sam did his best to shake off the lingering sensual haze clouding his brain after their encounter. It was so strange, the sudden lust that seemed to overtake his common sense whenever he was around Riley now. What had changed? What had inexplicably made him veer off his chosen path of being alone, of focusing on his work and raising his daughter? He didn't *want* to want her, and yet he did.

The most frustrating part for him though was that the awareness, the attraction to her went beyond just the physical. He cared about what she thought, enjoyed talking to her, loved her intelligence and sharp wit. And it all seemed completely out of his control, which was a real problem for him on so many levels. He didn't get involved with colleagues, especially ones who were so incredibly, inconveniently mesmerizing to him. But there was no denying their chemistry now. His lips still tingled from their kiss. He licked them and tasted her there. Sugar and mint and a hint of cherry.

Gah! He needed this gone. Right now.

He couldn't let Riley into his life. He couldn't protect her. Least of all from himself.

Sam mentally scolded himself as he got a glass of water then checked his emails at the counter. The best way to stop it was to go cold turkey, like a drug. That kiss would not be repeated. Sam wasn't looking for more than a professional relationship with anyone. He'd been there, done that, failed spectacularly and had the shattered heart to prove it.

Still, his curiosity about Riley remained. He wanted to know more about her. Everything about her.

Which was not possible because they wouldn't be seeing each other again outside of work. Speaking of work, he decided to talk to Riley on Monday at the hospital and confront the issue head-on, explain that the kiss had been a mistake. One they wouldn't repeat. He couldn't imagine her arguing since she didn't like him that way either.

Does she?

Yes, she'd responded beautifully to his kiss, but that could've just been the shock of it all.

Frustrated now in more ways than one, Sam strode into the living room, determined to settle things once and for all. None of this was real. It couldn't be. No one was lovestruck like that outside of cheesy romance movies. The holidays were always a stressful time and both he and Riley were overworked, which would explain it. They were both probably looking for an easy outlet for all that tension. Once January rolled around, all this would go away. Whatever *this* was. Until then, they'd avoid each other outside of work as much as possible. Problem solved.

Spork jumped up onto the couch beside him, dropping his octopus stuffie into Sam's lap before flopping over onto his back, legs in the air and tongue lolling out of the side of his mouth in a goofy doggo grin as he presented his belly for rubs. Sam snorted and shook his head. Oh, to be a dog, where everything was so clear, and the most important thing was having a good toy and good treats. Spork wanted affection, so he asked for it. End of story.

Emotions were what caused the problems, Sam decided. They turned minor diversions into major crises.

Which only proved his theory that they were best kept locked away so they couldn't make trouble.

Compartmentalizing was proving easier said than done though, because every time Sam closed his eyes, he imagined he could still smell Riley's cinnamon scent, still feel the softness of her cheek when he'd brushed the hair from her face, still hear the catch in her breath as she'd relaxed into his kiss...

He scrubbed a hand over his face. If he was honest with himself—which he seemed determined not to be—what worried him the most was all these messy feelings swirling deep inside him were ones he'd thought were long buried. The yearning for intimacy, the sense of breathless passion, the connection and care. He didn't have the time or the energy to deal with this anymore.

Sam sighed and stared at the wall across from him. Thank goodness he had Sunday off to recover. He could rest and recharge and sort all this out once and for all. Put it all in proper perspective before talking with Riley on Monday.

He started to relax. It would be all right.

Then his phone buzzed, and he peered down at his screen, expecting to see an alert or update from the hospital about one of his patients. Instead, he saw a text from Riley.

We need to talk.

She was correct, but that didn't stop the muscles in Sam's upper back from knotting.

He opened his messenger app and saw three bouncing dots then a new message.

Do you have time tomorrow?

He'd planned to push their conversation to Monday, but maybe it was better to get it over with sooner rather than later. So, he texted back, asking her when and where.

One thirty tomorrow. Meet in Radiology.

Sam took a deep breath then confirmed. Afterward, he messaged Hala to see if she could watch Ivy for a few hours the next day before leaning back against the couch cushions, torn between laughing and locking himself away until this all disappeared.

He loved the peaceful, ordered life he'd built for himself and Ivy. He could keep her safe here.

The chaos Riley caused inside him didn't seem compatible with that at all.

CHAPTER SEVEN

AT THE APPOINTED time on Sunday afternoon, Riley sat across from Sam in the reading room, doing her best not to notice how his biceps bulged enticingly beneath the soft-looking black sweater he wore. A muscle was ticking near his jaw again too, the one that went to town when he was irritated, or stressed, or both. When had she noticed that about him? It didn't matter. What mattered was after today, she wouldn't notice it anymore. He must be having second thoughts about their kiss too, right? That should make her feel better, that they were both on the same page. For some odd reason, it didn't.

All she knew for certain was this situation was banana pants stressful, and she wanted it over with.

She wanted to go back to her independent lifestyle where the only person she thought about 24/7 was herself. Not in a selfish way—in a put-your-own-oxygen-mask-on-first way. Instead, right now, Sam had seemed to infiltrate her every waking moment. Her every sleeping moment too, if the way she'd woken up in a sweat this morning—to images from her dreams of them together, naked and tangled in her sheets, limbs entwined—was any indication...

Lord, she was in a bad way here. And that wasn't good.

"Look, I'm sorry about what happened yesterday, this kiss," Sam said, finally. "I never should have done that."

Riley shrugged, nodding slightly. "It was unexpected, that's for sure."

"I don't even know why it happened." He dropped his head and rubbed the back of his neck. "I was ready to say goodbye…and then…" He sighed and closed his eyes. "It doesn't matter why it happened. It was inappropriate, and I'm sorry."

"Okay," she said agreeably, though she was feeling anything but. She felt cold and lost inside, unsure what was going on and why, but just knowing she had to make it through this or else everything would change, and everything had already changed so much, and she wasn't sure how much she could take anymore.

He looked up at her response, his eyes narrowed. "That's it? That's all you have to say? 'Okay'?"

Confused, she frowned. "Do you want to fight about it?"

"No." He shook his head and looked away again. "I just want to make sure it doesn't happen again."

"It was a kiss, Sam, not rocket science. Sometimes people just do things spontaneously." Seeing him so discombobulated about it made her wonder if he'd ever done a single unexpected thing in his life. And sure, it *had* been a mistake, but that didn't mean it hadn't been good. Better than good. It'd knocked her socks off in a way that hadn't occurred in years, but Riley wasn't going to flip out about it. "Living outside the everyday can be fun."

"It can also be dangerous. No, thank you. I like control, order, logic."

"I know," she said, her tone not exactly flattering.

"Like that's a bad thing," Sam grumbled. "Control keeps us safe."

"It also keeps us locked in a cage. And that's just sad."

"Sad how?" Sam scowled at her from across the room.

"In my experience, acting recklessly only makes people less safe."

Well, she couldn't argue there. Sitting there in a wheelchair, she was living proof.

The knowledge didn't make her feel any better. In fact, it only made her angrier. She didn't want to catch feels for Sam Perkins. Didn't want to moon over him and his biceps. Riley did *not* moon over men. From the age of sixteen, she'd dated lots of guys. Rebels, bad boys, hot guys, cool guys, cute guys, nerdy guys, and in one unfortunate case, an actual criminal. But in all those encounters, she'd been the one making the choices, the one with the power in the relationship.

Sam and her stupid attraction to him had turned the tables on her though. It wasn't just the fact that he was hot and nerdy and ticked a lot of boxes she was looking for with his smarts and his strength. She also sensed a deep well of pain and emotions that drew her in and made her want to help him, heal him, and that was like poison to her freedom. The longer she let this go on, the greater the risk she'd fall for him even more—she'd always been a sucker for wounded heroes—and then she'd end up *needing* him and not just wanting him and… Her sense of self-preservation kicked in and she rushed to offer, "How about we just agree to forget it completely and move forward as professional colleagues? Nothing more."

Sam looked pleased by that potential solution, but before he could respond, an alarm went off in the corridor indicating a Code Blue, meaning a patient had gone into cardiac arrest, had respiratory problems, or another type of medical emergency on the floor. Not uncommon in Radiology, since many of the patients they saw were to diagnose the cause of serious to life-threatening conditions sent from the ER. All the staff were trained to respond, including Riley and Sam. Without hesitation, they both hurried out of the reading room, heading toward a treatment room at the end of the hall where a blue light flashed above the door. Inside, they found a middle-aged man on an exam table, the top of his hospital gown open to reveal his chest as someone performed CPR. Riley rolled in and checked the patient's airway before grabbing an Ambu bag to administer oxygen to the patient as Sam took over chest compressions from the bedside nurse.

"Status?" he asked.

The charge nurse, who stood near a screen in the corner, read from the patient's digital chart. "Sixty-two-year-old male, admitted last night in preparation for a laparoscopic surgery today. He was brought here an hour ago for preliminary ultrasounds, then began having trouble breathing. His systolic blood pressure dropped to the low eighties. No history of heart problems. We shocked him at one fifty for a V-fib arrest a minute and a half ago before you arrived. Patient is still in V-fib."

"Thanks," Sam said. "Any meds given yet?"

"No," the charge nurse said. "We do have IV access."

"Let's give epi then," Sam said.

Riley didn't interrupt, since closed-loop communication was critical during a Code Blue. Too many people giving orders only confused the situation and risked the patient's life even more. At the next pulse check, they all rotated positions. The bedside nurse took over the Ambu bag for Riley, and Riley moved to the digital chart on the wall, while a radiology tech took over compressions for Sam. Sam moved to check the monitors and the defibrillator machine, which was charging again on the counter nearby.

"One milligram of epi in," the charge nurse said.

"Good." Sam stepped in beside Riley to see the man's chart the check the man's vitals again. "Good airway and ventilation but he's still in V-fib. Let's go ahead and shock again. Charging at two hundred joules." When a sharp, high-pitched beep sounded, he said, "Everybody stand clear." Once everyone had moved away from the patient, he pressed the large red button on the machine. The patient's body convulsed quickly. "Shock delivered. Resume CPR."

"Resuming compressions," the radiology tech said. "Ten seconds to pulse check."

At the ten-second mark, Sam took the patient's carotid pulse. "He has a pulse."

"Hold compressions," the charge nurse said.

"God job, everyone," Sam said. "Let's secure the airway and call ICU."

Once the team from intensive care arrived, and they'd successfully made the handoff, Riley and Sam went back out into the hall.

Instead of heading for the reading room again, however, Riley went for the elevators, pressing the down button. "I don't know about you, but I could use some fresh air."

Sam followed. "Me too."

They rode down to the first floor in silence, both seemingly lost in their thoughts as they proceeded through the lobby to a side plaza area. It was mid-December now, so the tables set up there for lunchtime during the spring and summer were stacked neatly against the wall, awaiting warmer weather again. Their breath frosted on the air, but at least Riley had dressed more appropriately than he had today, with a thick sweater and pants beneath her lab coat. Sam only had on his cashmere turtleneck and jeans. He'd left his jacket upstairs.

His mind kept flashing back to the tiny green elf costume though, and his fantasies of stripping it off Riley, but he hoped the cold and the lingering adrenaline rush from the code upstairs would shove those errant thoughts firmly away as they stood alone near the center of the courtyard.

Riley said, "Did you know there's a legend about this fountain? They say if you stand before the water and wish for true love with a true heart, it'll happen for you."

Sam snorted. He'd never taken her for a sappy romantic, but he must've been wrong because Riley arched a brow at him. "It's empty now. What does that mean?"

"No clue," she asked, her tone pointed. "Probably that we're a couple of losers."

"Perfect." He tucked his hands into his pockets to keep them warm. "I never took you for someone who bought into legends and myths."

"You think love is a myth?" Riley gave him some side-eye. "You were married."

Sam's chest pinched a little. He did not want to go there, but he'd walked right into that. "Yes. I was. And I loved Natalia more than my life. And now she's gone."

Riley exhaled slowly. "I'm sorry for your loss."

"Thank you."

She stared at the fountain again. "Is that why you keep to yourself so much?"

"Yes." He shrugged. "I want to protect myself and those I care for. Can't do that if I'm vulnerable, so I've conditioned myself to not get invested emotionally past a certain level. Like you have."

Riley gave him an incredulous expression, her salty side coming out in full force as she used air quotes for emphasis. "What do you mean 'like me'?"

"You keep to yourself as well. We've worked together off and on for a year now," he said, "and I've never seen you with anyone. Don't deny it."

She looked back at the fountain, clearly hating that she'd been that obvious and that he'd noticed. Several tense seconds ticked by before she answered, low enough that he would've missed it if he hadn't been watching her so closely. "No. You're not wrong."

"Riley!" someone called then, interrupting them.

It was Luna Norton, a physical therapist at the hospital. Sam had met her a few times, mainly at the diner she worked at that was owned by her parents. There were only two restaurants in town and one of them was also a bar, so when he and Ivy went out to eat, they went to the Buzzy Bird. Mark Bates was with her. Sam had met him briefly at the diner. He seemed nice enough, and completely besotted with Luna, poor man. "Hey, Dr. Perkins," Luna said to Sam as she reached them, but her attention was fixed on Riley. "Are you working today too?"

"I am." Riley smiled. "Just finished a code upstairs, so came down for a quick break. Why?"

"No reason." Luna's curious gaze darted between Riley and Sam, then fixed on Sam for a long beat, a warning in her eyes that Sam understood immediately because he'd used it himself where his daughter was concerned.

Hurt her and you'll die slowly and painfully.

Right. Sam shuffled his feet to maintain circulation in his chilled toes, wondering why Luna felt the need to warn him about Riley. They weren't involved nor would they be. That was the whole point of today. Which reminded him...

Once Luna and Mark went back inside, and Sam and Riley

were alone again, he ignored the pinch of regret in his chest and said, "I accept your offer."

"Huh?" Riley squinted up at him.

"What you said upstairs. We forget about the kiss and move forward as professional colleagues only. I agree that's the best way."

"Oh." She stared into the frozen fountain again. "Okay."

And just like that, it was over. He should be happy. Thrilled. Except he felt…*disappointed*.

Sam scrambled to figure out why as his analytical brain popped up facts like a scoreboard. Fact one: he'd kissed Riley. Fact two: she'd kissed him back. Fact three: that kiss had been the best thing to happen to him in recent memory, and now all Sam could seem to think about was doing it again, even though that was the absolute worst idea in modern history.

And that's exactly why he had to stick with this arrangement, for better or worse.

Sam sighed and pinched the bridge of his nose as they went back upstairs. In the reading room, Riley kept her attention firmly on the file in front of her, which was good because Sam didn't think he could get through this with those pretty blue eyes watching him. He should leave. He wanted to leave. But then he sat down again and asked, "Why do you use a wheelchair?"

Riley, still salty apparently, snapped at him over her shoulder. "Because I like the aesthetic. Why do you think?"

Yeah, he'd misphrased that question and now felt worse than before. *Idiot*. "I'm sorry."

Riley shot him a sour glare. "Look, why are you still here? We made a deal. The kiss is forgotten, okay? Leave me alone. It's fine. I'm fine."

"You're clearly not fine," he said quietly before he could stop himself.

She opened her mouth, closed it, then opened it again. "Not your problem, okay? I am not yours to fix."

Sam sat forward and scrubbed his hands over his face. "I don't want to fix you, Riley. I think you're great as you are. Better than great. Amazing."

Several long moments passed before Riley finally turned to face him, her expression guarded, and her gaze lowered as she said, "I was in a car accident. The car lost control on the ice and skidded into the bay. My parents died instantly. I broke my back in three places and had spinal cord damage. That's why I use the chair. The accident was my fault. They were only out that night because of me."

"I'm so sorry." He sat back, exhaling slowly. "Thank you for sharing that with me."

Riley nodded, looking up at him at last. "How did your wife die?"

"She was diagnosed with ALS at thirty-four and passed away two years ago, before I could find a cure for her. I failed my wife. I won't fail my patients."

They sat across from each other then, silent, as a new understanding hung heavy between them. Part of him was glad Riley had finally confided in him, but instead of quenching his curiosity about her, it only made him want to know more. Why did she feel responsible? He was sure that wasn't the case, but before he could ask more, his phone buzzed. He checked his screen and winced. "I've got to get home to Ivy. Hala needs to leave soon."

"Right." Riley turned back around to face her desk, her face flushed and her eyes damp. "Guess I'll see you on the next case then."

Sam stood, reluctant to leave after what they'd shared, despite their agreement. He pulled on his jacket and started for the door, unsure what to say to make things better between them. She stopped him before he reached the hall. "And, Sam? Thanks for telling me about your wife."

He gave a slow nod. "Thanks for telling me about your accident."

Then he walked away, that dreaded warmth in his chest toward her blossoming anew, telling him that his emotions were still involved where Riley was concerned, regardless of their deal. That spelled big, big trouble, because if he couldn't stop those emotions from spreading to his heart then all bets were off.

CHAPTER EIGHT

"THIS IS A TERRIFIC HOUSE, Riley. One of my favorites in the area. And it's close to your brother's place as well," Lynette Thompson, the Realtor, said as she led her into a nice ranch-style home with bay access. "It's been newly remodeled within the last three years, though I can see a few areas where accessibility might be a problem for you. The entrance out front, for instance, and the higher kitchen island and counters, out of reach for someone using a wheelchair or a scooter. All easily fixable by a licensed contractor though."

Riley looked around, taking in the crisp white trim and hardwood floors. She liked the contemporary style and the updated conveniences, such as the quartz countertops in the kitchen. "Can we look at the rest?"

"Sure thing." Lynette handed Riley a spec sheet on the property before leading her around from room to room for the next half an hour, ending with a large master bedroom and attached bathroom. The house was graceful and lovely, though it had been built in a different era without any thought toward accommodating those with mobility challenges. Still, Riley could envision how much better it could work for her with a few updates.

"It's four bedrooms, two and a half baths, so plenty of room for guests. Built in 1958 and sits on a third-of-an-acre waterfront lot. You're just a short distance away from the private beach and have picturesque views from your back patio year-round. There's even a boardwalk that leads from your patio down to the water. And with lots of windows and glass doors overlooking Buzzards Bay, it makes the indoor and outdoor living seamless. As I said, with a few modifications, I think it could work well for you."

"Hmm." Riley was already doing calculations in her head. She'd prequalified for a mortgage through her local lender, knowing how cutthroat the current housing market was, but she also wanted to bring a contractor through before signing on the dotted line to make sure all the necessary changes could be done within her budget. Trouble was, she'd been so busy lately, she hadn't had time to find anyone to do the work yet. "I think so too, but I'd like a second opinion first before I move forward. How quickly do you need my answer?"

"As quickly as possible, unfortunately," Lynette said. "You know how fast properties go around here. I'll hold other buyers off as long as I can, but I really need to know before Christmas, which gives you two weeks. The current owners want this done soon so they can enjoy their retirement in Florida."

"Okay." Riley pulled out her phone to make notes on her next steps. "I'll find a contractor ASAP then schedule another tour through the property with them. Thanks, Lynette."

"Sure thing, hon." The Realtor led her back toward the entrance and out to the brick front walk. Riley's vehicle was parked in the nice driveway beside the house, in front of an attached two-car garage. The neighbors were busy shoveling the sidewalks in front of their houses, lit by moonlight, the streetlamps and the glow from all the colorful Christmas lights in yards even though it was only 5:00 p.m.

"We'll talk soon," Lynette said.

"We will." Riley waved, then got back into her car to head home to pick up Adi. Today they'd announced in the media the grand opening of the long-awaited Ice, Ice Baby pop-up festival downtown, and she'd somehow lucked out and had the evening off. She'd promised her niece earlier that once the festival opened, they'd go, since Brock and Cassie were both stuck at the hospital a lot lately. As she drove through town, crowds were already filling the area, especially around the town square, which had been blocked off for all the vendors and the ice rink. For the first time that year, it felt like the holidays were coming.

But as she passed the building where she and Sam and the girls had played bingo the week prior, her spirits sank. She and Sam hadn't seen each other much since their talk in the reading room. He hadn't even had any cases on her docket this week, which was odd. Riley wasn't sure if he'd done that on purpose to avoid her or if fate had intervened, but either way, it didn't matter. They'd made the right decision putting an end to things after that kiss. Neither of them needed or wanted the complication. They were both just getting their lives back on track after trauma. No reason to screw it up now with messy emotional entanglements that may or may not last.

Not even ones as hot as Sam Perkins.

Adi was waiting impatiently for her when she arrived at her brother's house. Riley barely had a chance to go inside and change out of her scrubs and into regular clothes before her young niece all but tugged her out the door again to go to the festival. Riley at least made sure Winnie, a potty break outside, was locked safely in her pen with food and water before heading back downtown.

* * *

Sam didn't want to be here.

But as he weaved through the crowded town square, following his daughter from the parking lot toward the temporary ice rink, he knew there was no backing out. Ivy had been talking about nothing but Ice, Ice Baby for weeks, and Sam couldn't let her down, regardless of the fact he'd had less than ten hours sleep total this week due to being on call, in addition to his busy regular schedule. He'd barely had time to eat, let alone sleep a full night.

"I can't wait to skate, Daddy," Ivy called, bouncing on her toes with excitement in front of him. She glowed nearly as bright as the holiday lights around her. "Will you skate with me?"

Sam hadn't been on a rink since he'd been nine and gone on an ill-fated field trip with his school class. They'd met some hockey players—yes, they had hockey in California—and he'd had the crazy notion to impress a girl he'd liked in his class, Ida Thong. Unfortunately for Sam, he'd had no clue what he was doing and ended up making a fool of himself in front of everyone by face-planting on the ice right in front of Ida. Repeating that experience now with Ivy wasn't at the top of his to-do list, but his exhausted brain couldn't come up with a good reason to refuse, so he went with, "Maybe."

The entrance to the temporary rink was draped with strings of colored lights and ringed by crackling metal barrel fires all around the edge. Ivy stopped near a kid about her age who wore a stocking cap that had to be about eighteen inches long. She tapped them on the shoulder and the kid turned, grinning as they saw her. "Hey, Nic!" Ivy said, all but vibrating with energy. "I can't wait to ice-skate. It's my very first time!"

"You never skated before?" Nic asked, looking dubious.

Ivy shrugged. "No. Where are your parents?"

The kid pointed toward some vendor stalls nearby. "My dad isn't here, but my mom and my sisters are getting hot chocolate."

"Oh, I love hot chocolate!" Ivy rounded on Sam again. "Daddy, can we get some? Please?"

Based on the lines, Sam's first instinct was to tell his daughter they should rent skates first, before they ran out, but the words died on his lips at Ivy's eager smile. He hadn't seen her so happy since before her mom died, and he couldn't refuse. "Sure. Let's get cocoa, then we'll get in line for skates."

They headed toward the hot chocolate vendor stall, which was more of a tiny trailer that seemed too small for an adult human to stand upright in. A woman wearing antlers and a red-and-white-striped top was taking orders at the window. Sam and Ivy joined the back of a line with about six or seven people ahead of them.

While they waited, someone came up behind them in line, but Sam didn't turn around, at least not until he was tapped on the back of the leg. Then he glanced over his shoulder to find Adi Turner grinning up at him, missing at least one tooth.

"Hi, Dr. Perkins!" she said, waving up at him before stepping around him to Ivy's side.

Riley was there too, giving him a small smile from her chair. "Fancy seeing you here."

"Yes." Sam forced himself to breathe. He hadn't seen her in several days and had managed to convince himself his reactions to her had all been in his imagination. But it seemed all it took was one encounter and he was right back to a racing heart and tight throat. To avoid making a fool of himself, he turned back around to face the trailer. "Ivy is very excited to skate for the first time."

"Adi too, though this isn't her first time," Riley said, apparently unaffected by seeing him again. "She takes lessons. The festival's always a good time though. Everyone in town gets into the spirit. Never feels like Christmas to me until the ice rink is open."

Sam had to admit it was a jolly scene, with all those colorful lights, Christmas music coming from a live band playing on a makeshift stage set up on one side of the area, and those flames flickering in the night.

The line finally moved forward and the people in front of Sam reached the window, where they ordered ten hot chocolates. Either they had a serious cocoa addiction or they were part of a group. This would probably take forever. Just his luck.

Riley peered around him at the window then settled back in her chair, apparently coming to terms with waiting a while as she asked, "What holiday traditions did you have in California?"

"Natalia always handled it." The familiar sting of loss he felt when bringing up his wife had dulled, less like a sharp jab and more like a vague ache. Huh. That was new. "Most years we'd take off the week between Christmas and New Year's to spend a few days at the beach with Ivy."

"Sounds nice," Riley said, her tone tinged with a sadness that tugged at Sam's heart. "The holidays are tough when you're missing someone."

"True." Sam corralled the girls to keep them in line in front of him. "But I'm determined to make this Christmas special for Ivy. New town. New traditions. New memories."

"You're making a good start of it," Riley said, surprising

him enough that he turned around again to look at her. Her blue eyes sparkled, and his pulse tripped. Sam tried to tell himself it was just the cold December night and his exhaustion, but even he had to admit that with the snow lightly falling and the laughter and joy all around, the night suddenly seemed more magical.

"Next!" the reindeer at the window called and Sam stepped forward. "May I help you?"

"Four hot cocoas, please, with marshmallows and extra whipped cream."

"Right away, sir."

"You don't have to buy us hot chocolate," Riley said.

"My treat." Sam handed his card to the woman in the trailer, where another antler-bedecked reindeer bustled around behind her preparing his drinks, inserting the filled cups into a cardboard drink holder, then sliding it all out the window toward him. He tucked his card and wallet safely away again before picking it up the tray, along with some napkins, then turning to face the girls and Riley. "Let's find a table to sit down before I spill these all over myself or someone else."

They worked their way back through the crowd toward the rink, crossing some bumpy snow and icy sidewalks. It couldn't have been a smooth ride for Riley under the best of circumstances, and Sam was impressed with her ability to handle her chair. He told her as much.

Riley glanced up at him, smiling. "Thanks. I switched last year to an upgraded model that's more all-terrain, plus it has a power assist motor if I need help over grass or gravel."

"Which you're probably too stubborn to use," he added, not looking at her. He wasn't flirting. Nope. This was just small talk, no matter how enjoyable bantering with her was. He suddenly didn't want to leave now. In fact, he wanted to spend as much time as possible with the sweet scent of cocoa wafting around him and a gorgeous woman at his side.

"You know me so well," Riley said, shooting him a quick wink, which made Sam stop in his tracks.

He battled a sudden wild urge to toss the drink holder into the snow and pull Riley into his arms and kiss her silly instead. Which would be a direct violation of their agreement. Instead, he turned abruptly and headed for the first open table he saw, calling behind him as he prayed for more willpower to get through this night unscathed. "This way."

Riley wasn't sure exactly what was happening, but Sam's abrupt shift in mood bothered her. Yes, they had an agreement, but that didn't mean they couldn't be cordial to each other, at least in public. When they'd been waiting in line, he'd been charming enough, and he'd even bought them all hot chocolate. For a crazy second, it had felt like *something*.

But, of course, it wasn't. Sam had made it clear he wasn't looking for romance, and neither was she. She had too much going on already, with work and her new house hunt. She didn't want him that way anyway. Even if the sizzle in her nervous system said she did.

He led them to an empty table near the edge of the dining area and the next few moments were a flurry of distributing drinks and throwing away the cardboard drink holder. Which was good, because it allowed Riley to make a shift of her own, from sappy to salty where Sam was concerned. She didn't try to be deliberately prickly with people, but it had become a defense mechanism since the accident. And where Sam was concerned, her heart needed all the defenses it could get.

"Thanks, Aunt Riley," Adi said, snatching her cup and taking a swig before fanning her mouth. "It's hot!"

"That's why they call it hot chocolate," Riley retorted, shaking her head. "You know that."

"We should rent skates," Sam said, eyeing the ever-growing line nearby. "We don't want them to run out."

"I have my own skates." Adi proudly patted the *Star Wars* backpack she'd brought with her. "But Ivy needs some."

"I'll go grab them," Sam said, barely glancing at Riley. "You all stay here, so we don't lose the table."

"Yes, sir." Riley gave him a mock salute, which made the girls giggle.

Twenty minutes later, Sam returned with a pair of pink rental skates for his daughter and another, larger, black pair that Riley assumed had to be for him, because she certainly couldn't skate. Sam helped Ivy with hers before putting on his own. The girls had only finished about half of their cocoa but seemed eager to get out onto the rink.

"Can we go out now, Aunt Riley?" Adi asked.

"You'll have to ask Sam, since he's the ice king going with you," Riley told her niece. Sam looked over at her double entendre and Riley just raised a brow at him. As if it wasn't true. The man could turn his emotions off on a dime.

"Dr. Perkins is a king?" Adi asked, frowning.

"Does that make me a princess?" Ivy asked. "I've always wanted to be a princess. Like Elsa!"

Riley shook her head and chuckled at yet another ice reference.

Sam placed a hand on his daughter's shoulder while shooting Riley visual daggers. "You're always a princess to me, *yeobo*."

"Okay." Adi jumped up from the picnic table and nearly

fell in her skates on the uneven ground. The indoor facility where she took lessons had nice, even floors. "I'm ready!"

Sam and Ivy stood too, both as wobbly as newborn foals. Riley's heart did a little flip despite her wishes. The man could be so darn sweet when he tried to be. Like when he'd brushed the hair from her eyes, or when he'd listened to her story about the accident and not tried to give her the usual platitudes, instead really taking it in and then thanking her for sharing...

Warmth that had nothing to do with the fire nearby blossomed and grew inside her.

"Hold on to me as we go to the rink, so we stay together," he said, taking each girl's hand, one on either side of him as they traversed the short distance to the rink entrance amidst much giggling from the girls.

They stopped just outside to take off their blade protectors and Riley found herself calling to them, "I'll be cheering you all on from here."

So much for her salty queen act.

Adi and Ivy gave her thumbs-ups while Sam just watched her warily, then all three of them staggered out to the ice, holding each other for balance. Riley had skated out there so many times herself growing up. It was bittersweet now to watch others doing what she couldn't.

Someday, she reminded herself.

She sipped her cocoa, throat aching with both sadness and determination. She would get back out there again, no matter what. When she set her mind to something, she did it. Visions of her and Sam and the girls skating together, holding hands, laughing and teasing each other, being a family filled her head before she could stop them. The intense yearning hit so hard then that she had to bat away tears. Where had that come from? Yes, she missed her old life and old dreams, but that didn't mean she wanted Sam to replace them.

Did it?

She swiftly brushed her mitten-covered hands under her eyes. No. That was ridiculous. She'd just missed all this, that was all. Missed the camaraderie and fun. Missed the companionship and support. And okay, fine—maybe she'd missed seeing Sam the past week or so, if only in passing. She'd gotten used to his quirkiness in her reading room, and having it gone left a void. A Sam-shaped void. And she missed Ivy too, hanging around at the house with Adi, giggling and playing and doing all the stuff seven-year-old girls did. She hadn't known Sam and his daughter that long, but they'd somehow become a part of her life while she wasn't looking. And Sam was a good man, even if he wasn't the man for her.

I wish he was.

Riley froze at the sudden realization, blinking at the rink as the trio completed another pass around the ice. Sam looked over at her and waved, a wide grin splitting his handsome face, and she found herself wondering what it would be like to be loved by him.

Wait. What?

No way had her crazy attraction to Sam grown into more without her knowing. How could it have? They'd barely said two words to each other this week, and they had an agreement. No more kisses. No romance. No more anything beyond the professional. That's what she'd wanted—what she'd asked for.

But apparently her heart had other ideas.

She was still grappling with it all when the girls returned, followed closely by Sam himself.

Adi headed straight to Riley and hugged her over the side

of the wheelchair, exclaiming, "That was so cool! I didn't even fall once."

"Good job!" Riley said, her eyes fixed to Sam's over the top of her niece's head. What was she going to tell him? How was she going to deal with this? The last thing she needed was him going all possessive boyfriend on her, thinking he had to help her, cure her, like he had with his wife. She didn't want that, had never wanted that. Panic had her spiraling as she pulled away from Adi.

"I wish you could come with us, Aunt Riley," her niece said, snapping Riley out of it.

"Me too," Riley mumbled as she tore her gaze away from Sam's too-perceptive one. "Maybe next year."

"Is my cocoa still hot?" Ivy asked through chattering teeth. "I'm freezing."

"It is." Riley pushed the cup over to her. "Drink up, munchkin."

"After you finish, we have to go." Sam sat down beside his daughter to change back into his shoes. "You girls have school tomorrow."

"Do we have to?" Adi and Ivy whined together.

"Afraid so," Sam said, sounding wistful, like he wished the night could continue.

Riley got it. But she had to get out of there, had to go home and think this through. What a mess. She'd thought she and Sam had doused the fire when they'd decided to keep things professional between them. She'd thought she was safe from falling for him because she'd put him in a tidy friend box, but nope. He'd somehow escaped and now threatened to burn down all her barriers and put the future she'd thought she wanted at risk. It was all overwhelming and confusing and more than a little tantalizing, giving her new possibilities she hadn't expected before.

Distracted, she tapped Adi on the arm. "Get your boots back on too, then I'll race you back to our car."

CHAPTER NINE

"ALL RIGHT, MR. LANGSTON, your scans are done," Riley said to the older man on the CT table through the speaker system. "The tech will help you sit up when you're ready, and once you've changed, the orthopedist will talk with you in his office downstairs."

Harry Langston, the town auctioneer, fussed with the white hospital gown covering his top half, scowling through the glass at her. "He's always late. Not like you. You run a tight ship, missy."

"Dr. Warner is very busy." Riley hid her grin at the compliment. She'd known Harry since she was a girl and underneath his bluster, he was just a big softy. "Take your time then."

Still frowning, Harry allowed the tech to help him off the table and into the dressing room. Despite what he'd said about Riley running a tight ship, today, she was decidedly behind. She'd had a full schedule already, made worse by several emergencies that had needed to be worked in from the ER, including Mr. Langston, who'd hurt his back decorating the front of his auction house downtown. He'd claimed he wanted it to look nice for the extra visitors who'd come to town for the festival, but Riley suspected it was part of the ongoing rivalry between him and Arthur at the hardware store. Those two were always trying to outdo each other.

By the time Harry was finished, Riley met him in the hall.

"You're all set," she said, smiling at him. "Go on down to orthopedics on the second floor. I called them, and the nurse there is expecting you."

He gave her a repentant glance. "Sorry for my mood. My stupid phone isn't working right, even though I just got it. Won't save anything. Says my memory is full."

Riley frowned. She knew for a fact Harry had gotten his device the year before, because she'd been in the store at the same time getting hers, so it didn't sound right that it wasn't working. Harry unlocked the phone then handed it to her. She scrolled through, checking a few settings until she found the problem. "You have twelve thousand photos of your dog on here, Harry. How did you take so many so fast?"

He shrugged. "Bandit likes having his picture taken."

"Well, it's eating up all your memory." Riley sighed and handed the phone back to him. "I suggest backing up to the cloud then deleting them off your device to free up more space. Storing them all on your phone is the problem. If you need help doing the backup, call the guys at the phone store."

"Okay," Harry grumbled while Riley led him to the elevators, biting back a smile. Despite all their quirks and her salty reputation these days, she loved the people in her town and didn't mind taking care of them when she could. She pushed the elevator button, and the doors whooshed open to reveal Sam standing there.

Her breath caught, same as it had when she'd come up behind him in line at the festival. He still looked just as dreamy today, though she herself felt frazzled and frumpy after a busy morning. She smoothed a hand over her hair to make sure it wasn't sticking up too badly.

Normally she didn't care much about how she looked, but she'd been hyperaware of it all since that night at the festival, when she'd realized her attraction to him might have become something more. She noticed everything about him now. Like the tiny gold flecks in his dark brown irises, and the white evenness of his teeth when he smiled at Harry, or how his scrub pants clung to his muscular thighs and butt just so…

She didn't realize she'd been ogling until Mr. Langston cleared his throat.

Whoops.

"Excuse me, youngsters." Harry sidled past them to get into the elevator. "Need to get downstairs."

Flustered, she moved her chair to the side, only to bump into Sam's leg. "Sorry."

"My fault," Sam countered, stepping back fast as if she'd burned him.

Harry harrumphed and shook his head as the elevator doors closed. "Saints preserve me from love."

Well, that was awkward.

Riley turned to head back to Radiology and her next patient, cursing herself for not remembering that this one had been referred by Sam for recurring migraines. Normally she kept on top of her referrals, but time had gotten away from her. As Sam followed her to the MRI suite, she asked, "How are you?"

"Good. Can't remember the last time someone called me a youngster." He seemed affable today. Always mercurial, that was her Sam. Sometimes the man seemed like a mystery wrapped in an enigma to Riley. He took a seat in the other chair at the desk beside hers in the reading room and nodded toward the observation window. "We can get started whenever you're ready."

Right. Turning her attention toward the patient where it belonged, Riley reviewed the woman's file to ensure she was doing the correct testing. This was an MRI series of the brain to check for any vascular or structural changes or lesions that might be causing the patient's headaches. She signaled to the tech through the observation window to get the patient positioned correctly inside the machine. While that happened, she tried to make small talk with Sam to keep him from noticing how oddly she was acting around him today. Like leaning toward him without meaning to, as if drawn by an invisible connection. So strange. Whenever she caught herself, she leaned away again, embarrassed. She really needed to get control over this. "Did Ivy have fun at the festival?"

"It's all she's talked about for days," he said. "Now she wants skating lessons too."

"It's not a bad idea," Riley said. "I took them when I was little. It's good exercise, and that's one less gift to worry about for Christmas, right?"

"True." Sam looked over at her then, his dark eyes softening a bit. "It was fun having you and Adi there with us. I'm glad the girls found each other. It's helped bring Ivy out of her shell here."

Riley's chest pinched at this sweetness, and she kept her gaze on the file before her instead of the man beside her for fear he'd see what she was feeling in her eyes. "It's helped Adi too. After she lost her mom, we were all worried. She didn't talk for months, just beeped at people, imitating her favorite droid toy back then. Brock even took her to a speech therapist because of it, but they said it was trauma related and would go away on its own in time."

"Huh," Sam said, looking genuinely concerned. "Poor kid. Obviously they were right since she seems to talk fine now."

"Yeah. Some things just take time and patience." Riley shrugged. "Having Cassie return to town helped too. I think

Adi just missed having a constant female presence in her life. She missed having a mom."

Sam seemed to take that in a moment, his lips pursed. He did that a lot when he thought deeply about things, she'd noticed. She really needed to stop noticing stuff about him. It was becoming a problem.

Finally, the tech signaled the patient was ready, and they began the MRI. It took about an hour overall, and the patient had been given IV gadolinium, a contrast solution to make the blood vessels in her brain more visible. When it was over, Riley and Sam went over the results together while the tech helped the patient out of the machine and removed the IV.

"On the positive side, there are no microbleeds, lesions or changes to the white or gray matter volume," Riley said, studying the images on her computer screen.

"True," Sam agreed over her shoulder, his body heat chasing away Riley's chill. "But on the negative, I still have no clue what's causing my patient's migraines." He sighed and sat back, rubbing his eyes, looking about as tired as Riley felt.

"You look like you need sleep," Riley told him, her stomach gurgling from hunger. "When's your shift over?"

"An hour ago," Sam replied, his tone gruff with fatigue. "But my replacement hadn't arrived yet at last check and this lady needed help, so I stayed."

"Are they here now?"

He checked his phone then smiled, looking rumpled and ridiculously sexy. Riley looked away fast, her face heating from her naughty thoughts. "Yes, thank goodness. Now I get to go home to an empty house and eat leftovers alone."

He didn't sound too disappointed, but Riley had been around him enough by now to hear the note of loneliness underlying his tone. It tugged at her heart and before she could stop herself, she said, "Or you could come home with me and eat leftovers there. Brock and Cassie are both working, and Adi and her baby brother are staying at her nanny's place tonight since we were all working."

Sam looked a bit startled, and Riley realized she shouldn't have suggested that because of their agreement. And sure, they might have crossed the line a bit the other night by sitting together at the festival, but that was a different situation. Neither had planned for that to happen. It'd been pure fate. This was a direct violation. The hint of the forbidden in her suggestion had her long-buried bad girl sitting up at attention. She played it down in her mind. This wasn't a big deal. It was two colleagues sharing a meal. They'd chat about work and cases and eat, then call it a night. End of story. Never mind that Riley seemed to be waking up from fevered dreams of her and Sam—in bed together, doing all sorts of wicked and wonderful things to each other—a lot lately.

"Oh, uh…" Sam shifted in his seat, fiddling with some papers on her desk. "I don't want to impose."

He was giving her an out. She should take it. Except she didn't. "You're not imposing. I invited you. Unless you'd rather sit in your house alone."

The silence stretched taut until the uncomfortableness grew too great, and Riley faced her computer again, the weight of Sam's stare still on her making the back of her neck tingle.

Finally, he exhaled slowly, as if surrendering at last to the inevitable. "Okay."

Riley swallowed hard then looked back at him over her shoulder. "Okay. Meet me at Brock's after you're done. My shift is done now too."

Sam nodded then left to go back downstairs to brief his

replacement on the migraine patient's case. Riley finished up some last-minute documentation before clearing out and heading home.

Outside in the parking lot, she took a deep breath of crisp winter air before clicking the buttons to remotely start her engine and open her vehicle. It had started snowing again, and after getting inside and turning on the heat, she checked her email on her phone while waiting for the windows to defrost. Lynette had messaged her again about the house on the bay. There were apparently other people scheduled to see the house tomorrow, and she wondered if Riley had found a contractor to give her estimates on the upgrades so she could put in an offer. The short answer was no. Riley hadn't contacted anyone because she'd been too busy. But she needed to do so fast if she didn't want this opportunity to pass her by.

Too many had done so already.

Once the windows thawed, Riley put her phone away and found a favorite rendition of "Have Yourself a Merry Little Christmas" by James Taylor on the radio before pulling out of the employee lot and heading toward home.

Once there, she let Winnie out in the fenced backyard to potty then heated up the leftovers from last night's dinner. By the time Sam arrived, everything was in the oven, and she'd changed into comfy jeans, socks, and a red sweatshirt with a reindeer and a large candy cane on the front that said "Pole Dancer."

Sam knocked at the front door and Winnie immediately lost her mind, paws scrabbling on the hardwood floors as she tore around the house in endless laps that would hopefully burn off all her excess energy before Riley went to bed.

"Smells good in here," Sam said as he took off his coat and

hung it on a hook near the door before toeing off his snowy boots. "Anything I can help with?"

"The homemade mostaccioli and breadsticks should be done shortly, but you can set out plates and silverware, if you want." She led him into the kitchen and pointed out where things were kept. "We can eat in here at the island where it's cozier, or the dining room where we'd have more room. Your choice."

"The island works fine for me," he said, his grateful smile sending a fresh sizzle of forbidden attraction through her. "Thanks again for inviting me. I don't mind eating alone when I get home late, but it does get old after a while."

"You're welcome." To distract herself from the way her ovaries were jumping for joy because of his nearness, she asked, "You mentioned leftovers at your house. Does your nanny cook too?"

"No, I do. It relaxes me. Between the Italian dishes I learned from my wife and the Korean recipes I inherited from my mom, I can hold my own in the kitchen."

"Huh." Riley smiled, imagining Sam as a chef. "I was never much of a cook myself. Figured after the accident I wouldn't have to worry about it anymore because I wouldn't be able to reach stuff anyway. But then Brock had the contractors put in these adjustable-height countertops and other accessible amenities and now I don't have any excuses."

Sam chuckled, looking around. "Well, this kitchen is amazing."

"Yeah, it's going to be difficult to replicate when I get my own place."

"Maybe not." He shrugged. "Depending on what's in place to start with, the renovations could be more minimal than you think. I did all the work on our house back in San Diego myself to make it easier for Natalia once her condition declined. Kitchen, bathrooms, front entrance. All of it."

The oven timer dinged, and Riley grabbed a set of oven mitts from the counter to pull out the dishes of food, then set them on trivets on the island, using the time to gather her thoughts. She'd had no idea that Sam had handyman skills as well. Given all the other things he had going on that took up his time, she was intrigued. There were so many sides to him she'd yet to discover. She pulled out serving utensils from one of the drawers, then parked her chair beside his at the island to eat.

"Well, I looked at a house the other day that I really liked, but it needs a lot done to make it work for me," Riley said as she dished out mostaccioli for herself, then took a breadstick too. "But I need to find a contractor to look at it with me to give me estimates so I can put an offer in if it fits within my budget. She said tonight that other people are interested in the property too, but I haven't had time to find anyone yet."

Sam swallowed a bite of his pasta then said, "I can take a look at it, if you want."

Riley frowned over at him. "Really? Are you sure? Your schedule is crazier than mine."

He scoffed. "Shouldn't take long. And I enjoy doing it. I learned young to fix things around the house to save money and honed my skills over the years. I'm not licensed here yet, but plan to be soon, before I'd touch your project. I understand though if you'd rather find someone else, what with our agreement and all—"

"No, no," Riley said. "That would be great. I know you, so I'd trust your opinions, and from what you've just told me, you'll know what needs to be done."

"Okay then."

"Okay."

Sam grinned as he bit off a bite of breadstick, and any awkwardness between them disappeared, just like that. "You'd be doing me a favor too, honestly. I like working with my hands but haven't had a chance to do much with my building skills since moving here. Renovating things gives me a sense of accomplishment too. A job well done. Kind of like surgery, except the house is my patient."

"That's very Zen of you," Riley teased, relief washing over her. For so long now she'd wanted to get a place of her own, but it had never seemed like the right moment. Something else always seemed to take precedence and it became so easy to put it on the back burner and forget about the dream. But now, with Sam basically offering her everything she needed, it was all right there waiting. She resisted the urge to hug him and instead picked up her phone. "I'll message Lynette now and see when she can get us in again."

After dinner, Sam couldn't quite believe he'd volunteered to help Riley with her renovations. But even worse, he couldn't bring himself to regret it. After the festival the other night, she seemed to occupy most of his waking thoughts, so why not go all out and keep hanging around her, even it went directly against their agreement? Neither of them seemed too upset about that, and it made him question where she was at with all this.

She'd offered to give him a tour of the rest of the house so he could get an idea of the kinds of things she'd want him to look at in the new place. Now they were standing in the hallway outside her bedroom, and he couldn't stop imagining if the circumstances were different and they were living together, even if it would never happen. He felt hot and bothered and wished he could quietly slip away, but with Riley's wheelchair blocking his escape route, that was all but impossible.

So, he forced himself to focus on the details of the architecture, the wide entrance to the room with its pocket door that opened and closed with the push of a button, the wide windows across the room with glorious views of Buzzards Bay, and the huge closet with automatic height-adjustable racks.

Next, they went down a ramp to the house's lower level, where a gym had been installed, again easily accessible for wheelchair users. In one corner was a hot tub, and at the sight of it, Sam's traitorous brain immediately clogged with images of Riley, slick and wearing nothing but a towel, before he banished those thoughts fast. He didn't want to think about her like that. He didn't want to want her that way. He didn't want to open his heart only to be left behind again. And yet it seemed that was exactly what was happening.

His chest constricted and beads of sweat broke out on his forehead.

"I realize it's a lot," Riley said, breaking him out of his anxiety spiral over the realization that despite all his efforts to the contrary, she'd found a way inside him, a way to make him open and vulnerable again. She made him want to throw caution to the wind and lose control with her. And that was... scary and stupid and sinfully appealing. She continued as his pulse jackhammered in his ears. "I don't really need any of this though. Just the basics upstairs would be fine to start." Then her gaze flickered down to his hands hanging by his sides, and her blue gaze flared with surprise. "You're trembling. Are you all right?"

Her eyes met his, concern and something he didn't know how to interpret logically within them. His body, however, had no problem grasping what was going on as a sudden, fierce need burned through him, a hunger for her that stole his breath, with her bright blue eyes and her lush dark hair and her quick intelligence. He'd tried to explain it away as nothing but loneliness. Tried to ignore it, deny it. But he knew now he couldn't continue like that. He wasn't ready, but then he might never *be* ready again. Riley had proven herself to be loyal and true and courageous. He needed to find those same traits in himself and stop using his grief and fear of being hurt as excuses to keep people at bay.

People like Riley.

She continued watching him, and he found the tilt of her head far more endearing than he should. She'd mentioned Adi missing a mother figure in her life. Ivy needed a mother too, deserved more than he could give her. But that was a lot for anyone to take on, especially someone who prized their independence as Riley clearly did. He didn't dare ask her. Not yet. Maybe not ever.

"We can take the elevator upstairs," she said, after what seemed like a small eternity, leading him over to a gold-toned door set into the wall. "This is something else you don't have to worry about since the house I'm looking at is all one level."

"Oh, uh, great." Sam tried to cover his discomfiture as the elevator door opened. They'd had an elevator installed in their old house back in San Diego too, but this one was much smaller. In fact, if Riley stretched out both arms from her chair, he bet she could touch both sides. Fitting them both in there together would be a snug fit. He hesitated, thinking maybe he could claim a phobia, but no—they'd already ridden in elevators together at work, so that was off the table.

So, they both boarded, and Riley pushed the button, which was at the perfect height for her in the chair. When the door closed, it was a tight enough fit to make his internal temperature tick up a notch. Thankfully, Riley kept talking, giving him something else to concentrate on besides her nearness and how easy it would be for him to pick her up and kiss her silly until neither of them cared about that stupid agreement they'd made.

"Like I said, my biggest concerns are the things I use every day. The counters, sinks, showers, windows, closets. Those will be the most important to have fixed by the time I move in."

"Sure," Sam said gruffly as the elevator whisked them back up to the first floor. "It's just a matter of time and money."

"Everything's a matter of time and money." Riley snorted.

"Not everything," Sam countered, meeting her gaze, and now his skin felt too tight for his body.

"No, I suppose you're right," she said, her cheeks flushed as the elevator finally stopped and the door opened again, letting in a rush of blessedly cool air. "Not everything."

Sam held the door for Riley to exit first, then stepped out in the hallway after her. With the tour over and the air still sizzling with possibilities, Sam cleared his newly constricted throat. "I should be going. But thank you for dinner. And the tour. Let me know when the Realtor can fit us in."

"You're welcome. And I will." Riley smiled, looking around. She seemed happier tonight, more relaxed and open with him. He was enchanted. "It'll be hard to leave this place. I love it here. Even if my brother gets on my last nerve sometimes."

Sam pulled on his coat and shoved his feet into his boots, eager to get out into the frigid night to keep the fire inside him he now felt whenever Riley was around from scorching him alive. He pulled on his gloves and had a hand on the door handle, saying, "I'll talk to you soon."

"Okay. Be careful driving home," Riley said from behind him, forcing him to turn slightly to avoid hitting her with the door, and that's when he saw she'd left her chair behind in the hall in favor of a pair of forearm crutches. She chuckled at whatever she saw on his face. Probably shock. In the whole time he'd known her, he'd only ever seen her in the chair. As if reading his mind, she said, "I've done a lot of PT over the last year. I hope to get back to walking on my own someday without these."

When she reached out to take the door from him, she bobbed slightly, and Sam automatically steadied her with a hand on her arm, but she pulled away fast. "I'm fine. I don't need help."

Sam froze, embarrassed heat creeping up his neck. Of course she didn't need his help. She was perfectly capable of handling things herself, just as his wife had been. Sam clenched his hands at his sides. "Sorry. I shouldn't have... Sorry."

"Stop apologizing. Please." She sighed, her shoulders slumping. "I'm sorry too. I know people say I'm salty about my situation." She made a vague gesture over herself. "But after my accident, Brock treated me like I was made of glass and would shatter at the slightest touch. It took me forever to get him to back off, so I could figure out how to survive on my own again. And once I move out, I won't have anyone around to open doors for me or pick up a crutch if I drop one, right?" Before he could say anything though, her phone buzzed, and she pulled it out of her pocket, balancing on one crutch. "It's a text from my Realtor. She has an opening tomorrow afternoon. Would that work for you?"

"What time?" He fumbled out his own phone, his palms slick with sweat despite the chilly air swirling around them both from the outside.

"Around two?"

"I'm free," he said, typing the appointment into his schedule.

"Excellent." She texted back her agent then gave him a cheeky grin. "Thanks again for helping me with this. It's an immense help. Especially so close to the holidays. This time of year can be so hectic."

"True. But I like to stay busy," he answered. "It helps keep the ghosts away."

Silence settled between them then, and when Riley finally spoke, her voice was lower than before, a bit rougher too, pulling on his heartstrings. "I still miss my parents, especially knowing it's my fault they aren't here. If I hadn't gone out that night, if I'd just listened to them about the guy I was dating then, that he was bad news…"

It was the second time she'd blamed herself for their deaths and he felt compelled to say, "That accident wasn't your fault."

"How would you know? You weren't here. They went out that night to pick me up after my date dumped me. During an ice storm. If that isn't my fault, I don't know what is." At the slight tremor in her voice, Sam clenched his fists to keep from pulling her into his arms and kissing her pain away. "I've learned to live with it."

"You shouldn't have to though." His tone held all the conviction welling up inside him. "You're right. I wasn't there. I don't know all the details. But I do know without a doubt that you were not responsible for what happened to them, Riley. We all make choices, and we live with the consequences.

They could have sent a cab for you. They could have told you to ride home with someone else. They didn't have to drive there themselves. They chose to do that, Riley. And I can't imagine they would regret their decision. I know I wouldn't if I was in their place, rescuing Ivy."

She blinked at him, tears shining in her blue eyes, her mouth open like she wanted to say something to him. She reached out with her free hand, as if to touch him, and he leaned in toward her and...

The back door opened, and Adi ran inside, jarring them both back to reality. "Aunt Riley, why are you holding the front door open? I get in trouble when I do that."

Riley took a deep breath, as if trying to regain a little equilibrium. "Dr. Perkins was just leaving. And what are you doing home? I thought you were staying at Lois's tonight."

Brock came inside then too, closing the back door behind him. "For once the ER was slow and overstaffed, so I volunteered to go home. Hey, Sam."

"Hey." Sam raised his hand in greeting, feeling far too exposed for his liking.

"Guess what!" Adi continued, rushing over to them. "Ivy and I are the *head* goldfish. Which means we get to swim in front of everyone onstage and wave our fins at the audience!"

"Cool," Riley said as she closed the door again.

Sam crouched to put himself at eye level with the little girl. "I'm sure Ivy is excited too. She and Hala have been working on her costume. But being head goldfish means you both need to practice even more since you'll be in the spotlight. The play is only a week away now."

"The teacher said we don't have lines, so it's easier. She said we get to impoverish."

Riley looked at Sam, biting back a laugh. "I think you mean improvise."

"That's what I said," Adi said. "Improdise."

Sam chuckled and straightened. "Close enough. Who knew there were goldfish at the nativity?"

Adi ran back into the kitchen, where Brock stood in front of the fridge. "Daddy, can I have a Go-Gurt?"

"And on that note, I really am leaving this time," Sam said. "See you later."

"See you," Riley said, holding the door for him again as he hurried outside, grateful he hadn't embarrassed himself any more than he already had by kissing her again. If her brother had walked in and seen them... Talk about the rumor mill churning at the hospital.

And yet, as he got into his vehicle and began to pull away, he spotted Riley still in the doorway, watching him, looking as beautiful and bright as the Christmas Star, and thought that maybe people thinking he and Riley were a couple wouldn't be so horrible after all.

CHAPTER TEN

THEY SAW THE HOUSE the next day, which was how Sam ended up standing on the back patio, staring at the frozen splendor of Buzzards Bay. It was a good-sized outdoor space with Adirondack chairs and a small table that was included with the house. There was a small shed on one side as well, which he'd checked and found filled with hardware staples one might need around the house—lawn mower, Weedwacker, various tools, nails, screws, extension cords and a long length of rope. There were even a couple of inflatable toys for swimming in the summer. As he closed it back up, he realized how much he'd missed living near the water. There was a yearning inside him, growing stronger by the second, to spend more time here, to watch as the dark gray water lightened and changed as spring approached, to teach Ivy about the different animals that lived near the shore, to jog along the beach at sunrise. To walk hand in hand with Riley on the boardwalk as she used her crutches, stopping to kiss her near the water, hold her close and…

The thought froze him in place. He wasn't sure where that had come from, nor why, now that the thought was in his head, he couldn't seem to get it out. It should scare him witless to even consider being with someone like that again, in an intimate relationship. It would mean letting her into his life, his heart, his future. It would leave him exposed, vulnerable, quite possibly weaker and less in control. All things he'd steadfastly not wanted just a month ago, but now...

"So, what do you think?" Riley asked, joining him on the patio. "Can everything be done within my budget?"

"Based on my preliminary assessments, I think so," Sam said, glad to discuss something other than the uncomfortable emotions roiling inside him—deep affection, need, want, terror. He'd thought that by getting to know her better, his interest in her might fade. But it seemed the opposite was true. The more time he spent with Riley, the more time he wanted with her. She was brilliant in her career, passionate about those she cared for, and had obvious and genuine love for her family and community. She showered everyone in her circle with warmth and humor and concern—him and Ivy now included. If he'd been a man given to flights of fancy and fate, he'd almost believe their paths had been destined to cross.

When he realized she was still waiting for him to continue, Sam cleared his throat and added, "I'll still need to confirm supply costs with nearby retailers first, but you should be well within budget."

"Good!" Riley clapped with excitement. "I'll go tell Lynette I'm buying a house!"

Sam watched her go back inside, knowing the house was perfect for her: bright and open, the creative design somehow managing to perfectly merge the nature outside with the warm, cozy interior. There were even extra guest rooms so the girls could each have their own when they came to stay with her. Or if Riley decided to start a relationship and have children of her own at some point.

Except the thought of her being with anyone but him made him feel a streak of possessiveness that nearly made his knees buckle. Where had *that* come from? Riley didn't belong to him, and he didn't belong to her.

But you wish she did...

Perplexed, Sam shook off the strange thought. He didn't want a relationship. He didn't want romance. He didn't want to risk getting his heart eviscerated again.

Do I?

Just a month ago, he would've steadfastly said no. Now? He wasn't so sure.

Things had changed between him and Riley recently, and while he was still processing it all, he also knew that those changes hadn't been all bad. He felt more connected now— to the town and to her. Felt a part of things again in a way he hadn't since Natalia was alive. Those were things he'd missed as well. Things he'd thought had been gone from his life forever.

Until now.

Deep in thought, he went back inside to join the discussion between Riley and her Realtor about the amount of the offer given the renovations that would need to be done. Once they'd hammered it all out, based on Sam's preliminary estimates for the work, the Realtor called the owners and made the offer, which they verbally accepted on the spot.

Riley was thrilled. Sam was too, on her behalf.

"Congratulations," Lynette said. "I'll get the paperwork ready, and we'll move forward."

"Any kind of time frame for closing?" Riley asked.

"I'd say after the first of the year sometime, considering Christmas is just two weeks away now." They left by the front door this time and the Realtor stopped at her car, parked near the curb, and turned back to them. "Happy holidays, you two. You make such a cute couple!"

Sam just blinked at the woman, too stunned to respond.

Riley didn't say anything either, at least until her friend had pulled away. Then she turned to Sam and shook her head. "No idea why she thinks we're together."

"Hmm," he said, following her back into the house. It was a little warmer today, with a slight southerly breeze. The air stirred the hair around Riley's face, making Sam's fingertips itch with the urge to trace his fingers over her cheek, to see if her skin felt as soft as he remembered. Her sweet cinnamon scent teased his nose, and her warmth beckoned him closer. But it wasn't just sexual attraction anymore, Sam realized, though that was still as strong as ever.

A horn honked in the distance, snapping Sam back to reality, and he realized he and Riley had been watching each other this whole time, the moment stretching between them as heat raced through his chilled body.

Before he could second-guess himself, Sam leaned down and kissed her again. She made a soft, sexy sound and Sam couldn't get enough. He wrapped his arms around her, picking her up from her wheelchair and holding her to him, tangling his mouth with hers as the magic from their first kiss returned full force. Her breath mingled with his, her lips soft and warm beneath his own. If they hadn't been standing outside, in full view of everyone on the main street through town, he might have kept going. As it was, he pulled away slowly, feeling like the kiss had gone on an eternity, though it could only have been a few delicious seconds.

Had it been a mistake? Probably.

But Sam couldn't bring himself to care anymore.

He'd tried running, tried keeping everyone at bay all the time, tried avoiding Riley, tried denying his feelings, and it had been exhausting. Every time he saw her, their connection grew stronger, and the memories swarmed back, the feel of her mouth beneath his, her soft hair in his hands, her breasts brushing his chest as she clung to him. The scent and taste and feel of her... He couldn't resist anymore. He wanted to celebrate the rush of blood in his veins, the life-affirming surge of adrenaline that reminded Sam he was still very much alive and still very much a man.

Now he just needed to figure out how to move forward.

Riley was trying to figure out Sam Perkins while in her weekly PT appointment with Luna the next day. He'd kissed her twice now, and the way he looked at her sometimes was enough to scorch her panties, but he seemed to be holding himself back. Each time she thought they might take the next step forward, he seemed to move two steps back from her. It made no sense. She knew he was still dealing with his wife's passing, but this was ridiculous. Either he wanted her or he didn't. He needed to let her know.

"Earth to Riley," Luna said, giving her a flat look. They'd been doing passive range of motion exercises to help Riley warm up her hips, knees and ankle joints to keep them flexible and healthy. Over the last year or so, she'd worked hard to not only keep her leg muscles from atrophying, but to build new muscle mass too, all with the hopes of moving to the crutches permanently and leaving the wheelchair behind. "It's time to move to the bike."

"Sorry," Riley said, hiding her blush by wiping a towel over her sweaty face. "Distracted, I guess."

"Everything okay?" Luna asked, as Riley used her upper body strength to shift herself from the workout bench to a stationary recumbent bike beside her. It was designed especially for paraplegics, and the hospital had ordered it earlier in the year. In the quest to get Riley walking again, Luna said they had to address her circulation as part of the overall picture. Since then, Riley had utilized the bike as part of her weekly visits. Luna strapped Riley's right leg in the holder and her foot to the pedal then did the same on her left. Then she attached electrodes to Riley's right thigh and gluteus maximus muscles before stepping back. "Ready."

"Thanks." Riley flipped the switch on the control panel and chose the high-intensity mode, which involved four minutes of hard exercise with an equal interval of easier training to increase her blood flow and pulse, accelerating oxygen uptake and enhancing her heart's pumping volume. Once she'd really gotten going, Luna sat on the bench Riley had just vacated to keep an eye on her and make sure she wasn't overtaxing herself on the bike by keeping her talking.

"So, what's distracting you?" Luna asked again. "Please tell me it's something juicy and salacious. There hasn't been any good gossip around the place in months."

"I put an offer in on a house," Riley puffed. It wasn't a lie—she was thinking about that. But she was also thinking about Sam and their kiss yesterday. Not that she'd tell Luna about that. The last thing she wanted was the town talking about her and Sam, especially since they were still figuring out what was happening themselves. "Lynette said the closing should be after the first of the year."

"Wow. That's fantastic! Congratulations," Luna said. "Where's the new place located?"

Riley gave her all the details, still puffing slightly but not too winded. "It needs some renovations though." When she realized she'd talked herself into a corner, she tried to play it off as nonchalantly as possible. "Did you know Sam Perkins also builds things? He offered to do the work for me."

"I did not know that." Luna sat forward. Why had she brought up Sam? Why? Too late now though, as her friend was giving her a Cheshire cat smile. "So, you and Sam have been spending a lot of time together, eh?"

"It's not like that." *Liar.* It was totally becoming like that. The heart rate monitor on the machine beeped at the sudden uptick of her pulse before Riley calmed herself. Stupid bike. She gave Luna an annoyed glance as she took a swig of water from the bottle attached to the bike, still peddling away. "He's helping me with the house. That's all."

"Sure." Luna grinned. "And he's your colleague."

"So?"

"And his daughter and Adi are friends."

"What are you getting at?" Riley snapped, beyond irritated now.

Luna shrugged. "Nothing. I think it's great that you two found each other. Lucille mentioned seeing you both at the festival and said you looked good together."

Riley stopped herself from telling Luna exactly where Lucille could shove her observations by scowling down at the digital screen in front of her as it tallied her progress on the imaginary course she was riding on. "We're just friends. And Lucille needs to mind her own business. After the way she outed Brock and Cassie on the town's Facebook page and dogged both you and Mark *and* Madi and Tate, I'd have thought you'd have stopped listening to her gossiping on principle."

"True." Luna shrugged then checked her watch. "Like I said, it's been slow around here. I'm sorry." She reached over and patted Riley's leg. "I really am happy for you, Riley. You deserve to find your someone too. Whether that's Sam or someone else, you need love."

"I don't need anything," she countered, wishing that were true. But since the day she and Sam started getting closer, she'd feared it wasn't. Not anymore. Despite all her determination to stay independent and prove she could do it all on her own, he'd somehow gotten past her barriers and made her see that maybe alone wasn't the best way to go. Riley pedaled harder, wishing she could ride away from her lingering fears about what commitment might mean for her but knowing she couldn't. "Sam's a good man."

"I'm sure he is." Luna sat forward, narrowing her blue eyes. "He seems extra good for you."

"I don't know what you're talking about." Even as she said it, Riley felt Luna's eye roll. "Okay, fine. We've kissed. A couple of times. But that's it."

"Kissing's good," Luna said, smiling.

"It was good," Riley conceded. "But now I'm not sure…" She struggled to find words to describe what was happening between her and Sam and how she felt about it all. "I don't know how he feels, and I'm scared that I'm going to lose the freedom I've worked so hard for, and it's all just messy and difficult, okay? So please don't say anything to anyone else about this right now."

"I promise." Luna leaned in, lowering her voice even though they were alone in the PT room. "Do you think Sam's The One?"

If Riley hadn't been strapped to the bike, she might've fallen off it she was so startled. Yes, Sam ticked a lot of the boxes of what she was looking for in a partner. He was smart and sweet and funny and thoughtful—and helpful to a fault. And he seemed to temper her more impulsive side well with his more logical approach to things. But she wasn't thinking too far into the future yet, not when her prognosis changed on what felt like a daily basis. She was taking things week by week at this point. "I do like him. A lot. But I'm not sure about more yet."

"Why not?" Luna frowned.

Because the future was complicated, with their pasts and their working relationship and his daughter. Neither one of them seemed ready to be in a relationship again, and Riley did not have the time or energy for pipe dreams. She'd worked too hard to get where she was now to surrender it all for a man who wasn't willing to let her have her freedom. And while she enjoyed being with Sam, liked how he treated people with respect, no matter who they were, liked how he obviously wanted her too. But sometimes wanting wasn't enough. She couldn't afford to fall for him without knowing he'd be there to catch her.

Luna was still waiting for an answer, so Riley said, "I told you, it's complicated."

"Love always is," Luna said, giving her a sympathetic look. "You both need to talk. Stop running away from this just because you're scared. Trust me, I know how that goes."

"We're just being practical here. We lead very different lives."

"Different can be good."

"If both people are on the same page about it," Riley countered. "Sometimes I'm not sure Sam and I are even in the same book."

The bike finished its course and shut down, and Luna helped her undo the straps holding her legs to the machine before handing her the towel.

"Well, just don't give up too easily before you know what

you've got, okay?" Luna said. "Trust me, the best things can happen when you least expect them. And the future you need isn't always the one you expected."

CHAPTER ELEVEN

THAT NIGHT, Sam was on edge as he drove through the lightly falling snow toward the Turner house. Not because of the weather, but because Ivy had come home from school that day and asked if she could spend the night at Adi's again so they could keep practicing for the Christmas play together. Sam wasn't sure how much practice being a goldfish took, but apparently it was a lot.

"Why are you mad, Daddy?" Ivy asked him from the passenger seat.

"I'm not mad, *yeobo*," Sam said, forcing his face to relax.

He was stressed after sitting through rounds of meetings at work all day. What they didn't tell you about when you accepted a department head position was the endless paperwork and bureaucracy that came with it. Yes, there was prestige and a nice bump in salary, but there were also days where the job was a real pain in the—

He inhaled deeply and rolled his tight shoulders, focusing on the road again until they pulled in under the portico in front of the Turner house a few minutes later. Ivy hurried out of the car while Sam shut off the engine, then he joined her at the front door. "I just want to make sure they know they don't have to pick you up from school tomorrow."

That, and he hoped to see Riley again, however briefly.

Yeah, he was a besotted fool.

"Okay," Ivy agreed, holding the old flip phone he'd given her last year in one hand and her overnight bag in the other.

Sam rang the bell then waited, his anticipation building until Riley answered the door, her hair piled atop her head in a messy bun. She was wearing a ruffled Christmas-patterned apron with streaks of flour across the front of her chest, which drew his attention there, reminding Sam of their kiss the day before. She was using her crutches tonight, and when she saw him, her face flushed, and her mouth opened as they both blinked at each other.

Riley found her voice first, which made sense since Sam wasn't sure he was capable of speech just then. "Hi, there. Come on in." To him, she whispered, "I didn't expect to see you tonight."

"Ivy!" Adi called, bounding into the living room where they were.

"I…uh…" Sam started, his words as jittery as his pulse. "I'm not staying. I uh…just wanted to let you know that I'll pick Ivy up from school tomorrow to take her to the hospital party. She'll text me when she's ready."

"Okay." Riley tilted her head adorably. "Cassie said it's no problem, though, if you have an emergency or something."

He nodded, noticing for the first time the smell of baking— something comforting and rich with sugar.

She gestured at her messy front. "We're making cookies for the hospital Christmas party tomorrow. You're welcome to stay and help if you want. It's just me and the girls tonight, since Madi and Tate are watching baby Ben, and Brock and Cassie are both working."

"Oh," he said, stepping back from the door. He hadn't planned on going to the party. Too many people. But he already wanted to spend more time with Riley, and he was pretty sure that urge would only worsen as the night went on. "I don't know..."

The girls ran over to join them. "Come on, Daddy," Ivy begged. "Please? It'll be so much fun!"

In the end, Sam couldn't resist the three faces looking back at him. He stepped inside and closed the door behind him, the tension inside him lessening almost immediately. "Okay. I'm all yours."

Exclamations of glee erupted from the girls before they raced down the hall to put Ivy's overnight bag in Adi's room, with Ivy telling Adi, "I brought my new skates with me. They're so cool!"

Riley smiled, shaking her head. "So, you got her the lessons, huh?"

"I did," he said as he took off his coat and boots. "You said it was a good idea and I believed you. They're the same skates as the ones she used at the festival, except white with glitter unicorns on the side. Ghastliest things I've ever seen, but she loves them." He shrugged. "She'll be going to the same rink as Adi too, but Ivy doesn't start until after the first of the year."

"You're a good dad," Riley said as she led him into the kitchen.

"I try." Her compliment made him feel ridiculously flattered, which was silly, but he didn't seem to be able to control his reactions around her anymore, and he was tired of trying. He stopped to pet the overly excited Frenchie dancing around his feet. "How's Winnie tonight?"

The dog gave a satisfied whine as he scratched behind her ears.

"I know," Sam said, grinning. "You and Spork need to meet."

"Who's Spork?"

"Our mutt."

"Ready to make cookies!" the girls shouted, their stockinged feet sliding on the hardwood floors as they ran back into the kitchen.

Sam noticed out the window that it was snowing harder now, the large flakes helping to set a very cozy scene. Growing up, they'd never had much money for gifts. And after Natalia's death, Christmas had become just another day to him. Tonight, though, he found himself excited for the upcoming holiday in a way he hadn't been in years.

They set up four frosting stations at the kitchen island, each person getting their own pan of cookies and frosting utensils, with bowls of different-colored frostings and sprinkles in the middle for everyone to share. As they worked their way through four dozen assorted stars, bells, reindeer and snowflakes, Sam was pretty sure more frosting ended up in their stomachs or on the girls' faces than on the cookies. Even Winnie got a dollop or five when some was dropped on the floor. Food coloring stained Sam's fingers, and the cuffs of his dress shirt, but he was so charmed by the whole affair he didn't even care.

After they finished, the girls got ready for bed while Sam and Riley handled the kitchen cleanup, working as a team to clear away the chaos. When they were done, Riley made them each a cup of peppermint tea, which they took into the living room to sip.

"That was fun," she said, taking a seat on the couch and setting her crutches to the side. "Thanks for helping."

"My pleasure," he said, meaning it. "I haven't done that in years."

"Making cookies was a tradition around here growing up. It felt right to revive it this year."

"Going to bed, Aunt Riley," Adi said, climbing up on Riley's lap to give her a kiss. "See you in the morning."

"Good night, munchkin," she said, kissing the top of her niece's head.

"Night, Daddy." Ivy clambered up beside Sam to hug him tight. "I love you."

"Love you too, *yeobo*," he said, hugging her tight before letting go. "Get some good sleep."

"We will," the girls said in unison before running off toward Adi's bedroom at the far end of the hall. The door closed with a resounding *thunk* behind them, cutting off their whispers and giggles. Sam bet they'd be lucky if they got a few hours of shut-eye that night, but they'd be fine.

Oh, to be that young again.

Once they were alone again, he and Riley sipped their tea as the snow continued outside, Sam's thoughts whirling like a blizzard in his head. He should talk to her, tell her how he was feeling. But what if she didn't feel the same? He felt like a gawky teenaged boy, which was probably why he ended up blurting, "About the kiss yesterday..." at the same time Riley said to him, "We should talk."

They both blinked at each other a moment before setting their cups aside and shifting slightly to face each other on the sofa.

"You first," Sam said.

"Okay." Riley took a deep breath. "I like you, Sam. A lot. Probably more than I should. But we made an agreement, which we've already violated several times. Based on the fact you've kissed me twice now, I think you like me too, but I can't read you. And I just need to know what we're doing here, because I don't want to get hurt again."

His brain had snagged on the *I like you, Sam. A lot* part, even though she'd kept talking.

"I don't want to get hurt again either." He needed her to understand, even though he wasn't sure he fully understood himself. "When my wife died, it nearly gutted me. We were partners, in every sense of the word. Losing her was like losing half of myself. I could barely function for months, just going through the motions of life on autopilot, and that's no way to live. I need to be fully present, for my patients, my daughter, my life. And the only way I could ensure that happening was by suppressing my emotions. I'd done a pretty good job of it too. Until I met you."

Riley watched him for a long moment, biting her lip. He'd never wanted to be a set of teeth more in his life. "What made you change?"

"You." Sam scrubbed a hand over his face. "You made me change. Don't ask me how or why, but I'm different now than I was even a month ago. I'm feeling everything again because of you, and I don't know how I can go back. I'm not sure I even want to."

She stared down at her hands in her lap, frowning. "That doesn't answer my question."

He sighed. "I like you too, Riley. So much it scares me."

Riley looked up then, their gazes locking as she swallowed hard, hesitancy and hope flaring in her blue eyes. "I'm scared too. I've tried to be independent for so long now, giving that up is hard."

"I don't want you to give that up," he said, his heart thumping in his chest. "I like you just as you are, Riley. Exactly as you are."

His urge to hold her and comfort her and kiss her broke through his self-control like an avalanche. Sam reached for

Riley, pulling her to him and burying his face in her hair, unable to fight the pull of their connection any longer. "I don't know what we're doing either, but I know I don't want it to end."

Her gaze traveled over his face then, as she realized that he'd quickly become her favorite thing: his warm dark eyes, his firm lips, his golden-brown skin and his chin with the little divot in the middle. She traced her fingertips over each of his eyebrows, down the bridge of his nose, over his mouth. They'd have to be quiet. Very quiet. And the knowledge it had to be secret made it hotter somehow.

Riley craved closeness with him, desire burning her from the inside out. Since the accident, she'd worried she'd never have this again, would never find someone who'd accept her completely, the good, the bad and the broken parts. Yet here was Sam, saying he wanted her just as she was. He saw her, really saw her, and that was a rare and precious thing. They might not have a clue how this would end, but there was no way she was turning her back on it now. Not tonight. Maybe not ever. "Let's go to my room."

Sam stood and swept her into his arms so fast, Riley gasped. She did love a bold man. As he carried her down the hall, she rested her hands on his shoulders, her nose buried at the base of his throat, inhaling his good Sam scent of pine and soap and crisp winter chill.

After locking the door, he let Riley slide slowly down his front until her toes barely touched the floor, his big hands at her waist, his warmth surrounding her, comforting her, driving her wild with lust. Fingers shaking slightly, she slid her palms down his biceps to rest on his forearms, their faces close.

Sam skimmed his lips over her left eyebrow, across her cheekbone, then settled his mouth into the notch just below her earlobe. Spirals of pleasure radiated out from Riley's center, like a prism of bright color shimmering over her skin as he nuzzled her neck.

"I want you so badly I ache," Sam whispered against her neck, lifting his head so his mouth rested against her ear as he pulled her closer still so she could feel the truth of it for herself. "I haven't been able to think about anything else since you came out of that dressing room in your tiny elf costume."

"Yeah?" Her voice came out husky as she arched against him. "And what are you going to do about it?"

"This." Sam kissed her slow and hot and deep, his legs bracketing her own, bracing her as his hands moved lower still, gripping her butt, rocking her into him, teasing the juncture between her thighs just right. Riley moaned and dug her hands into the front of his sweater, needing more, but not wanting to let him go.

Finally, both of them breathless with need, Sam picked Riley up and set her on the edge of the bed. They each tugged off their shirts and pants, leaving her in bra and panties and Sam in just jeans and socks. She licked her lips at the sight of his toned, lithe torso. She couldn't wait to explore every inch of him.

But he seemed to have other ideas first, opening Riley's legs to step between them, sliding his hands up her thighs so both of his thumbs pressed gently against her slick folds through her underwear. She stifled a muffled curse into his mouth and slid her fingers into his hair. Then he spread her thighs wider as one of his thumbs found her most sensitive nub through the lace of her underwear. He rubbed in slow, gentle circles, varying the pressure depending on how she gasped and moaned, finding what she liked best.

Riley groaned low as Sam bent over her, nipping her earlobe, his hot breath panting against her cheek. "You're so sexy."

Then he knelt before her, one hand holding her in place as he tugged off her panties with the other, exposing her to him completely. He swirled his tongue over her, then sucked gently, her grip in his hair tightening as her other hand scrabbled for purchase on the covers beneath her. Riley urged him on silently, arching into him, biting back her cries of pleasure, imagining what he'd feel like inside her.

Then Sam hummed against sensitive flesh and Riley went over the edge, her whole body vibrating as orgasm struck, washing her away on a tidal wave of endorphins and bliss until, finally, she came back to earth, chest heaving as she gazed up at Sam. He stood near the bed, watching her as he removed his jeans and boxer briefs. "Condom?"

"Nightstand."

He put one on then stretched out beside her, his erection brushing her hip. She was tired of waiting and wrapped her arms around him, pulling him atop her. Sam braced his weight on his elbows on either side of her head, his body pressed along hers as he settled between her legs, and she couldn't stop herself from reaching between them to stroke him. Riley took her time, running her loosely circled fingers up and down his shaft as he lavished attention on her breasts before finally settling into position between her legs again, his tip teasing her until she thought she might explode. "Hurry."

Sam laughed. "I like it when you're demanding."

In response, Riley pulled him down for another kiss as he entered her slowly.

"You feel amazing," he breathed, moving inside her. Riley lost herself to sensation, gripping his shoulders so tight her nails left little crescent-shaped marks, taking him deeper, holding him closer. She might not be able to feel her legs, but everything else was working just fine.

Sam buried his face in her neck, their soft moans swallowed in kisses and sighs.

"Yes. There. *Please*," Riley whispered as she changed angles, guiding him to what she liked best. Sam did not disappoint. He was watching her, his dark, fathomless eyes full of heat and yearning and desire. Before Riley knew it, she went over the edge again, climaxing hard, which sent Sam over the brink too. He went whipcord tight against her, his eyes closing until he collapsed atop her then rolled to her side, pulling her close, his heart racing against hers. Riley kissed his ear, too jelly-boned and satiated to do more. After a while, Riley expected him to leave, or pull away, but instead Sam burrowed closer. She laid her head on his shoulder and placed her hand on his chest.

"That was wonderful," he said, his tone sleepy. "But I think we need to go slowly. Is that okay?"

Riley exhaled with relief. "Yes. That's what I want too."

He got up then to use the bathroom, and Riley watched his retreating back, glad that he seemed happy, because that made her happy too.

And maybe, if they worked this right, they could both be happy, together.

Sam woke again a few hours later, taking far longer than he should have to realize he wasn't alone and this wasn't his bed.

To be fair, he had a bit of a deep-sleep hangover. Between work and Riley and the approaching holidays, the last few days had been a blur of work emergencies. He sighed, remembering the last few hours. Making cookies. Making love.

Riley sighed in her sleep and curved her warm body more tightly against him, dealing him a death blow right in the feels. Being with her had been a revelation—sweet and shocking and shattering.

Sam took a deep breath and shifted to look over at her, finding Riley rolled up in the comforter like a burrito with only a puff of her shiny dark hair peeking out from beneath the covers. His heart squeezed with the urge to kiss her awake and repeat what they'd done earlier, maybe try a few new variations too.

Except…

He sat up and glanced at the clock on her nightstand. The girls would be up soon, and he needed to get out of here before that happened. To him, "taking it slow" meant keeping it a secret, at least for now. He needed to go home, take a shower and get to work so no one would know he'd slept here. With Riley.

Oh, God. What if Brock and Cassie were home? He hadn't heard anything, but that didn't mean anything. As tired as he'd been, a bear could've walked through the house and he might not have woken up.

Holding his breath, Sam inched toward the side of the bed, allowing himself a sigh of relief when Riley never so much as quivered. He hit the bathroom again, got dressed in his clothes from the night before, then snuck out of the bedroom to fumble for his boots and coat in the dark living room. So far, so good. The last thing he wanted was to explain to her brother what he was doing with Riley. Especially when he still wasn't completely clear on it himself.

Was it a relationship? A fling? A "friends with benefits" situation? He had no clue. All he knew was that being with her had been glorious and he wasn't ready to share that with anyone else yet. Based on what Riley had said last night about not wanting to get hurt, or lose her freedom, he assumed they were on the same page there. Good.

Sam scratched his unshaven jaw. Flings and friends with benefits arrangements usually meant meaningless, no-strings, no-emotional-involvement kinds of sex. But that wasn't what he'd experienced last night with Riley. He took his boots over to the sofa to put them on in the dark, the moonlight streaming in through the windows highlighting the holiday decor, glitter and fairy lights and garlands galore.

Riley had mentioned while they'd frosted cookies that Adi had been given free rein with the design, and it showed. Sam had the same problem at his house because of Ivy. Apparently, according to seven-year-olds, decorating a house meant covering every visible surface to within an inch of its life.

Which turned his thoughts to Riley's new place. He pictured her living there, decorating for the holidays, trimming the tree and baking in her new kitchen. Maybe she'd have Ivy and Adi to help her. Maybe Sam would be invited again as well after he finished the renovations. Maybe...

For a second, he allowed himself to imagine what it might be like to live with Riley, create a new life, a new future with her. The three of them sitting in the living room of the new house with Spork, watching the views of wintery Buzzards Bay through the windows, a tree glowing cheerily in the corner as they played games or read stories or streamed corny Hallmark movies on the TV.

It sounded wonderful.

With a sigh, Sam opened his eyes and returned to reality. He couldn't get carried away here. They still had a lot to contend with. Their pasts. Her need for independence. His need for control. Then there was the fact that his emotions were involved now—no point in denying it—and he was frightened. He felt confused and conflicted and completely out of control.

He had to be logical about this to protect them all. He stood to pull on his gloves and found Riley at the end of the hall, watching him from her wheelchair. She'd somehow snuck up on him without him knowing, still wrapped in the comforter and nothing else, her blue eyes shadowed and her dark hair tangled and sticking up all over her head. "I thought you'd left."

"I'm going now," he said quietly, bending to give her a quick kiss before heading for the door, ignoring the spike in his blood pressure from her nearness. He pulled his keys from his coat pocket, every fiber of his being telling him to go back to her, carry her back down the hall and get back into bed. "Don't want the girls to see me."

"See what?" Ivy's groggy voice came from the hall. She stumbled in, rubbing her eyes, her pj's crooked from sleep. "Why are you here, Daddy? Is it time to go home?"

Sam froze, his gaze darting from his daughter to Riley, then back again.

Fortunately, Riley moved faster than he did. "No, munchkin. Your dad forgot something last night, so he came to pick it up on his way into the hospital."

Ivy squinted through the dim light at him. "What'd you forget, Daddy?"

"Um…"

My sanity.

He searched for something, then held up his hands, wiggling his fingers. He hated lying to his daughter, but he could hardly tell her the truth.

"My gloves. It's cold and I needed them to keep my fingers warm."

Adi soon toddled in to join them, climbing into Riley's lap in the wheelchair. "Why is everybody up? It's time to sleep."

"I know, sweetie." Riley kissed her niece's head. "Sam just needed to get something first."

"And now I'm going." He opened the door, praying the slap of cold air on his face would wake him up from this nightmare. "Ivy, I'll see you after school."

With that, he rushed out of the house and over to his car, knowing this was a disaster. The girls talked to each other and the adults around them. All it would take was one word to the wrong person and the gossip machine in town would kick into overdrive. Everyone would know he and Riley were sleeping together. He started his engine to let it run while he cleaned off his windows.

Sam had to take control of this situation and prevent it from getting out of hand. Protect himself. Protect Riley. And most importantly, protect Ivy. He wasn't sure how to fix it yet, but he would. Because that's what he did.

CHAPTER TWELVE

"Don't tell me you unwrapped your Secret Santa gift early and found Dr. Perkins inside, because if that's the case, there's gonna be a lot of single hospital workers who change what they put on their wish lists for next year," ER Nurse Madi Scott said as she stood beside Riley near the wall at the annual staff holiday party at Wyckford General.

Riley glanced across the crowded event room to where Sam stood, talking with several other doctors. She still wasn't sure how she felt about him leaving the way he had that morning, as if he'd been embarrassed or felt guilty about sleeping with her. Neither was a flattering reaction. Since then, they hadn't had a chance to talk, but each time their eyes locked across the room, her breath went a little haywire. Sam had been an amazing lover, seeming to know what Riley needed before she even knew it herself. Memories of the way he'd felt against her, inside her, filling her in a way that went beyond physical, in a way she hadn't experienced in years, kept floating through her mind at inopportune times. Like now. Riley felt wound tighter than a spool of Christmas ribbon.

Madi watched her closely, too closely, tapping the toe of her white sneaker against the floor, her coy smile letting Riley know that her friend wasn't buying her act where Sam was concerned. But there was no way she could know about them being together, regardless of what the girls might've said to other people. The gossip machine was good, but it wasn't that good.

"Seriously," Madi said. "I can tell something's bothering you. Might as well tell me now and save me the trouble of stuffing you with chocolate cake at the diner to get you to talk. Unless you want cake, in which case I'm always game for that."

"I'm fine," Riley said. And she was. She'd been fine before Sam had come into her life, and she'd be fine if he left. Even if it felt like a knife to the chest just thinking about it now. Besides, what would she tell Madi? That they'd had sex, but beyond that she had no clue what they were doing? Not exactly a stellar relationship report. If all this was even becoming a relationship, which, given Sam's reservations about all that, was unlikely at best…

"Sure you are," Madi said, not sounding convinced at all.

Riley took a deep breath. Her body was still tingling from last night, which was a nice change from the usual numbness. What they'd done the night before had been far more than sex for her. It had been a reawakening. The first time since her accident that she'd recaptured the old magic of intimacy she'd been missing so much. She'd had sex and orgasms over the past two years. She was human, after all. But it hadn't been as easy and carefree and wonderful as it had been with Sam. He'd seemed to enjoy their time together as much as she had, and while she didn't know every detail about Sam's life yet, she did know he wasn't a wham-bam-thank-you-ma'am sort of guy. He'd want to proceed with things. Of course he would.

She stifled the giddiness and uncertainty that had threatened to overwhelm her all day.

She was a strong, independent woman. She didn't need any man to make her happy or complete.

Now if her heart could just get with that program, she'd be all set.

Riley glanced his way again before she could stop herself, and just seeing him made her feel tangled up and twisted, which was enough to raise her anxiety levels to just short of panic. She wasn't in love with Sam. She wasn't. She didn't want to be in love.

"Does Brock know yet that you've found someone?" Madi asked.

"I have not found someone," Riley snapped. "Just because you and Tate are floating around on the Love Boat doesn't mean the rest of want to buy a ticket, okay?" She crossed her arms, feeling decidedly too exposed. Why couldn't people just mind their business? Hadn't they gotten a big enough piece of her after the accident, when everyone learned about what had happened?

Across the room, she watched Sam excuse himself and followed Lucille Munson through a doorway at the back of the room. Riley nibbled on cheese and crackers from the plate she'd made upon arriving at the party and cursed the itchy Santa hat on her head. Normally she liked these parties, but she wasn't in the mood for it now. The only reason she was staying was because Sam had been talked into playing Santa for the staff members' kids and Adi was going to be there, along with Ivy.

"Hey," Madi said after a moment, apparently taking Riley's silence for offense. "I'm sorry. I didn't mean to pry. I just really hope you find happiness again, Riley. You deserve it."

And now Riley felt bad. Madi was the nicest, sweetest person she knew. Riley knew her friend's concern came from a place of genuine caring. The same was true of Brock and most other people in town. But just because their concern was real didn't make it any less suffocating. If fact, what Riley wished for most right then was for everyone to stop worrying about her and what her future might look like and to just let her get on with it.

She found herself staring at the door Sam had disappeared through again, wondering if he had problems with his Santa suit. Maybe she should check on him...

"Psst... Dr. Turner?" someone called to Riley from the entrance nearby.

It was Daisy Randall. Riley excused herself then went over to talk to her. "How are you?"

"Good, thanks." Daisy looked better than she had during her last appointment. The PET scan results had come back unchanged, which was a good thing with ALS. It meant she had more time. How much? No one could say for certain, but then no one really knew how long anyone had left in life. Riley had learned that lesson the hard way. "My mom went to get the car. We were here to get lab work done and fill a prescription at the pharmacy. But I wanted to stop by and wish you happy holidays since I won't see you again before Christmas."

"Aw." Riley gave her a hug, their wheelchairs clacking together between them. "And happy holidays to you too. Do you and your family have plans?"

"Nah, we're sticking close to home for now. Enjoying the quiet."

"Sounds good. I'll be doing the same." Riley smiled. "Did I tell you I got a house?"

"How awesome!" Daisy beamed. "Tell me about it."

Riley did, including the fact that Sam would be helping her with renovations. Which reminded her—she needed to call Lynette about getting a set of keys so they could go in and take measurements. "I'm excited and can't wait for you to see it when it's done."

"Me too! And it'll give me incentive to live that long," Daisy added.

"Hey, new treatments are being discovered every day," Riley said. "Don't give up yet."

"Never." Daisy shrugged. "Just being realistic. But I swear I'll see your house, Doc. That's a new goal going on my vision board at home."

"Vision board? Maybe I should try one of those."

"Maybe. I'll let you get back to your party," Daisy said, peeking through the door. "Looks like fun."

"You want to come in?" Riley asked. "It's mainly staff and their kids, but Sam's playing Santa."

"Dr. Perkins? Really?" Daisy seemed as surprised as Riley had been at hearing the news. She checked her watch. "I wish I could, but Mom's waiting. I'll see you at my next appointment." She waved and turned away, then stopped and called back, "And happy New Year, Doc!"

Riley returned to her spot against the wall just as Adi and Ivy arrived. Her niece ran over and scrambled up onto her lap. "Aunt Riley, is Santa here yet?"

"Not yet, kiddo." Riley ruffled her hair. "But soon."

"Hey." Brock leaned against the wall next to her. He must've been pulling office hours in their dad's old clinic that day, because instead of scrubs he had on trousers and a shirt and tie beneath his lab coat. His stethoscope was still around his neck too, meaning he'd probably left in a hurry. "We miss anything?"

"Just mediocre snacks and warm eggnog." Riley shrugged as her niece raced over to where Ivy stood watching a man making balloon reindeer. Or at least that's what they called them. They looked more like dogs to Riley. "Where's Cassie?"

"Consulting on a facial reconstructive case," he said. "She probably won't make it."

"Lucky her."

"I see your holiday spirits are alive and well." He chuckled, resting his head back against the wall.

"My spirits are great," she grumbled, knowing she needed to tell him about buying the house. Now seemed as good a time as any, so she said, "I need to tell you something."

Brock laughed outright now. "What? That you and Sam Perkins have a thing going?"

"What!" Riley turned to look at him so fast she almost gave herself whiplash. "Why would you say that?"

If the rumor mill got ahold of what they were doing, it would be awful. She didn't think she could take being the focus of all that attention again.

Her brother shrugged. "I have eyeballs, sis. You two have been giving each other puppy dog looks for weeks now."

"Have not!" She knew she sounded childish, but then so was this conversation. She didn't owe anyone an explanation for how she lived her life. "And why is it any of your business anyway?"

"Calm down, Salty Queen," Brock said just as the door opened across the room and Sam stepped out. Brock narrowed his eyes, then laughed. "Sam is Santa?"

"Yes." She tried to refocus the conversation on more important matters. "I need to tell you that I—"

He pushed away from the wall as Adi and Ivy raced toward where a line was forming to see the big guy in red. "Sorry. It'll have to wait. I need to keep my daughter from climbing your new boyfriend like a Christmas tree."

"He's not my boyfriend! We work together, that's all!"
Riley yelled after him, too loudly given that everyone within
range of her turned to look at her, including Sam. As usual,
she couldn't read his reaction, especially when he had that
big white beard on, but it didn't matter.

"I bought a house," she told Brock bluntly. She'd tried
to ease into it but, given the situation, that wasn't working.
"My closing is after the first of the year and I'll be moving
out shortly thereafter."

Brock just blinked at her. "What?"

"I bought a house," she repeated, feeling a little bad about
telling him like this, but there never seemed to be a good
time and, well, she needed to get on with her life. Besides, it
wasn't like she'd planned to stay with him forever anyway.
"It's on the bay, not far from you, so I'll still be able to watch
Adi if you need and we'll still see each other a lot. I just really need a place of my own now, for privacy, and that way
you and Cassie have more room too."

"But things are going so well the way they are. I thought
you were happy living with us." His expression was an odd
mix of surprise and hurt. "Are you sure you're ready to be
on your own?"

"I *am* happy at your place, and I'll always be grateful for
you taking me in after the accident, but yes. I'm ready to be
on my own." She squared her shoulders. "This is for the best."

"Is it?" Brock crossed his arms, narrowing his gaze. "Is
the new house accessible? If not, how are you going to get
around and do things by yourself? Have you thought of that?"

Affront quickly burned through her guilt over dropping
a bombshell on him at the staff party. "I'm not an idiot. Of
course I've thought of that. I've got it taken care of. A contractor is going to be renovating it for me before I move in.

I'm using your house as my guide because you did such a good job. Quit worrying about me."

"I can't stop worrying about you," Brock growled. "You're my sister."

"Exactly. You're my brother, not my keeper or my boss. I'm moving out. Deal with it," she said, mirroring his obstinate posture. "Fighting about this is stupid. We're both grown adults. We can both do what we want. I can take care of myself. Always have, always will."

"Who's doing the work for you?" he asked, ever overprotective. "Are they licensed?"

"Which part of 'not an idiot' didn't you understand?" she asked, again probably too loudly, since people nearby were watching them now. She'd hoped Santa's arrival would give them cover, but apparently not. "Believe it or not, brother, you're not the only one who knows how to get things done." She thought about lying to him about who was doing the work for her but figured he'd find out soon enough anyway, so she came out with it. "And Sam's doing the work for me."

"Sam Perkins?" Brock's nose scrunched in disbelief. "What the hell does he know about renovations?"

"He renovated his own house back in California. He's been doing them for years. It's his hobby, he said. And he has experience with accessible homes. He's perfect for the job."

"Really?" Her brother did not sound convinced. "I don't believe it."

"I don't care what you believe." She'd known her moving out was going to be an issue. Brock had always been way too bossy for her taste, and with his previous golden boy stature in town, it had made him way too big for his britches. She'd thought the accident had tempered his attitude, but it obviously hadn't. Thirty-two years of resentment, coupled with the stress of not knowing what was happening between her and Sam, congealed into a flaming hot mess of anger. "Why can't you let me have this, Brock? For three decades I've lived in your shadow, never quite reaching the spotlight no matter how hard I tried. Now, finally, I get to have this one thing for myself, and you still can't be happy for me. All you want to do is control me and keep me under your thumb. Well, no more. I've had enough!"

"Daddy!" Adi yelled as she ran over to them. "Santa said he'll bring me a seven-foot-tall Darth Vader for Christmas!"

Brock's blue eyes still blazed with fury as he glared at Riley, and she knew their discussion wasn't over—just paused. Fine. She was glad she'd put it all out there. It was past time. And if it was news to him, all the better. She'd kept it inside too long.

To his daughter, Brock said, "We'll talk about Santa later. Can you go get me a cup of eggnog?"

"Sure!" Adi said, skipping off, completely oblivious to the sizzling tension between her father and her aunt.

"First of all," Brock said, which was never a good conversation starter, "I don't know what the hell you're talking about. Living in my shadow? You were the baby of the family. You got all the attention and never even had to try. I had to practically bend over backward just to eke by."

"Whatever," she snapped. "Everyone in town loved you! The big hero!"

"Hero?" He gave her an incredulous look. "After Kaede died, I was a wreck. You know that. I couldn't even get out of bed for days. And when I did, it was just to make sure Adi was still okay. What kind of heroics is that?"

She opened her mouth to answer, but he talked right over her, which only annoyed her more. An ear-splitting scream ripped through the air from somewhere near the dais, where Sam was sitting with a kid on his lap, but the fight was going too strong now for either of them to pay much attention. They hadn't had a row like this in decades, and it was long overdue.

"You got away with everything growing up, Riley. Everything. Late nights, breaking curfew, running around with the wrong crowd. Anyone would look golden compared to that. And if I tried to do the opposite just to get a bit of attention, can you blame me? And after all I did for you after the accident too."

"I never asked you to do any of that," she countered. "I've told you over and over how grateful I am that you took me in, and I am. But I never asked you to do it."

"So I was just supposed to leave you to fend for yourself?"

"Yes! Maybe if you had, I'd be out of this chair already from necessity."

"Oh, do not put that on me. If you're going to blame anything for what happened to you, then—"

"What? Blame myself? I do, believe me. I know that accident was my fault, Brock. I don't need you to tell me that, okay? I think about the fact that our parents are dead because of me every single day!"

When Sam emerged from the back room, dressed as Santa, he asked himself for the umpteenth time how the hell he'd been talked into this. But he already knew why: because someone needed help and it was his duty to answer the call. So now here he was, at the front of the room on a dais, swathed in hot fabric and fake white fur stuck to his neck and chin, pretending to be jolly old St. Nick on short notice.

He glanced across the room and spotted Riley talking to Daisy Randall in the doorway. He'd tried to avoid looking at her as much as possible before changing for fear someone would see his feelings written all over his face. Last night had been a revelation for him. The way she'd responded to him, the sounds she'd made, the taste of her on his tongue... At first he'd thought sleeping with her might have broken the spell between them, but the opposite was true. The more he got of Riley, the more he craved. She made him believe in the magic of Christmas again. She made him feel better, less alone. She made him forget everything but her—including right now.

Lucille, dressed as a North Pole helper for the party, cleared her throat, letting him know the line was ready for him.

Right. Showtime.

He nudged the big bag of toys on the floor by his feet and gave a hearty *ho, ho, ho.* "Welcome, kids and kids at heart! Who's ready to come up and get a gift from Santa and to tell me what you want for Christmas?"

The children in line, including Ivy and Adi, jumped and clapped and whooped for joy. Santa was a legend to them and now Sam was representing him today. He swallowed hard and gestured for Lucille to send the first child up. The whole party was a bit much for him, but Wyckford General seemed to go all out for its staff and their families.

The first few children were easy enough, asking for the normal stuff—toys, sports equipment, tech gadgets. Then came Adi. She climbed up onto his lap, immediately called him Dr. Perkins, then asked for some giant *Star Wars* thing, and since Sam had no clue what it was, he said he'd do his best to bring it to her. He'd mention it to Brock later just in case.

Ivy went fine too. He'd made note of all the things she'd

wanted and would do his best to get everything on the list, whether locally or online. He'd already purchased the train set she'd liked the day they'd played bingo, and just had to find time to pick it up from the store.

He saw a few more kids then, the line steadily decreasing in length as he kept the visits short and sweet. And while the holidays were not bittersweet for him, he still loved seeing the joy and wonder on children's faces this time of year and how people were nicer and more considerate to one another. And yes, Natalia's death had dulled his happiness for the past couple of years, but now he felt like a bit of his old spirit was back. And while he could kid himself all he wanted about the source of that new spark, the truth of it was that it was all because of Riley.

He glanced over to where she was talking to her brother against the far wall. They seemed deep in serious conversation, and her face was flushed, but before he could wonder if he should be concerned, the last kid in line was plunked down onto his lap by Lucille. It was a little boy who looked to be about three.

"Hello!" Sam said to him. "What's your name?"

After squirming a bit and poking a knee far too close to Sam's privates for his comfort, the boy blinked up at him, wide-eyed. "R-Ronnie."

"Well, Ronnie…" Sam adjusted the youngster on his lap to a more comfortable position. "Why don't you tell Santa what you want for Christmas?"

"No!" the little boy shouted, struggling now to get down, his face red and his expression belligerent. "I want my mommy!"

He glanced over to see one of the labor and delivery nurses dressed in pink scrubs standing near the sidelines, looking apologetic. Sam gave her a nod and a smile to let her know it was fine, then held on to Ronnie a bit tighter as the kid made a valiant effort to escape. His small legs swung wildly, and this time his heel caught Sam in the shin, sending a painful jolt up his right leg. He gasped and automatically reached for his leg, allowing Ronnie precious time to reach up and tug his beard off. Then the boy screamed—an ear-splitting, blood-curdling keen that only a terrified toddler could produce, followed by something warm and wet soaking through the leg of Sam's Santa suit. Pee. Wonderful.

"Oh, God." The poor mother ran up to collect her sobbing child. "I'm so sorry, Dr. Perkins. Ronnie's usually such a good boy. He was hungry and I should've taken him through the food line first, but I'm on my break and thought this would be faster."

"No, no," Sam assured her, wincing slightly as he tugged the wet material of his pants from his leg. He looked out into the room then, to see who had witnessed his humiliation, but found everyone watching Riley and Brock as they had a rapidly escalating argument. As the mother carried young Ronnie away, the room quieted enough for him to hear the yelling coming from across the room.

"I think about the fact that our parents are dead because of me every single day!"

Oh, boy.

Riley had told him as much the other night, and he'd assured her that the accident hadn't been her fault. He still believed that with every fiber of his being, but she obviously didn't. He stood to go back to the dressing room to clean up and change, when Adi ran back to her father with a cup of eggnog in her hand.

"Here, Daddy," she said excitedly into the quiet. "Aunt Riley, is Sam spending the night again tonight, since Ivy is?"

Sam felt the gasp that went through the crowd over every inch of his prickling skin. He froze, not sure what to do. His worst fear was being vulnerable, exposed, and now his deepest secret had been shared with a room full of people not known for being discreet when it came to gossip. His chest constricted and his mouth felt hollow as Riley's gaze met his across the space.

Time slowed again, but not in the romantic way it had before with them. This was more like a slow-mo disaster.

Brock glanced from Riley to Sam then back again, his tone turning decidedly accusatory. "What the hell is my daughter talking about? Are you sleeping with Sam Perkins? In my house?"

Riley opened her mouth, closed it, then opened it again, her cheeks deep pink now. "That's none of your business!"

People were whispering and glancing between Sam and Riley now, clearly enjoying the show, and all he wanted to do at that moment was hide. Burrow himself away somewhere safe and dark and protect himself and Ivy and Riley from whatever wanted to harm them.

But he knew Riley wouldn't want that, and he didn't know what else to do other than explain himself, so instead of changing, he stepped off the dais and headed across the room. "Brock, if you'll let me explain—"

"I don't want to hear it from you, Perkins. I want to hear it from my sister," Brock said, his gaze steady on Riley. "Are you and Sam sleeping together? Is that why you want to move out all of a sudden?"

She shot visual daggers at her brother. "I want to move out so I can get you out of my business! You have no right to question me or what I do." She grabbed her chair wheels and started to move toward the door. Except partway there, she got caught up in a tree skirt that had been knocked askew by the crowd. She struggled to get it out of the way, and without thinking, Sam rushed over to help her.

"Get away from me!" she all but snarled at him, unshed tears glistening in her blue eyes, nearly breaking Sam's heart. "I've got it myself. I don't need you and I don't need your help. Just leave me alone! For good!" She yanked hard at the tree skirt, and it ripped in two, freeing her chair wheel at last. She'd obviously had it with everyone by this point and just wanted to be alone. He should have known that, should have given her space, but it seemed he'd failed. Again. "And go change your clothes. You smell like pee!"

She rolled out of the room and toward the elevators, leaving him behind to stare after her, his wet, stinky pants sticking to his leg and his shattered heart in pieces on the floor.

"Daddy!" Ivy said, sniffling as she came up to him. "I want to go home now. Everyone's staring at us."

"I know, *yeobo*," he said, placing his hand atop her head. He'd known better than to open himself up again, because it only led to pain in the end, and now it wasn't just him who was the center of everyone's negative attention—it was Ivy too. His hurt nearly made him stumble, but he had to be strong for her. "Let me change, and then we'll go. Why don't you and Adi go and use the restroom before we leave?"

"Sam," Brock said as the girls left, and the room's attention shifted away from them at last. The man looked shell-shocked and more than a little chastised. Good. Whatever had started that fight, Brock should have been adult enough to not have had it here in front of everyone. Sam was angry too. Angry and hurt and left completely torn asunder. His first instinct was to go after Riley, but she needed time to cool off. They all did. Best to leave it alone, give it time, then sort through the aftermath. Though something in his gut told him it was over. It never should have started. He knew better than to trust his heart and his emotions. He couldn't protect Riley from hurt, that much was clear. Just like he hadn't been able to protect his wife. He just wasn't good enough...

And yet he'd gone and fallen for Riley anyway.

"Did you know those giant animated Darth Vader things cost upwards of a thousand dollars?" Brock was saying. "Not to mention they're almost impossible to find. Maybe you should think about that before you make a promise you can't deliver on."

He stalked off, leaving Sam alone. Great. He'd pretty much disappointed everyone now. As he walked back to the dressing room in his urine-soaked pants, he decided Brock was right. He should have thought about a lot of things before making promises he couldn't deliver on.

CHAPTER THIRTEEN

THE NEXT WEEK passed in an awkward blur of longing and regret for Riley where Sam was concerned. She regretted the way they'd left things at the party, and how she'd lashed out at him when he'd only been trying to help her, but she'd been hurt and embarrassed and all she'd wanted to do at that point was get away from everyone to calm down and collect herself. But she'd also expected him to come after her at some point. When he hadn't, she hadn't been sure how to interpret that.

They'd only had the one night together, after all, and while it had been spectacular, Riley also knew how skittish Sam was when it came to privacy and relationships. They'd blown both of those things out of the water at the party, in front of half the hospital staff. Since then, she'd not heard anyone directly discussing the big fight in front of her, but it was apparent people *were* talking about it, about her, by the way they stop talking whenever she was nearby.

So yeah, she and Sam had steered clear of each other since the party.

She wasn't actively avoiding him. She was still at work, still seeing her patients, and assumed he was seeing his to, but their paths hadn't crossed at all. Which was strange because, while they were both busy, the hospital wasn't that big, and they'd usually at least pass in the halls. So maybe he'd gone out of his way not to see her.

One person she *was* sure was avoiding her was Brock. Since the party, they hadn't said two words to each other, which for two people living under the same roof was hard to do. Their whole argument had escalated way too far, way too fast at the party, and she felt bad about it. But Riley also still stood behind the fact that what she'd told him had needed to be said. He'd seemed stunned by her words, but what surprised her more was his denial about her being in his shadow all this time. How he felt like he'd had to fight for attention because she'd taken all of it.

It was the farthest thing from the truth, but also oddly fascinating. In all these years, she'd never really looked at their situation growing up from his perspective. She supposed maybe she had gotten away with a little more, but that was because their parents had always been so focused on Brock's accomplishments.

Hadn't they?

Well, whatever. It was done. Over with. Both her fight with Brock and her fling with Sam.

And while it hadn't felt temporary to her, it was probably good it was over because they still had to work together, both at the hospital and on her new house. Which was where she was now, waiting for Sam to show up to take measurements. Riley had come earlier, bringing Adi with her, because yeah, she was nervous to see Sam alone again.

Would he be angry with her? Resigned to the end of their... whatever it was? Sad and stressed, like she was?

"Can I go out on the patio?" Adi asked her as they stood in the kitchen. She had her skates around her neck, the laces knotted together. Riley had picked her up at the rink after her last lesson before the holidays.

"Uh, sure," Riley said. "But stay away from the beach. It's

too cold. It's icy but not fully frozen through yet. It's not safe to walk out on, okay? And keep your gloves on."

"Okay." The little girl went outside to play with her toys as a knock sounded on the front door.

Sam.

Riley's pulse jittered with nerves. She wasn't ready for this. She wished they could go back to before that stupid party and redo it all to not have that stupid fight, to not draw the attention of everyone in the room to them and all their secrets.

Another knock, and Riley took a deep breath before smoothing a hand down the front of her sweater. She'd used her crutches today since it had been a while since the last snowfall and the streets and sidewalks were clear now. She hobbled to the front foyer and said a silent prayer for strength as she opened the door to find Sam and Ivy on the stoop. He had a frown on his face and a toolbox in one hand. Ivy had her backpack.

"Come in," Riley said, flashing a nervous smile. "Adi's out back on the patio, Ivy, if you want to play with her."

"Cool! Thanks," Ivy said, skipping off to find her bestie.

It seemed she'd recovered well enough after the trauma of the other day. Riley only hoped she and Sam could do the same, but she had her doubts. He walked past her into the hallway, the breeze carrying his good Sam scent, and she found herself inhaling deep as she closed the door. She'd missed him, even if it had just been a few days.

"Where do you want me to start?" he asked when she returned to the kitchen. His voice sounded lower, gruffer, than it usually did, and she wondered if he was nervous too. He'd laid out different tools on the granite island—tape measure, pencils, a laser guide—and was shrugging out of his coat to reveal a dark green sweatshirt underneath. He looked comfortable and casual in his jeans and work boots. Handsome too. Riley fought the urge to throw her arms around him and hold on for dear life.

He wasn't hers to hold.

"Uh, wherever you think is best. You're the expert."

Sam snorted as if she'd made a joke, then picked up his tape measure and a pencil and headed for the master bedroom to check the closet and bathroom. Riley tagged along behind him, feeling as useless as tits on a bull. Given that she needed both hands for her crutches, she couldn't even hold the tape measure for him. Not that he asked. Generally, he seemed to give her an extra-wide berth, going out of his way to make sure they didn't touch at all, even in passing.

Guess that answered her question about what the future held for them.

Finally, when he'd checked all the closets and bathrooms and returned to do the kitchen last, Riley couldn't stand it anymore. She waited until he'd crouched in front of a set of lower cabinets then said, "I'm really sorry about what happened at the party."

He straightened, focusing on typing his measurements into his phone as if she hadn't spoken. She glanced through the sliding glass doors to where Ivy and Adi were playing on the back deck. Ivy was trying on Adi's skates.

"You have every right to be mad at me," she added.

"I'm not mad at you, Riley," he said finally. "I'm mad at myself."

Now it was her turn to frown. "Why? What did you do?"

Sam continued measuring the kitchen. "I failed to protect you. I made bad decisions where you're concerned, and now we're paying the price for that. I'm sorry."

Hackles rising, she gripped the edge of the island tight. "Bad decisions?"

"Yes. I thought I was ready to get involved again. I thought I could compartmentalize what was happening between us. Control it. Keep it from causing issues in other areas of my life. I couldn't. And because I couldn't, I caused you stress and upset and created a rift between you and your family."

It took her a moment to process all that, but when she had, her anger rose. "Wow. So, you're saying this is all your fault?"

"Yep." He crouched again to measure the dishwasher, and she did her best to ignore how good his butt looked in those jeans. She did not need to be looking at that right now.

"Wrong." She hobbled over closer to him so that when he stood once more, they were facing each other. "This was not all your fault. I did plenty on my own before you ever showed up in your Santa suit, buddy. And just so you know, that rift between me and Brock was a long time coming, okay? You don't get to control that narrative either, sir."

"I'm not trying to control anything, Riley. I'm just stating the facts as I see them."

"As you see them. But not necessarily as things are."

A muscle ticked near his tense jaw. "And how do you think things are?"

"I think we both took a chance on being together and it was always going to be rocky at first. I thought you were the kind of guy who wouldn't run at the first sign of turbulence. I thought you were the overprotective alpha type. Kind of like Brock. Apparently, I was wrong."

His lips tightened a bit at the direct hit on his vulnerabilities. "I'm not running. I'm being logical."

"Oh, really? Because from where I'm standing it looks an awful lot like avoidance."

For a second, it looked like Sam wanted to argue more about that, but then he turned to put his coat back on. "I have what I need here." He shoved his phone back into his pocket. "I'll get quotes on supplies and then—"

The rest of his words were drowned out by a scream from outside—a heart-ripping, life-in-danger sound that had both her and Sam running out onto the patio to find both girls gone.

"What the—" Sam took off down the boardwalk leading from the patio to the beach with Riley doing her best to keep up on her crutches. She prided herself on her independence and being able to do everything other people could, but sometimes being differently abled really sucked.

"Adi? Where's Ivy?" Sam shouted as they reached her niece. "What's happened?"

Adi was sobbing so hard all she could do was point out toward the bay, where a dark hole was visible in the frozen ice on the bay, maybe fifteen feet from shore. Riley knew the drop-off around there was sharp and deep, and her stomach sank to her toes. She remembered Ivy trying on Adi's skates.

"Did she go out on the ice?" Riley asked.

Adi nodded, her breathing jagged as her teeth chattered so hard her words stuttered. "I—I told her not to go. Not like the r-rink. The bay—the bay kills p-people. K-killed my mom, and now I-Ivy t-too!"

Sam swore under his breath and ran back up the boardwalk to the patio and headed straight for the shed, where he grabbed a coil of rope then ran back. He tossed Riley his phone before tying the rope around himself in a makeshift harness then handed her the other end. "Call 911. I'm going in to get my daughter."

"Wait!" Riley yelled after him. "Sam! You can't go out there. It's too dangerous!"

"I have to!" He stopped at the edge of the frozen bay and turned back to her. "If we wait until help arrives, it will be too late. I was on a volunteer rescue dive team back in San Diego. It's not quite the same circumstances, but I do have some training. I can't lose Ivy! She's all I have left."

Riley dialed 911 as Sam slowly made his way toward the hole in the ice. She reported their emergency, and the dispatcher told her fire rescue was five minutes out. Sam was right. That would be too late.

She's all I have left...

Her chest squeezed at his words, knowing that wasn't true. Not anymore. He had Riley too. If he still wanted her.

From the ice, Sam yelled back at her, "Wait for my signal to pull."

Sam dropped to his knees about five feet from the hole and crawled the rest of the way, the ice cracking ominously beneath his weight. Then, in the blink of an eye, it gave way and Sam dropped into the frigid depths. Riley choked back a scream as he braced his gloved hands on the edge of the new hole he'd just created, taking a deep breath before going under again to search for Ivy. Based on his body mass and the temperatures, Riley knew he had about thirty minutes before becoming hypothermic. Now they had two clocks running: one for Ivy and one for him. She prayed he'd save them both before time ran out.

Sam pulled himself out once more, then disappeared again beneath the surface. Riley counted the seconds, praying that Sam knew what he was doing, her hand tightening around the rope. Maybe all that upper body work she'd done with Luna in PT would finally pay off. Each time she closed her eyes, flashbacks of the accident slammed into her with debilitating force. Trapped and submerged in the freezing, unforgiving darkness as her injured parents drowned before her eyes, with Riley paralyzed and helpless in the back seat. She refused to be helpless ever again.

"Aunt Riley, it's them!" Adi yelled.

Her eyes opened wide to see Sam pop out of the water one last time, this time clutching his daughter's limp body. He finally gave Riley a thumbs-up and she dug her feet into the sand and tugged with all her might. Adi picked up the slack behind her and pulled too.

They hauled on the rope at the same time Sam boosted himself and Ivy up onto the surrounding ice sheet with one arm until only his booted feet remained submerged in the bay. Each yank on the rope drew them closer to the shore now, and thankfully the ice held beneath them. Once they were ashore, Riley dropped the rope and hobbled over to help him with Ivy.

"Adi," she told her niece. "Go back to the house and get my coat. We need something warm and dry to wrap Ivy in until the medics arrive."

The little girl raced back up the boardwalk.

Sirens echoed in the distance, but they were still a few minutes out, if Riley had to guess. Ivy's little face was blue from the cold as Riley checked for a pulse. "She's unresponsive and not breathing. Starting CPR now."

Riley gave two breaths, then Sam started chest compressions on his daughter. Ivy's tiny chest rose and fell with each ventilation, which only made the stillness afterward that much more disturbing.

"Come on, *yeobo*," Sam pleaded. "Breathe. Please just take a breath."

They continued CPR until Ivy convulsed as she choked. Riley turned the child over onto her side where she coughed and vomited up seawater. Adi had returned with her coat, and Riley took it to wrap Ivy up in as the medics and fire rescue finally arrived. Sam was holding Ivy to him now, rubbing her back as tears streamed down his shivering face. "I thought I'd lost you too, *yeobo*."

Riley reached over to touch his arm as the medics ran down to take over. "She's going to be okay."

"I'm going with her to the ER," Sam said, stating the obvious. He'd allowed Tate and the EMTs to get Ivy onto a gurney and loaded into the back of a nearby ambulance, but otherwise he was in charge. He clutched the Mylar blanket they'd given him tighter around himself and took a large gulp of hot tea someone had shoved into his hands after the chaos. Honestly, he could have been drinking sludge for all he tasted it. His attention was focused solely on his daughter now. No, that wasn't entirely true. He was also aware of Riley there, with her too-pale face and worried eyes. They'd been through hell just now and it showed. He didn't imagine he looked any better. But she'd stayed by his side through it all. Helping him save Ivy. He would never forget that. The EMTs gestured for him to get in the back of the ambulance with Ivy for the ride to the hospital, and he turned to Riley. They still had so much to say to each other, but now wasn't the time. "I'll call you once I know more."

She nodded and handed him back his phone. "I'll be praying for you and Ivy."

"Thanks." He wanted to say more, to apologize for everything that had happened since that party, to tell her how he felt, to ask her not to give up on him, on them, to beg her for another chance. But it would have to wait until later. So instead, he cupped her cheek, her skin cold beneath his touch. "Talk soon. Take care."

"You too," she said, turning her head slightly to kiss his palm. Then she stepped back beside Mark Bates, who was there with fire rescue.

His heart swelled with warmth as the doors closed and the rig took off, sirens blaring as they raced toward Wyckford General. The EMTs had replaced Riley's coat with heated blankets around Ivy to keep her warm, and they'd started her on high-flow oxygen through a face mask, along with IV fluids—all routine care for drowning patients. They'd also done a preliminary exam for spinal injuries before loading her onto the gurney, but thankfully hadn't found any. She'd left Adi's waterlogged skates behind on the beach. He'd have to buy a new set for Adi, but it was a small price to pray for his daughter being alive and hopefully well.

Ivy wasn't talking, just gripping Sam's hand for dear life. His mind still raced with what-ifs. What if he'd not reached her in time? What if the CPR hadn't worked? What if she had permanent brain damage from being underwater so long, not breathing? Sam rubbed his eyes with his free hand, the Mylar blanket crinkling around him each time he moved.

"Okay, Doc?" Tate Griffin asked him.

"Yeah," Sam replied. While having an analytical mind was good on many levels, it could also turn against you at times, causing anxiety that fed on itself. It hadn't happened to Sam in a while, not since he'd left San Diego. But this near miss with Ivy had triggered him again. "Just exhausted."

As they neared the hospital, he wished Riley was there with him. Her ability to calm and refocus him was just another reason to love her. He froze at the realization. Yep. It was true.

I love Riley Turner.

Sam's eyes sprang open at the feel of Ivy squeezing his hand tighter. "What is it, *yeobo*? What do you need?" He brought her chilled hand to his lips to kiss it.

Ivy swallowed hard, the monitors she was hooked up to beeping as her core body temperature updated to ninety-five. A good sign. "I said, can Riley come live with us and be like another mommy for me?"

"Oh, uh..." Taken aback, Sam wasn't sure how to answer. He hadn't gotten that far yet, let alone heard Riley say she loved him too. Plus, marriage was a big deal. Did either of them even want that? He didn't know but wanted to reassure his daughter. "How about we talk about this later, after we get your prognosis."

Ivy wrinkled her nose. "What's a frogdosis?"

Sam laughed then, a mix of relief and thankfulness and tension release. "Prognosis. It means how well they expect you to recover."

"We're here, Doc," Tate said as they slowed to a halt.

The next several minutes passed in a blur as the back doors of the rig opened at the ER entrance to reveal Brock and nurse Madi Scott waiting for them. They got Ivy unloaded then Sam followed the team inside as Tate gave them a run-down of what had happened, Ivy's condition and the treatment so far. Sam only let go of Ivy's hand once when they moved her from the ambulance gurney to a hospital bed in one of the ER trauma rooms.

Sam stood to the side of the bed as Brock ran the team's assessment and treatment plan. There was a reason you didn't treat your own family members; it clouded your judgment, and he couldn't afford to make mistakes now.

"What's her O2 level?" Brock asked.

"Ninety-one percent," Madi said, checking the monitor as she helped remove Ivy's wet clothes before covering her with a gown and more blankets.

"Okay. Let's get an EKG to check for bradycardia, please." While Madi placed the pads on her small chest, Brock did a neurological check on Ivy. "Hey, kiddo. Can you tell me your name?"

"Ivy Perkins."

"Very good. And how old are you?"

"Seven."

"Excellent. What month is it?"

"December."

"And where do you live?"

"Wyckford, Massachusetts."

"Perfect."

Then Ivy added, "I used to live in San Diego, but then Mommy died, so Daddy and I moved here. It's nice. And Adi's my best friend!"

"Yes, she is." Brock grinned before winking at Sam, letting him know his daughter was okay. "GCS score of fifteen."

"Is Riley your sister?" Ivy asked Brock, frowning.

"Yes."

"You were yelling at her at the party."

Brock stopped and looked from Ivy to Sam then back again. "I was. And that was wrong of me. I shouldn't have done that."

"No, you shouldn't," Ivy scolded him. "I get in trouble when I yell at people."

Brock glanced up at Sam again, this time biting his lips

as if holding back a smile. To Ivy he said, "Yelling is hardly ever a good thing to do. Especially with my sister."

Ivy seemed to think about that for a moment before asking, "Are you still mad at her?"

"No. Not anymore. I wasn't mad at her anyway." He shrugged. "But I need to apologize to her."

"I like Riley. I asked Daddy if she can be my new mommy," Ivy told him before Sam could stop her.

All eyes suddenly turned to him again, but instead of feeling exposed, this time Sam puffed out his chest and stood tall. He loved Riley and he didn't care if the world knew. He and Brock had a mini standoff across the bed, then Brock finally lifted his chin slightly in a show of acceptance and a bit of the tension still lingering inside Sam relaxed.

Brock continued with the exam, asking Ivy to breathe as he used his stethoscope on her chest and back. "Some rales noted on left side on exam. Slight cough observed. Signs of aspiration. How's the EKG looking, Madi?"

"So far, so good," Madi said, checking the strip. "No dysrhythmias noted."

"Great." Brock examined Ivy's abdomen next. "And no gastric distention. Let's get a core body temp on her and an initial chest X-ray to check for delayed or developing pulmonary edema. Pending those results, we'll repeat it again after eight hours to check for any changes. Also, get a blood glucose and ABG from the lab. Classify her as a grade two drowning and let's put her on observation and monitor her condition until the next chest X-ray. Keep her hydrated and warm under observation until then, please. Thanks, everyone."

Brock then took Sam to a small conference room across the hall and closed the door. "I owe you an apology."

"I don't care about that right now. I just want to know my daughter will be okay," he said, sitting on a chair against the wall. His clothes were still damp, and his boots squished with each step. He hadn't taken time to change after the rescue. All his focus had been on saving Ivy.

"We'll know more after the observation period. Symptom development can be delayed because of the hypothermia," Brock said, walking over to a nearby cabinet and pulling out a fresh set of scrubs and a pair of hospital socks, the kind they usually gave patients to wear. He handed it all to Sam. "Get warm and dry, then we'll talk more, okay? I'm due for a break, so I'll buy you a coffee in the cafeteria."

He left without waiting for Sam's answer, meaning it wasn't up for discussion. So be it. The guy would be Sam's new brother-in-law if things went to plan, so he needed this to go well. He took off his sodden clothes and boots and exchanged them for the fresh scrubs and socks, then found an empty plastic bag to store his wet stuff in until he could get it home. Once he was done, he went back out to check on Ivy before joining Brock at the nurses' station to head downstairs. He could use the caffeine to keep awake, since it sounded like they'd be there a while.

"So, you and my sister aren't just a fling? You're a couple now?" Brock waited until they got their drinks and found a table in a quiet part of the cafeteria to bring up the subject, not far from where he'd sat with Riley that one late night that felt like forever ago. "How long has that been going on?"

"Not long." Sam shrugged, wincing slightly at the pain in his shoulder. He was going to feel the rescue in the morning. "And we're not a couple. I mean, I'd like to be, but I'm not sure that's what she wants now, so..."

"You talked to her at her house earlier?" Brock's expression remained frustratingly neutral, so Sam couldn't read whether he was happy about the news. Based on the fight at the party the other day, it was hard to tell.

"I did, but the way we left things…" He scrubbed a hand over his face. "I don't know where things stand with us."

"Riley is my only sibling, Sam. And despite going at it sometimes, we take care of each other." He toyed with his cup of coffee, scowling down at the dark liquid inside. "She's been through a lot. I just want to make sure she's protected."

"I know. Me too," Sam said. "I've been through some things too."

"Well, despite what's happened in your pasts, I saw how Riley looked at you, like you're her favorite present, and I saw the same goofy expression on your face too, so maybe give it another try. Love isn't necessarily easy, but it's always worth it, if it's real."

Sam was too tired for this. "I know. I know it's worth it. But I'm still trying to wrap my analytical brain around the fact that for some crazy reason, I seem to have fallen hard for your sister after only a couple of weeks. But we just feel right together. And no matter how hard I try to logic my way out of it, that's the truth. Have you ever felt that way about anyone? Like fate had brought you together?"

Brock snorted. "Cassie and I were only back together a few weeks too when I knew."

Sam sat back and sighed. "I care for Riley, and I want a future with her, however that looks for us. I never expected to find love again after my wife died, but my past has taught me how precious it is. I don't want to lose this chance with her."

Brock smiled at last. "You're a good man, Sam. And while I don't appreciate you two sneaking around behind my back at my house, I think you two will be good for each other.

And Ivy is a pure joy. It's not easy being a dad on your own, is it?" He sat back as well, shaking his head. "I'm not gonna lie. It nearly killed me. I felt like I was stretched too thin to be any good to anyone who mattered. Hell, it got to the point my daughter wasn't even talking like a human anymore."

Sam snorted. "Riley told me."

"Then Cassie came back to town, and she somehow broke through all that noise. Don't ask me how, but she did. I've always believed when you know, you know."

Sam took that in then sat forward to check his watch. "You really think Ivy will be fine?"

"I do." Brock switched back into doctor mode again. "She's very lucky. The cold water helped her. Slowed everything down until help arrived. You're a hero, Dr. Perkins."

"Can I get that in writing, please?" Sam laughed. "Might come in handy when I start the renovations on your sister's new house."

Brock chuckled. "She'll still be salty sometimes."

"I wouldn't have her any other way."

They finished their drinks then returned upstairs. Brock went to grab a new patient while Sam returned to Ivy's room to sit by her bedside while she slept. She looked as tired as Sam felt, but at least she was alive and well. He pulled out his phone from his pocket to check his emails and found a text from Riley.

Just checking on you. Hope everything's okay.

That heart emoji at the end made him smile.

He sent her back a quick text telling her they were okay, with a smiley face at the end, then settled into his chair for a nap.

He didn't get to sleep long, however, before he heard Ivy's small voice say, "I'm sorry, Daddy. I just wanted to see what it was like out there. It was cold. It was so cold. And dark." Tears trickled down her cheeks. "I tried to yell when I fell in, but it was like the ice squeezed all the sound out of me."

"Don't cry, *yeobo*," he said, leaning in to kiss the top of her head. "It's all going to be okay."

Ivy was quite for a while, so long that Sam wondered if she'd fallen asleep again. But then she looked at him, her expression serious. "Adi says that you like her aunt Riley."

Sam had wondered how he'd talk about with his daughter, but it seemed fate had intervened yet again. "I do. Very much. In fact, I love her."

"You do?" Ivy looked up at him again. "So we'll be a family again?"

"I hope so." His chest squeezed with sweetness.

They sat there for a while as Ivy seemed to process that. Then she asked, "Can I still be in the Christmas play tomorrow?"

He'd forgotten all about that with everything going on. It was twenty-four hours away, and he'd have to double-check with Brock to be sure, but if he cleared Ivy, Sam would be okay with it. He told his daughter as much.

"Yay!" She clapped. "I'm going to be the best goldfish ever!"

They settled back into quiet again after that, Ivy snoozing while Sam sorted through things in his head. It was still hard for his analytical side to grasp how quickly things had happened in his life here. Riley had brought light and warmth to his life, just like she had to all the people she cared for. She had made him smile, laugh, *feel* again.

He remembered something Cassie Turner had told him

once when she'd first persuaded him to move to Wyckford almost two years prior. She'd given up everything to return home and marry Brock, basically starting all over again, just like Sam.

I realized my life would never be what I'd once planned, but that didn't mean it was over.

Sam knew now that was true for him as well. He still had things to do and people to love—one very determined, very independent, very passionate radiologist.

And sure, she was salty sometimes, but he could be a difficult person to live with too, fussy and exacting to a fault. But the past few years had taught him it wasn't so much the differences that mattered; it was the ways you were alike with someone. Control was a fallacy, one he'd chased for far too long. Much better to take what came your way and make it better, support those around you and stand strong through good times and bad. That's what survivors did.

He closed his eyes again, wholly overwhelmed at the idea of a future with Riley. She'd given her all today to help rescue Ivy and it meant the world to him. His spirts lifted, buoyant like a helium balloon. He and Riley had things to talk about. Not over text, but face-to-face. Baring his soul was not in his nature, but for a chance at forever with Riley, he knew he had to open his heart to her completely and risk it all for love.

The next night, Riley dressed in her favorite red sweater and jeans for the Christmas play, then looked at herself in the mirror. She hadn't seen Sam or Ivy since the accident, and while they'd texted updates to each other since then, she was anxious to see them with her own eyes to make sure they were all right. Sam had seemed oddly vague with details, so she wasn't sure what to expect.

"Riley?" Brock called from the living room. "Get a move on!"

"I'm coming," she yelled back. "Be there in a minute."

Speaking of squirrelly, her brother had been acting weird too. They'd made up after their fight, they always did, but he was also vague whenever she asked him questions about Sam and Ivy, giving her only the driest of details. Which only made her nerves worse.

Things between her and Sam hadn't exactly been going swimmingly before Ivy fell through the ice. In fact, she'd called it off completely at the party, so she couldn't really blame him for being chilly toward her now. She'd hurt him badly, when she'd known he really had only been trying to help. He wasn't a do-gooder. He'd shown her in so many small ways over the past few weeks that she was more than her injuries. Shown her that true freedom sometimes meant forging connections with others. And now she realized just how much she loved Sam. But she'd ended it all herself— over before it had really started because of her stupid hang-ups about independence.

Sam didn't want to steal her freedom; he wanted to support her so she could soar.

With a sad sigh, Riley grabbed her coat and bag and joined the others in the living room, all too aware of Brock watching her, eagle-eyed. She'd deal with it, whatever happened, because that's what she did. But there would always be a Sam-sized hole in her heart.

As Brock helped her with her coat, he gave her a sidelong look. "Everything okay?"

"Fine," she said flatly. "We're going to see goldfish in Bethlehem."

Brock looked concerned, but thankfully didn't push it.

At the school, Riley forced a cheerful smile until she

thought her face might crack. Adi's teacher had saved them seats in the crowded school gymnasium, near the aisle for Riley's wheelchair. Brock rushed Adi backstage while Riley sat out front with Cassie. The place was packed, standing room only, as she scanned the crowd for Sam. She spotted him a few rows ahead, sitting with Hala and her husband. Riley tried to get his attention, but he kept his attention on the program in his hands.

Brock found them just as the light went down and the play started. While the play progressed, Riley did her best to focus on the stage instead of Sam in front of her. The Nativity production ended up being adorable, complete will a plethora of animals and sea creatures from all over the globe that couldn't have possibly ever been in the ancient Middle East, but they increased the number of parts so every child in school had a role onstage. There was even had a sing-along, with all the standard carols and the audience encouraged to participate.

After the pageant was over, everyone returned to the lobby to enjoy light refreshments, but Riley stayed behind, making some lame excuse about needing to call the hospital for something. Sam stayed too, she noticed, and she couldn't stand the suspense anymore, so she unlocked her chair wheels and rolled down to see him. She stopped about a foot away from him and met his gaze, her pulse tripping anew as she saw all the emotions there. So many things she hadn't dared hope for but wanted so badly from him—care, devotion, respect, love. That last one stole her breath.

"Hey," Sam said, his voice a tad husky. "How'd you like the play?"

"It was great. How's Ivy?"

"Good."

"And how do you feel?"

"Sore," he said, rolling a shoulder then wincing. "I'm getting too old for that stuff."

She bit her lip. "Do you really want to talk about the play?"

"No," he said, reaching over to pull her onto his lap before she even realized what he was doing. At first Riley froze, then she relaxed into him, his arms around her waist as she pulled back to see his face, concerned. "You're shaking."

He tucked her head beneath his chin, rocking her back and forth gently, as if she were the most precious thing in the world to him. Her heart grew three sizes bigger with love for him too as she buried her face into the base of his neck. "Better now," he whispered against the top of her head. "I missed you."

"I missed you too," she said, eyes closed. "I'm so sorry for what I said to you at the party. I never meant to hurt you. I was angry and frustrated with the situation and I lashed out, but it wasn't your fault. I'll do better in the future."

"It's okay. I should have given you space in that moment. I knew that's what you needed, but my need to help overrode my common sense." Eventually, he leaned back and cupped her cheeks, bringing her gaze to his. "So I'm sorry too. And we'll both do better. Together. Thank you for helping to save my daughter. Thank you for seeing me and bringing light back into my life. I love you, Riley Turner, and I want a future with you. Ivy does too. She's crazy about you too. Will you have us?"

She blinked to clear the tears gathering in her eyes, the cracks in her heart that had been there for years now beginning to mend. "Say it again."

"I love you."

She kissed him then, only to pull away when a chorus of

cheers and applause echoed from the lobby. Riley looked over Sam's shoulder to see their friends and family and half the town in the doorway, watching them. Riley laughed, burying her face in his shoulder. "Well, I guess the secret's out now."

"Guess so." Sam pulled her closer and kissed her again, seemingly not caring at all.

This time when she pulled away, Riley was breathless with wonder and hope. "I love you too, Sam. I thought doing everything by myself made me strong, but now I realize that without connection, without people I care for supporting me, I can't do anything. I can't wait to create forever with you and Ivy. And I can't believe I saw you for over a year and never took much notice, then boom. Feelings!" Pressed up against him as she was, her heart pounding in time with his, Riley never wanted to move again. "And I adore Ivy too. Of course I'll have you both."

Sam's embrace tightened around her as he kissed her again. "Good. Now tell me what you want for Christmas."

She shook her head, smiling from ear to ear. "Nothing. I have everything I want."

"Me too." Sam smiled then kissed her once more, and Riley put *everything* into it—her promise to be with him always, her hope for the future, her forever love for him and Ivy. Her very own family of three under the tree.

EPILOGUE

One year later...

"ARE YOU SURE we'll have enough popcorn?" Riley asked, her tone sarcastic.

Sam made a face at her from across the massive island in their new kitchen, which was currently covered in enough red-and-white-striped popcorn bags to feed an army.

"I only made ten batches," he said defensively. He'd spent a lot of time calculating just how much they'd need. "We have twenty guests coming, so that should be about right. Everyone loves popcorn, so I think we'll be lucky to have a kernel left over for ourselves."

"Better grab one now then, I guess." She shrugged, adjusting her crutches to grab the nearest bag.

"Help yourself," Sam said, distracted. Now that he was looking at it, maybe his calculations had been wrong. "Actually, maybe I better make another batch..."

He'd just added more popcorn kernels to the popper when he felt Riley's arms around his waist. "On second thought, it's not popcorn I'm craving," she murmured, kissing the back of his neck until he shivered.

They'd been engaged six months now and were still going strong. Sam couldn't get enough of her, and the feeling seemed to be mutual. He turned to kiss her, careful to avoid banging into one of her crutches. She was using them more than the chair now. To say Sam was impressed was the understatement of the century. He knew how hard she'd worked to get here, and he was so proud of her he could burst.

Riley pulled away slightly. "When is everyone coming again?"

"Fifteen minutes. Not enough time for what you're thinking."

"Damn." She slid away again to look out the window over the sink.

He and Ivy had settled even more into life in Wyckford since moving in with Riley. Now, in addition to his duties as head of neurosurgery at Wyckford General and his ALS research project, he also spearheaded a local charity called Natalia's Place, dedicated to providing accessibility resources and home renovations for those in need in the area. Everyone should be comfortable and safe where they lived, and it gave Sam a chance to donate his handyman skills to a good cause.

A win-win for everyone.

Riley was still busy as ever at the hospital and with helping to raise Ivy. The two had bonded even more, with Ivy calling Riley her "S-Mom," short for "second mom." It made Sam's heart so happy to know his daughter, *their* daughter, had someone as kind and loyal and strong as Riley in her corner.

He leaned his hips back against the kitchen counter while the corn popped and caught Riley as she passed by him, pulling her close once more. Having everyone over to their newly renovated place for the first time was a big deal, and he felt a little nervous.

"Stop worrying," she ordered him. "You already know everyone loves you. And they're going to love the house too. It's gorgeous. You did an amazing job!"

He took a deep breath and realized it was true. He and Ivy were a part of this town now, and it was a part of them. They made a difference in the lives of the people around them, and that was all Sam had ever wanted. Well, that and Riley, whom Sam loved with all his heart and soul. She felt the same about him. He knew because she told him every day. Told Ivy too. They'd truly become a family.

"Thank you," he said, resting his forehead against Riley's.

"For?" she asked, her dark brows furrowing.

"A million things. Mostly for not giving up on me when all this started."

Sam kissed her fast, letting her go just as Ivy came into the kitchen.

"I can't wait to see Adi," Ivy said, clapping. "When will she be here?"

Riley looked at the clock in the kitchen. "Soon. Looks like it's snowing again, so they may have slowed down because of the weather."

"Yeah. Daisy texted and said she and her mother might be a little late for that reason."

"Better safe than sorry," Riley said.

"That's what I told her."

Daisy was holding her own right now, not getting any better, but not getting any worse either. She worked from home now as a web designer rather than going into an office and overall was making the best of her circumstances. She'd also joined a support group at the hospital, to talk about her experiences and share resources with others in similar situations.

"How's the book coming?" Sam asked his daughter.

Ivy sighed. The therapist she'd started seeing after her fall through the ice had suggested journaling for Ivy, to work out her trauma over the accident and her grief over losing her mother. "Writing is hard."

"No lies detected there," Riley said.

"Do I have to do it?"

Sam shrugged. "You don't have to, but maybe if you take some time away then come back to it, you might feel differently."

"Maybe." Ivy seemed like eight going on eighteen sometimes, and Sam shuddered at the thought of impending teenager-hood in a few short years. The doorbell rang then, and Ivy jumped. "I'll get it!"

A moment later, his daughter led the new arrivals into the kitchen—Brock and Adi, followed by Cassie with their baby. Brock carried a large plate covered in plastic wrap balanced on one hand.

"Sorry we're late." Cassie looked around the kitchen. "The roads were a bit dicey. This place looks beautiful!"

"Thank you," Sam said, taking the plate from Brock and unwrapping it to find brownies before setting it on the island where people could help themselves to snacks. "And I'm glad you made it safely. Please make yourselves comfortable. We figured we'd wait until everyone was here to give the grand tour."

Brock kissed Riley on the cheek before grabbing a beer from the fridge. "Great work, Sam."

For the next half hour, a steady stream of people crowded into the house. Madi and Tate. Luna and Mark. Cassie's dad, Ben. Daisy and her mother. Even Lucille and grumpy old Mr. Martin. Once everyone had arrived, taken the tour, then settled into the living room with their popcorn and snacks, Sam moved to the front of the room near the large flat-screen TV and cleared his throat.

He looked out at everyone and thought about how empty his life would have been if he'd not taken that final, huge risk and opened his heart and soul to Riley, to the people of this town. Sam felt immeasurably blessed. "Thank you all for coming. These past couple of years have been a lot for me and Ivy and Riley, and we just want to thank you all for being there for us. We hope we can return the favor, and tonight is just a gift from us to you. Enjoy the show!"

Then he took his seat beside Riley on the sofa, Ivy on his other side, and Riley squeezed his hand at the cheerful opening credits rolled on *It's a Wonderful Life*. No matter what the future held for any of them, they had everything they needed right here in this room, all of it built on a foundation of love.

* * * * *

*If you missed the previous story in the
Wyckford General Hospital quartet,
then check out*

Her Forbidden Firefighter

*And if you enjoyed this story,
check out these other great reads from
Traci Douglass*

An ER Nurse to Redeem Him
Home Alone with the Children's Doctor
Single Dad's Unexpected Reunion

All available now!

BROODING VET FOR THE WALLFLOWER

SUE MacKAY

MILLS & BOON

This story is dedicated to those who care for sick animals.

You people rock.

CHAPTER ONE

'KATE, YOU HAVEN'T had the privilege of meeting one of our past colleagues, Finn Anderson.' Jackson gave him a cheeky grin. 'Finn, this is one of our vets, Kate Phillips.'

Finn knew his friend well enough to know from the look in his eyes that he had ideas about how well he and Kate might get along. As far as he was concerned, Jackson could think again. It wasn't happening. He was only back home for his brother's wedding before returning to Scotland and his fantastic job there in a fortnight's time. He was not looking for a new relationship. The last one hadn't gone cold yet, and the lessons learned would probably prevent that from ever happening. He was not open to sharing his life and all he'd worked for ever again. As for his heart—that was locked down as tight as possible.

As he turned to meet the woman standing beside Jackson, his stomach dropped. Never had he seen such a beautiful woman. Classic features enhanced by long, straight, strawberry-blonde hair and drag-him-under fudge-brown eyes. Then there was the figure to die for. Surely she came with a warning tag? Like a serious warning about how he would combust if he touched her, or even stood too close to her.

Kate looked at him and said, 'Hello, Finn. I mightn't have met you but I've heard a bit about you.'

'Hello, Kate. Yes, I seem to remember there're times when Jackson does exceed the sensible levels of idle chatter.' Especially when he was on a mission to interfere in his friend's life, as he had been ever since it had gone down the gutter more than three years ago. All Finn could hope for was that Jackson would continue to keep his trap shut about his past. His pal might be a pain about some things, but he felt certain he could trust him on that one. It was his story to share, no one else's, and he had no intentions of doing that with anybody. Not even a stunning woman who had him looking twice to see if she was for real. Which she most certainly was.

'Yeah, right.' Jackson grinned.

Finn stepped closer and said quietly, 'Knock it off, pal.' This was his first time home to New Zealand in nearly two years and next time he took a break from work he intended exploring parts of France. Yet he had to admit it felt surprisingly good to be here. He couldn't be ready to return home, surely? It was good to catch up with friends but returning permanently wasn't yet an option.

He was still getting over how his fiancée, an accountant to boot, had bankrupted them. Not them so much as him, because she hadn't had any finances to begin with. It had been a terrible time facing up to what she'd done and dealing with the resulting consequences. The money she'd told him she'd spent on wedding plans had instead been sucked up at the casino, along with lots more that she'd shrugged off as their living expenses. There'd even been a loan he'd known nothing about until the bank had foreclosed on it and started the whole process that had seen him left with little more than the clothes he'd stood up in. He'd lost his veterinary business, wasn't allowed a loan of any kind for four years, and all the money he'd earned since had gone to paying back debtors even though he wasn't obligated to do so.

Living on the other side of the world was helping to put it all behind him, but not the fact he'd struggle to ever again trust someone with the things that mattered most to him. Love, family, and working for his own pleasure and gain. Not only had Amelia financially ruined him, she'd broken his heart. She'd been the love of his life. He might've forgiven her if she'd been willing to do something about her gambling problem, but she'd laughed at that idea, saying it wasn't a problem and she could stop any time she chose. Nor had she once apologised for ruining everything for him.

She'd also stolen from clients of the accounting firm she'd worked for and consequently had her accreditation taken away. Harder to swallow was that a year ago she'd married a wealthy man and had recently had a baby. That news had torn him further apart because it had shown how far she'd go to set herself up for life. Telling him she was pregnant when it had been an out and out lie had been the final kick in the guts for him because she'd actually shown him a positive test strip she'd got from a pregnant friend. All to keep him at her side until she'd found someone else to give her the lifestyle she craved, and that the casino hadn't provided. To think he'd fallen hard and fast for her, and had no idea who she really was. Once bitten, so the saying went, the rest of which was now his motto.

'Relax, Finn.' Jackson brought him back to the here and now, probably well aware of where he'd gone. 'This is a party. You're meant to be enjoying yourself catching up with old friends.'

He couldn't argue with that. The Lincoln Vet Clinic staff were in a room at the pub to celebrate winning clinic of the year for their work with the racehorses bred and trained around Lincoln and when they'd heard he was in town they'd made sure he came along. 'It's great seeing everyone.' He glanced at Kate.

And meeting new people.

Down, man. He wasn't staying around after the wedding.

'You're a local?'

She smiled. 'Cantabrian through and through.'

That smile could wreck any intentions to remain aloof. He took a step back. 'It's not a bad place to live. I do miss certain aspects.' On the days when he forgot why he'd left in the first place, and, face it, those days were rare. The humiliation over what Amelia had done was never far from the surface, along with the pain in his heart. Throw in his complete lack of trust and he was a screw-up.

'You don't intend returning home?' Kate asked.

'Not in the foreseeable future. The job I'm doing is too good an opportunity to toss it aside.' More importantly, he needed to stay away until he'd totally sorted his head out and knew how he was going to move on from the past. Might be years before that happened.

When he and Amelia had first got together, it had been wonderful. It hadn't bothered him that she'd wanted to live in Wellington where she'd grown up. It was natural to support his partner, right? She'd had a good job with a top company in the CBD and he had been happy to set up a veterinary practice on the edge of the city. Little had he known what he was letting himself in for when she'd suggested she look after the financial side of his business He hadn't had a clue that she knew what she was doing in more ways than legal when it came to rigging the books. Nor had he known about her gambling habit until it was too late. Her greed had got in the way of honesty. It wasn't as though she'd been raised in poverty. Her parents were hard-working and did well with their grocery business.

'What field are you working in?' Kate asked.

'I'm working for a rural practice that deals big time with Aberdeen cattle breeders.'

'Bet that's interesting.'

'It is.' Those eyes were sucking him in too easily. He took another step back.

Jackson nudged him. 'Let's join everyone else and get closer to the fire.'

'Good idea.' Winter was making itself felt today, though not a patch on the winters he'd experienced in Scotland. They were something else. Just thinking about them made him shiver.

He shook himself mentally and glanced at the beautiful woman before him. His skin tingled, making him all hot and bothered. How was he going to get through the evening and come out sane? Because he wasn't coming out any other way. Until now he'd believed it was a given that he stayed clear of temptation as the consequences could be destructive and he wasn't prepared to take that risk again.

'I'll get a drink first. Would you like one, Kate?' Hopefully the barman would take an hour to pour the drinks, giving him time to settle back to normal. Looking at Kate as he waited for her answer, he felt a surge of pure lust strike. She really should be on the cover of a fashion magazine. But then, for all he knew, she might already be.

'G and T, thanks.'

'Me, too,' Jackson called over his shoulder.

Finn headed to the bar, unable to shake Kate from his mind. She was something else. Beautiful beyond words, yet she didn't come across as overly confident. Or was it that she wasn't cocky? There was a stillness about her that suggested she took no crap from anyone, and thought things through before opening her mouth. Again, he was probably wrong, because what would he know when it came to reading women? But no denying she didn't appear to be aware of her beauty in a full-on kind of way.

He was surprised at how easily she intrigued him. No woman had done that since Amelia, who he'd got involved with quickly, believing he'd found the love of his life. She'd reciprocated just as strongly. Showed how wrong he could be. Something to remember when he was sitting up and taking notice of Kate after he'd sworn off involvement of any kind other than the occasional brief fling. And that was not happening with this woman stirring his blood. He sensed she could get too close too fast and thereby hurt him. He had no idea where that came from, but he'd trust his instincts even though they'd failed him in the past with Amelia. He was clear he wasn't setting himself up for a fall.

Just as well he was home for only a short period. That'd save him making an idiot of himself, along with getting Jackson off his back. Jackson had never liked Amelia and seemed determined to interfere in getting Finn back on his feet. Bring on the return flight to Britain. He needed his own space and that was impossible here in Canterbury with everyone determined to get him out amongst it and shove his ex-fiancée completely into the past. Amelia *was* his past, but the ramifications of what she'd done weren't and were unlikely to ever totally go away. There was a huge warning hanging over his head.

Remain wary.

Not hard to do. Until tonight, it seemed. That'd come right once he sorted his mind.

'I'll take those drinks to the table.' A soft feminine voice slipped through his thoughts, tightening his fingers into his palm.

There were only three glasses. 'I could've managed,' he said abruptly, then felt bad. Protecting himself came with problems. 'But thanks. Here's yours.'

Why had Kate come across to join him? Was she the kind of woman who always offered to help out? Or had he inadvertently stirred her blood too?

'Thanks.' Her smile went straight to his head. And his groin.

Too many of those and he wouldn't be able to account for anything he said or did, despite his best intentions. 'Any time.' He winced. Not any time. He wouldn't be seeing Kate after tonight, no matter what.

'Is your job permanent, or are you restricted by immigration laws?' Kate asked as they crossed to the table where Jackson was.

'Permanent. My mum's British so there was no issue when it came to applying for work over there.'

'That's handy.'

'Saves a lot of hassles, which is good. I'm not into hassles,' he added lightly, because he didn't know what else to say without getting too intense. For some reason she did that to him even though he'd only just met her. Not a good look if he intended remaining remote, which he had to do for his own sake.

'Something I understand,' Kate replied. Strange how her beauty was so out there and yet her voice was quiet and calm, not saying look at him in any way, unlike other women he'd met who weren't half as beautiful. 'You like living on the other side of the world?' she asked.

'Yes.' It put distance between him and the past. And unfortunately his family and friends, whom he missed a lot.

'So you don't intend returning to New Zealand any time soon?'

It was as though she was sussing him out, but that couldn't be, surely? Or had he tweaked her interest in the same way she'd done to him? 'No. At the moment I'm enjoying the work, along with the knowledge I'm acquiring, so I won't be quitting my position in the foreseeable future.' Time to turn the conversation off him and onto Kate. 'What about you? Travelled a lot?'

Thought you weren't going down this track.

If he hadn't been watching her he wouldn't have seen the shadow that crossed her face or the sharp touch she made to her upper abdomen. What was that about?

'Twice to Oz is my lot. I keep thinking I'll head away on my OE one day but it never happens. Guess having a long overseas experience isn't at the top of my bucket list.'

It was something a lot of Kiwis did before settling into their careers. 'What is, then?' Why the heck did he keep asking questions when all he wanted was to put space between them?

'Making the most of my career. I love being a vet. It makes the thought of travelling seem a little redundant.'

'Are you more into domestic animal health? Or do you work rurally?' He did need to shut up or she'd be getting the wrong idea.

'I far prefer looking out for dogs and cats. Though tonight's all about horses.' She looked around the crowded room, a soft smile lighting up her beautiful face. 'I'd better mix and mingle a bit. We're meant to chat to the horse breeders as they were a big part of us winning the award.'

'No problem. I'll catch up with the guys I used to work with.'

And take a breather from wondering what it would be like to hold you in my arms.

But he was unable to take his eyes off that sensational backside covered in tight black jeans as Kate strolled away. What if he let go his restraints and had some fun for one night? It wasn't as though that'd be setting him up for a fall. He'd be back on the other side of the world in fourteen days.

But while Kate had been quick to ask him about his career, he had no idea what she might be thinking about anything else. She seemed able to keep her thoughts to herself far better than he managed. She hadn't come on to him, nor had she pushed her own veterinary knowledge to prove she was his equal, as a couple of vets he'd recently met in Scotland had done. Kate was almost too good to be true. *Almost.* No woman was that good. And if he wasn't bitter, then what was he?

Kate put her cocktail glass aside and leaned one elbow on the bar while she watched people letting loose on the dance floor. The pub had provided music for the evening and just about everyone was getting into the mood and letting their hair down. Or swinging their bodies all over the place.

If only I had the same confidence.

Unfortunately, after the put-downs she'd had about the state of her body from the few men she'd been intimate with since her marriage collapsed, she'd become ultra-cautious about showing too much of herself to anyone. Especially her horrific scars. Throw in how Hamish had gone off her and walked away as though their marriage meant nothing, and her self-confidence was rocky at the best of times. Not that she'd be exposing any part of her body while dancing, but she didn't want to attract attention. Focusing on the crowd, she admitted she'd like to have some fun without thinking about everything that had gone wrong for her. 'Everyone's gone crazy.'

Beside her, Finn laughed. 'It says a lot about the evening.'

Thoughtlessly she said, 'Think I'll try a bit of dancing,' surprising herself. Was it her way of asking him to join her? Could be, she admitted. He was quite something to look at.

He obliged. 'Want a partner for that?' Finn asked, then looked as surprised as she felt. Hadn't he meant to ask her?

Tough. At worst, they'd dance and go their separate ways. At best? She had no idea other than her fingers itched to touch him. He was so gorgeous her breathing was off beat, and she couldn't ignore him for long.

'Sure, why not?' Might as well have some fun, and forget everything else for once. Watching closely, she saw heat creep into his cheeks. What was going on? Was he as insecure as her? Had someone done the dirty on him too?

Well, buster, the night is nowhere near over and you are something else.

The usual tightness around her need to let go and relax was loosening unexpectedly. Getting up close to that muscular body would be a treat. A few dance moves could only be good, and as he had made it clear by talking only about work that he wasn't into her, she wasn't setting herself up to be hurt further along the way.

Don't forget he'll soon be heading away again.

How could she forget when he'd talked about how much he enjoyed his life in Britain? There was nothing to fear about getting too interested in him. There wasn't enough time. A one-nighter would be the best thing for her if she followed through on the heated sensations filling her. What was wrong with having some fun and not waiting for the put-down that always came these days? What was wrong was that she didn't do it any more.

But for some inexplicable reason, Finn was getting to her in ways she didn't believe possible. Finn might even enjoy spending time up close with her. If he did notice her scars, which she'd do her utmost to prevent, he might be the first man in a long time not to reject her, though she knew she was dreaming there. After the last failed attempt at a relationship because the guy couldn't handle the mess her body was, she'd come to the conclusion it would be wise to run solo and forget trying to find that special someone to trust with her love, so her heart would remain intact.

Yet here she was, considering a short fling—a one-off and not a relationship—which said a lot about how much Finn was getting to her. He was the sexiest man she'd met in ages. What was there to lose other than her pride if he couldn't handle the sight of her? And face it, she should be able to hide the scars for one night. Covers on and lights off were the way to go.

At the beginning of any relationship with a man she'd liked enough to take a chance on, she'd always told him what had happened and how her body wasn't pretty, but even that hadn't been enough to halt the shocked expressions from appearing when she did expose herself. The front of her body was scarred from here to Africa and back, and, apart from her ex-husband, the men who had seen it had made comments about how beautiful they'd thought she was until the moment they'd set eyes on the rest of her body and slowly over the next days or weeks they'd withdraw and go find a prettier woman to have fun with. Went to show how shallow beauty was, and kind of meant the chances of her finding that special someone to spend her life with were remote. Unless she got over herself.

But it was hard to forget the looks those guys had tried to hide. So now rule number one was get to know the man well, learn to trust him not to hurt her before she finally stripped off for him. That had meant no intimacy in her life since. Yet here she was, thinking otherwise about Finn, which made no sense whatsoever. Maybe she was tired of being sensible.

Now you're sounding like you get down and naked with lots of men.

Which couldn't be further from the truth. There'd been very few over the last couple of years since Hamish walked out of her life three months after they'd returned from Australia's Northern Queensland and the holiday from hell. He'd had an epileptic fit in the sea and she'd raced into the water to get him, even knowing there were stingers about. Saving Hamish had been more important than worrying about getting stung.

The irony was that Hamish was fine once the lifeguards got him back on dry land and pumped the water out of his lungs, while she was in agony when they hauled her out and up onto the beach. They sent her to hospital, where doctors did all they could to help her, but there was little they could do about the stings from the jellyfish except prescribe pain relief. They told her that in most cases the lines left by the stings would disappear after a couple of weeks. Kate was one of the unlucky few to be permanently scarred. The front of her mid torso was not pretty.

She'd already felt insecure and unworthy after Hamish had struggled to cope with her new look, which had added to her insecurities when she'd started dating again. The scarring wasn't the reason Hamish had left her—apparently he preferred his secretary between the sheets to his wife. It hurt even more that he'd hesitated over leaving her because he'd felt guilty about what had happened that day in Queensland and said it constantly reminded him how it was his fault she'd gone into the water so he'd stayed with her longer than he'd wanted. That had made her feel both angry and rejected.

On one level she knew she was overreacting about how her body looked, but it was hard to ignore and move on. Especially as she'd grown up always hearing how beautiful she was. Occasionally she found herself thinking that it would still be great to have a short fling with a man so good-looking he knocked her socks off. And with Finn not staying around there'd be no repercussions or looking for more fun because he'd be gone in no time at all.

Yeah, sounds perfect.

If only she had the guts to make it happen. If only he didn't see the mess that was her abdomen. If only a lot of things.

When Finn took her elbow to lead the way out amongst the heaving crowd, unprecedented heat shot up her arm. Wow. If one small touch could do that, what would it be like to make out with him? Pulling away, Kate turned to face him, and instantly wished she hadn't. He was smiling at her, looking a little stunned too, as though he'd felt her heat under his hand. What would he think if she ran off the floor and went outside to grab a taxi to take her home—alone? But then she'd never been a coward, other than when it came to her body, so guess that meant she was staying right here, doing the moves.

Forget the moves. Finn's body was a part of the music, almost flowing with the beats. Her throat dried as she watched, mesmerised, forgetting to dance.

'You got lead in your boots?' He grinned.

'Bricks.' Forcing her limbs to move, she did her best to dance, but it was a poor version of her usual style.

'Here, perhaps I can help.' Finn took her hand and spun her around under his arm, spun her back to face him, and kept her hand tight in his. 'That's better.'

It was more than better. Her body had relaxed so suddenly she didn't know if she was coming or going. All she was aware of was Finn. Up so close, his body brought flushes to every area of hers. Just as well he wasn't staying around or she'd be a goner for certain. Tonight was her limit when it came to spending time with him, and the night was young. She spun around again, turned back to him, grinning like an idiot. A very confused idiot. 'Far better.'

'I think so.' Those amazing hips did their thing, still moving in sync with the beat, setting her heart racing at an unbelievable speed.

Looking into Finn's blue eyes and seeing that similar surprise coming back at her, she wondered what was going on. Seemed he hadn't expected to feel attracted to her. Yet he was. It was obvious in the way he kept touching her arms or her hips or her waist, and then abruptly pulling back. She couldn't remember when a man had affected her so sharply—if at all—other than Hamish. Her feet tripped over each other.

Instantly Finn caught her and tucked her in close. 'Careful. Can't have you face-planting on the floor.'

'It wouldn't be a good look.' She wound her arms around him and held tight. Not that she was going to drop to the floor, but any excuse to hold his divine body worked for her. Right now a one-nighter did seem the perfect finish to the evening. And quite likely, if his reactions to her were an indicator that they might be on the same page. Strange how the usual warning lights weren't flashing in her head. Finn was that wonderful?

Oh, yeah.

When the music was stopped so everyone could take a break and top up their drinks, Finn walked with her to the bar and asked, 'Another drink?'

'Thanks.' She'd prefer a kiss but she wasn't rushing. Every moment spent with Finn was the best.

He nodded at the queue at the bar. 'We could be waiting a while.'

'Let's get some fresh air in the meantime.'

He looked at her, his mouth lifting at the corners. 'Good idea.'

The breath she'd been holding leaked across her lips. Phew. They *were* on the same page. Weren't they? She was being quite forward for her. Usually she was the one putting the brakes on when it came to getting close to a man. Said a lot about Finn and how he was affecting her.

Out in the foyer they headed for a quiet, darker corner, now hand in hand. Then Finn was hauling her up against him, his mouth finding hers. Her head spun as she pressed her lips against his. He tasted wonderful, like an aphrodisiac. He *was* an aphrodisiac. His tongue was in her mouth, touching, teasing, turning her on so fast she couldn't keep up. It was as if she'd never had sex before, or hadn't known it could be this wonderful, when they were only kissing for the first time. From top to toes, her body burned with need.

Suddenly Finn set her back, away from his body. His arms dropped to his sides as he took a step away, staring at her as though he'd never seen her before. She stopped breathing, stopped pulsing. What was going on?

'I'm sorry. I can't do this.'

The words blasted through her head like a bullet. 'What?' Rejecting her already? Without knowing anything about her? No way. 'Finn, what's going on?' She thought she was speaking firmly but her voice was shaky.

'It wouldn't be fair on you. There are things about me you don't know.' With that, he turned and strode out of the pub, out of her life. Gone, leaving her aching, shocked that he could do such a thing so abruptly. Almost as if she'd drawn him into something he didn't want, something he'd gone along with to oblige her. But he had said it wouldn't be fair on her.

Damn right it wasn't fair. Despair sliced through her. Once again she'd been rejected, this time for a different reason than usual, one she didn't understand. Worse, it had happened so suddenly.

'I'm sorry. I can't do this.'

Hamish's words hung in the air, making her shiver. But this time it hadn't been Hamish saying them. That was Finn walking away as though she meant nothing more than a pesky fly. He hadn't said anything else, and she was supposed to accept that? Of course she would, because that was what she'd done in the past. It was who she'd become: a coward when it came to getting close to men.

Kate hugged herself tight. Talk about confusing. She and Finn had danced together and he'd appeared to be happy. He'd been the one to pull her into his arms and start kissing her. Not that it had crossed her mind to back off. She'd wanted his kiss. This was a whole new experience. They'd only started kissing; he hadn't seen the scarring that had driven other men away. But he'd still walked out of the building.

Guess she should be grateful that she wouldn't be exposing her weakness. Except she didn't like that at all. For once she'd actually believed she might've been able to overcome those fears enough to have a wonderful night. Now she'd never know. Finn had gone. It was probably for the best, but it still hurt. She'd wanted him more than she could believe. Which had to be a warning in itself.

Best she head home and take a cold shower, though she'd already cooled off a lot as she watched him walk away. Finn might heat her up fast and have her body craving for him, but he wasn't her type if he could do that so abruptly. If she hadn't seen the shock and disappointment in his eyes she'd have thought he was too confident and sure of himself for her liking. But seeing those expressions made her wonder if there might be a lot more to this man than she could begin to imagine.

He was so damned sexy it was scary. And exciting.

And whatever she'd imagined happening was over before it had even begun. He'd rejected her, as others had before him.

CHAPTER TWO

'OF ALL THE veterinary clinics around Christchurch, why did Finn have to get a position at Darfield Animal Care?' Kate muttered as she drove to work on Monday morning. 'It's not like there aren't other rural vet places in the region.'

Be reasonable.

She'd been working out at Lincoln when they'd met and he wouldn't have a clue that she'd changed jobs. Her chest tightened. She had to get over herself. When Peter had announced to everyone that Finn Anderson was coming on board she'd nearly had a fit. She'd spent the last seven months pushing him out of her head at the moments she felt lonely and in need of some man company, and here he was about to start working at the Darfield clinic.

If she'd known he was taking up a position with the company she'd have turned down the job of Head Domestic Vet in the same clinic and stayed working for the company in their Rolleston branch. No, she wouldn't have, because that would've meant forgoing a pay rise and running the clinic, which she was thrilled to be doing and had been aiming for since she'd first signed up with the company a few months ago. One thing to be thankful for was that Finn would spend a lot of his time away from the clinic working on farms, so they wouldn't be constantly bumping into each other between patients.

But the problem was that she could still remember that sizzling kiss as if it happened yesterday. Hot, steamy, a turn-on like none other she'd experienced in a long time. Now she really did have to file that memory in the trash bin. It was not getting to her again. Not at all. If she started getting hyped up over that kiss when Finn was around, then she had only to remind herself of him saying 'I can't do this' and her head would be back in place. She was not getting into another relationship. Especially not with Finn when they'd be working for the same company because when it fell to dust, which it would because all hers always did, then it would be too awkward.

So she wasn't heading into work early to be in work mode when Finn turned up for the weekly meeting and be introduced to everyone? She wasn't claiming her space before he filled the air with his persona that had her re-thinking her determination to remain single?

'Shut up, head.' She turned into the clinic and groaned.

Finn stood beside a ute, glancing around as her car rolled forward, looking too good to be true.

Her hands tightened on the steering wheel. How could one kiss do that? She hadn't been that much into him.

Whatever.

From the moment the boss had told everyone he was joining the company she'd found herself wasting too much time thinking about him. So much for what he'd said as he'd walked away from her. But he had added that it was nothing to do with her. Climbing out of her car, she drew a breath and plastered on a tight smile. 'Hello, Finn.'

'Kate? Are you working here?' He sounded nonplussed, as if he'd been blindsided.

'I changed companies about four months ago.'

'Why?'

'I bought a house out here so it made sense. Being on call is a lot easier now.'

'I can see that. You're happy with the change?'

I was fine until I heard your gravelly voice.

Sexy didn't begin to describe it. Her body suddenly felt hot.

'I am.'

I was until I learned you were starting here.

She got her gear out of the boot and slammed it shut. 'What brought you back home? I thought you intended to be away for some years.'

'My brother and his wife are having a baby and I'd like to be around when he arrives. I've missed my family a lot.' He shrugged. 'Plus the northern winters are horrific.' He sounded quite relaxed. Obviously he hadn't spent the past seven months remembering their kiss.

Unlocking the side door, she said over her shoulder, 'I guess those are as good as any reason.' Had he thought about her at all?

'I think so.' He closed the door behind him and followed her through to her room. 'Do you ever help out with the rural side of things?'

'Very rarely. They have to be really short-staffed for that to happen.'

'So we won't be working together.' Did he have to sound quite so relieved?

Or was she looking for trouble? Quite likely. He'd walked away from her, remember? How could she not remember that whenever she thought about their kiss? He wouldn't want to be all over her now, which should help keep her hormones under control.

'Sometimes you'll have to help out in the clinic. But not often,' Kate added. She should be happy about that, but a little gremlin was teasing her, making her wonder what it would be like to work alongside Finn Anderson.

There was no pretending Finn didn't exist. Nor could she go round giving him the cold shoulder. If that was even possible. So becoming friendly colleagues was the only way this was going to work. Anything deeper would mean trusting him not to hurt her and she didn't do that these days.

Her head spun. Time for a change of subject. 'Go ahead and look around the place.'

'Good idea,' Finn muttered more to himself than Kate as he walked out of her room. He'd already been shown around by Peter, but anything to get away and be able to breathe properly for a moment was good. Of all the people he'd expected to work with, Kate was not one of them. She was the reason he'd applied for this position and not gone knocking on the door at Lincoln Vet Clinic where he used to work.

Hands on hips, Finn shook his head as he stared around the small operating room. So much for avoiding Kate. He'd walked into this eyes wide shut. Then he'd mentioned missing his family. He never, ever, talked about anything personal to anyone. Sure, for most people it wasn't a big deal to admit missing family or friends, but for him that was admitting his heart was involved and his heart was in lockdown. Yet he'd opened his gob and blurted it out to Kate.

For crying out loud, he definitely lost his marbles when he was around her. So much for thinking she hadn't wangled her way into his head that night when he'd kissed her. She'd been lurking in there from the moment he'd walked away without a backward glance. That had been one of the hardest things he'd done in a while.

Imagine if he hadn't left when he did. She'd touched him in such warm, intriguing ways he hadn't known in a long time that he suspected he might never have let her go. Not that he had really. Over the months he'd spent weighing up whether to return home or continue with the career he was carving out in Scotland, he'd told himself it was only because he missed his family and mates, but Kate had been hovering in the background all the time, memories of holding that firm yet giving body against him and those beautiful brown eyes haunting him.

Seeing her get out of her car just now had set his blood heating and his toes tensing, terrifying him to realise how vulnerable he really was. He wasn't going to think about all parts above his feet. So much for believing returning to Canterbury was the right thing to do. After almost four years since breaking up with Amelia, he truly believed he'd finally laid his past relationship to rest and could get on with making the life he wanted, which included keeping control over his heart. He'd paid off his debts and finally begun saving for his own property. Things were on the up, though not when it came to trusting a woman enough to be in his life. Chances of that happening were remote.

But just seeing Kate, already he was in deep trouble. Shaking his head, he concentrated on checking out where everything was kept in the operating room. He was not going to spend his day thinking about Kate. What was the point? Even if she was the most beautiful woman he'd ever set eyes on, plus sexy as all be it, he was not getting involved. He couldn't lose control of his thinking around another woman.

Last time the end result had been appalling, and he doubted it would be great if he tried again. He wouldn't be bankrupted again—because he'd keep a firm grip on things even if the woman he might find wanted to be in control. And he certainly wasn't handing his heart over to be decimated once more. It wasn't going to be straightforward getting on with his future dreams as he'd probably spend all his time looking for problems and even find some that didn't actually exist. He'd become vulnerable, not something he liked to admit.

With Amelia, he'd fallen hard and fast, and had believed her when she'd sworn she loved him, that she'd do anything to make their life wonderful. He'd believed anything was possible when he was in love with such a wonderful woman. She really had blindsided him, and he'd paid a huge price. Like the fool he'd been, he'd believed her when she'd said she was pregnant despite having already learned how devious she was.

So no falling for Kate allowed. The attraction that flared just talking to her had to back off. *Now.*

What were the chances?

Keeping his distance at work would have its difficult moments but he was sure they could get along fine and not overstep the mark when it came to being workmates, and possibly even friends. Fingers crossed that was how it turned out.

* * *

Kate stood at the reception desk looking at the list of patients for the day, wishing she hadn't come in early, trying to ignore the image of Finn as he walked towards her. Even in outdoor clothes suitable for getting down and messy in paddocks as he checked over animals, he looked sexy. But then, some men just did, and this one in particular seemed to make a habit of firing her up when she didn't need it. 'How come you came in early?'

'I was antsy to get started. New job and new people always have me buzzing to get started.'

How come he didn't look as if he was buzzing? 'You've got keys to the place?'

'No, that's why I was hanging around outside, hoping someone would turn up soon. Peter was meant to give me a set on Friday but he was still out on a job when I was coming in to see him, so it never happened.' He looked around the room as he continued.

Avoiding her? Could be he was as uncomfortable about this as she was. But then, why would he be? He hadn't wanted to stay around to see the night out last time they met.

Banging on the front door had her spinning around. A man stood there holding a springer spaniel in his arms, looking frantic. 'Oh, dear.'

Finn beat her to the door and opened it. 'What's happened here?'

Kate called across the room, 'Archie, come in. What's Pippa been up to this time?'

'She's got fish hooks in her paw and mouth. I had to cut the nylon between one in the foot and the other end in her lip as each time she moved she put pressure on them and squealed like she'd been stabbed with a knife.'

Kate shuddered. 'Come through.'

Finn closed the door again and followed them into the surgery. 'Want a hand?' he asked as he helped Archie place Pippa on the table and kept a firm hand on her so she didn't try to leap down to the floor.

Not really, but she wouldn't be churlish. She had to start out how she meant to carry on. 'Sure,' Kate replied. Anyway, it was always better to have an extra pair of hands when the dog might be frightened and snap at her. It was well before opening time so no other staff were here and this sort of situation required two people keeping the dog calm as she worked on the injuries. In fact, they could both do that and get it sorted quicker.

Archie was stroking his pet. 'The boys went fishing last night and didn't put their gear away when they got home. Pippa was snooping in the shed after I let her out for her morning pee and this is what she found. I could wring their necks, the idiots.'

Pippa was known to find all sorts of things that were not good for her, but fish hooks were new. 'Do you know how many hooks are in her mouth?' Kate asked as she pried the dog's mouth open.

'I counted two. Don't know if she's swallowed any though. She was gagging on the way here.'

That didn't sound good. 'I'll need to take an X-ray of her oesophagus. Then we'll give her a strong sedative while we get those hooks out. If that's okay with you?' she added, knowing Archie never blinked at spending what was necessary when it came to his pets. But she had to ask. It was company policy to outline treatments and expenses. Not that she wouldn't anyway.

'Do whatever you have to.'

'It'll mean keeping your dog here for a few hours,' Finn said before looking to her. 'There're two hooks in this paw as well, one firmly embedded in the pad.'

'Need opening up to remove? You can't cut it and push it through?'

Finn shook his head. 'I think that might cause more harm than an incision.'

'I'll leave you to it, Kate.' Archie looked at Finn. 'Thank you, too.'

'Archie, sorry, I've been remiss.' Because she was struggling to accept Finn now worked here, like it or not. 'This is Finn Anderson. He's just started with us as a rural vet so you'll probably get to see him whenever any of your stock require a vet.'

'Hey, Finn, good to meet you. I breed Charolaise cattle and keep a tight watch over them, which regularly involves you guys.'

'Brilliant. Right up my alley. I've returned from Scotland where I was involved in looking after Aberdeen herds.'

Archie reached out to shake his hand. 'Sounds good to me. Right, I'm out of here. Give me a bell when Pippa's ready to go home, Kate.'

'Will do.' She'd found two hooks in the dog's mouth, just as Archie had said. The throat looked red and swollen too. 'Right, my girl. I'm going to give you a sedative to keep you calm while we fix this.'

'Starting with an X-ray?'

Finn. For a moment she'd forgotten him, being totally involved in checking over Pippa. 'Yes.' So he didn't entirely rule her mind. Thank goodness for something. Checking the bottle of sedative she'd got from the drug cupboard, she attached a needle and inserted it into the back of Pippa's neck.

Finn was rubbing the dog all the time, keeping her calm.

Kate ignored how that made her feel. 'Hold her still, please.'

Within moments Pippa was sprawled flat on her belly, unaware of anything going on.

'I'll carry her through to the X-ray machine if you show me the way,' he said. 'She's not light.'

'I'm not arguing. She's big for her breed.' The whole litter was, but Pippa was the largest. Before leading the way to the operating room where the X-ray machine was, Kate rubbed the dog's head. She'd known this one from the day she was born as she'd had to do a caesarean when the bitch couldn't push the pups out. 'Through here.'

Finn followed, holding his heavy bundle against his wide chest. It would be lovely to be held there. He was gorgeous. No matter how she felt about them working together she wasn't about to stop thinking that any time soon. Instead she had to learn to ignore the heat that any stray glance generated throughout her sex-starved body.

Flicking the light switch, Kate took a deep breath as she grabbed the machine and rolled it over to the table where Finn was laying Pippa down. His large hand was gentle as he rubbed the dog's flank.

Lucky girl.

Day one, before opening hours at that, and she was already in a dither about the new vet. 'Why did he come here and not go to Lincoln where his mate was?'

The sound of a throat being cleared had her spinning around to come face to face with Finn.

'Because this is my ideal job.'

Her eyes widened and her cheeks were heating up something horrible. 'I didn't mean to say that out loud.'

'So I gathered.' He locked intense eyes on her. 'We're going to have to make this work, Kate. I'm here for the long haul.'

'So am I,' she retorted. Straightening her already tight back, she added, 'We'll be fine.' Then she sighed. This wasn't working. 'It is good to see you again, Finn.' It wasn't quite true. Their abrupt ending last time got in the way of that. On the plus side, maybe she could really get to know him and get over that brief interlude.

'Thanks.'

That was it? Fair enough. He was being sensible. So she'd try and follow suit. Lining up the X-ray plate above Pippa, she asked Finn, 'What about your time with the cattle you were so keen about? Has that made a difference to what you want to do going forward?'

Finn rolled Pippa onto her side with no resistance. The drug had done its job. 'It had got me thinking about what I could do with cattle around here as well as working for Peter. He knows I'm interested in setting up a specialty unit,' he added quickly.

'He's open to anything, is Peter. You didn't want to work somewhere else over that side of the world before you returned home?' Might as well keep the conversation flowing and her mind focused on Pippa's problems.

He shook his head sharply. 'No. It was fun living north of Aberdeen, and the Scots are wonderful people, but I can't see myself living permanently anywhere else but in NZ.'

'Something we have in common.'

'Don't you mean something else? We obviously both enjoy working with animals.'

She relaxed a little, even managed to smile. 'Can't argue with that. Right, stand back.' She waited until he'd moved away from the table before pressing the button to take the X-ray. Within moments she had the answer to whether they'd have to operate. 'She didn't swallow any hooks.'

'That's a relief.'

'It certainly is. I think the gagging is because of a small piece of bone in the oesophagus, which'll slowly make its way through her system.' Collecting a clipper to cut through the metal hooks and a kit to suture the wounds, she asked, 'You want to deal with the paw while I deal with her mouth?'

'More than happy to.'

'There's a largish hole in the back of the tongue where one hook's gone through. Could be the one that was pulled when Pippa tried to stand on her foot.'

'Need stitching?'

'Hopefully not. It would be better to let it heal naturally as the hard ends of the thread will aggravate her more than the wound. I'll give Archie antibiotics and pain reducers to feed her over the next few days.'

The room was quiet for a while as they both worked on fixing Pippa.

When Kate stepped back from the table, she rubbed her lower back. She'd never got used to bending over a table while working on an animal. 'Thanks for your help.'

'Glad I was here.'

The door opened and Peter, the owner and overall boss, walked in. 'Morning, you two. I see you're already hard at work.'

'Archie turned up at the door with Pippa in his arms. She'd managed to get hold of some fish hooks.' Kate began clearing away the needles and thread.

'Where do I put her?' Finn asked.

'In the next room.' She opened a door and headed for one of the cages. 'This is our recovery room.' She watched as he knelt down and slid Pippa inside the cage so carefully it almost brought tears to her eyes. Bet he was just as gentle with the humans in his life. A big softie on the inside, not quite as much outwardly. He hadn't been with her. Not if the way he'd walked away from her that night was anything to go by after saying he had issues he was dealing with.

She had to admit it had been for the best. If they had gone further and become intimate, she would not have wanted to see his eyes widen with shock and hear derogatory words spill from that divine mouth if he saw her scars. It was hard to take from anyone, but for some inexplicable reason she thought it might've been even worse coming from Finn.

'There you go, Pippa.' Finn stood up and turned to Peter. 'Great way to start the day.'

'You were obviously early. Couldn't sleep for the excitement of meeting everyone?' Peter grinned.

'Absolutely.'

'Well, you've met Kate, and worked with her already, so that's a start.'

'I agree,' Finn said, not mentioning the fact they'd already met.

'I'm going to put the coffee on shortly if either of you want one,' Kate told them as she dumped the wipes she'd used to clean the table.

'Count me in for coffee, unless Peter has other ideas,' Finn replied. 'I haven't had my caffeine fix yet.'

'Give me five.' She turned away from those intense sky-blue eyes and focused on the computer screen to enter Pippa's details and email Archie a message saying his dog was fine and would be good to go home in a few hours.

'Jack's surgery's been cancelled,' Di, the vet nurse, called through another door leading into Reception. Seemed everyone was turning up for work now.

Kate went through to see her. 'That must mean he's healing nicely.'

'His owner says his foot's looking good and he's running around like crazy once more. You must've removed the seed causing all the trouble the other day despite not being certain about it.'

'Hopefully that's the case. Surgery on his paw would've made life difficult for a few days for him and his owners.' Grass seeds between dogs' toes were a continuous problem, especially for those with long hair on their paws.

'Shall I make the coffee while you do what you have to out here?' Finn asked from behind her.

Turning around, she saw him press his lips together firmly. Did she rattle him as much as he did her? She drew a breath. This had to stop. If she just acted naturally these feelings of annoyance that he was on her patch would eventually subside. 'White with one,' she answered. It wasn't necessary he make the coffee but he'd offered and she'd accept. First step towards plan 'friendly'. Yes, she'd changed it from colleagues to friendly workmates already.

Ten minutes later, when she entered the tearoom, she struggled to dampen the heat filling her. Finn was sitting at the far end of the room and there were two mugs of coffee on the table in front of him, as well as an empty chair next to his. The last place she wanted to sit when the sparks were going off inside her. She remained on her feet and reached for the closest mug. 'Thanks.'

'Any time.'

'Have you met any of the others yet?'

'Only Di and Mark.' Mark was another vet.

'Let me fix that.' Kate went out to see who was around and brought them through to the tearoom, where she introduced everyone. Within a short time everyone had joined them, and Finn was welcomed like a long-lost friend. They had been down one rural vet since Gavin had been knocked down by a bull he was supposed to be vaccinating. It had put pressure on everyone as the hierarchy had waited until they knew if he'd return to rural veterinary work or settle for domestic duties.

'I'm not going to remember everyone's names straight up.' Finn chuckled as he drank his coffee. 'You'll all have to be patient with me for a while.'

Peter strolled into the room. 'Since everyone's here I'll grab a few minutes of your time before we get on with the day, though I'm sure those of you who have to work outside will want me to drag this out.' The heavy clouds were now bucketing rain and not looking like stopping any time soon.

There were pluses to working inside the clinic, Kate mused as she focused on Peter and not Finn.

'First of all, welcome to Canterbury Vets and especially

the Darfield clinic, Finn. We're glad to have you on board. Any questions?'

Finn shook his head. 'Not so far. I'm pleased to be here and look forward to working with everyone.'

Even her? Kate sipped coffee and stared at the tabletop. So far he'd been friendly enough. Working together with Pippa had gone well and been no different from working with any other vet in the practice.

'We've been asked to have a tent once more at the local school pet fair in April, where we can discuss various matters with pet owners. As we know from the past, we'll get kids bringing in their dogs, cats and rabbits for us to see and check over. It's all good fun and we sell loads of toys.' Peter looked at Finn. 'It's a community event, and we usually get a few new customers out of it.'

'I'm happy to start putting lists together of what we'll need and who wants to volunteer for the day,' Kate said.

Peter nodded. 'Thanks, Kate. The lists are still there from last year but could do with some updating.'

'Anything I can do to help?' Finn asked.

'You can work with Kate from the rural perspective,' Peter suggested. 'Some youngsters bring along their pet calves. Mark, you look like you want to say something.'

Kate scowled. Thanks, Peter, she thought, but he was only getting things sorted for the day.

Mark said, 'Count me in too. It's actually fun as a vet being out there amongst the locals and not behind a table with a sick animal and worried owner.'

Within minutes Kate had a list of volunteers and everyone was getting up to start their day. 'That was easy,' she said to the room in general.

'We all know you're a pushover when it comes to hand-ing out the tricky jobs.' Mark laughed.

She laughed back at him. 'For that you get to do the poop collections.'

'Knew I should've kept my mouth shut.' Mark headed out of the door.

Turning to put her mug in the dishwasher, Kate found Finn watching her with an amused expression.

'What?'

'Where did you come up with that idea from?'

'Poop collections? They're for real.'

'I did not come down in the last rain shower.' How that smile got to her, made her hot in places best not thought about right now. 'We're going to be in a tent, not wander-ing around the grounds with animals.'

'Damn, then I'll have to find another ghastly job for Mark.'

Di appeared at the door. 'Vicki's here with Frankie, Kate. She's due an allergy shot.'

'Vicki or Frankie?' she quipped, then shook her head to clear Finn out of it. 'Coming.' She needed to do some serious work on not being distracted whenever he was near. 'See you later,' she said as she stepped around him.

'I'll take a look at Pippa while I'm waiting for Peter.'

Peter had taken a phone call and gone to his office.

'If that's all right with you?' Finn asked, as though sud-denly realising he might be treading in her domain.

'Go for it. Let me know if anything's changed.' Friendly co-workers, right?

'All's good with Pippa. She's awake and alert, but not mov-ing much,' Finn told Kate when she'd finished with the miniature schnauzer named Frankie.

'So she's not licking her paw. That's good.' Kate stood up from the computer. 'Are you working out in the fields today? Or is it all about orientation?'

'I'm heading out to Kirwee once Peter's gone through some data with me and handed over a set of keys. I've got a Highlander bull to see. He's got suspected bovine virus diarrhoea. Apparently not the first on this particular farm, and there's likely to be more, since the farmer was slow in separating him from the herd.'

Kate winced. 'Now I remember why I prefer working with domestic animals. Antsy bulls are not my thing.' The animal would be moody because of the symptoms. 'I hope you're very careful around this one.'

'I'm very cautious around all bulls, antsy or not. Especially Highlanders with their huge horns poking out sideways and able to impale me in an instant just by turning their head to see what I'm doing.' It was one thing he did fear. Those horns were evil.

'Glad to hear it. I've heard a couple of stories of vets and farmers being injured or worse by horns.'

'Haven't we all? I'll let you get on with your patients and go see what Peter's got to show me. Catch up some time during the day.' He closed the door behind him, denying the fact he'd said that. He'd meant to say maybe they'd bump into each other over the week, not catch up as though they'd sit down and have a yarn, but it hadn't come out like that. No wonder her beautiful fudge eyes had widened. He could drown in those eyes. So big and warm, even when she was keeping her distance.

Oh, yes, he knew she'd been brassed off in the tearoom. The annoyance in her eyes had been a dead giveaway. He hadn't done it deliberately. It had been a thoughtless move and to have shoved her coffee across the table to another spot would've suggested he was affected by her. Something he wasn't letting on. They had to get along. It might take some practice on his part, but he'd make sure they did. For everyone's sake. Especially his.

CHAPTER THREE

'DAMN AND BLAST,' Kate muttered when she headed outside the clinic to go home at the end of the Friday evening session. She was tired, her back ached from too many operations earlier in the day, and now her car had a flat tyre. 'Just what I need.'

Tossing her bag on the front seat, she popped the boot and cleared the assorted boxes and bags of gear off the spare tyre. 'Why do I carry around so much junk?' Most of it was there for times when she was required to help an injured animal outside the clinic, but at moments like this she wished she were less OTT about having absolutely everything she might need, and then some.

The tyre was heavy to lift out of the well. Leaning it against the back of the car, she hunted around for the jack and spanner, and sighed with relief when she found them in the bottom of the well. This shouldn't take too long, she thought. It wasn't the first tyre she'd ever changed.

'Here, I'll give you a hand.' Finn was striding across from his ute.

She hadn't heard him pull in. That was a good sign, as it meant he didn't feature in her mind all the time. 'I've got this.'

'Don't be stubborn, Kate. I'm not leaving, so you might as well step aside and let me do the job.'

'And if I don't?' Why was she being so stubborn? Because Finn was right; that was exactly what she was doing. If it had been Peter or Mark she wouldn't have refused the offer.

'I'm being a gentleman. Make the most of it.' His smile was flippant but his eyes were sincere.

'It doesn't happen often?' she asked, stepping aside because the sooner the job was done, the sooner she could head home, and put distance between them.

'I do my best.' Kneeling down, he placed the jack under the axle, then stood to use his foot to operate the lever.

Another retort came to mind, but as she looked at Finn her heart clenched and she kept it to herself. He was being kind, and didn't deserve any grief because she had issues with men. Throw in the fact that he wound her up fast just by being here and she was all over the place with knowing what to do about her reactions to him. 'Thank you for doing this.'

'It's all right. I'm sure you'd have it under control in no time but there's no way I could've walked away.'

'I know.' The thing was, she truly did. She mightn't have had much to do with him all week but it came through loud and clear he was a gentleman—when he wasn't walking away from a kiss and the sensuous sensations that had caused. Of course, he might've done that because he *was* a gentleman and didn't want to take advantage of her. Not that he had been because she'd been ready for some fun, but he wouldn't necessarily know that. 'What brought you here at this hour? I'd have thought you'd be long gone.' It was the end of the week and anyone not needed was well and truly gone.

'I need to top up with some drugs for a farm visit I've got lined up in the morning.'

Nothing unusual in that. 'How's your first week been?'

'Brilliant. There're a lot of farms on the books to keep me busy, and so far the farmers I've met have been friendly and ready to take advice.' The wheel was off and Finn was lining up the spare onto the studs. 'Very similar to where I worked at in Scotland.'

'You don't sound like you're missing that place.'

'I haven't been back in Canterbury long yet, so no. But I doubt I'll miss more than a couple of friends. Where I was is a beautiful part of Scotland, but not the sort of place where I'd want to live for ever. Too bleak and cold. Summer lasts weeks, not months. At least here we know when it snows that there will be extremely hot temperatures in the summer to make up for it.'

'You into skiing by any chance?' Mountains ran down the centre of the South Island and there were ski fields not far from Darfield.

'I did some when I was growing up, and got more into it in Scotland. I intend to keep on with it now that I'm back, though winter's a way off right now.' He suddenly looked annoyed, but she had no idea why. The tyre was on and he was fastening the bolts so it couldn't be because there was a problem there.

'Not a lot of snow to be found at the moment.' She'd love to see those long legs swishing down the mountainside.

You wouldn't be with him.

There was a point.

'What drugs do you want? I can get them while you finish up.'

'Thanks.'

Why hadn't she thought about it sooner instead of hanging around watching Finn? The answer was in the question really. He was quite an eyeful. 'What do you need?' she asked sharply.

After he told her what he wanted, he stood up and surprised her. 'Feel like going to the local for a drink? I haven't got any reason to rush home and thought it would be nice to have a yarn with someone I know.'

So he wasn't desperate to spend time with her, only in need of some company. Not as settled in yet as he made out to be? Her instinct was to decline but she hesitated. She did understand he was new to the area and it couldn't hurt to be friendly. Mightn't hurt, but she'd be a mess by the time she got home if she did go. It was part of doing the friendly thing, not the hot, sexy, 'I want your body' one. And one drink wouldn't hurt. Hopefully she could manage that without getting in a bigger dither over him.

'Which pub are you thinking of?'

'That one around the corner from here. The Hunters' Retreat?'

'Yep, that's it. Okay, let's do it.' She turned for the door leading inside. 'I'll be back in a minute with those meds.' *After I've checked my make-up and tidied my hair.*

'No rush. This is all but done. I'll put the damaged tyre in the back. You need to get it repaired asap in case it happens again.'

'There's a tyre shop along the road. I'll drop it in tomorrow morning.' She headed inside without a backward glance, which was hard because all she wanted to do was turn around and drink in the sight of Finn. Where had that come from when she'd been comfortable and not distracted—much—while talking about skiing? He went and suggested they go to the pub together and suddenly she was melting on the inside. It was going to need to be an ice-cold drink to cool her down.

Her hair was in a lopsided, messy ponytail. Tugging the band off, she brushed the knots into something tidier. A girl had to look her best when she was with a jaw-dropping, good-looking man. Except when at work. As for her make-up, it wasn't too bad and she didn't want to look as if she was going all out to impress him. But it was so tempting. Her lipstick was in her hand before she thought about it. Okay, what the heck? It was normal to put some on when-ever she was going anywhere unless it was to help a ewe give birth to a lamb.

'Shall we walk?' Finn asked when she rejoined him and handed over the drugs he'd requested.

'Why not?' It would be good to get some fresh air after a day inside. It might also go some way to helping her cool down. 'It's barely five hundred metres. Besides, parking there's often a nightmare on Friday nights. It is the locals' favourite pub.'

'So I heard.'

Walking beside Finn didn't quite cool anything. His arm had a habit of rubbing against her shoulder when-ever she dodged an uneven patch on the footpath. Not many of them but enough to make her even more aware of her colleague. Yes, keep thinking about Finn like that and hopefully she'd get over this unusual reaction. Think about the scars and that would certainly put everything into perspective.

'Are you living in the township or further afield?' he asked.

'I bought an older house with a half-acre section on the back street about a year ago. I'm supposed to be doing up the house but there's never much spare time. One day I'll get it done.' When the mortgage was a little less eye-watering she'd put in a new kitchen and bathroom. Since her house-mate had moved away there was less spare money to spend. She needed to get someone else to rent the spare room. 'I'm a beginner when it comes to painting.'

'Can't say I've done a lot either, though my ex and I were starting to do up the house we bought in Welling-ton,' Finn told her.

'So like mine, not a new house?' An ex, eh? Another thing they had in common.

'A nineteen-twenties bungalow in Karori. It was a cold hole as they didn't know about insulation back in the days when it was built. Winters were hell, but nowhere near as bad as Scotland.'

Kate shivered despite the warmth. 'I hate the cold, which is why the first thing I replaced when I moved into the house was the fireplace. It was in rough condition. I probably burnt more firewood last winter than everyone else around here put together.'

'Got a local farmer on hand with lots of trees to fell, by any chance?' Finn laughed.

His laugh was warm and friendly, and added to the heat coursing through her. 'One or two.' He could move into her house for winter and she wouldn't need any firewood. Except she'd then need a lock and key on her hormones.

He took her elbow as they reached the pub door. 'It's certainly busy.'

It would be rude to pull away when his hand felt good against her skin. It really had been a while since she'd enjoyed the simple touch of a man. So much for thinking she didn't need one in her life, if this was how she reacted to Finn. 'Where are you living?'

Closing the door behind them, he took her elbow again and led them to a table with bar stools. 'I'm temporarily renting a flat in West Melton. What would you like to drink?'

In other words, ask no more. 'G and T, thanks.'

The scowl that had been growing disappeared. 'Be right back.'

What was wrong with asking where he was living? It wasn't a big deal, surely? But then she was still getting to know him and he often didn't seem to like talking about himself. Which could make for a quiet evening, she mused, because she liked getting to know people, even when it was this man.

'Hi, Kate.' Peter appeared beside her. 'I see you're with Finn. That's good. He needs to get to know all of us so he'll feel settled and not think of leaving.'

'He only started this week.'

'I know, but I'd hate to lose him. He's darned good at what he does and getting new vets isn't easy these days.'

Quite a few were going offshore once they'd qualified and not all were returning home in a hurry, if at all. 'I don't think Finn has any intention of moving away. He's home for family.' She glanced over at him coming their way, then back at Peter.

'Good.' Peter's face broke into a smile. 'Finn, good to see you out and about.'

'Hey, Peter. Can I get you a drink?' Finn placed a glass in front of her.

'Thanks, but if I don't head home my missus will have something to say about cooking dinner being a waste of time. See you both next week.'

'Bye.' Kate turned to Finn. 'Sheree, Peter's wife, is a hard case. She'd never make him go without his meal, but she does let him know what she thinks whenever he's late. When they were young and raising their three kids, she was a vet nurse and running the home, while Peter was doing extra papers and setting up his own practice. I don't think it was easy for either of them.'

'I bet it wasn't.'

'You haven't thought of starting your own practice?' With his experience in Scotland, it would make sense.

Finn all but poured beer down his throat before putting the glass back on the table heavily. 'I had one once. Before I left for Britain. It was in Wellington, not rural. I had to close it down.' Definitely not happy talking about his past.

There was a lot to Finn she had no idea about, but she got his reaction in bucketloads because she was reluctant to talk about her past too. Especially her trust issues. Did he have those too? 'I didn't mean to upset you.'

'I guess you won't be the only person at the practice to ask me, merely the first.'

'Everyone we work with is genuinely nice and they'll want to get to know you. It's not like they want to learn some gossip to spread around. If they did, they'd have been on the Internet by now.'

Finn's eyes darkened, and his nod was abrupt. 'Don't I know it.' More beer went down his throat, then he sighed heavily. 'I was engaged to be married at the time. To an accountant. She bankrupted us.' His words were abrupt and there was a load of hurt in his face.

Kate wished she could reach out and take his hand in hers, hold him tight, but she sensed he wouldn't appreciate that at all. Nor would it help her determination to keep her distance. 'I bet that's still a bitter pill to swallow.'

His eyes weren't so sky-blue now, more a dark, gloomy shade. 'Very.'

She'd also bet he wouldn't have a lot of trust these days when it came to women. What his ex had done would have been devastating, not only to his dreams of owning his own business, but more than that, his heart must've been shattered. Her chest tightened. She was completely in sync with him on that one. 'I am really sorry for over-stepping the line.'

'You weren't to know.'

'Of course not.'

His smile was tight. 'Obviously no one mentioned it at work in Lincoln after the party.'

Kate shook her head. 'Not at all.' She opted to grin and hopefully lift his mood, along with hers. 'Everyone was so stoked at how well the party went, they didn't talk about anything else for a week.'

Sipping his beer, Finn slowly relaxed and finally gave her a genuine smile. 'Thanks for not making a big deal out of it. It's in the past and I'm moving on, setting up a new life, which I hope will include a specialty business.'

'Going to Britain was to put distance between you and your ex?'

'That and to earn some decent money so I could rectify some of the debts.'

Wow. That said a lot about the man. Declared bankrupts weren't obliged to pay back money owed to creditors. They couldn't obtain a loan for a set period of time either. It must've been a few years back when Finn lost everything if he was legally able to start a new business now, but then he hadn't said he was doing that yet. Of course, he probably didn't have the funds either.

'You're too quiet,' he growled. Worried about what she might be thinking?

'And you don't like that. Fair enough. I am getting my head around what you've told me, but, rest assured, I'm not making a big deal out of it. From the little I've seen of you this week, I can't imagine you'll be sitting still and not making a successful future for yourself.' Picking up her glass, she tapped it against his. 'Here's to you.'

Finn tapped back. 'Thanks, Kate.' He looked around for a long moment, as if deciding something. Once more he surprised her. 'Feel like something to eat? I'm starving.'

'Me too. I'll have fish and chips.' So much for one drink and going home. She still should do that but right now she felt comfortable with Finn. She wanted to offer to get the meals but instantly thought he'd probably think she was being sympathetic about how he'd lost his money, so she kept quiet on that score. Anyway, for all she knew he might be floating in money by now.

'Blue cod or snapper?'

'Definitely cod.'

'You're my kind of woman.' His smile slipped. 'I mean—'

This time she did grab his hand for a brief moment, and instantly felt a flare of heat. Letting go fast, she said in a shaky voice, 'If you'd said you were having hoki I'd have walked out the door.' Not really, but the air between them had suddenly got heavy again and needed lightening. He also needed to see he could trust her to have some time out together without getting deep and worrisome.

'Hi, Kate. Finn. Thought I'd let you know Pippa's doing fine. No one would believe she'd got those hooks in her foot on Monday.' Archie stood between them. 'Thank you both so much.'

Kate laughed to herself. There was never a lot of privacy at this pub. Just as well she'd removed her hand from Finn's before Archie had appeared.

'That's the best news,' Finn told him. 'How did the boys take what had happened?'

'They got a bollocking, but to be fair they were both very remorseful. It won't happen again.'

'Good to hear,' Kate added her bit. She'd heard from one of the vet nurses that Pippa was doing well with no side effects. 'Let's hope we don't see you for a while.'

Archie shrugged. 'What are the chances?' He turned to Finn. 'We've got four dogs, two cats and the herd of cattle I told you about. Something's always happening to one of my animals.'

'To be expected when you've got that many.' Finn was looking more relaxed by the minute.

'I'll leave you two to it and get home. Thanks again,' he said before heading away.

'The good side to being a vet,' Finn said. 'I'll go order the food.'

Kate watched him moving through the crowded tables, a head above nearly everyone. His dark blond hair was a mess and fell over the edge of his shirt collar. His shoulders were firm, not tight as they'd been when he'd mentioned his past. The back view was good, and when there was a gap in the crowd and she could see his taut butt the view got even better. That was one sexy rear. A ten out of ten.

Quickly swallowing a big mouthful of gin and tonic that wasn't as cold as it had first been, she looked away, trying to find something or someone to focus on until the heat in her veins backed off. It was a fail. There were no interesting distractions. But recalling that night and those words, 'I can't do this', might do the trick. Those words had resonated in her mind time and again whenever she thought about Finn. Now that they were working together she needed to keep his statement foremost in her mind as there was no way they were going to be more than friends.

No man she'd liked enough to get close to had wanted a bar of her once they'd seen the damage done to her skin, and she particularly did not want that happening with Finn. Why was she attracted to such shallow men? Just because she'd been born with good facial looks it didn't mean she was perfect all over, inside and out. Nobody was.

Not saying Finn was shallow from what she'd seen so far though. In fact, when she wasn't being careful, he had her thinking the impossible—getting up close and inde-cent with him. But recalling how he'd repeated Hamish's words 'I can't do this' did pull the brakes on a little. Add in that he had a lot of baggage and she needed to be even more cautious. He wasn't going to accept her so easily, if he even wanted more from her. Nor could she blame him. She was still getting over Hamish leaving her and he hadn't done half of what Finn's fiancée did to him.

Finn placed napkins and salt and pepper shakers on the table. 'Shouldn't be too far away. The kitchen's humming.'

'They have a good rep for their food.'

'What were you thinking about?' he asked. 'You appeared to be miles away.'

Getting way ahead of myself when I'm not sure what I want.

'Thinking how my two fur babies will be curled up on my bed waiting for me to get home and light the fire.'

'I'm picking dogs, not cats.'

'Bang on. My neighbour's daughter looks after them when I'm late home, which is a big help. It also gives her some money to buy the things teenagers can't seem to do without.'

'I heard there's a pet day care in town. It's amazing how many people have dogs these days and go that extra distance to make sure they're looked after when they're at work.'

He wasn't suggesting she shouldn't leave her boys at home, was he? 'It's a small centre as most people have large properties and their pets are fenced in so they can wander around all day without getting into trouble. Mine are well past that puppy stage where everything is an adventure so I have no concerns about leaving them at home. Charlotte takes them for a walk after school, and feeds them if I'm late.'

'You'd be the last person I'd expect not to have all the bases covered. You're a vet and a caring woman.' He drained his beer. 'Want another drink?'

It wasn't far to walk home. She could indulge for once. 'Yes, thanks. How about I get them?'

He shook his head. 'Tonight's my turn. You can offer some other time.'

She gave him a smile. 'Offer? Not pay?' He really was great to be with when she wasn't coming up with every reason in the book to hold him at arm's length, or jump his bones.

'You read me too easily.' Picking up the glasses, he headed back to the bar.

And she watched him again. Should've asked for a double serve of ice, she conceded as her skin warmed. He'd sounded certain when he'd said she was a caring woman. Wow. He was getting to her in more ways than the one where her body overheated.

Should've gone home while she could without looking silly.

CHAPTER FOUR

'I'LL DRIVE YOU HOME,' Finn told Kate when they were ready to leave the pub. She had said she'd walk but there was no way he'd let her now darkness had fallen. He'd only had two beers, with fish and chips thrown in, so he was good to drive.

'Cheers. That'd be great.'

Too easy. With this woman he was always looking for the problems, not the straightforward acceptance that they were working partners. It was proving difficult to put her out of his mind. Even at work, when they were busy with animals and their sometimes distressed owners, she slipped into his head. Like unfinished business that needed dealing with. But that couldn't be right. Finding an ideal woman for his future wasn't part of his game plan.

'Let's go.' Shoving his hand in his pocket to prevent himself taking her arm because that would seem too keen, he headed for the door and held it open while she stepped past him, teasing his nostrils with the scent of spring flowers.

Kate flicked her hair back from her face. 'The temperature's barely dropped a degree since we got here.'

'Is your house cool in summer?'

'It gets a bit stuffy if I don't leave windows open.'

'That's safe to do?'

'With the dogs roaming the section it is.' There was a softness in her voice whenever she mentioned her pets.

'Do they come first in your household?'

'First, second, and third. I love them to bits. They came from a couple out this way who were moving into a retirement village and felt it was unfair to keep them in such a small space after living on a farm. I had been thinking about getting Labrador puppies but the time needed for training seemed daunting when I've already got a lot on.' A light laugh fell between them. "Besides, I'd be too soft with them, and they'd never have grown up into sensible dogs.'

He believed her. 'How old are the two you've got?'

'Rusty's four and Sam's three.'

A phone rang. It wasn't his call sound.

Kate pulled hers from the bag slung over her shoulder. 'Charlotte? What's up?'

Finn found himself moving quicker to keep up with her.

'How did that happen? I thought I'd shut the gate this morning. Charlotte, it's not your fault, okay? I'm on my way. I'll be five minutes, no more.' She gripped her phone at her side. 'Rusty's hurt himself. Charlotte says his front leg is at an odd angle and he howls every time he moves.'

This time Finn didn't hesitate to take her hand to keep Kate steady as they raced back to the clinic, where he had his vehicle unlocked in an instant. 'Which way?' he asked as he turned the ignition on.

'Left, then second right. The little brat jumped the fence and got his leg caught in the wires. Charlotte thinks it was injured when he fell further. He was swinging when she found him.' Kate brushed the back of her hand over her face. 'So much for being a sensible, serious vet. This is doing my head in. What if—?'

Finn cut her off. 'Don't go there. Wait until we've assessed the injury.' He'd be there to support her, and do whatever was required for the dog too. Which probably meant taking him back to the clinic.

'We? Thank you.'

His heart sank. 'You didn't think I'd help you?'

'Finn, I'm not thinking straight. Of course I didn't think that.'

The beating in his chest returned to normal. 'You're a stressed mum,' he said lightly. Imagine how she'd be if this had happened to a child of hers. The sort of mother any kid would be lucky to have. And any dog, he admitted with a wry smile.

'That drive on your right. Charlotte's opened the gate for us.'

Lights were on inside the house. The girl was probably as stressed as Kate. 'Want me to bring my gear in?' Who knew what they might need to make Rusty comfortable?

'Yes. I've got a kit in the laundry but you'll know your way around yours.' She was out of the car, running up the steps to the front door.

Bag in hand, he followed the voices inside. Kate was kneeling by a couch where a cocker spaniel lay, panting fast. A continuous low moan was audible, making Finn want to touch Kate on the back so she'd know she wasn't alone. Instead he knelt beside her, and said to the girl hovering over the couch with tears spilling down her face, 'Hi, Charlotte. I'm Finn, also a vet. How did you get Rusty inside?' He began feeling the twisted leg while keeping an eye on the dog in case he reacted badly to the touch.

'He hopped in very slowly, crying all the time.'

Kate put her hand on the dog's head, and rubbed his back with her other hand. 'That's the boy. Easy, easy.'

'I don't think the leg's broken. I suspect a torn ligament,' Finn said. 'We need to take him for an X-ray. I don't want to do too much checking out until he's sedated and best I do that at the clinic.'

'Agreed,' Kate said, still stroking her boy. 'We're probably going to have to do surgery, aren't we?' Asking that showed how upset she was. She knew the answer.

Touching her shoulder, he nodded. 'I'll do it if it's necessary.'

'Thanks.'

No argument whatsoever. That had to be a plus. He'd have thought Kate would insist on taking care of her beloved pet. There was still lots to learn about her. 'What about your other dog?'

'I'll take Sam home with me,' Charlotte answered before Kate had a chance. 'He's used to our place.'

'He'll be restless with Rusty not there,' Kate pointed out.

'I know, but he can sleep on my bed.' Charlotte finally smiled.

'Your mother will not be pleased.'

'Tough.' Charlotte grinned, then turned serious. 'Will Rusty be all right? It wasn't my fault. A kid was taking his puppy down the road and Rusty went spare.'

'That's not like him.' Charlotte stood up and reached for the girl, wrapped her in a hug. 'Stop blaming yourself. I know you'd have been looking out for him.'

Opening his kit, Finn found the vial for pain relief and attached it to a needle. 'Here we go, Rusty. Just a quick jab to make you comfortable on the short trip to the clinic.' The needle slid into the flesh on the back of the dog's neck and Finn pressed down on the syringe. 'There, all done.' Already the dog was quietening down.

Kate gave him a tight, heart-wrenching smile. 'I definitely owe you a drink and dinner now. Thank you for helping.'

He lifted Rusty into his arms. 'Will you stop saying that? You'd be doing the same if this was the other way round.'

'True.'

Once the dog was loaded onto the back seat of his ute and Kate had locked up after Charlotte had left with Sam, they were on their way, Kate sitting in the back, rubbing her pet's head.

'You're a big softie,' Finn told her.

'I know. It's bad enough when this happens to someone else's dog, but I feel sick when it's mine. Have you got any pets?'

'Not yet. There hasn't been a lot of time since I returned home, what with finding somewhere to live and getting other things sorted out.' Like talking to his lawyer about a mortgage now he was almost free to get one again, and tying up everything he owned so that if he ever made the mistake of falling in love with the wrong person he'd at least still have his assets. Not that they were the most important of everything he'd lost with Amelia.

A glance in the rear-view mirror brought on a rare longing for a woman to go home to at the end of the day, to sit down and relax over a meal and share their days with. When he wasn't being too self-protective he could admit to how much he missed having that special someone in his life. Plus the dreams for the future that went along with that. Family.

He shivered. This was plain crazy for him to be thinking like that. He wasn't going there at the moment when it appeared that Kate had no one to share those things with either. She hadn't phoned anyone since getting the call from Charlotte so he'd stepped up. Seeing her distress about her dog was sad. But he wouldn't be there for her all the time. He was not going down that route no matter how much he was beginning to like her.

'Have you got family around here?'

'Mum and Dad recently moved to a new subdivision in Lincoln, which is a huge downsize for them after spending the last twenty-two years on fifty acres out near here in Kirwee. They thought it was time to go, but I'm not so sure. Dad's always trying to find things to do and now mows lawns for half the people in their street.'

'Sounds like a man with a big heart.' Was that where Kate got hers from?

'He is. My brothers have moved away. One's a doctor in Taupo, and the other's a civil engineer working in Western Australia.'

'Bet you miss them.'

'I do. Big time.'

'I felt that way about my brother, and Mum and Dad, when I was in Scotland.' They were the main reason behind why he'd returned home ahead of time, hoping he was ready to get on with making a new life on old turf. The nagging memory of kissing Kate had been a teaser, not a solid reason to come back. Though he had thought about her as though he'd missed a wonderful opportunity by walking away from that kiss; an opportunity he was still reluctant to risk everything on.

But the fact he'd never forgotten Kate told him he wasn't as in control of his feelings as he'd like to believe. Throw in the fact he knew he'd done all he could while away to put Amelia behind him, and the time had definitely arrived to move forward.

Another glance in the mirror at the beautiful woman in the back. No. No matter what happened between them, he wasn't going so far as to involve his heart. That would be a serious move and there was a lot to learn about Kate before he even considered giving in to the intense sensations of longing she caused. She might be creating havoc in his head and body, but that was as far as she was going. He was not looking to tie the knot with another woman. Never.

'Have you ever been in a permanent relationship? Or married?'

'I'm divorced.' She looked up at him as if to ask where that came from, then she glanced back at Rusty. 'I found the man of my dreams and got married six years ago. All was going great, or so I thought. Then we went away on holiday to Port Douglas for what I believed was to be a lovers' retreat, only Hamish had apparently fallen out of love but was giving it one last shot. Three months later we split up. End of everything.' Kate hadn't looked up from Rusty while telling him that.

Finn felt for her. What she'd told him was a bland outline with loads of pain behind the words. He understood the need to play it down, not drag sympathy out of others. It didn't get you anywhere and made you feel worse. 'Life's a bitch,' he admitted.

'Sure can be.'

He turned into the clinic parking yard and the automatic lighting came on.

Behind him, Kate was talking to her pet in a velvet voice that tickled Finn's skin and had him questioning himself about remaining aloof, especially now he knew she'd been hurt. He thought he wanted to make her feel better, and himself along the way, which went against everything he believed would be right for him. Scary to say the least.

'Here we go, my boy.' Kate opened the door and began helping the dog out.

'I'll open up and turn some lights on inside.' He headed for the main entrance, focusing on what he had to do for the dog, and not himself. Turning around, he hesitated when he saw Kate leaning over, holding Rusty's collar as she carefully led him towards the clinic. He was wobbly on his feet, but making slow progress. 'Do you want me to carry him?'

'No, we'll be slow but we'll get there. He's not moaning so the painkillers are working.'

Finn did lift the dog onto the X-ray table. He wasn't letting Kate struggle with the weight and difficulty of picking up an injured animal. Rusty wasn't huge but neither was he light. 'There we go. You want me to handle everything?' Kate had said yes earlier but he wanted to be certain and not cause any awkwardness between them. He also really wanted to do this for Kate. He didn't have an answer as to why, other than he liked her and she was hurting over her pet, like any client.

'Go for it. I'd only start seeing things that probably aren't there.' Her smile was tight. A little shudder touched Kate. 'Is this what parents go through every time their child hurts themselves? It must be hard on them.' Her face filled with worry.

'It must be.'

Her head shot up, and the worry disappeared in an instant, to be replaced by shock. 'I'd better stick to dogs. I wouldn't cope.'

What was going on? If he didn't know better he'd say Kate was overreacting to something she knew nothing about. There again, how well did he know her? 'I'd say most parents have to dig deep at times to cope with their children's problems and accidents. It must be normal.' He adjusted the X-ray machine over the dog's leg.

'Of course you're right. I was having a panic moment.'

'You have panic attacks?' he asked as he checked the screen to make sure he was taking a picture of exactly where the fracture appeared to be.

A blush crept into her perfect face, making her look vulnerable and even more beautiful. 'No.' She stepped back from the table so he could take the image. 'But I've always been a bit of a worrier when people or animals get hurt.'

Not quite a full answer, he suspected, but he'd let it go. It wasn't his place to start asking deep and meaningful questions. He'd like to know the answers, but then Kate would get the wrong idea and think he was trying to get close to her. Which couldn't be further from the truth. Either that, or he was lying to himself. 'Here. Come and look at this.' He stepped aside from the screen so he didn't have to breathe her scent.

Kate stared at the image. 'That needs surgery.'

'Yes. Can you put Rusty under while I get organised?'

'No problem.' She opened a cupboard and got out the required drug to administer.

* * *

Kate handed Finn a needle with suture thread to close the wound where he'd stitched the ligament back together in Rusty's leg. 'You're good.' Careful and exacting with his work. He'd just gone up a few notches in her view. Then there was the view of his alert eyes as he worked, and one thick blond curl that kept falling over his forehead that had her itching to shift it.

'This is my workmate's family.' Finn looked at her, his eyes crinkled at the corners. 'Can't send her boy home with any problems.'

For the first time since Charlotte had phoned, she laughed. Really laughed. She was probably being OTT with relief and drowning the stress that had gripped her, but she felt good. Her boy had a way to go. He'd suffer some pain and wouldn't be able to use that leg much for a while, but he'd eventually be running around again like the crazy dog he was. 'Now I know I can be a vet nurse if required. Though I know I'd want to interfere all the time.'

'We'd better get you both home. What if I drive Rusty home to your place and you take your car? Then I can carry him inside for you?'

She'd never finished her second drink at the pub so she'd be fine behind the wheel, and Rusty wasn't so heavy she couldn't lift him. 'Thanks, but I'll be fine. You've done more than enough already. I truly owe you a meal and beer now.'

'That won't be necessary.'

She shrugged at his sharp tone. 'We'll see.' He obviously wasn't pleased she'd turned down his offer of more help. But they'd spent more than enough time together tonight and the last thing she needed was Finn in her house, breathing the same air, taking up space with that long body, while she wandered around keeping an eye on her pet and reminding herself Finn was only there as a colleague. Not a prospective father of the children she wanted some day. That idea had slipped into her head when they were talking about dogs and families and she hadn't been able to get rid of it since. She'd always wanted a family and had thought Hamish was on the same page. Turned out he wasn't on the one about being faithful and loving his spouse for ever. 'I'll go and unlock the car.' Anything to get away from that look of annoyance coming her way. He'd be glad to see the back of her now.

But when she turned from the car to go back inside to get Rusty, Finn was walking towards her with her pet in his arms.

He was so caring and kind despite having been badly hurt. Her heart thumped once. She clenched her hands to prevent herself from leaning forward and kissing those sensual lips. Hell, she wanted to kiss him more than anything. To say thank you. To taste him again. To know him a little better.

Finn placed Rusty gently on the back seat and closed the door. 'I'll lock up. See you tomorrow.' Turning, he strode away.

Her heart crunched. Just like the first night when they'd met. Back straight and head high. At least he hadn't said, 'I can't do this.' He had no idea how he affected her. Something to be grateful for. It would have been downright embarrassing if he'd known what she'd been thinking and feeling.

Kate's heart slammed shut.

I am not letting him in.

There was too much at stake. He might've been loving and careful with Rusty, but that wasn't enough to start letting go of her fear about being rejected yet again once he'd become intimate with her. Nothing would ever be enough to take that risk.

Inside the clinic, Finn scrubbed the operating table harder than necessary in an attempt to alleviate the frustration brought on by Kate damned Phillips. She'd sneaked under his skin without a blink. One moment they were chatting over a drink and the next he was tight for her. A tightness that hadn't abated ever since. Not even when she'd got the call about her dog. Seeing her pain and fear for her pet had only increased the longing filling him to be there for her.

Kate was in his head all the damned time. Laughing, being serious, caring for an animal, talking to patients and staff. She never left. Had he fallen a little bit in love with her when he was home seven months ago? Was that why he hadn't forgotten that kiss?

He tended to fall hard and fast. He had with Amelia anyway. A shiver tightened his skin. Kate was not Amelia. Except he didn't really know her that well. But she wouldn't be a vet if she were anything like Amelia. Vets were kind and caring people. And like him, she'd been on the receiving end of a lot of hurt from her ex. Was he messed up, or what? Only one thing was certain: he was not going to be sucked in and made a fool of ever again.

He hadn't forgotten the taste of Kate's lips under his when they'd kissed. Nor had he forgotten the sudden shock he'd experienced as he'd relaxed and felt excited while kissing her. It was the reason he'd abruptly walked away—to protect himself. He'd been blunt with her, and knew she'd been shocked about that, but there'd been no way he could follow up on that sensational kiss. He had shoved her out of his mind with a fierceness that suggested he'd tried too hard to forget her. It hadn't worked. There'd been weeks when he hadn't thought about her, but then there'd been many more times when she'd crept into his head to tease him, especially when he'd begun to think of returning home sooner than he'd originally been going to.

Now he was back permanently he needed to deal with this before it became too difficult. He was not leaving home again. He'd missed it more than he cared to admit. Especially his family and friends. No one, not even Kate, was going to cause such havoc with his head or heart that he'd walk away from what was important to him again.

He threw the wipes in the bin, switched off lights, and headed outside. Time to get out of here and go home before any other distracting diversions cropped up.

When he pulled up outside the flat, the owner was crossing the lawn towards him as though he'd been waiting for him to get home. 'Hey, Finn, got a moment?'

It was well after ten. This couldn't be good. He opened the front door and flicked on some lights. 'What can I do for you, Harry?'

'Sorry to be the bearer of bad news, but the house has sold. The purchaser offered the price I was wanting if the property changes hands within two weeks.'

'You are kidding me.' Two weeks? It had taken a month to find this place. Unless he rented in the city—which he did not want to do—he was going to be hard pressed to find somewhere else in such a short time. There weren't a lot of rental properties around Darfield. So much for relaxing.

'I am really sorry, Finn, but you did know it was on the market.'

'I did.' He might get lucky and find somewhere quickly. Now that he'd started at the vet clinic, someone there might know of something available. 'I'm pleased for you, seeing as how your father needs to be in partial care.' He'd known the house had been on the market for more than six months, overpriced from what Finn had seen, but as he'd been desperate to settle somewhere he'd taken the flat. 'I must've brought you some luck.'

'Sorry, but them's the breaks. I'll ask around at work in case someone knows of a place available for rent.' Harry worked for a mechanical company in Darfield.

'Thanks, Harry.'

The man walked away, obviously relieved to have got his mission out of the way. He must've been dreading telling him, since he'd been waiting for Finn to come home.

Finn stepped inside and closed the door behind him before heading to the fridge and grabbing a beer. It was late but he wouldn't sleep anyway. First Kate playing with his mindset and now this. Maybe he should've stayed in Scotland, not come home to get on with turning his life around.

Sinking onto the couch and stretching his legs out in front of him, he tipped his head back and stared up at the ceiling. 'It's a slight setback, nothing catastrophic.'

The cool beer took some of the heat out of his overactive mind. He'd sort it. It might even turn out to be for the best. Peter had mentioned some rural properties around Darfield and Kirwee had cottages that the owners rented out. One of those would be ideal, and way better than living in suburbia. Yes, he'd find somewhere else that he'd be happy to go home to at the end of the day. Absolutely.

'Wonder how Kate's feeling at the moment?' Hopefully Rusty was quiet and not causing her any more heartache.

It was too late to phone and find out. He had no idea what time she went to bed, but the hour was late. Bed. Kate. Instantly he was tight. The next mouthful of beer did nothing to cool him down. The image of that beautiful face and shapely body was doing a number on him. Leaping up, he grabbed his keys and headed outside, dropping the empty bottle in the recycle bin with a loud clang on the way past.

His steps ate up the footpath as he charged around West Melton, crossing streets, going along the grassed walkways, around the children's playground, out to the main road running between the city and Darfield, and still his body was tight. He did another circuit.

'Morning, Finn,' Kate greeted him late the next morning at the vet centre when he went in to write up notes on the cattle he'd been inspecting. 'You look tired.'

Lack of sleep did that. 'I'm good. How's Rusty?'

Her shoulders tightened. She must've got the message he wasn't in the mood for conversation and wasn't pleased with him. 'Sore and stiff but as hungry as usual. He's in one of the crates out the back. I don't want to leave him at home yet.'

'I can understand that.' She'd be worried if she wasn't around to watch over the dog. He sat down at the desk and clicked on the computer screen, focusing on work and not Kate, who thankfully left the room to call a dog and its owner into the treatment room. The sooner he got these notes done, the sooner he could leave and put some space between them.

But twenty minutes later she was standing in front of him. 'Finn, since you're here, do you think you could take a look at Rusty's leg for me? It's very red and looking a little swollen.'

'Of course. Give me a minute to finish this and I'll be there.' Why ask him when she was just as capable of dealing with the injury as he was?

'Thanks. I've looked at the wound and know there's an infection brewing, but I'll feel a lot happier if you take a look in case there's anything I've missed. I'm probably overreacting but that's me.'

'Kate, you're a big softie.' Hadn't he said that last night? 'I do understand though.'

'Because you're a softie at heart too?' Her mouth lifted slightly.

He must be back in the good books. 'Who? Me? Not likely.' Only with those who were important to him. Plus the animals he treated. And Kate. No, not Kate. His hand gripped the mouse as he clicked hard on the X to close the screen. Yes, Kate.

Shoving back the chair, he stood up.

Kate was heading down the hall to the room where animals were put in crates while coming round after surgery or some other treatment.

He followed slowly. There hadn't been a lot of sleep last night. Funny thing was that it was Kate who had kept him awake, not the fact he had to find somewhere else to live in a hurry.

She was lifting Rusty onto the table when he entered the room.

'Hey, I could've done that.' He liked to do his bit, and helping a colleague was right up there. Except that, while he did work with Kate, she was more than a colleague. She was a friend in the making. That was it. A friend. Nothing more.

'I'm good.'

Didn't he know it? 'When did you look at Rusty's leg?' The crepe bandage was loose.

'Half an hour ago. He'd been whimpering more than he had earlier, and I like to keep an eye on injuries for any animal I'm working with.'

'Especially your own pet.'

'Yeah.' Her gaze was fixed on his hands as he unwound the bandage and exposed the red wound site.

Glancing up, he saw that her teeth were digging into her bottom lip. He mock growled. 'Don't do that, Kate. Rusty's going to be fine once I give him some more antibiotics. So far the infection's mild. I'll give him a heavy dose to stop it in its tracks.' He looked firmly at Kate. 'If that's all right with you.'

'It's what I'd do.' She rubbed the dog's head so softly Finn wanted to touch her in a similar way to reassure her all would go well with the surgical site.

Of course, he resisted. 'I'll fetch the injection and get this done. Have you got any more appointments this morning?'

'One more at midday. A schnauzer with grass-seed allergies needs a top-up of corticosteroid.' Kate suddenly looked all-in.

Could be he wasn't the only one who'd missed out on sleep last night. 'Want me to stay and do that? I've got nothing on for the rest of the day.' Other than talking to letting agencies about rental properties, and he could do that while sitting in Reception waiting for the schnauzer.

Back to that lip-nibbling thing, Kate looked from Rusty to him. Something was bugging her.

'What's up? You look as though you've got a problem.'

Her ponytail slid from side to side when she shook her head. 'Not really. If you're serious about dealing with the last appointment, then I'll take you up on your offer. Thanks.'

'Sorted. You get out of here while you can.' He saw her rub her lower back and stepped closer to the table and Rusty. 'Go and open your car. I'll bring this fella out.' The dog could walk but it would be awkward and painful for Rusty and Kate, and *he* wanted to do something more than seeing to her final appointment for her.

When Kate didn't argue he had to wonder what was bothering her, but he refrained from asking as the answer might be something he didn't want to hear. They were getting on fine and he didn't want to mess with that. As he followed her out to the car, longing for a deeper relationship sprang up. Kate was lovely, inside and out. The kind of woman he could lose his head over. Right now he should be putting the dog down and running for the hills. Except he really didn't want to. Despite all the warnings he'd gone through while striding around West Melton last night, he did not want to turn his back on Kate.

So he placed the spaniel on the back seat, closed the door, and headed back inside without another word.

CHAPTER FIVE

'THERE YOU GO, RUSTY. All snug and dry.' Kate closed the crate and stood up. She could've left her pet at home in the laundry room with Sam but she liked to be able to keep an eye on him. The wound was healing well and he did use the injured leg at the moments when there were interesting objects to pursue in the yard, but she'd spend the day worrying he'd hurt himself if she left him at home.

'How's the infection?' Finn asked from the doorway.

'Clearing up fast.'

'Glad to hear it.' Finn sounded more relaxed this morning than he had on Saturday. He must've had a good weekend. 'Peter's in the tearoom waiting for everyone to turn up.'

'Coming.' They opened up half an hour later for patients on Mondays so everyone could get together to discuss any problems that had arisen over the past week.

'I've made your coffee,' Finn told her.

'Thanks.' Following him into the staff room, she felt good. The weekend had been quiet. She'd visited her parents and helped her dad bottle too many kilos of tomatoes. Now, seeing Finn looking so at ease and as handsome as ever was warming her throughout. Not that he was supposed to do that. Friendly colleagues only. Easier said, apparently.

Finn went to the bench and picked up two full mugs. 'Here you go.'

Taking her drink, she sat down next to Peter, and, when Finn took the seat on the opposite side of him, sighed with relief. She was getting used to having him around, just as she'd intended from the start, but it was difficult to remain calm at the times when he sat next to her. If only she could ignore the humming in her veins. He got to her all too quickly. 'Morning, Peter. How was your weekend?'

'If you don't count the fact that the motor mower blew a couple of valves, then perfect.' Peter grinned. 'A mechanic I am not.'

'You should've called round and got mine,' Kate told him.

'And spoil a quiet afternoon? No, thanks. Seriously, the mower will be back in working order later today.' He looked around. 'Still waiting for Mark, I see.'

'He's dealing to a cat that's had a claw torn out,' Di said. 'He said to go ahead without him.'

'Right, then let's get on with things.' Peter filled them in on progress with the school pet fair arrangements. 'That's about it from me. Anyone got something to tell us?'

A lot of head shaking went on around the table.

'Good. The only other thing I want to mention is that Finn is looking for a place to rent, so if anyone knows of somewhere, or hears of one, please let him know.' Peter turned to Kate. 'You haven't taken in anyone since your last boarder left, have you?'

'No-o.' Finn was the last person she wanted living under her roof. They were getting along well but she couldn't see that going quite as smoothly if they spent more time together. She'd have to be ultra cautious and when it was in her own home and the one place she could relax completely, it wasn't a good idea.

'That could be an answer to your predicament, Finn.'

Shut up, Peter.

She glanced at Finn and saw his jaw tighten. This was the man who'd leapt in to help her with Rusty on Friday. The guy who'd taken her to the pub for a drink and a meal. He'd been nothing but good to her, though often a little edgy. 'You can take a look at the room if you'd like,' she said in a rush. 'It's got a bed and dresser so you wouldn't need to bring any furniture.'

His chest rose and fell. 'Thanks, Kate. It's good of you to offer but I've got every agent in the area on my case so hopefully something should turn up soon.'

Fingers crossed he was right. She'd heard that he'd had difficulty finding a place last time and it hadn't been more than a few weeks ago so chances were he would have the same problem now. 'Why are you moving out of the flat you already had?'

'It's been sold and the purchaser offered a good deal if the property changed hands quickly. To be honest, I did agree to a short time frame to get out if it sold and in return had a lower rent so I can't complain.' His smile was rueful. 'Silly me.'

Finn was not silly. Far from it. 'Here's hoping you find a place you like.' Deep breath. He'd know she wasn't keen on him moving in. She doubted he'd be that willing either. 'If not, you are welcome to use my spare room.'

Looking around to make sure everyone had left the room, Finn leaned back in his chair. 'Thank you, Kate, but we both know we're still trying to make this work so that we're comfortable around here, and sharing a house would only add to the pressure.'

Or it could go some way towards cementing their friendship, except she wasn't so sure about that. 'I thought we were getting along fine.' If she didn't think about how she'd wanted to kiss him the other night. She could be grateful he'd left before her feelings had really taken over and she'd made a fool of herself. She was not prepared to face that a second time from Finn. Or anyone.

Di appeared in the room. 'Finn, your first visit's been cancelled. I've rung Monty to see if you could go to his farm earlier than arranged but he's in town at the moment so you've got nothing on for the next hour or so.'

'Guess that means I'll hang around here and give Kate and Mark a hand. They seem to have a long list of patients this morning.'

Kate was on her feet. 'We do. I don't know what it is about Mondays, but it's nothing unusual. Can you take one of Mark's as he's obviously busy with that cat?'

'On to it.'

So Finn needed accommodation sooner rather than later. He had to find somewhere else. It was a bad idea for him to move in, but there wasn't a lot she could do about it now that she'd made the offer. It was up to Finn what he did with it.

She followed him out of the room and went to get her first patient. 'Barb, come through with Jetson.'

A middle-aged woman led her Alsatian into the treatment room and got him up to sit on the examination table. 'How's things, Kate? Busy as usual?'

'You bet. No rest for vets.' She laughed, a little tightly but she was wearing her professional face.

'I hear there's a new vet started here. Quite a looker apparently.'

Word got around fast in small towns. 'Finn Anderson. He's mostly doing farm animals but, having said that, he's working in here this morning.' That'd give Barb someone to look out for and satisfy her interest. 'Now, what's up with Jetson?'

'He's not eating properly. It started last week and first I thought he'd eaten something bad, but after two days I decided it had to be something else. He doesn't have much energy.'

Jetson wasn't on any medications, nor had he had a vaccination recently, so she could rule those out as causes. 'I'll check his body for pain in case he's injured internally.' As she felt over the dog's stomach and ribs she asked Barb, 'Has he been stressed about anything out of the ordinary lately?'

'Not that I've noticed.' And Barb would. Her dog was the most important part of her life.

Jetson was remaining still, his eyes watching Kate's every move. 'Any changes to what you feed him?'

'No.' Worry was building up in Barb's face.

'No fractures or internal wounds as far as I can ascertain.' She'd do an X-ray if no reason for the lack of appetite showed up. 'I'll check his teeth now. Not chewing can be a sign of a broken tooth or an infection in the gums.'

'He hasn't touched a bone for more than a week.'

That should've been the first thing Barb mentioned but Kate understood what it was like to be stressed about your four-footed buddies, and this woman didn't have Finn around to make sure her pet was given the best going-over. Finn. His name slipped silently across her lips. He'd been brilliant with Rusty. He'd also fully understood how she'd been hurting for her boy. She wriggled each of Jetson's teeth, moving slowly along the bottom row then the top.

Suddenly Jetson jerked his head away. 'Grr.'

Pulling away, Kate said, 'Think we know what's causing the loss of appetite. The last tooth I touched was loose, but there could be more. I'm going to sedate him before I go any further.' Putting her fingers inside a distressed dog's mouth while he was fully awake was not an option now she knew where the problem lay. 'I'll get Di to give me a hand.'

Returning with the nurse, Kate told her what was required. 'Is the operating room free this morning?'

'Yes,' Di said. 'Until eleven when you've got two cats to de-sex and a metal pin to remove from the leg of a sheepdog.'

'Then I can use the room now if necessary. I'll take this guy in there shortly. Finn can take over some of my appointments once Mark's ready to do his.' Sometimes things worked out well, when she wasn't thinking how she preferred Finn wasn't in the building. If he'd been out in the field as he was meant to be Jetson would have had to wait until she'd finished her operating schedule to have his problem dealt with. It wouldn't have been an issue but she liked to keep animals calm and comfortable, and giving him too much sedative while waiting wasn't good when she had to put him under later.

Within moments of the sedative being dispensed into the back of his neck, Jetson was asleep, and Kate could examine his mouth thoroughly. 'Two loose teeth and swelling in the gum along with an infection. I'll take an X-ray to find the cause.'

As she rubbed her pet's back, Barb asked, 'Will you be removing teeth?'

'It's very likely, but until I can see exactly what the problem is I don't know what I'll be doing. It could be that he's got a slither of bone stuck in his gum that's causing an infection.'

'Sounds like surgery might be necessary.'

'Yes, it could be.' With Di's help Kate took Jetson through to the room next door to x-ray his mouth.

When she returned without the dog, Barb's face crumpled. 'You're going to operate.'

'There is something embedded in his gum between the two loose teeth that has to be removed if we're to stop the pain and the infection. Are you okay with me carrying on?'

'Just do it. Make him happy again.'

'Di will bring you a form to fill in and sign. We'll keep Jetson here for the day, and I'll phone you as soon as I've finished the surgery to let you know how it went.'

Finn walked in. 'I hear you want me to carry on with your patients now that Mark's back on board with his.'

'That would be helpful.' Of course, as the clinic manager she could've just said that was what he'd be doing, but it wasn't her style. 'Finn, this is Barb Newton. It's her Alsatian's mouth I'm going to remove an obstruction from.'

'H-hello, Finn. I heard you'd started here. Welcome to Darfield.' Barb's face was turning pink.

Kate knew all too well what that was like.

'Thank you, Barb. It's a great area to be in, and the practice is excellent. You've brought Jetson to the right place.' He smiled and Barb's colour deepened.

'I—I'd better sign the form you mentioned, Kate, and get out of your way.' Barb turned for the door.

Finn reached over to open it for her.

Kate was laughing to herself. The man was hot, and, it seemed, setting off firecrackers in lots of women. 'I like your advertising. Never hurts to put us out there.'

'If I get bored being a vet, I'll know what to do next for a career.' He grinned.

'You'll never get fed up with veterinary work. You're passionate about it.'

His grin widened as he tilted his head to one side. 'You think?'

'I know.' Kate turned away before her face outdid Barb's for colour. Damn him for being able to tip her off centre so easily—with a grin. What happened to never letting a man get close again? They *weren't* close. No, but keep up these thoughts and the feelings that came with them and there'd be no stopping her trying to get there. Heck, he could not move into her house. No way. She'd never keep her distance. Unless he saw her scars and then he'd be gone. Out of her life for ever. She'd have to pull on her big girl's hat once more and pretend it didn't hurt, when it always hurt—badly.

'Kate? You all right?'

'I'm fine, thinking about what I have to do with Jetson.'

'Try again, Kate. You're not fooling me one little bit.'

Fighting the urge to throw herself at Finn just because he understood her a little too well, she turned slowly. 'We need to get back to work, Finn.'

'You're right. We do.' The disappointment coming her way was huge.

In looking out for herself, she'd let him down. He was

vulnerable too. She'd never deliberately hurt him, but with her insecurities it wouldn't be hard to do. More than ever before, she couldn't stand the thought of Finn's eyes widening in horror and awful words spilling from that beautiful mouth. 'I'm sorry.' She'd hurt them both. Like it or not, she was starting to care too much for Finn and every step came with a price. Most of which she was afraid to incur, for fear of having her heart broken a second time.

Finn watched Kate walk into the room next door and swallowed hard. By walking away she'd done the right thing by him. She was saving his heart, whether she knew it or not. He was more than a little smitten with her, but that did not ease the fear of being used and decimated again. Returning home because he missed his family and friends was all very well, as was starting to get on with making a life for himself in the one place he wanted to live permanently. But that wasn't easy. Far from it.

Without even trying, he was unwittingly edging beyond the boundaries he had set. All because Kate often managed to make him forget his fears momentarily. It was not wise. Sooner or later his trust would be tested and he had none to give. If Amelia could knowingly rob him of love, and of everything he possessed, and of his self-worth, then he'd be an absolute fool to risk it again. Even worse was how she'd offered him hope in following up on the dream to have a family and then taken it away with her horrific confession. 'I am not pregnant, never was. That positive test was not mine. You were an idiot to believe it was real.' Talk about a deal-breaker. How could he ever trust a woman with his heart again?

That he'd never forgotten what it had felt like to hold

Kate and kiss her the night he'd met her even once he'd been back on the other side of the world was huge. But it didn't change anything. He was not ready to follow through. He'd never be.

'Finn, you've got two people with their pets waiting to see you.' Kate had returned.

Did she know what he was thinking? Was he easy to read? Of course not. He was being paranoid. 'I'll be right there.'

'I'll take one before I see to Jetson.'

He shook his head. 'That won't be necessary.' When her eyes began to widen, he nodded. 'Seriously, I'm not going to let the team down. I was just having a moment of indecision, but I'm sorted.' For now, at least.

Her face softened. 'Nothing's ever easy, is it? I'm sure you'll get your accommodation sorted in no time.'

Her misunderstanding was a relief. 'I will.'

Hopefully not by moving in with you, Kate, because I'm starting to see I'd never handle having you so near all the time.

It was bad enough bumping into her at work, but then he got to go home, and she wasn't anywhere in sight. Except when he went and invited her to the pub, and ended up at her house and then bringing her dog here to operate on.

Checking the screen to see which person to call in, he headed out to the waiting room while Di wiped down the table from the last animal. 'Pauline Clark?'

A young woman stood up and lifted a cat crate from the chair beside her. 'That's me, and this is Scratch.'

'I'm Finn Anderson, your vet for this visit. Come through.'

Pauline was eying him up. 'I heard about you when I

dropped the kids off at school. Everyone seems to know there's a new vet in town.'

She could look all she liked, but being single didn't mean he was interested. The point was, he'd made himself unavailable to protect himself, and keeping Kate at bay was hard enough. No other woman would be able to unsettle him the way she did, so it was easy to walk into the treatment room with Pauline and not really notice her other than as a cat's owner. 'So what's Scratch's problem?'

'He's losing fur non-stop,' Pauline said as she lifted the tabby from the crate and held him in her arms.

Finn took the cat and placed him on the table so he could get a better look.

Di moved up and held Scratch still, which was good because Finn didn't feel like having claws ripping his skin through his gloves. 'There are quite a few bald patches. Have you changed his diet recently?'

'Yes. He seemed to be less energetic so I got a different brand of biscuits about four weeks ago,' Pauline answered.

'Did that improve his energy levels?'

'A little. Then the fur started coming away in clumps, but I didn't think about the biscuits being a reason for that.'

'There's no sign of ringworm, which could've been a cause.' No allergies were recorded in the cat's file, and Scratch wasn't on any medications. 'I suggest you take him off those particular biscuits and go back to the original ones. Also I can recommend some other foods to boost his energy levels.' Finn glanced at the screen in front of him. 'He's getting on in years so it could be he's slowing down.'

'Shh. He'll hear you.' Pauline laughed, then said more seriously, 'Thank you so much. You've made me feel a lot happier. I'll give away the biscuits and buy whatever it is you're suggesting.'

'Di, show Pauline the options we've got so she can get Scratch started.'

'Will do.' Di lifted Scratch off the table and cuddled him. 'Come on, little man. Let's get you something yummy to eat.' Which meant Di would give the cat one of the treats she kept at her desk.

As Finn made his way back out to Reception for the next patient, he heard Kate talking and laughing in the operating room. Was someone else in there with her? He couldn't hear anyone. Maybe she was talking to her unconscious patient. That way she wouldn't get answers she didn't want to hear. He smiled to himself at the zing in his step. He shouldn't feel like this, but there was no stopping him. Kate did that to him. He hated to admit it, but it seemed he didn't have a lot of control over his emotions when it came to her. So moving in with her was out. A cave would be safer.

Right, get on with what he was here for. 'Jonathon Bell?' Not Kate Phillips.

An elderly man stood up with a leash in hand that was attached to a mixed breed, mid-sized dog. 'That's us.'

'Come through.' Finn closed the door to the waiting room behind them, and shut his mind down on all things Kate and his future, and got on with work. It was the only way to get through the day and come out sane.

That or a phone call from a rental agent telling him they'd found him somewhere to live.

CHAPTER SIX

'ANOTHER WEEK FINISHED.' Kate raised her glass to every-one sitting around the table in the tearoom after the front door had been locked behind the last animal needing attention for the day. 'It's been a busy one.' She was more tired than usual. A glance in Finn's direction reminded her how often she'd lain in bed throughout the week thinking about him. At least he hadn't been across the hall in the other bedroom or who knew what she might've done?

'It certainly has,' Mark agreed before taking a mouthful of his beer. 'Glad it's you on call, Kate.'

'What's everyone got planned for the weekend?' Finn asked.

'Anything that has nothing to do with sick animals,' Peter retorted, then grinned. 'As little as possible.'

'You know what we haven't done for a while?' Kate asked before putting her brain in gear. 'When was the last time we had a staff barbecue?'

'About two months ago,' Di answered. 'Want to have another?'

So much for thinking straight. She'd really blown her determination to keep Finn at arm's length. But she could hardly say no now. 'Let's. We can have it at my place.' Because that was what they usually did. 'If I get called out it's not as though you don't all know your way around.'

Strangely the idea was perking her up, shoving the exhaustion aside. It was something to look forward to. She could see more of Finn without being alone with him. That had to be good for a lot of reasons. Or possibly not. He'd get to see her home and how she lived. But if he moved in, he'd learn even more about her. Anyway, she couldn't retract the offer of her spare room any more than she could the suggestion of a staff get-together.

'I'm on,' Di said.

'Count me and Sheree in,' Peter added.

'We'll be there,' Mark said.

Kate went round the table, getting the same answer from everyone, including Finn, who asked, 'How does this work? Do we all bring meat and salads?'

As Kate went to explain her phone rang. It was the clinic number, which had been switched over to her phone. 'Here we go.' Stepping away, she said, 'Hello, this is Kate Phillips at Darfield Animal Care.'

'Kate, Dave Crocker. There's been an accident on the West Coast Road involving a horse float with two horses on board. Can you come?'

The local cop sounded stressed. 'On my way, Dave. Can you tell me how far along the road the accident happened?'

Heads turned and everyone was suddenly quiet, listening to her side of the conversation.

'About twenty k's from town,' Dave told her. 'I don't think the horses are in good nick.'

Wonderful. As she listened she mentally ran through her kit, making certain everything she could possibly need was there, including sodium pentobarbital in case she had to put either of the horses down. Not that her kit wouldn't have everything but she could never be too sure. 'See you shortly.' Hanging up, she turned to the others. 'That was Dave. A small truck spun into a four-wheel drive towing a horse float. Two horses have been injured, possibly critically. I'm off.'

Finn was on his feet in a shot. 'I'm coming with you.'

As she opened her mouth to say he didn't need to, he cut her off.

'Two badly injured horses? Two vets are better than one.'

She couldn't argue with that. 'Grab your gear. We're out of here.' As she headed away, she called over her shoulder, 'Someone fill me in later about the barbecue. You know I'm happy with anything going.'

'I'll text you,' Di returned.

Her car was already running when Finn leapt into the front seat. 'Any more details than what you said inside?'

'Dave thinks one horse might have a broken leg, but he added it's mayhem in the float and no one's game enough to get close enough to find out what injuries the animals have.'

'What about the driver towing the float?'

'An ambulance is on its way for her. She was thrown through the windscreen. It must've been a massive impact.' When Kate hit the main road she pressed hard on the accelerator. Dave had said 'don't dally' so he'd back her if one of his colleagues tried to stop her.

'Sounds like the truck hit her vehicle very hard,' Finn commented, unaware she'd had a similar thought. Then he tightened his seat belt.

'It's all right. I won't go too fast, but Dave sounded extremely worried and the fact the horses are kicking and trying to get out of the float means we need to get there as soon as safely possible.'

'I'm all good, Kate. I want to get there asap too.'

They didn't talk much after that. Kate was concentrating on driving and Finn went through his kit to find vials of xylazine to help with the pain the horses would be in. 'How we're going to administer this when they're so restless is something to think about.'

'I don't fancy being kicked,' Kate agreed. 'Out of my way,' she growled at a slow campervan, and, glad they were on a straight stretch of road, indicated before pulling out to pass. The kilometres were disappearing but it seemed to take for ever to reach the accident site. Finally she spied red and blue lights flashing on top of a cop car. Easing off the pedal, she heaved a sigh of relief. 'Now the real fun starts.'

Finn placed his hand over hers. 'We've got this.'

In other words, they were together, a team. A good team. That made her feel happy. So did the feel of his warmth on her hand. 'We have.' Pulling over onto the grass, she pulled on the brake and shut off the engine. 'That's Dave coming our way. Have you met him yet?'

'No, I haven't.'

'He's a good guy. Believes in being there when people are in dire straits, and also has a firm hand when it comes to dealing with out-of-control teenagers.'

'I like him already,' Finn said as he pushed out of the car.

'Kate, the horses have quietened a little but everyone's staying back in case they get upset again. The owner, Doria, is in the ambulance, and her husband's on his way here to see what's going on with the horses.' Dave nodded over at Finn. 'Hello, I take it you're the new vet?'

Finn stepped around the car with his hand extended. 'Finn Anderson. Pleased to meet you, though not in the circumstances I'd prefer.'

Kate wasn't hanging around to play nice and friendly. The plight of the horses was worrying her. The fact they'd quietened more likely meant shock was taking hold, and they could still react violently when approached. Unfortunately there was no avoiding that she and Finn did have to get close to administer drugs and see what the injuries were.

As she reached the float Finn touched her elbow to indicate he was right there with her. His second light touch since they'd arrived. She'd never felt the need to have another vet alongside her when faced with a serious accident involving animals, but his touches calmed the turmoil in her belly so she could focus better on what was important.

The float was on its side. Plywood and fibreglass were strewn everywhere, as were the aluminium sheets that had once kept the horses protected inside. A lump formed in her chest as she regarded the two mares sprawled in the carnage, their legs twitching and their mouths frothing. One was on her side, while the other was seated on her butt and trying to stand, groaning in agony.

'This doesn't look good.' She took a couple of steps closer, Finn with her. Pointing to the closest horse, she said, 'I'll take this one.' Placing her kit on the ground, she leaned over the mare trying to stand, and made observations of the breathing rate, heartbeat, and then began assessing the mare's body externally without touching her, and all the time aware of her movements. Fortunately those were getting weaker as the pain and shock took over. Not that Kate wanted the animal to be suffering those. 'Back right leg fractured. Ribcage compressed.' There were bleeding abrasions in many places but those weren't urgent.

'Fractured left back leg, and possibly the left front leg on this one,' Finn replied moments later. 'There's also an indentation on her head on the same side.'

Kate locked eyes with him. None of this boded well. 'Pain relief first.'

His nod was brief. 'Let's do one at a time so we can assist each other in case either horse reacts badly.' He didn't add that they'd be in a direct line for trouble if that happened.

'This one first. She's still jumpy.'

Finn delved in the kit and held up the syringe and xylazine. 'Agreed?'

'Yes.' Carefully reaching over to the horse's neck, Kate found the triangular spot used for injections and reached behind her for the needle Finn was holding out. Under her hand, the horse flinched and raised her head a few inches. 'Shh, it's okay, girl. We're going to help with the pain.' She held her breath as she slid the needle under the skin, her heart beating heavily as she squeezed the plunger and hoped like crazy the mare didn't jerk her head around or try to get away from her. Within seconds she was withdrawing the needle and sitting back on her haunches, sweat beading between her eyebrows. 'Phew.'

Finn said, 'Well done.'

'One done, next one coming up.'

'My turn to be in the firing line.' Finn stood up, reaching down to help her up too. He gave her hand a small squeeze before getting the second syringe and ampule and moving close to the mare. As he leaned down the horse's nostrils flared and she banged a hoof on the ground. 'It's all right. I'm here to help you.' His voice was so soft Kate smiled. If only he were holding her.

Tyres screeched on the road and then a door was slammed shut.

The mare hesitated, her head still as she appeared to be listening, and Finn made the most of the opportunity. He had the needle in her neck fast and pressed down to empty the drug into the horse, then stood up to step back.

A man appeared beside Kate. 'What's happening? Are the horses in a bad way?'

'Are you the owner's husband?' Kate asked.

'Yes, I am. I should be on the way to the hospital but someone had to come and deal with this mess.'

It must be hard for the man. Kate immediately got down to business. 'I'm Kate Phillips, a vet from Darfield, and this is Finn Anderson, a vet from the same practice. We have just given both horses painkillers. One has two broken legs and other injuries, and the second one has a fractured leg and possibly broken ribs.'

The man swore. When he calmed, he said, 'Sorry but this is a nightmare. Doria dotes on these two. How am I going to tell her what's happened?' It seemed he might understand what probably lay ahead.

These horses weren't going to get back up on their feet without major surgery and a very long recovery, and even then it wouldn't be an easy process for the animals. Kate glanced at Finn, who grimaced, before saying to the man, 'There is a possibility of operating and placing pins in their legs but in reality that's going to be very hard on the mares. If there are multiple fractures around the site, then I wouldn't recommend it.'

Kate added, 'We won't know what we're faced with until X-rays are done.' Which wouldn't be easy. 'For that the horses need to be moved onto trailers and taken away from here to their stables.' They'd need to be unconscious during the process of moving them.

The man stared at the mares. 'I'm Colin. Sorry, didn't say earlier.' He knelt down beside one mare. 'Hey, Cass, girl, I'm here.' He reached out to stroke her.

'Careful,' Kate warned. 'They're not their usual selves.'

But Cass didn't flinch. She obviously knew Colin's touch. He looked up at Kate. 'You're going to have to euthanise them.'

Was that a demand or a question? 'The odds point that way, but it's not my call. You and your wife need to decide how far you want to take these mares in terms of treatment and how they'll get around during the coming months.' Her heart was hurting for the couple and their mares. She hated the days when she had to put an animal down. It never got any easier.

The man stood up. 'Decision made. I can't bear the thought of these two in pain and probably never getting back the full use of their legs. See to it, will you? I'm going to the hospital to be with Doria.'

'Hang on, mate.' Dave stepped up. 'There's the matter of getting the horses moved away from here.'

'It'll have to wait. I need to see Doria and make sure she's all right.'

'Is there someone you can call to come sort this out?'

'What about these vets?'

As Kate opened her mouth to explain they didn't do

that, Dave said, 'It's not their job. They'll euthanise the horses but someone else has to remove the animals and the remains of the float from the roadside.'

'I'll call our neighbour to come with his trailer and a couple of guys to help him,' Colin croaked.

Finn had his kit open. 'I'll give each mare another sedative. Then I'll follow up with the sodium pentobarbital.'

A second sedative wasn't going to harm the horses, and would prevent any movement if either of them got stressed again. 'I'll take care of this one,' Kate told him. She might hate doing this but she wasn't about to leave it all to Finn. That was hardly fair. The sadness in his eyes told her he felt much the same as she did. Then again, find a vet who didn't and that person shouldn't be in the job.

Colin coughed. 'Thanks, both of you. It's hard, you know? I've got to tell Doria.' He was choked up, and his eyes were watery.

'Go and make that call, Colin,' Kate said. He didn't need to watch the process. 'Then get on the road to the hospital.' She moved away and took the syringe with an attached sedative capsule from Finn. 'Thanks.' On her knees, she kept a firm eye on Cass as she rubbed the spot on her neck where she'd insert the last needle. 'Good girl. Just a small prick and you'll go to sleep.'

Then another prick and you'll never wake up again.

Kate blinked. Focused. It was necessary but awful all the same.

Back at the clinic, Finn took both kits inside to top up the drugs and syringes they'd used. Night had fallen and everyone had left for home. He felt flat after euthanising those mares. This was when he liked having others around to lift his spirits. 'Kate, once we've done this, feel like a wine since we didn't get to finish the first one?' He'd do whatever it took to keep her here a bit longer, and hopefully put a smile on her wan face while lifting his own spirits.

'Best idea ever.' The front door closed with a bang. 'I'm not ready to go home yet.'

'We could go to the pub for a meal.' That'd keep her at his side for a while longer. Then he sighed. Talk about sounding desperate. But it had been a long time since he'd had that special person he could download with. Tonight it would be different because Kate had been there with him, and had had to do the same thing to one of the mares.

'I'm not hungry.' She took the vials he handed her and placed them in her kit. Her voice sounded as flat as he felt.

'Time for a career in banking?' he quipped in an attempt to lift the mood between them.

'Think I'll try my hand at commercial gardening. Only thing that'd die would be the plants.'

'Aww, Kate. Come here.' Finn took her in his arms and held her tight. 'This side of the job's a bitch.'

'Totally.'

Her body folded into his and her arms went around his waist. Her head lay on his chest and he could feel her breaths at the vee of his shirt. Damn, he'd missed this. Worse, he hadn't even realised it hadn't been there. He'd been so focused on putting Amelia and the past behind him that he hadn't thought about anything else. Now he was looking ahead and it wasn't quite as bad as he'd thought. There might even be opportunities for happiness—and love. He stood straighter, pulled back.

'Finn?' The beautiful face that filled his mind at all

sorts of moments was looking up at him with puzzlement. 'What's going on in your mind?'

Wouldn't you like to know? You'd probably run for your car and speed away if I told you.

'It was hard dealing with the horses so I was relaxing with you.'

'Then you stopped.'

'I'm not sure if holding you is the right thing to be doing.' He could do honest with this woman far too easily. About some things anyway. It was those other things that frightened him. Mentioning how good she made him feel would be a game-changer he wasn't prepared for. 'Let's have that wine.'

Pushing up onto her toes, she brushed a light kiss on his mouth. 'I'll get it.' She walked away from him.

Was that disappointment on her face because he'd been honest? Surely not. That'd suggest she had similar feelings to his about having someone to share tragic events with and that didn't make sense. But she'd kissed him—softly, and so tantalisingly he wanted more. More kisses and more of her company.

Was Kate taking a shine to him? Did she want something stronger than a workplace friendship? He should've said he'd changed his mind about having a wine but for the life of him he couldn't find it in him to do so. Spending time with Kate was starting to feel too good. She brought him alive in ways he hadn't known for a long while, ways he'd been intent on denying himself to remain safe.

He wasn't only thinking about sex but also about sharing the things that made a real life. A home, family and friends. Those were what he'd grown up believing in, only to have the possibility slashed from under him. Yet here he was opening up ever so slightly to thinking he might find them all because Kate had a way of sneaking under his radar.

Her voice interrupted the errant thoughts. 'Unfortunately we didn't really have any choice. The two mares were in a serious condition. The owner's husband gave us the go-ahead.' Kate pointed to her phone and mouthed 'Peter' to him.

He took the bottle out of her hand and found two glasses in the cupboard to fill.

'No, it wasn't pleasant.' Kate paused, listening to Peter. 'Great. I'm looking forward to it. Sounds like there'll be way too much food as usual.' She wasn't smiling. Her mind was most likely still on the mares and not tomorrow night's barbecue. Or could she be thinking about kissing him again? Yes, please.

When Kate placed her phone on the table Finn handed her a glass. 'Get some of that inside you.'

'Oh, Finn, it never gets any easier, does it?' She wiped a tear from her cheek.

'Nope, afraid not.' Leaning closer, he wiped a second tear from her other cheek. 'But you were kind and gentle with Cass. That's what counts.'

Kate watched him as she took a large mouthful of wine, her eyes filled with a longing he didn't dare put a name to.

He took a sip of his drink and placed the glass on the table beside him, not looking away from Kate's gaze for a second.

Kate leaned sideways and put her glass down too, still watching him.

Simultaneously they reached for each other, their mouths meeting, touching, tasting, feeding that longing he'd seen in her eyes and known inside his heart. This was Kate, the woman who'd played with his mind for months, the woman he'd kissed once before and never forgotten what it had felt like.

Kate.

He tightened his hold around her, drew her even closer so her breasts were pressed against his chest, her stomach pushing into him. She was wonderful.

Kate's tongue was on his, sending his need spiralling out of control. Her lips were soft under his. Her hands firm on his butt. He was in paradise, returning the kiss with everything he had.

It wasn't enough. He needed to feel her skin, to touch those breasts, to get even closer. 'Kate?' he whispered against her mouth.

Her lips sealed against his again, kissing him back fervently. Then Kate lifted a leg up to his waist, then the other, and her arms were around his shoulders. 'Take me, Finn.'

His eyes popped open and he looked at her. 'You have no idea how much I want you.'

'What's stopping you?'

'Nothing.' Holding that wonderful body tight against him, he carried her into the office and closed the door to keep the world out. He didn't bother with lights. He could find his way around Kate so easily it was wonderful. It wasn't the wisest thing he'd done but there was no stopping the need pouring through him. And, he suspected as Kate kissed his neck and chin, no stopping her either.

As she slid down his body to stand before him, her hands were reaching for his trousers, undoing the zip to take hold of his erection. One touch and he was nearly gone. 'Stop, Kate. We're doing this together.'

She grabbed his hand and placed it against her moist centre.

When had she discarded her trousers? Touching her heat sent sparks flying throughout his taut body, teasing, tantalising. Damn she was amazing. So sexy. He was losing control far too quickly.

'Finn, lift me up against the wall so I can ride you.'

Then she was holding onto him and sliding down over him and he was brushing her heat and they were coming together.

The next thing he knew was Kate cuddled up against him with the wall at her back and her short breaths hot against his chest. 'Kate.' He stopped. What could he say that would be better than what had just gone down between them? Nothing. He brushed a kiss over her forehead, then another on her lips.

She stared at him and a sensual smile grew on those lips. 'Wow.'

'Yes, wow.' He stepped back and pulled his trousers up from around his ankles.

Suddenly Kate jerked, and reached for her trousers too, turning her back slightly as she did.

'Kate? You all right?'

'Couldn't be better.' She tossed him a crooked smile over her shoulder, then zipped her trousers and turned back to face him looking a little confused.

'You're not regretting this already?' He'd be gutted if she was. Though he knew he had done something he'd sworn not to, he did not regret it at all. How could he when Kate was so wonderful?

'No, Finn, I am not. It's only that we're supposed to be friendly colleagues and nothing more.'

He laughed. 'Friendly colleagues? Is that how you see us?'

'I did. And if we're to continue working side by side it might be the only way to go.' Her smile dimmed. 'Except I can't imagine that any more. Not after what I've just experienced with you.'

'One day—or should that be kiss—at a time, eh?'

Her shoulders lifted, fell away again. But her smile remained. 'Deal.'

'Come here.' He wrapped his arms around her and held her close and tight. He hadn't felt so comfortable with a woman in a long time. Not even the few he'd dated on and off in Scotland had given him a sense of belonging. Which was downright scary. But he couldn't pull away. Not yet. He had to hold Kate just a little bit longer first.

Then the phone spoilt everything by ringing loud and clear.

'At least whoever it is didn't call ten minutes ago,' Kate said with a grin as she picked up the instrument. 'Kate Phillips of Darfield Animal Care speaking.' She looked as if it was hard to focus on reality and not what had gone on in here moments ago.

Finn grinned as he waited for the call to finish.

'Got a cat that needs some stitches in a paw coming in,' Kate told him when she put the phone down. 'It's one way to get back on track.'

'I can stay around to help with the cat if you want,' he said, not ready to leave her.

Kate shook her head firmly. 'I'll be fine, thanks.'

'You want me to go.'

'I think it's best, don't you? I mean, what happened was awesome, but work is intervening and I don't want to mix the two.'

She was right, but a little gremlin made him say, 'Not really.'

Taken aback, Kate stared at him. 'We're meant to only be friends.'

'I know, but seems there's more to this than either of us expected. We've kind of blown that theory.' When she didn't say anything he stepped closer and brushed a kiss over her lips. 'See you tomorrow.'

And hard as it was, he did walk away. Because Kate was right. They were becoming friends, not friends with benefits. Except they'd blown that out of the water and needed to cool down and see what they really wanted next.

As he drove back to the flat he thought about moving in with Kate if he couldn't find anywhere else. Only a few hours ago he'd rung the rental agencies and received the same answer—nothing available in the district. So far the choices were: going into the city where there were rentals available, or staying with Kate for as long as it took to find what he required.

Moving to the city would be a drag when he worked out here. But sharing a house with Kate would be tricky. Exciting, sure, but despite that incredible sex he was still afraid of his heart being broken again. Because she had just got in deeper than ever and he still wasn't ready. Sharing her house would mean they'd more than likely carry on with what they'd started today. While he'd be on tenterhooks all the time, waiting for the crash, the damaged heart. Basically the whole nightmare he was determined never to face again.

So staying with Kate looked nigh on impossible. He wanted to kiss her, make love to her, again. Admit it, he wanted to get to know her better. To share day-to-day occurrences with her. Which meant setting himself up to be vulnerable.

Silly man. That could not happen. She was so beautiful inside and out it wouldn't take much for her to have him in her hand to do with as she pleased. It would be impossible to resist her, which would be fine until he remembered he wasn't prepared for a life partner and pulled back. They'd need to spend all their time avoiding each other. Not comfortable at all. And not easy to do when sharing a kitchen and a lounge.

The alarm went off and Kate rolled over in bed with a sigh.

Finn knew how to kiss like the devil. He'd stirred her up even more when he'd made love to her. Her body hadn't stopped craving him ever since.

Damn it, Finn. How do you do this to me?

Try as she might to deny the afterglow of last night, it was impossible. It was also impossible to deny that Finn was waking her up in unexpected ways, which would only lead to trouble because the day would come when she'd have to expose her insecurities. She'd been lucky last night not to have exposed the scars. They hadn't turned on the lights as there'd been enough moonlight coming through the window for them to carry on as they'd started. But if he wanted more from her, and she believed he might, she was ready for a lot of things but not to show him her body and have him stare at her as though she was the ugliest thing he'd ever encountered.

Okay, an exaggeration, but she'd been hurt by other

men who hadn't been able to refrain from saying the first thing that had popped into their miserable minds. She had to remember Finn would be protecting himself after his previous relationship.

The alarm repeated its loud drumming. Five minutes gone already, spent thinking about the one person she shouldn't be. Finn Anderson had a lot to answer for.

After a shower she dressed in jeans and a blue tee shirt before scoffing down tea and toast. She fed her dogs, and took them for a walk along the street as Rusty had little difficulty with his damaged leg now. After that she went in to work. The clinic only opened in the morning on Saturdays but no doubt she'd be called in some time over the afternoon. Mark said he'd take any calls once the barbecue was under way. She was grateful for his generous offer, though it didn't seem fair on his wife and kids. Then again, she'd covered for him three weekends ago when he'd had a family party to attend out of town.

'Hey, Di, I got your list of who's coming and what they're all bringing this afternoon, thanks.' They'd opened the door and already people were arriving with their pets. 'Doesn't seem like there's much for me to do.' She'd hit the grocery store after work to get snacks and mixes for drinks, plus some frozen desserts.

'You know how it works.' Di laughed as she brought their first dog of the morning into the treatment room with its owner. 'Tipsy's due for a parvo jab.'

Yes, thought Kate, she knew how everyone always brought more than enough for an army to eat, and the men shared the cooking on the barbecue while the women watched out for the kids and enjoyed a drink. It was always a good way for everyone to relax together and seemed to keep the usual staff grizzles at bay. This would be the first one Finn attended, and she was certain he'd fit right in. He did with everything else.

'Too well,' Kate decided as she watched him turning steaks on the barbecue, beer in hand, and laughing with the guys.

'He gets on with everyone, doesn't he?' Di was watching Finn too. 'Has he found anywhere to live yet?'

'Not yet. He's got another week left before he has to get out of the place he's renting.' By then hopefully he'd have found something because after last night she couldn't see them getting along comfortably while sharing her home unless they continued having a fling, something she was trying not to think about. 'I didn't realise how difficult it was finding rental properties out this way.'

'There aren't that many places to rent and it's harder in summer for some reason. I have heard that some townies think living out here will be wonderful, then along comes winter and they suddenly miss the lights of the city and the shorter drive home in the dark after work.' Di shrugged. 'I don't think Finn's one of those.'

'Definitely not.' He'd talked about living in Scotland and the freezing winters and lack of people around in the worst times, but not once had he said he hadn't enjoyed it. Except for the cold, he'd seemed to love his time there.

'I think it would be cool if he moved in with you.' Di gave her a wink. 'Who knows what might come of that?'

'Nothing,' she snapped. When Di grinned, Kate said, 'It can't. We work together.' Hell, even she was getting tired of that excuse. Especially after last night.

'So what? Mark and Dorothy worked together and look how that worked out.'

'They do have a great marriage.' Kate sighed. 'But they're them and I'm not looking for a partner at the moment.' Something else that was getting tiring.

'Kate, you got a minute?' Finn was walking across the lawn in her direction, wearing his serious face.

Her heart sank. This felt wrong. As if he was about to tip her world upside down. Hadn't he already done that? And didn't she feel a teeny bit excited about everything? 'Sure.'

'I'll start putting the salads out,' Di said and left her with Finn.

'What's up?' Her heart rate was rising rapidly. They couldn't live together in the same house. She needed to put space between them. Needed to remember how men had treated her in the past.

'This is not what I thought I'd be asking of you this soon, if at all. Especially now that we've got closer.' He drew a breath. 'Can I take you up on your offer?'

Her head spun. What to do? She had made the offer, but that was before they'd had sex.

'It's all right. I'll move to the city.'

'No, you won't.' She couldn't say no, could she? She'd have to find a way to protect her heart but she couldn't make him leave the district when he worked here. Besides, everyone would think she wasn't being nice when she'd already said it was fine. 'Come inside and I'll show you around.' If only they hadn't had sex. But they had, and now they had to get past it if Finn was going to share her home. Or they could go crazy and have lots of sex so she could get this need out of her system.

'I know this isn't what you wanted, but I've run out of options. It's a week sooner than I have to move but all the agencies say it's not looking hopeful. Also the owner hassles me every day to get out so he can do the few maintenance jobs that are part of the sale agreement, and, to be honest, I've had enough of him always asking if I've found somewhere to live.' Finn sounded flat, which was unlike him.

Turning to him, she said, 'It's all right. We'll make it work. I like having someone in the house. It gets a bit too quiet at times. That is, except when the dogs are super energetic. Though their conversation skills need some work.'

Finn smiled tightly. 'You're a champ. I know last night has made things awkward, but we're grown-ups, we can move on from that.'

'True.' Her heart plummeted. He was right. Only thing was, she would love some more of those kisses and the sex that had followed. Spinning around, she headed for the bedroom that was to become Finn's. 'Have you got your own furniture?'

Stepping into the room, Finn looked around. 'Not a thing. The last place came furnished.'

'No problem. The bedroom has everything you need.'

'You've got it all sorted, haven't you?'

'I try to be organised.' Didn't always work out but still. 'When were you thinking of moving in?'

'Tomorrow. If that's all right with you. Otherwise it'll have to be after work one night.'

She winced. Nothing like no time to get prepared, but then she probably never would be so might as well get it over and done. Once Finn was here, she'd be able to stop wondering how she'd cope, and get on with doing whatever it took. 'I'll get you the keys so you can bring your gear around any time you like. I'm on call tomorrow so might not be around all the time.'

Back in the kitchen she looked outside. Everyone was gathered around her large wooden table, filling plates with food. 'Looks like they're starting without us.'

'Come on. Let's join them and I'll get the keys before I go home.'

'If you forget, there's a spare back-door key hanging on the back of Rusty's kennel. He'll probably give it to you.' Rusty had followed him around the yard from the moment he'd turned up for the barbecue. 'He obviously doesn't blame you for his injured leg.'

'He seems fine now, doesn't he? I know he isn't running or going for long walks, but nor is he limping.'

Her boy was doing fine. 'Thanks to you.'

'I'll take that.' His smile lightened her further.

If a smile did that, how was she going to manage to stay on track with him living in the house? It might prove very interesting over the coming weeks. Or months? How long would Finn end up living here? He hadn't even unpacked a bag yet and she was wondering that? Time to get out amongst everyone and put some space between them. But as she stepped off the deck to join her friends, her hand touched her abdomen, reminding her why she got in such a pickle when it came to letting a man into her life. But Finn was only renting a bedroom, not moving into her bed—or her heart.

At the table, she grabbed a plate and concentrated on placing steak and salads and potatoes on it. Her head was spinning. Her heart was not getting involved. It couldn't be. Too risky. Somehow she felt if she truly started falling for Finn, she wouldn't be able to stop. It would hurt worse than ever when he walked away.

What if he didn't?

What?

Why wouldn't he? The man she'd loved so much that she'd believed they'd be together for ever had, so why would she expect another one to stay with her? But Hamish had already stopped loving her when she had been attacked by the stingers, and had only stayed with her afterwards because he'd felt guilty about her coming into the water to save him when he'd had an epileptic fit. 'I can't do this any more.' Yes, those words still reverberated around her head at times. That was when she'd finally learned he'd taken her to North Queensland for a holiday in the hope of finding he could still love her, and not because they had been so in love that he'd had to spend time away with her in an awesome location. His secretary had won in the end.

'You all right?' Finn asked quietly beside her. 'You've gone awfully pale.'

Glancing at him, she felt a tight squeeze in her chest. No, she wasn't all right. This man had also said something very similar last year. The words still reverberated around her head at awkward moments. *I'm sorry. I can't do this.* Even though his words weren't backed up with the same unbelievable truth that she was no longer loved by her man, they had the capacity to upset her all over again. Best to keep that to herself. 'I'm good. Need to eat some food, that's all.'

He stared at her in disbelief. 'I can move into the city,' he reiterated.

She was letting Finn down. Or he thought she was. 'No. Really, no. You're staying here.' Strange how that felt the right thing to say when her head and heart were in disagreement with each other. 'I mean it. In fact, let's let everyone know now.' Then there'd be no backing out on her part.

'Only if you are absolutely certain, Kate. I don't want to upset you.'

'Didn't I just say that I am certain?' He could see through her. Surely he had his own doubts about what he was about to do? If he didn't, then she'd read him wrong.

'Yes, you did. Okay, ready for this?' he asked through one of his gorgeous smiles.

'Totally.' She put her plate down and tapped the side of a glass with her fork. 'Listen up, everyone. Finn's moving into my spare bedroom tomorrow as it seems there're no rentals available around Darfield at the moment.'

'Need a hand moving your gear?' Mark asked.

Finn grimaced. 'What I've got goes in the back of the car just fine. I haven't been back in the country long enough to amass lots of furniture or anything else, but thanks for the offer.'

'Kate's got more than enough of everything inside this house,' Peter said.

'Make me sound like a kleptomaniac, why don't you?' Kate retorted. 'But I wouldn't mind if some of you did come tomorrow and help me move some furniture out to the storage shed.' She had been wanting for a while to have a bit of a clean-out but needed some manpower to lift the furniture.

'Count me in,' Peter said.

'And me,' Mark added. 'What time?'

'Sort it with Finn so he can have help lifting his cases out of his vehicle.' She tried to laugh as she picked up her plate. Not easy when she was suddenly in a flurry of nerves about Finn coming to live with her. 'Come on, everyone. Let's enjoy dinner.'

So I can pretend everything's all right and I am not worrying about how to deal with that sexy man wandering around my house at all hours.

She took her plate and sat down next to Sheree. 'How're you getting on with the wedding plans?' Their daughter was getting married in three months and Sheree had taken over organising everything.

'Not bad.'

As Sheree filled her in on everything, Kate tried to settle the nerves tightening her. It was official. Finn was going to be living with her. Everyone had accepted it as though it was an everyday occurrence. Which it probably was, even for her. She had been thinking about finding a new housemate, just hadn't expected to feel so disorientated by the one she'd got.

She looked around, her gaze coming to rest on Finn sitting with Mark and Campbell, Di's partner, chatting away as if he didn't have a worry in the world. Why would he? His housing problem had been solved. He was fitting in with everyone very well. He was back home for good. But there were times when she felt he struggled with feeling at ease with his life. Obviously he hadn't got over what his fiancée had done to him and was constantly on guard. He probably had as many trust issues as she did, if not more.

Sheree nudged her. 'He's quite a catch, isn't he?'

Kate swallowed as her face warmed. Why was everyone trying to pair her up with someone? Mentioning Finn as though it were the ideal answer to her problem? 'Good-looking for sure.'

'That's not what I meant.'

'No, I surmised it wasn't.'

'Kate, I know you've been hurt in the past so I get that you're not in a hurry to find a man to share your life with, but Finn might be worth taking a second look at.'

Here we go again.

Why couldn't her friends leave her to sort out her life herself? Because she hadn't done a good job so far? Probably.

'I hear you, but I'll make the decisions about my private life, thanks, Sheree,' she said with a smile. No way did she want to upset her friend, but neither did she need any interference over how she conducted her life.

Sheree laughed. 'Just giving you the heads up. Now I'll shut up.'

'Thank goodness for that,' Kate said before realising she was still watching Finn. Yep, he was definitely doing her head in, and he hadn't moved in yet.

CHAPTER SEVEN

'KATE, WE HAVEN'T discussed the rent,' Finn said the next morning, dumping his three cases in what was to be his bedroom. Over the hall from Kate's. Too damned close by far, but then it could be at the end of the street and it would be too close. How the hell was he ever going to get any sleep knowing Kate was so near to him?

When she gave him the figure, he said, 'That can't be right. It's way too low.' He wasn't here for charity.

Kate looked a little flummoxed. 'It's all I ask for.'

He tried for light-hearted. 'I get it. I do all the house-work, cook every meal and mow the lawns.'

'Bang on.' Her smile was tired, but at least it was a smile.

'Kate, it's still not too late to change the plan.' Though he'd be gutted if she changed her mind now. He'd spent a lot of the night thinking about it and knew it was the best option as long as Friday night didn't get in the way. There'd been a lot of reminiscing about that too, and how Kate had felt in his arms and how hot and wonderful her body had been as they'd made love. Getting to know Kate better had to be a good thing because deep down he felt something soft and caring for her. Something like love, though not really love. Because love was not allowed. Too dangerous for his heart.

Snap. No more smile. 'We are not going over this again. We've made an agreement and we're sticking to it. Anyway, it's too late. If you found something in the city you wouldn't be moving in today. You'd have to go shopping for furniture and everything else required to live in a house.' Turning her back on him, she strode inside, leaving him to deal with his gear.

'Fair enough,' he called after her, not sure if she'd heard.

A car turned into the driveway. He wasn't alone. Peter and Mark were here to help store whatever Kate wanted out of the house. They'd get on with the job and then he'd go give the flat one last tidy up, leaving nothing for the owner to complain about, and then come back to settle into his new abode. Hopefully he'd then get to spend time with Kate and talk about anything but the fact she didn't seem happy for him to be here.

Though it might be best to get over that hurdle sooner rather than later so they could move on more comfortably.

'Finn.' Kate was back, this time with both dogs at her side, as if they were bargaining chips or something.

'Aye?' He put out a hand to Sam and got a short nudge with his nose.

Kate's smile was firmer this time. The kind that always knocked on his heart. 'When you're finished putting my things in the shed, bring the others in for a coffee and left-over cake from the barbecue.'

Was this her way of apologising for being abrupt? She didn't owe him one, but he'd let it go as he didn't want to cause any more tension between them. 'Give us twenty minutes. There's not a lot to do.' She'd already pointed out what she wanted removed from the rooms.

'I've still got to give the flat keys back,' Finn told Kate an hour later when the guys had left. 'Do a bit of vacuuming.'

'I'll come and give you a hand,' she told him.

'That's not necessary.'

'Maybe, but I'd like to.'

He wouldn't argue. This was a way to get over the hurdle between them. 'Then let's get it done.' It would make the job less boring having Kate doing some of the cleaning. Face it, Kate made everything less boring just by being around.

'I'll take my car in case I get called in to the clinic.'

'Come with me, and if that happens I'll go with you.' It seemed pointless to take two vehicles to West Melton. 'Want me to put the dogs in their kennels?'

'They'll be fine in the yard. We won't be all day.'

But they were later than planned. When Finn pulled out of West Melton he noted Two Fat Possums, a bar slash café, in the row of shops, and made an instant decision. Pulling into the car park, he said, 'I'm starving. Let's have a late lunch.'

Spending time with Kate on neutral territory would be a way to quieten his busy mind and heart. He wasn't looking to ask a load of questions, but it would be good to clear the air by having a relaxed meal and light conversation. If that was possible.

'Good idea.' Kate was out of the ute in a blink, smoothing down her shirt and brushing her hair back behind her ears.

She looked good enough to eat. Yep, he was starving for

more than food. Now he'd become her housemate it was going to be harder not to follow up on those feelings, especially as his body knew hers a little better now. 'My shout.'

Her hair swished back and forth across her shoulders. 'I owe you for operating on Rusty.'

'You don't, but I'm not going to waste time arguing.' There'd be other opportunities to take her out for a meal. 'Have you been here before?'

'A couple of times. The food's great and there's great seating outside in a covered courtyard.'

'Not possum meat, I hope.'

'What else would they have?' She laughed, a deep, sexy sound that had him longing for her. Damn it, he had to get beyond these feelings or he'd never get a proper night's sleep while he lived in her home.

He went with seafood pizza even though Kate had been joking with him about possum meat.

'You don't trust me?' She grinned.

'Nope.' He could fall into that grin and not come up for air for a long time. 'I do enjoy a good pizza though. Like a beer? Or a wine?'

'I'll have a soda since I'm on call. What about you?' She had her cash card in her hand. Probably didn't trust him not to take over and pay for lunch.

'Same.' He went to find them a table in the outdoor area. She was right. It was shaded but warm, and the tables were spaced so that he didn't feel as if they'd be sitting so close to the next table that conversation would be impossible.

Kate placed the order number in its holder on the table, along with two sodas on mats. Sitting on the stool, she glanced around. 'I haven't been here for a while.'

'Where did you live before moving to Darfield?'

'After Hamish and I broke up I flatted in Lincoln while I saved to buy a house. I wanted something to call my own. It gave me security and confidence over what I chose to do.'

So her ex had made it hard for her to believe in herself. 'Running your own life, eh?'

She nodded. 'With no one to change the plan.'

'There's something secure in owning your own home.' One day he'd be able to do that again. Next time he'd make sure no one could take it away from him. Kate might not be the sort to do what Amelia had, but he would struggle to trust anyone that much again.

'There sure is.' Her soda was going down fast. 'I believed Hamish and I had that together. I know, that sounds trite, but that's how it was for me.'

'Nothing wrong with that. I felt that way about Amelia. My fiancée,' he added in case he hadn't mentioned her name when he'd told Kate about her.

'It puts the kibosh on trust, doesn't it?' Now there was a haunted look on Kate's face that twisted his gut.

'It sure does.' He wanted to say more but was worried he'd say something that'd upset her even further. Nor did he want to expose more of his distrust about relationships. Looking around, he saw the waitress approaching with their meals. 'Those look good.'

Kate settled further onto her stool, looking relieved. 'Sure do.'

They ate in silence until a young child at a table in the corner started crying and shoved his plate away. 'I don't like fish.'

'You did last week,' the man with him, presumably his dad, replied quietly.

'Did not.'

Kate smiled. 'The joys of parenthood, eh?'

'I wouldn't know,' Finn said quietly. When the truth came out, his heart had broken all over again.

'Would you like to be a dad one day?'

Absolutely. It would be wonderful. He filled his mouth with pizza. It wasn't happening.

Kate was looking at him with disappointment. She wanted to learn more about him. As he did about her. Okay, he'd do his best to open up a little and see where that went. But he sure as hell wasn't telling her how Amelia told him she was pregnant in an attempt to keep him with her until she found someone else to give her the life comforts and money she craved.

'I'd love to have a family to call my own. Little horrors running around my home and making me laugh and cry and adore them to bits.' How was that for a genuine answer? More than he usually put out there. 'I'm just not ready yet.' Not likely to ever be, but that was for him to know.

A glimmer of a smile appeared. 'Little horrors, eh? Dad used to call us those when we were very young. Usually followed up with an ice cream.'

'Must be a generational thing, because it was the same in our home growing up.' Something they had in common, apart from their careers, and broken hearts. 'Does that mean you'd like a family one day too?'

'Definitely.' Kate forked chips into her mouth.

Okay, he got it. Ask no more. For now. 'You've had a quiet day so far for being on call.'

Swallowing, Kate shook her head at him. 'Thanks. Bet I get something now.'

'Yeah, the moment the words left my mouth I knew I'd set you up.'

'That's how it works.' Taking a sip of her drink, she said, 'You seem happy to have moved out of that flat.'

'Now that I have, I am. I was never overly happy with the place, a bit too cramped, but it was somewhere to put my head down at night while I got organised with what I want long term. Unfortunately time ran out too soon.' He'd got into the groove of saving every dollar or pound he earned, first to pay off debts incurred by Amelia and then to build up some funds so he could buy a house or set up a vet practice in the near future.

Though that second option didn't seem as important now, since working at Darfield Animal Care was ticking all the boxes for him. It was a good practice with excellent vets, and the staff were friendly and focused. A glance at Kate reminded him who his favourite colleague was. Had he made a mistake moving in with Kate? Especially after their hot night at the clinic? Too late. Whatever the answer, he had already moved in. He'd keep looking for somewhere else in case this didn't work.

'I was a bit surprised when I saw the flat. It doesn't appear to have had any maintenance for quite a while.'

'Never, if you ask me. I don't think there's a lot of spare cash in that household. But I couldn't turn it down when I'd taken weeks to find somewhere to rent.' Finn ate the last piece of pizza and pushed his plate aside. 'That was perfect.'

Kate nodded in agreement. 'It's not a bad place for casual meals. I—'

Her phone rang.

Glancing at the screen, she shrugged. 'Guess it had

been too good to be true. Hello, this is Kate Phillips from Darfield Animal Care. How can I help you?'

Finn drained his glass. They were on the move. No such thing as a second round and more conversation about themselves. That had to be good, though he did like getting to know Kate. She was lovely, and while she had issues from the past she was getting on with her life. She had a job she seemed to love, and had bought her own home, had two dogs as well. He could learn from her. Was she content? Or did she get lonely at times? As he did after a long day at work and going home to an empty place to cook a meal with no one to share it with? At least that would be different for the coming weeks until he found a permanent place to rent.

Kate slid her phone into her pocket and stood up. 'I need to go to the clinic. A poodle has eaten her owner's pills. Quite a list of them, by the sounds of it.'

'No time to waste, then.'

Wish I'd brought my car, Kate thought as Finn drove them back to Darfield. She could do with a break from him. He was too much. Too sexy, too good-looking, too desirable. He'd only moved in today and she was already in a pickle.

'Want a hand with the poodle?' he asked.

'No, I'll be fine. Drop me off and head home.' Having him in the same space at the clinic was the last thing she needed right now. 'I'll walk back after I'm done.' Lunch at the Two Fat Possums had been great. They'd relaxed together, talked a bit more about themselves, but she could only take so much Finn air before her body started to get wound up and need release—with Finn. They needed to have a big argument over something so she'd have an excuse to ignore him.

Ha! She laughed. She really did come up with some mad ideas at times. All to protect herself from getting hurt.

'What's funny?'

'I have no idea.' It was the truth. It wasn't funny that she had to think of ways to keep Finn at arm's length. 'Just a random thing.'

'I see.'

Bet he didn't. Instead he'd probably be thinking she was a fruit loop. Which might have him looking harder for somewhere else to live. Then she'd be disappointed about that. No winning for Finn. Or her.

Yet when she got home after treating the poodle and there was no sign of Finn or his vehicle, she had to remind herself they weren't a couple and that he'd be coming and going as he pleased while staying with her.

A note sat on the bench.

Gone to see Mum and Dad, having dinner with them. Finn.

See? They were housemates. 'Okay, boys, let's go for a walk.' Grabbing the leads, she headed down the drive with her dogs running around her excitedly. Once they were clipped onto their leads, she opened the gate and turned towards the main road.

During weekends Darfield was quiet apart from the supermarket and takeaway outlets. The majority of retail properties were about farming equipment and supplies, and other outdoor requirements. As they walked past the bakery Kate sniffed the air and caught a whiff of something delicious she couldn't recognise. On the job late, by the smell of it.

Despite the burger and chips she'd had earlier, her stomach did a flip. Seemed it was hungry again. Around the corner she stopped at the Indian takeaway and ordered lamb korma for one, then continued walking her dogs along to the park where teenage boys were skating on the rink, making a racket as they did spins and flips.

Finally back at home she fed Rusty and Sam, then sat down in front of the TV with the korma to watch a crime programme. The house felt eerily quiet. The dogs lay in their beds as per normal. No traffic was going along the street. All perfectly usual and yet it seemed different. Because Finn would be here later and she couldn't wait to see him, to find out how they'd get along with this arrangement. Yes, she was totally out of sorts. He had got to her in lots of ways, the hardest to accept was that she was starting to think more of him than just a friend.

Whenever they'd worked together on a patient they'd been a team. No difficulties over who did what, or how either of them did a procedure. They just got on with what was required. She was always aware of him whenever he was near and that hadn't happened with other men she'd known since Hamish. He was continually in her head space, winding her up with an image of his to-die-for smile. As for his lovemaking—that was something else. Blood-heating, heart-pounding, toe-tingling kisses that had her yearning for more. A lot more.

Except for her there was one huge wall in the way of getting close and intimate. Her scars. Shoving her plate aside, she stood up and went to the bathroom where she lifted her tee shirt and lowered her jeans. The scars no longer horrified her. She was used to them. The problem lay in what men had said about them. Running her fingers over her skin, she stared at herself. Her skin wasn't rough. Enough time had gone by for the scars to soften. Unfortunately they hadn't lost much of the angry reddish pink colour, and that was what seemed to draw the attention of the men she'd tried to be intimate with.

Looking up, she studied her face. Her skin was perfect, nothing marring the light tanned shade. Her eyes were big and, yes, beautiful. Her lips were naturally full and sexy. But none of that mattered. It was what was on the inside that counted. When she was growing up, her parents had made certain she understood that, and mostly she'd agreed, though there had been a time in her teens when she'd got a bit too big for her boots and used her beauty to get what she wanted. It hadn't lasted long. She'd overheard two boys saying they wanted to get into her pants and see if the rest of her was as good, and from then on she'd made sure any guy she spent time with liked her for who she was, not only her face.

What would Finn think if he got to see her naked? Would he make awful comments like those she'd heard before? She couldn't see him doing that, but she could imagine him shuddering and turning away without a word—which was as horrific as what others had voiced. Guess she'd never know what his reaction would be because he wasn't going to see her without clothes on. So, end any thoughts about getting closer. They had to remain friends, no more, and hopefully no less.

Pulling her clothes straight, she went back to finish her dinner, only the korma didn't taste as appetising as it had a few minutes earlier.

It was nearly ten when the programme finished. Kate took the dogs out for a pee then let them back in to go to their beds. Leaving the outside light on, she had a quick shower and got into her bed with the crime story she was currently reading. When Finn got home she turned the bedside light off and snuggled down under the lightweight duvet, pretending all was well in her head.

Finn walking through the house and down the hall to his bedroom opposite hers said all was not quite as good as she'd like it. Finn was the man waking her up from what felt like a long sleep. It had been kind of like that over the months since she'd decided no more dating after the last man walked away. Not only was she waking up, but she was beginning to hope. She was already feeling a little bit in love with Finn, though not so much that she couldn't back away, and it was as though a whole new world was opening up. An exciting world where love was guaranteed, where children were included, and nobody gave her grief over something she couldn't change.

Dream on.

Early the next morning Finn parked outside the joint bakery café where they made the best ever breakfasts and right now he was starving. He hadn't slept well. The bed was perfect: firm yet soft. The house had been quiet except whenever the dogs did a lap of the hall, obviously making sure Mum was still there. But it was the goings-on in his head that had kept sleep at bay.

In other words, Kate. This morning he hadn't been ready to chat over toast as though everything were all right so here he was, about to order breakfast and then go in to work where he'd see Kate at the weekly meeting.

Kate was ruling him. Not that she'd be aware of it. He hoped not anyway. How had he got to this point when he was so determined never to fall in love again? Did he love Kate? No, he did not. But it felt as though he was well on the way. Living with her was making it difficult to keep the lid on his emotions.

'What would you like, Finn?' the woman behind the counter asked.

He recognised her as the owner of a herd of cows he'd vaccinated a couple of weeks ago. 'Bacon and eggs with hash browns, thanks, Heather. Plus a large long black double shot.' He desperately needed caffeine to wake him up fully.

'Coming right up.'

He had picked a quiet moment. No truckies in sight and too early for mothers stopping in for their morning fix after dropping the kids off at school.

'Got a lot on today?' Heather asked as the coffee machine hissed.

'I'm heading out to Rangiora later in the morning to look at some sheep with facial eczema.'

'Nice.'

'All part of the job.' He grinned, finally letting go some of the tightness gripping him.

'You can have it.' Heather placed a large mug in front of him. 'Breakfast won't be long.'

'No hurry.' Once he'd eaten he'd still be early arriving at the clinic and no doubt Kate would already be there. She seemed to like to get her day sorted before everyone else turned up. He hadn't heard her moving around the house when he'd left. Keeping low until he'd gone? His laugh was taut. They did need to get along normally or the days when he was in the clinic would be tough along with the evenings at the house.

'Morning, Finn. You left early.' Kate smiled warmly as he strode into the office forty-five minutes later.

'Morning. I was too late leaving Mum and Dad's last night to stop at the supermarket and get some groceries so I went to the bakery for breakfast.' That was true. 'I'm sure you wouldn't have minded if I helped myself to whatever was in the pantry or fridge, but I was starving and a big breakfast did the trick.'

'Your mum didn't feed you enough?' she asked.

'More than, but my appetite seems out of hand lately. Too much time spent walking around farms maybe?'

Hadn't he done that in Scotland? 'Better than being inside all day.' Her gaze cruised his body, heating him when that was the last thing he needed right now. Or any time.

What? He'd gone off sex? With a woman who had the ability to pull him in close emotionally? Absolutely. 'You'd like to be outdoors on the job?' So far she'd always said she preferred the domestic side to the work they did.

Her thick plait swished across her back when she shook her head. 'Not really. Winter can be harsh, and anyway I prefer dogs and cats to cows and bulls. Sheep are all right, but they're so dumb.'

'You want intelligent animals to treat?'

'If I have to talk to them when I'm checking them out, then of course I do.' She sounded serious but there was a mischievous gleam in her eyes. Lightening up?

The front door crashed open. 'Finn, give me a hand, will you?' Mark called. 'I've got an Alsatian in the back of my car that's been hit by a truck. Not looking good.'

Kate leapt to her feet. 'What can I do?'

'Open the operating room and turn on some lights,' Mark yelled, his voice full of dread.

'That bad?' Finn was tight behind him when he reached the back door of his SUV.

'Yep. Toby belongs to my neighbour. One of their kids left the gate open when she set off for school.'

The dog barely responded to being lifted out of the vehicle and carried inside between them. As soon as Toby was laid on the table Finn swung the X-ray machine above him. 'We'll start with finding out the real damage.'

'Broken back leg for a start,' Mark replied as he arranged the dog in a way that they could get a clear picture of his organs and ribs.

'Stand back,' Finn warned as soon as Mark was ready.

The X-rays showed three fractured ribs with both lungs perforated. Blood was oozing from Toby's mouth and his breathing was getting more laboured by the minute.

'What do you think?' Finn asked Mark.

'His owner said to do all I could to save him.'

'I'll help you with the surgery if you'd like.'

Mark's nod was abrupt. 'Thanks.'

'You two carry on here and don't worry about the meeting.' Kate spoke up behind them, giving Finn a fright. He'd forgotten all about her while dealing with Toby. 'Unless you want me to take your place, Finn?'

'No, I'm good here.'

'I know, but you have got a lot on today.' Her voice was tight, as though she'd prefer he didn't do this. She was in charge of the domestic side of the business after all.

But she had other things to do that he couldn't. Glancing her way, he found her watching him closely. 'I'll manage. Toby needs help now, and you've got a meeting to run.' It was true. Peter wasn't coming in this morning and it wasn't *his* place to run the meeting.

'Fine.' She left the room in a hurry.

So much for getting along. That had gone down the drain the moment an emergency cropped up. Turning to Mark, he asked, 'Want me to administer the anaesthetic?'

'You do that and I'll get ready to open Toby up. Hopefully we're not too late. His breathing doesn't appear to have altered much in the last few minutes.'

That had to be because it was already about as slow as it could be without actually stopping. Finn kept that to himself. Mark would be fully aware of the situation.

Much later, Finn tossed his gloves in the bin with relief. 'We did it.'

Mark high-fived him. 'We did. Thanks for your help.'

'Kate would've done the same,' he said.

'I know. But she's got a lot on today with Peter being away and the operating list chock-full. We don't usually do surgical bookings on Monday but there's been so many people wanting to bring their pets in for one thing or another we had to do an extra list.'

She hadn't mentioned that to him but then she didn't have to, he supposed. 'I'm going to grab a coffee and head out to Rangiora.' He wasn't hanging around where he wasn't needed. He and Kate would have enough time together tonight when they were at home.

'How did it go with the extra op list?' Finn asked Kate as he cleared the table after dinner.

'All good.' Peter had stunned her when he'd phoned early to ask her to step in for him as he had to take Sheree to the doctor. The man never stepped away from work no matter what arose in his private life. She'd phoned before heading home only to be told it was a false alarm and that Sheree was fine.

'I'd have been shocked if it wasn't.'

'What?' She stared at Finn, completely at a loss as to what he was talking about.

'Ah, hello, Kate. I mentioned the surgical list.'

She huffed out a breath. 'Sorry. I was miles away.'

His face tightened. 'So I see.'

'Finn, stop it. I was thinking about something else, that's all. Nothing to get your knickers in a twist about, okay?' Even to her, she sounded a bit harsh. 'Sorry again. I take that back. It's been a busy day.'

'It must've been, because I don't wear knickers. Not lacy G-strings, anyway.' His smile was tentative, as if he expected her to lose her cool again.

'You're saying you go commando?' Where the hell did that come from? This was Finn, the man she was trying to remain immune to, and she'd asked if he went without underwear? Bloody hell. She was in deep trouble if nonsense like that poured from her mouth whenever she wasn't being careful around him.

'No comment.' His smile was cheeky and not giving anything away as he wiped the bench and set the dishwasher to start.

The second night into the rental agreement and this was happening. Kate walked around Finn to get the kettle and filled it to make tea. Anything to keep busy and quieten her overactive mind. Holding a mug in both hands would keep them out of trouble. 'Want tea or coffee?'

'No, thanks. I'm going to watch something on TV. If that's all right with you,' he added sharply.

'Why wouldn't it be?' She spun around to face him, her

hip bumping into him. She reached out to steady herself and came up against his chest.

Her hands were instantly encased in Finn's and she was being drawn closer to his sensational body. Raising her head, she found him watching her with a longing that undid all her resolve to remain cautious. 'Finn,' she croaked over a suddenly dry tongue.

Beautiful suck-me-in brown eyes locked on him. 'Finn,' she whispered.

His breathing stopped. Just like that she had him in the palm of her hand. 'Kate,' he whispered back. But then that was what he'd wanted as he drew her in against his body. Wrapping his arms around her, he leaned back to look at her, to absorb her beauty and heat and sexiness. Instantly he was tight, so damned tight he ached for Kate. She was so gorgeous it was impossible to ignore these sensual feelings she engendered within him.

Before he could say anything more, her mouth was covering his, kissing him as though she'd been wanting this for ever. He knew how that felt, because he'd been longing for Kate from the moment he saw her when he walked into the clinic on his first morning working there. Of course he'd denied it, but it was true. Had been all along. And having sex with her the other night had not dulled the need one little bit. Now he was returning her kiss like a starved man. Which he was. Starved for love and sex and being part of someone's life.

Damn, she tasted wonderful. Felt even more wonderful. Her body was soft and strong, hot and warm, demanding and giving. He leaned in closer, held her tighter, and continued kissing her while losing all thought about anything but Kate.

Until she slid her mouth away and looked directly at him.

His heart sank. She was bailing.

'Your room or mine?'

Did he just hear right? 'Yours.' His bed wasn't as big as hers. Yes, he had seen inside her bedroom to know it was very feminine and the bed ever so welcoming with its big, soft eiderdown.

His hand was in Kate's and he was being pulled down the hall into her room and then they were on the bed, back to kissing while their hands began exploring each other.

Then Kate stopped.

'What's up?' Apart from his erection.

She got off the bed and closed the curtains. Returning to the bed, she lifted the cover. 'Let's get underneath this. I'm a bit cold.'

'Sure.' Though every part of him was on fire, he'd agree to anything right this moment.

Then they were under the cover, legs entwined, hands and mouths busy, and he had no idea whether it was hot or cold. Just damned sexy. 'Kate, you're beautiful,' he murmured as he kissed his way down between her breasts.

She stilled, her mouth paused on his neck.

What had he said wrong? She *was* beautiful.

Then her tongue slid over his belly button and she relaxed. So did he. So much so she drove him to the peak with her tongue, licking, touching, bringing him to the brink.

'Slow down,' he groaned and lifted her over him so he could touch her and keep her from driving him insane with need. Then he touched her moist sex and knew little after that, other than when Kate climaxed she cried his name on a husky tongue and tightened around him as if she'd never let go. He drove deep inside her again and again until he couldn't hold back any longer and let go to the heat and need expanding throughout him. 'Oh, Kate, sweetheart, you are beautiful.'

Why did she shiver when he said that?

The next day at work Kate wondered if Finn was avoiding her as she didn't see him once at the clinic. He did have a busy schedule but he usually came in at the end of the day to top up whatever drugs or equipment he might've used. Was he having second thoughts about where their *friendship* was heading?

Please not that. So far their lovemaking had been beyond amazing. There'd been a moment when she'd nearly freaked out last night when she'd realised Finn would be able to see the scars if she didn't darken the room. Pulling the curtains had made all the difference and relaxed her to continue having a wonderful time. Later, when they had been lying curled up together, she'd kept a tight hold on the duvet for fear it might fall away, and when Finn had got out of bed saying he was going to his room the relief had been quick to appear. As much as spending all night together appealed, she wasn't ready for him to see her scars.

Until now she'd always forewarned the few men she'd slept with but she couldn't bring herself to do that with Finn. She liked him too much. To watch him walk away would be harder than ever to cope with. He was special. Of course it would happen. It always did, but first she wanted as much time with Finn as she could get. Which might be seen to not being honest with him. She shivered at that thought. She was always honest. But her heart was in danger here, and that came first. Though she was risking it by having so much time with Finn, she still worried he might already be changing his mind about their fling.

When she got home that night Finn was already there and preparing steaks and salad for dinner.

She relaxed. She'd been overthinking everything, as per usual. 'Hey. You're busy.'

He threw her a grin. 'Hope you like baked potatoes.'

'I like anything I don't have to cook. How long before you want dinner? I've got to take the dogs for a walk.'

'I did that when I got in. They were champing at the bit to get out so I figured it was the least I could do to make them happy.'

'Talk about a perfect housemate.' He didn't have to do that. 'I'll have a shower, then.' At least he couldn't say he'd done that for her.

'I'll pour you a wine while you're doing that.'

'You haven't got a beer.'

'I was waiting for you to get home.'

There was a skip in her step as she made her way to the bathroom. Finn made her feel happy with his easy way of getting on doing things. Having him here was getting better by the day.

She'd be quick in the shower and join him to make the most of everything.

'How do you like your steak?' he called after her.

'Medium rare.' Was there any other way?

'Perfect.'

No, Finn was the perfect one around here. She glanced over her shoulder and found him watching her with a smile.

She'd bottle that and take it out whenever they weren't seeing eye to eye, which, hopefully, wasn't often.

CHAPTER EIGHT

SATURDAY DAWNED BRIGHT and sunny. The mountains in the background were clear. Kate had a bounce in her step as she walked the dogs around town before breakfast. Since Finn moved in it had become her new way of walking, happy and light. 'You're going to be home alone, guys. I'm going to the school fair.'

If they were lucky Charlotte would pop over, though she was going to the fair with her friends from school too. 'I'll take you for another walk when I get home,' she promised.

Back at home she headed for the shower. Finn had already left as he and Mark were setting up the vet clinic's stall at the school. It felt strange to be able to wander around the house in only her towel, something she hadn't done since he moved in. The sex was plentiful and breathtaking every time. So far she'd managed to keep her secret by staying under covers or not stripping off completely, but it couldn't last. She knew that, and dreaded the moment she'd have to explain what had happened in Northern Queensland. The longer she put it off, the harder it would be when the time came to open up with Finn.

She threw bread into the toaster, and made some tea, then sat on a stool while she waited for the toast. The benches were spotless, and not a single cup or knife lay in the sink. Finn was very tidy, whether that was his norm or he was being ultra careful in her place, she didn't know. He usually cleaned up after himself at work, so this probably was his way. Which had her making sure she put anything she used straight into the dishwasher and not in the sink to rinse later. Talk about getting around on tiptoes whenever he was here.

The phone rang. 'Hi, Di. What's up?'

'Can you grab the box of toys from behind my desk on your way here? I forgot them in my hurry to get home last night.'

'No problem.' Time to get cracking. 'Are you already at the school?'

'Yes, and it's busy. Not only with stallholders setting up, but people with their pets are turning up already and the fair doesn't open for another hour.'

'That's enthusiasm for you. Right, I'm on my way.' As soon as she swapped the towel for jeans and a shirt, and got the dogs into the car, because now it did seem like a good idea to take them. They could do some socialising, which always went down well and also exhausted them so they slept for hours afterwards.

Finn saw Kate pull into the car park and went across to get the large box Di had asked her to pick up, wondering what sort of reception he'd get. Lately Kate sometimes seemed to run hot then cold as if she was hiding something from him, and that raised alarms. He couldn't bear the thought she wasn't completely honest with him.

Like he'd told her everything about his past?

His shoulders sagged. Good point.

'Morning. Oh, hello, you two.'

Her dogs were on the back seat of her car. He reached in and put leads on them. 'You're having a family day out, eh?'

Rusty bounded off the seat and around his legs, followed quickly by Sam. Finn kept hold of the leads in case they decided to do a runner. Though he doubted that would happen, they weren't used to being in crowds as far as he knew.

'I decided they might as well be here as at home alone. They're usually well behaved around people and other dogs.' Kate had the boot open and was lifting out a huge carton.

'That what Di wanted?'

'Yep.'

'Here, you take the dogs and I'll get that.'

'Cheers. It is heavy.' With the leads in one hand, she picked up a small backpack in the other. 'Some of the emergency equipment I've brought just in case something happens to an animal.'

'Or someone brings their pet for a check-up.' He laughed. Doing a lot of that lately. 'I hear we'll get a bit of that. Freebies all round.'

'Peter mentioned it to me too. He says that we'll pick up some new clients through it so it's no big deal.' Kate walked beside him, keeping the dogs on her other side, obviously happy too. 'I'm actually looking forward to the day. It's quite different from a normal work one.'

'Hi, Kate. Glad to see you've brought your dogs,' a woman of similar age to Kate called out as she came towards them.

'Hey, Lisa. You manning the dog training tent?'

'I am for the first couple of hours, then some more in the afternoon.'

'Lisa, this is Finn Anderson. He's working with us now.' Kate turned to him. 'Lisa and a friend run dog classes for all ages.'

'Hello, Lisa. Do you get a lot of attendees?' Dog training was big business, though whether that was the case out here in Darfield he had no idea.

'Unbelievable the number who come. It never used to be as busy in previous years, but I think more people are getting dogs and aren't always up to speed on training them.'

'I can believe that. There seem to be more dogs going through the clinic than I expected too.' He loved dogs and would get one once he was more settled. A sideways glance at Kate and longing gripped him. Spending the past week sharing her house had opened him up to the possibility that he could finally let go of the past that held him stuck in his belief he couldn't trust another woman to care about him as much as he cared for her. If only he didn't have this nagging sense she might be holding something back, that was.

Kate must've picked up on his thoughts because she gave him a quick glance followed by one of her devastating smiles. 'It's a fact—more people are taking dogs into their homes and lives than ever before.' Then she turned back to Lisa. 'Sorry, but we'd better keep moving. I've still got more cartons to get out of the car and set out in our stall.'

'Probably see you later on. We need to arrange a shopping trip,' Lisa told her.

'Good idea.'

'A shopping trip, eh?' Finn grinned.

'You bet. Not that I *need* any new clothes, but, hey,

why not?' Kate looked a little embarrassed. Not used to spending up large?

Finn laughed. 'You're female. Clothes shopping is a given with most of you. And your friend Lisa is at the top of the list for that. Or are you better at it than her?'

'No comment.'

'In other words, yes.' Bet she didn't put her money into the gambling machines in the hope of buying something glamorous and expensive.

Down, boy. That was uncalled-for. You know Kate is careful with her money.

She had a mortgage to pay off, for one.

'The op shops like me when I get around to having a clean-out of my wardrobe.' Her face flushed redder. 'Not that I do it very often.'

'Hence the full wardrobe in the third bedroom.' He'd put his empty cases in that room the day he'd moved in and unpacked. They hadn't fitted into the wardrobe for all the clothes already taking up space.

'We balance each other out. You had three cases when you came to my place. They'd only be a start for me if I had to pack up and move.'

'Guess you're not shifting house any time soon, then.'

Her smile dipped. 'Probably not.'

And he'd thought she was more than happy with her house. Guess he didn't know her as well as he thought. On a positive note there was time ahead to improve on that. He did not want to go back to the awkward atmosphere that had hung over them some nights after work last week. They mightn't be getting into a relationship but they could do better than they'd managed so far. 'Good, I'm safe for a while.' He gave her a big smile to show he was not trying to be a pain in the backside.

'Just don't ask for more space for clothes, or you might have a problem.' Her smile had returned, though a little tentative. Then she changed the subject away from herself.

'If you do decide to get a puppy, then I strongly advise you using Lisa and Mary's training school. They have a very good reputation.'

'Good to know.' So Kate remembered him saying weeks ago that he would like to have a dog. What else did she remember? Hopefully he hadn't said anything too personal during the times they'd been together away from work. He did tend to keep a firm brake on what he told people about his past, but Kate had a way of getting under his radar without even trying.

Face it. That was something that he liked about her. Her ability to have him talking about things that he usually kept close to his chest made him feel he'd found a woman who wasn't all about herself and would not use him for her own purposes. But then he also hadn't met a woman since Amelia who brought him alive in a rush of heat and need so that he struggled with keeping her strictly in the 'friend with benefits' mode, which was worrying. Especially now, when he wondered if Kate was being as open as he'd first believed. He didn't want to move away but it might come to that to protect himself from falling in love and being hurt.

As they neared the clinic's stall, Rusty bounced around in a circle. 'Settle, boy. That's Di, yes, and you know you have to behave around her and everyone else.'

Di came over and rubbed both dogs on their heads. 'G'day, guys. Thanks for the box, Kate. We're nearly set up and there's a large space on the stand for all these toys to go.'

'I'll give you a hand with them,' Kate said. 'I'll just tie these two up somewhere out of everyone's way for now.'

Finn put the carton down and went to see how Mark was getting on with the table they'd use when anyone brought a pet in to be checked over. 'Looks like you're all sorted.'

'Took five attempts to get the legs straight, but hopefully it'll be good now. We can hang back and wait for the fun to start.'

'It'll probably be more waiting than doing.'

Kate's laughter came from behind him. 'From what everyone's told me we're in for a busy day. I thought I warned you.'

'I hoped you were exaggerating.'

Mark shook his head. 'Not likely. See, here we go and it's not even nine o'clock.'

Finn looked around to find a teenage girl carrying a cat basket walking towards them. 'Hi. I'm Finn, a vet. Does your cat need something?'

'Hi, Finn. I'm Samantha and this is Lucky and she's been crying all night. Not like her at all. I can't find anywhere that she's hurting though.'

The cat had been crying and he had to check it over? He looked at Kate and got a smug smile for his effort.

Right, you're on, girlfriend. I'm going to give this cat the best going-over it's ever had.

Crying could suggest something serious. Or a teenager who wanted attention via her pet. Then it struck him what he'd thought. Girlfriend? Kate? Not likely.

Swallowing hard, he turned to the girl. 'Come over to the table and I'll examine Lucky.'

'Sure. What's it like being a vet? I've always wanted to be one but Mum says it's not always nice when you have to do awful things to the animals.'

Again he glanced across to Kate and felt heat in his face when she grinned at him as if she were saying 'told you so', which she hadn't, but still. She'd pay for that. In the nicest possible way, of course. He'd make sure she cooked dinner tonight, or bought in takeaways. 'Well, Samantha, your mother's right to a point, but there are many more times when it's the best job ever. Think of making a dog wag its tail again after having been hurt, or hearing a cat purr when you put her kittens on her belly.' He lifted Lucky out of the crate, and had to hold her tight when she tried to do a bunk. 'Hey, Lucky, no, you don't.'

Samantha reached for her pet and held her close while smoothing her fur. 'There you go, Lucky. This vet's going check you out to see why you cry so much.'

'Hold her on the table so I can feel all over her body.' He waited until Samantha had the cat on her haunches, still with a firm grip on it, before he began to carefully touch along her spine, then her ribs, and next her legs. 'All good so far.' Not a single reaction. 'Now I want to touch her stomach. She might not like that so be ready to hold her tighter.' Again no reaction. Finn straightened up. 'I think there's nothing wrong with Lucky. Maybe she's not crying but singing to you.'

Samantha stared at him. 'You think I don't know a cry when I hear it?'

Ouch. He needed to be more careful about what he said. 'Sorry, I know you do, but Lucky didn't get distressed whenever I pressed her firmly and she would've if she had any serious injuries.'

Samantha suddenly smiled. 'Thanks, Doc. I mean, you are an animal doctor, aren't you? I'll take her home and bring my dog in for you to check out.' She swung Lucky up and into her basket. 'See you soon.' And away she went.

She was barely out of earshot when Kate and Mark started laughing.

'That went well, Doc,' Kate said through her laughter. 'This is starting to look like it might be a fun day.'

'Your turn next.' Finn grinned. 'I'll be right behind you, taking in every word you utter.'

'As long as it's not Samantha and her dog, though I suspect she'll want you to deal with that one.'

Di was laughing too. 'You forgot to try and sell her a toy for her cat.'

'Great. Now I've got to be a salesman as well.'

'And a dietician.' Kate pointed to the array of bagged dry pet food, then tapped other containers. 'These are bones, by the way.'

'I'm going to the coffee cart,' Mark interrupted them. 'Anyone want a hot drink?'

'I'll come with you,' Finn said when the order grew to five coffees of varying types. He'd have gone if Mark was only getting one. He needed to get away from the women giving him a hard time about how he wouldn't know a plastic bone from a real one.

'I can't believe how fast the day went,' Finn said as he helped Kate unload the boot of her car at the clinic after everyone had packed up the stall once the crowd had finally dispersed. 'The hours flew by.' It was now nearly five.

'That's because it was a lot of fun,' Kate answered as she hefted a carton half full of toys out of her boot. 'We sold a lot of these.' The carton contained the remainder of what had been in four boxes at the start of the day.

'Anyone would think it's Christmas the way sales went.' He stretched his back and rolled his shoulders before lifting the medical equipment out of the boot and closing it. 'I'm looking forward to a drink on your deck when we get home and watching the sun go down behind the mountains—if we're not too late.'

Bit of a mixed message there. Your deck and then he'd said home as if it were his too. Despite his concerns in a way it was, but becoming to feel more and more like the go-to place when he was ready to unwind after a hectic day—with Kate, of course.

She dumped the carton in the storeroom and headed outside again. 'See you there, then. First one home pours the drinks.'

'Or grabs the shower.' He stank after all the dogs, cats and guinea pigs he'd held and lifted and rubbed.

Kate laughed and leapt into her car. 'See you there.'

In the shower? Now there's a thought.

He'd love nothing more than to slip in behind her and lather that beautiful skin with soap. But first a challenge hung between them. 'You're on.'

Too late. She was halfway out of the entrance and heading for home.

Home. There it was again. Something he hadn't really had since his relationship with Amelia went south. He'd loved that feeling of belonging—to his home, to Amelia, to his life really. Except for Amelia, he missed it all. Even the bad days because they were as integral to life as the good ones. Since he'd moved into Kate's house there'd been more good than bad, but it had only been a week.

They mightn't get along perfectly but they got along well enough for him to now be following her back there for a shower and a drink on the deck, ignoring his concerns.

He wasn't rushing, letting her get ahead, while he relaxed in the warmth exuding from his body. Perhaps he'd barbecue the chicken he'd bought at the supermarket yesterday, make a salad and bake some spuds to go with it all. Funny how his enjoyment for cooking had returned. Another small sign he was letting go the past and moving on as he'd hoped to.

When he parked up and went inside he could hear Kate singing to herself in her bedroom. 'You done with the bathroom?' he called.

Had he been that slow driving back? She usually had long showers. He'd often been tempted to join her under the water but sensed she might not appreciate that. So far he hadn't seen her fully naked. Somehow she always managed to remain partially covered with the duvet or clothes. Was that behind what she wouldn't talk about? If she *was* hiding anything. Whatever it was about, he didn't want to ask for fear of losing the closeness they had created together. See? She had got to him all too easily, which made him happy and wary all in one.

'Sure am. I feel so much better.'

The air was warm and moist in the hall outside her bedroom. The scent of roses teased him, heated parts of him that needed to remain cool. But couldn't. Kate did that so fast sometimes it was a wonder he could still walk.

The shower was on hot. Flicking it to cold, he got under the water and groaned as the chilly water poured all over him. Damn, it was freezing. Gritting his teeth, he withstood the chill until his skin was covered in goose bumps and the need tightening him lessened, then he flicked the tap back to hot, and got on with scrubbing himself hard all over in an attempt to keep Kate out of his mind. It worked to a point where he was finally clean and calm enough so that when he wandered out to the deck she didn't appear to notice anything out of the ordinary about him.

'Here, I got you a beer, but if you'd prefer a wine I can pour one.' She passed him a glass and a bottle, her smile beautiful, her eyes shining.

She was dressed in butt-hugging jeans that left nothing to his imagination, and a blouse that drew his eyes to the line between her breasts. 'Beer's good,' he said and took it from her. The bottle was cold, the beer chilly as it ran down his throat, but it did nothing to cool the parts of him that were overheating.

'It's been a fun day. Nothing like I'd expected,' Kate told him. 'I knew we'd be busy with people wanting us to see their animals, but I hadn't realised so many kids would be coming up to us wanting to show how great their pet was compared to everyone else's. It was sweet.'

'Even Samantha with her pets, and then her grand-father's dogs, was fun once she got over trying to impress us all.'

'A vet in the making, I wonder.' Kate was standing right next to him and he could still smell roses.

'Were you like that as a teenager?'

'What? Chatting up the male vets in town?' She grinned. 'No way. I was too shy.'

'You? Shy? I don't believe it.' Somewhere along the way that had changed. There was nothing bashful about Kate. She did get hesitant at times when her past was mentioned but that was nothing to do with being shy. And today she'd been full-on happy and laughing with everyone and joining in all the races with pets, taking one or the other of her dogs with her. An ideal woman, if only he could trust her completely with his heart.

'Kate, sweetheart, you are beautiful.' Kate lay on her stomach, pressed up against Finn's gorgeous body, and breathed deep. Could Finn make love or what? That had been an amazing experience. The best lovemaking in for ever. There'd been no hesitation. He seemed to always want her for herself, not her beautiful face, but then he still hadn't seen what usually messed with her hope of love. Her fingers were spread across the scars. By not having to watch the horror appear in his eyes when they made love, she felt Finn had given her something so special she'd give him her heart if he would only open up to her more. Something she knew he wasn't doing, no matter how close they were getting.

'What are you smiling about?'

She blinked. So much for thinking he'd nodded off. 'That was amazing.'

'It was.' He leaned in and kissed her lightly. 'Is. I'm still feeling it.'

Laughter bubbled up her throat and spilled out between them. He really did make her feel so good. 'The perfect ending to a great day.'

'Who says that's the end of it?'

Her eyes widened. This was definitely different from anything she'd experienced in the past few years, even when she was still with Hamish. She shivered. This was not the time to be thinking about her ex. That was insulting to Finn, and her. Getting in a knot about her ex was spoiling this wonderful time with a man she was getting to care for more every day.

Rolling onto her side, she reached for him, and caressed him until he was tight and throbbing once more, making her hot and horny too.

Then Finn moved, and flipped her onto her back, touched her once and she was right there, ready and pulling him into her.

Finn woke to the sound of the shower door closing. A light sound that shouldn't have disturbed him so he must've been waking anyway. Reaching out to the other side of the bed, he felt the warmth where Kate had been lying. A picture of her under the spray of the shower had him up and striding to her bathroom in an instant. He was going to do this. It was another step in letting go of his fears. The urge to hold her against him, run his hands over that hot wet skin while he kissed the back of her slim neck, was huge. Damn, he was hardening again. Unbelievable.

Kate was standing under the shower, her face turned upward, her arms crossed under her breasts, her back to the door.

Sliding the glass doors apart, he stepped in behind her and slid his arms around her, tucked her in against him.

Kate instantly froze. 'Finn?'

'Who else?' What was going on here? Every muscle in her body felt tense. 'Kate, what's wrong?' He kept holding her. She hadn't pushed him away and he sensed she needed his strength, though why he had no idea. 'Kate, has someone hurt you in the past?'

Her shoulders rose, then dropped again.

He waited.

Slowly Kate turned in his arms, her face devoid of any emotion. But her eyes were fixed on him. She was waiting for something—from him.

Leaning in, he brushed a light kiss on her mouth before looking down her body to where her arms were tight against her upper abdomen. Below them scars crisscrossed all over her skin. Unreal. Her skin was a mess. But it was only skin. This was still Kate. Looking up, he gasped.

Her face was frozen, though pain was starting to emerge. She was terrified he'd make some obscene comment. He knew it, which meant someone else already had. 'Kate.' With one hand, he rubbed her back lightly. With the other he lifted her arms away, then touched her stomach as gently as possible. 'You are the most beautiful woman I've ever known.'

Her eyes widened but still she said nothing.

Leaning down, he kissed light trails all over her front, touching the scars, her breasts and neck.

He touched her breastbone. 'Beauty is on the inside too.'

'Too?'

'Absolutely. These scars are skin-deep, Kate. How you got them might've been horrendous. I don't know yet, but they don't make any difference to the wonderful woman I know.' Was this behind her mood swings? If so, surely she'd have realised he'd find out some time?

Tears coursed down her face, making his heart ache for her. 'I have changed since this happened. Men saw me as beautiful until I exposed myself in front of them.'

Hence why she kept the covers on the bed when they made love. 'When were you going to show me?' It did hurt that she hadn't done so at any point since they'd got together sexually. Not that she'd think about it when they were making out, but surely afterwards she would have?

'Did you think I'd treat you badly too?' Face it, trust was one of her issues and he understood that well, so he couldn't really get too upset about this.

Kate looked away, and drew a breath before locking her eyes on him again. 'I'm sorry. I kept putting it off because we were getting on so well and I didn't want that to stop.'

Fair enough. He understood too well, and could swallow his pride. 'Come here.' He wrapped his arms around her and held tight until the water started going cold. Reaching behind Kate, he turned it off and opened the shower, not letting her go. 'Come on. Let's get dry and tucked up in bed where it's warm.'

When she got out of the shower with him, he sighed in relief. She'd been so afraid of his reaction it made his blood boil. Obviously someone had been insulting about those scars. Someone? Or more than one man she'd tried to get close to? Who were they? Give him five minutes alone with them and they'd never do something so horrid again.

Picking up a towel from the rack, he began to rub her all over, drying her, showing her he didn't give a damn about the marks on her skin. Why would he? 'They're skin-deep, Kate, nothing more,' he repeated. He had to ignore how he felt about her not having told him from the start because he did want to move forward and trusting Kate had to be a part of that.

Nothing more than skin-deep.

Kate burst into tears again as she stared at this man drying her off. Not once had she seen his eyes widen in horror. There hadn't been a glimmer of shock. Finn accepted her as she was. Just like that. If she hadn't already begun falling for him, then she was certainly getting in deep now.

Then he wrapped her in her robe and swung her up in his arms to carry her back to bed. When they were both under the cover Finn pulled her close. 'How long ago did this happen, Kate? If you want to talk about it, that is.' He sounded cross, as if she'd let him down.

But then she had. She'd always been ready to explain if anyone asked, but so far no one had. Instead they'd thrown their hands up in horror, made awful comments and disappeared out of her life. Then along had come Finn and she'd wanted to hold onto him for as long as possible.

'It was when Hamish and I were in Northern Queensland on that holiday I mentioned weeks ago. It was stinger season.' She knew her voice sounded flat, emotionless, but it was how she coped when telling the few people she had about what had happened.

Finn shuddered. 'I've heard those creatures can be nasty.'

'They are. All the beaches have stands where bottles of vinegar are placed so that if you get stung you can pour it on the area to relieve the pain.' Vinegar hadn't helped her that day. 'Hamish went in swimming despite the warning signs saying it was stinger season. Though he did wear a full wetsuit. He's an epileptic, and he had a fit while he was in the water. He'd gone quite a way out.'

She could see him now, splashing in the water, trying to wave to her and not succeeding. Fortunately she had seen what was happening. 'I saw him go under and thought that wasn't right somehow. When he came up again I recognised what was happening and raced in to haul him out, shouting for help as I went.'

Finn's arm tightened around her. 'You weren't wearing a wetsuit?'

'No. I had no intention of getting into the water at all, given it was stinger season. The surf lifesavers came out immediately. First they got Hamish out and while two dealt with him one came in for me. I was thrashing and screaming, trying to rush up onto the sand, but the pain from the stingers was unbearable. The guy dragged me onto his board and paddled like fury back to shore where someone poured vinegar all over me and others dried me and gave me water. Not a lot anyone could do, except wait to get me into an ambulance.'

She paused to let it sink in with Finn. She still couldn't believe he wasn't throwing his hands up in horror, and she well knew what to look for. 'I spent two nights in hospital and was told most people lose all trace of the scars over a period of time.'

'You were one of the unlucky ones.' He brushed a kiss on the top of her head. 'That must've been hard.'

'Not at first. I didn't get stung anywhere but my front between my bikini top and thighs. I mean, it's not as though my face was made to look awful. That would've been difficult because everyone would see and I know now their reactions would've been uncomfortable to say the least.'

'So what happened for you to change your mind?'

The hardest part of the whole episode.

'Hamish.'

Go on, get it over.

'At first he was sympathetic, and said he felt bad because if he hadn't had a fit then I wouldn't have gone into the water. It's not like he could help it. I'd do it again if I had to. It's what people do. Some people,' she added with a hint of bitterness. 'Sorry, but I still get upset.'

'You're allowed to. It's normal.' Finn brushed a kiss over her mouth, just like other times, no change. No withdrawal.

'Then three months later Hamish left me.' She could still see the look of despair on his face, as if he'd been doing his best by her and she'd failed him somehow. 'One night he was being snippy and when I asked what his problem was, he said he couldn't take it any more and that he was leaving. With that he got up off the sofa, went to his office by our bedroom to collect two cases of clothes he'd pre-packed and walked out the door.' She drew an unsteady breath and took another look at Finn to make sure she hadn't read him wrong, that he wasn't put off by any of her story.

He looked thoughtful, and when he noticed her watching him he asked, 'He left because of what happened in Queensland?'

'No. He'd only been staying on because it was his fault I went into the water and got so badly stung. Hearing that hurt as much as anything. The last thing I needed was for him to hang around out of guilt and nothing to do with loving me. That was over. His secretary was more alluring.' Kate couldn't help it. She smiled. 'She didn't stay around long. Got a new job and a new man.'

'No wonder you're smiling.' Finn smiled, then grew serious. 'Going back to when we met, I now understand why you looked like I'd stuck a knife in your chest that night I backed away from our kiss.' He sounded sad and apologetic all in one. 'I'm sorry, Kate. As I said at the time, that had nothing to do with you. It was me dealing with what

Amelia had done and how I was nowhere near ready to get involved with another woman.'

Kate looked hard at this man who was making her the most comfortable she'd ever been with her body since that horrible day in Australia. 'I think I started to figure that out the night you told me what she'd done to you. You had no idea what I was hiding either.'

'Kate.' He paused. 'I get why you never let me see your body at first, but surely you must have known the time would come when I would see and want to know what had happened?'

'Yes, I did.' She sat back and clasped her hands together in her lap. This would go one of two ways. She could only hope Finn would continue to be understanding. 'The few times I was intimate with men I told them first, figured it would make things easier.'

'It didn't?'

'They both looked horrified but said things like it didn't make any difference. One of them I never saw again after the first night. The other guy hung around for a few days pretending he was coping but eventually he left too.'

'You didn't trust me enough to do the same? I did notice how you always kept covered when we weren't pressed so close together I couldn't have seen you anyway.'

Here we go. 'The first time we made love, it just happened. We were upset about putting down those horses and got together in a hurry. Raising the subject would've been a passion killer for sure.'

Finn was watching her with an unreadable face.

That hurt, but she couldn't really blame him. Digging deep, she continued. 'After that, I wanted to be with you so much I put it off. Being intimate with you has been so wonderful, and has made me happy about myself, and you. I should've told you. I know that. But I kept thinking one more time and then I'll tell him.'

'You have trust issues, too.'

Not the answer she was expecting, but then this was Finn and she didn't do well when it came to reading him. 'I do. We do.'

'I can't promise not to hurt you, Kate, but, believe me, it won't be deliberate if I do.'

'I can live with that.' Not that she knew where they were going with their relationship yet.

'You do understand you're beautiful, don't you?' Finn slid a hand under her robe to lie on her abdomen, making her relax further. 'These are a part of life, a sign that you're kind and put others before yourself. Wear them with pride, Kate.'

She stared at him. 'You are amazing.' He had no idea what he'd done for her. 'Thank you so much.'

'For what? Being honest? That's easy.' He wrapped her in a hug and held tight.

Kate could not believe this. All she'd ever wanted from a man was to be accepted for all parts of her and here Finn was showing it was possible. She burst into tears. Doing that a lot tonight.

He rubbed her back as she sobbed. Another good point for Finn. Hamish had always disappeared in a hurry whenever she'd cried, which meant she'd learned not to most of the time.

Slowly she quietened. 'Thank you, Finn. You have no idea how good you've made me feel.' Almost back to the woman she used to be, though she'd never be quite the same. Life's lessons had a lot to say. Now she could see that she'd always overreacted after Hamish had left her. He was supposed to have loved her for ever, and instead had made her uncomfortable about the scars because if he couldn't handle them, then who could?

'Stop it, Kate. I get that it's been a difficult time for you, but from now on don't let the past get in the way of what you want in the future. You can have it all if you don't let other people destroy your dreams.'

'I am finally starting to see that. You've upped the ante for me.'

Blimey, Finn certainly knew his way into a woman's heart. He was wonderful. But caution still held her from leaping into his arms and never letting go. He had said he had trust issues and so far she didn't know how deep those went after all the time since his relationship with Amelia had gone so hideously wrong. Amelia had done a number on him that would take some coming back from. It wouldn't be easy to let another woman into his heart or anywhere near his possessions.

Only time would show Finn that he could trust a woman he might care about. She wanted to be that woman, and because of that would hold back from throwing herself at him. Hopefully, living here, he might get to see she was worthy of his trust, because she didn't have it in her to do to Finn, or anyone, what Amelia had done. 'Maybe you should heed your own advice,' she told him gently.

'Valid point. I'll see what I can do. Now shall we move on and enjoy the rest of the evening?' Without waiting for her answer, Finn rose from the bed and found his shirt and shorts. 'Stay there. I have an idea on how to finish this evening.'

A few minutes later he returned with a glass of wine each. 'Dinner in bed.'

It was easy to laugh. She felt so good. It was as though a boulder had been lifted away, and she could breathe freely for the first time in more than two years. 'Cheers.' She tapped his glass with hers, still unable to fully accept he hadn't hurt her when he saw the scars.

Finn took the tray back to Kate's bedroom and set it on her bedside table. 'Toasted sandwiches with ham, cheese and red onion.' Easy to make and easier to eat in bed than steak and salad.

'Great.' Kate was smiling softly, as though her life had changed for the better this evening.

All because of his reaction. He had no doubt about that. She'd been expecting the worst and he hadn't delivered. There was no need. He didn't see the scarring as a problem. 'Can't say I've ever had a dinner date in bed before.' He was still reeling at what her ex had done to her though. Or, for that matter, the other men. How could anyone be critical of her scars? They weren't pretty but they did not mean there was something wrong with Kate. She was beautiful inside and out, and marks on her skin were never going to alter that.

'If this is a date, then I'd like more of them.'

He watched her face begin to colour up and, before she got too flustered, said, 'I'll have to see what else I can come up with.'

Was their fling about to become more meaningful? Was he ready? Not when he still had so many trust issues of his own to deal with. It had hurt to hear Kate say she'd put off telling him about the scars. That suggested she didn't fully trust him. She was right not to. He hadn't, and still wouldn't, mention how Amelia had fooled him into believing she was pregnant. That would mean going further than he was prepared to do.

On the other hand, Kate was wonderful, and he wanted more of her. To him Kate's bombshell had been a fizzer. It didn't matter that Kate wasn't physically perfect. Perfection was a little too OTT at times.

So, the big question for him. Did he want to be in a relationship with Kate? Did he only want more sex without serious commitment? Or did he want the whole show? He knew what he wanted. He just didn't believe he was ready. Despite the delay in revealing her biggest fear, Kate was honest, and he knew she was trustworthy. But deep inside he still didn't accept he could let go and totally trust anyone with his heart. Not yet. Not even Kate. Because he was beginning to fall for her, she had the power to hurt him so much and that was something he could not face again.

Yet he did so want to have more with her. What if he lost any chance with her by not leaping in and going for the lot? Better to be careful, than be hurt. Or was it? He had no answer to that at the moment. Kate was also vulnerable. She'd been hurt by her husband and he couldn't be responsible for that happening again either. So did he continue looking for somewhere else to live or stay here and see how everything played out?

Kate nudged him. 'If you're trying to think up other crazy dates, then stop. It's sidetracking you and I'd prefer to enjoy your company now while we eat these scrumptious sandwiches with our wine.'

'Fair cop.' Focus on the moment, and stop questioning

everything. He bit into a sandwich and agreed it was delicious, even if he'd made it.

'This was not how I expected the day to end.' Kate was smiling to herself.

'What were you expecting?'

She shrugged. 'Hadn't a clue really, but hot sex with a dinner-in-bed date was not it.'

'The unexpected is often the best.' Especially when it included sex with a stunning woman. He looked at the empty plate. 'Do you want me to make some more sandwiches?' He had made what he thought was a lot.

'Not for me. I've pigged out enough.'

'I'll put the dogs on dishes duty.'

'They'd love you.'

That was love he wasn't afraid of. Moving closer to Kate, he finished his last sandwich and went with feeling happy. It was kind of special sitting in bed with her, having a wine and eating dinner. Yes, he could get to more than like doing things like this on a regular basis.

'You know I'm not going back to my room tonight, don't you?' He couldn't leave her tonight when she'd bared her fears to him. She might get the wrong idea and think he'd been put off by what he'd seen despite saying otherwise.

'I'd tie you to the headboard if I thought there was a chance of that happening.'

'Sounds kinky.' He chuckled.

CHAPTER NINE

THE DAYS FLEW BY. Having Finn in her life made everything seem wonderful. The sky was bluer, the sun warmer. Her heart felt lighter. Kate stretched out in the bed three weeks later, smiling from ear to ear. She and Finn were getting along so well she had to keep pinching herself to believe it was real. She had a store of memories involving hot, sensual sex most nights to prove it was all true, but there were also the nights they didn't share the sheets because one or other of them was exhausted after a busy day at work. On those nights she'd love to curl up with Finn and fall asleep in his arms, but it wasn't to be.

That was when she missed Finn the most even though he was only across the hallway. Apart from the night he'd seen her scars he always went back to his bed after they made love and so it made sense that when they didn't he didn't come to her bed at all.

She couldn't help feeling superfluous to requirements when he didn't want to make love. It wasn't because her body made him cringe because he'd done it before then. She suspected he wasn't ready for more than they already had going, and worried that he was seeing this as a fling with no real future. That he might never want more from her. It was hard to take as she was falling for him more and more by the day and therefore putting her heart on the line. Better to try to win him over and lose, than back off completely without knowing what he felt. Or so she kept telling herself when the doubts flared.

Woof. Woof.

In other words, *Where's our food? And why aren't we out walking already?*

Sam and Rusty were at the door.

'Coming, guys.' No rest for the wicked, or the busy vet.

Dressed and out in the kitchen, she filled her pets' bowls and made a plunger of coffee to give her a kick-start to the day.

Finn had left a note on the bench.

Hey, there. Gone to visit a goat farmer who has animals with mastitis. See you later. X

She smiled and blew a kiss in the air. He made her heart sing. It seemed strange having the house to herself. Most mornings she and Finn bumped around each other in the kitchen and bathroom as they got ready for work, laughing and chatting as though they'd always done that. At the end of the day they usually shared dinner, though he visited his parents one night a week and some nights went to see his brother. She'd been a bit disappointed when she hadn't been asked to go along even once because it kind of said they weren't in a serious relationship. Finn usually made up for it when he got home and joined her in bed for a busy hour, wiping out any concerns she had about where they were at.

He hadn't talked any more about his past. It seemed he'd told her all he was willing to, and she had to accept that, like it or not. She was happy to have got her problems out of the way and was starting to be herself in all respects. The old Kate had no hang-ups about herself and was willing to share all she had. Finn's ready acceptance of her had opened her heart to possibilities for her future, even *their* future.

Picking up the leads, she muttered to her boys, 'Let's go somewhere different today.' She'd do something out of routine, all because she felt happy. She'd drive to Kirwee and walk around the park and the showgrounds so they could run free for a while. Nothing like a good walk to get the day under way. Along with coffee, which she needed to feel fully awake. Lately she had been feeling more tired than usual, which had to be because of all the activity she and Finn got up to.

After filling her coffee holder, she headed out to the car with the dogs bouncing along beside her. Life was good, when she wasn't worrying about what Finn thought of their relationship that didn't appear to really be a relationship. Not one where they were getting serious about each other anyway. Friends with benefits still best described what was going on, which dampened her spirits because she did want more.

Her heart was getting involved deeper and deeper by the day, but she doubted Finn's was. He might have lightened up with her, but he still held a lot back. It was there in the way he didn't share more than his body, meals and work. Maybe that was enough for now, and she was rushing things, but she'd waited a long time for a man like Finn to come into her life and it was nigh on impossible to go slow. He was everything she wanted. And some.

'Feel like a meal at the pub?' Kate asked Finn on Friday after the clinic closed. 'I can't be bothered cooking and I am not expecting you to do it either.'

'Good, because I had no intention of doing anything

more exciting than ordering in takeaways.' He was ready to sit down with a beer and unwind from a busy week dealing with too many goats with mastitis and sheep with blowfly strike. The second one had had him showering so often his skin had become very dry. Going to the pub with Kate was a perfect end to a busy day. She'd soon make him laugh and forget work.

'Whichever we go for, it's my shout.' Kate had changed out of her scrubs and dressed in those jeans that highlighted her cute butt and flat stomach while doing indescribable mischief to his libido.

It wasn't hard for her to grab his attention. He was smitten with her. She gave so much of herself even though there were still moments when she held back, as if more than the scarring was an issue. Either that or she only wanted some fun and nothing more.

It had been a busy week at night-time, which had nothing to do with animals. And that, plus not knowing what Kate thought, made the decision he'd been mulling over since a phone call he'd received from a rental company earlier in the day difficult. Suddenly there were two houses available and he had to make up his mind fast about which one to take as there were other people also desperate for rental accommodation. Peter was a mate of the agent, hence him getting first dibs.

Finn's problem was that he also had to decide whether to carry on living in Kate's house or move out. He knew he'd miss sharing the evening meals and other everyday things if he went, which worried him, though not as much as it once would've.

They were great together. Everything was going well. Almost too well. As it had done last time he'd got into a serious relationship. Though he doubted Kate saw it as serious at this point. She still held back on her feelings just enough to have him wondering what she thought about them together. Something he also avoided thinking too much about.

Except the time had come to decide what he really wanted going forward. Stay on with Kate and see how it worked out, or set himself up in another property and take time to get closer to her? If that was possible with his fear of being hurt again still hovering in the background, though not as strong as it used to be.

'Hello, Finn? Are you with me or not?' Kate sounded peeved.

'Making a call on what to do about dinner,' he said. 'Let's go to the pub for a drink first and decide what to do about eating after that.' There'd be a crowd there so serious conversation would be difficult with all the noise going on around them, which might give him time to think more about the rental properties and what he was going to do. He was coming to enjoy living in the community, which added to the ease of settling down. Not as much as he loved being with Kate, by a long way, but he could admit to wanting to settle down and this was a step in the right direction.

'We have a plan. See you there.'

'Let's walk. The parking's always diabolical there.' Not waiting for an answer, Finn took Kate's hand and led them outside, locking the door behind him. 'Any plans for the weekend?'

'Mow Dad and Mum's lawns since they'll be home next week. Mine need a cut too. Otherwise not a lot.' She glanced at him as if he might have a plan for them to do something together.

He wasn't taking her to see the houses. Not when he was in two minds about whether to ask her if he could stay on with her or go it alone while he got himself more set up for the future. This was something he had to decide for himself, by himself. Kate was important to him, but he wasn't letting her that close. Not yet.

'I have a couple of chores to do in the morning, then I want to check on the goats I've been treating all week.'

'Sounds exciting.' She smiled sadly.

'The thing is, it is in a way. I like getting out on a farm amongst the animals. It reminds me why I became a vet in the first place.'

'And why was that?'

Surely he'd mentioned it before? 'I love the outdoors and animals so it's a given really. I once thought of doing medicine—as in for humans—but figured I could have my cake and eat it too if I became a vet. Then I went and set up a city practice instead, which made no sense at all.'

But he had been in love with Amelia and doing what he'd believed was the right thing by supporting her and moving to her home town. This time he'd do it differently. He was working rurally, and planned to have a specialist practice on the side later on. No rush for anything. One step at a time. Like with Kate. If there was going to be a next time with her, as in a relationship involving everything from love to trust to having a family, he had to get it right for both hearts involved. 'Not everything goes according to plan, does it?'

Her laugh was tight. 'Can't argue with that. I suppose it would be too boring if everything ran true to schedule.

Though there are things I wish hadn't gone haywire for me, I'm still happy with most aspects of my life.'

'I'm glad to hear it.' Had she moved on from her scarring all because he'd seen it and hadn't made a big deal out of it? Or had she already been inching closer to that all on her own and he'd helped her by being honest? She deserved better than how her ex had treated her. But who didn't?

Stepping inside the pub, he paused. 'Unbelievable. It's only half full and nowhere near as noisy as usual.'

'Make the most of it,' Kate answered. 'You still want a beer?'

'Please.' He named the brand he preferred. 'I'll be over at that table in the corner.' As he watched Kate make her way through the tables to the bar, his heart was heavy. So he *was* going to move out of her place. He had to. Despite caring so much for Kate, he was not ready to give his heart away completely. He hadn't seen the houses yet, but he liked the sound of the small one-bedroom cottage on a twenty-acre block owned by a couple who lived on the property too. The agent had arranged for him to see it at ten in the morning plus meet the owners. The other house was further away and larger, so, for him, less appealing.

'Here you go.' A glass of beer appeared in front of him.

'That was quick.'

'Helps to know the bar lady. Or her cat anyway.' Kate sat her derrière on a stool and lifted her glass to her lips, bringing heat to his skin thinking about them trailing kisses all over his body.

'You seem to have a lot on your mind tonight.' She cut through his quandary. 'Want to share? Halve the load?'

'Not really. Thanks all the same, but I'd prefer to sit

back and unwind after the crazy week. Were you busy in the clinic today?'

Kate stared at him for a full minute, disappointment darkening her eyes, before she shook her head and sipped her G and T. Finally she answered quietly, 'No more than usual.'

He'd blown the relaxed atmosphere he craved between them. But telling her what was going on in his head would've done that too. Even more so. Except the time was fast approaching when he had to tell her what he was doing. He'd wait until he'd chosen which property to rent. Of course he was putting it off. He didn't want to see more disappointment in those beautiful eyes. And he wanted just a little more quiet time with her. He cared for Kate. More than cared, and was on the way to falling in love with her, so he did not want to hurt her in any way.

'Think I'll head home after this.' Kate held her glass between them. 'I don't feel like fish and chips tonight.'

In other words, she'd changed her mind about spending time with him. Fair enough. He was letting her down.

Kate closed her father's garden shed with a bang and headed for her car. She'd hit the local supermarket to grab some groceries before going home to mow her own lawns. The headache she'd earlier swallowed paracetamol to kill was still throbbing behind her eyes. A sleepless night tossing and turning for hour after hour had done its number on her, especially as she'd been exhausted already.

Something was up with Finn and she knew she wasn't going to like whatever it was. He'd been in a right old mood at the pub last night. Definitely hiding something, which got her back up. For months Hamish had hidden the fact he'd fallen out of love with her and when she had learned what was going on she'd been equally hurt that he didn't love her and that he hadn't had the guts to tell her, blaming the stinger incident for his reticence.

Apparently she and Finn weren't a couple, weren't in love, but they had shared a lot lately, so why the hell couldn't he be straight with her? Her blood was fizzing as she thought about his attitude last night and how he'd shut her down enough for her to know he was not being open with her. That really annoyed her. Even if they were only friends with benefits, she deserved better.

But—and it was a huge but—she had to tell him her news. No holding back as she had about her scars. This had to be done, and sooner rather than later.

When Kate pulled up in her driveway beside Finn's ute she didn't know whether to be pleased he was home or worried about the outcome of what she had to tell him. Lugging the grocery bags inside, she called out, 'Hi there. How's your morning been?'

No reply. Was he outside somewhere?

She began putting the groceries away, and felt her skin tighten. Turning around, she saw Finn leaning against the door frame. 'Hello. You look worried. What's happened?'

For a long moment he said nothing.

Her heart began thumping, and the headache intensified. 'Finn?'

'Kate, I've found a house to rent and as it's available immediately I'm moving out today.'

She grabbed the edge of the bench to hold herself upright. Hadn't seen that coming, had she? Yet it did explain why he'd been short with her last night. 'You never said a word, even when I asked what you had planned for this morning.'

'No, I didn't. I have been in two minds about whether to rent or carry on living here.'

'The house won, I see.' She knew she sounded angry but, hell, she was sad more than anything and that was an emotion he wasn't going to know about.

'I had two to look at, and the one I'm going to is just along the road in Kirwee. It's a one-bedroom cottage over-looking paddocks. Ideal, really.'

Ideal? Living with her wasn't so great after all. 'Here I was thinking we were getting along very well and that we had something going between us.' She was losing her cool. Blame it on the headache and the pain in her heart. Blame it on the news she had yet to tell him. Hell, blame it on anything. It didn't matter. Finn was leaving—today.

He moved into the room and sat on a stool. 'Kate, I am so sorry. We *are* getting on well, and that doesn't have to stop. The thing is I'm not ready to be in a full-on relationship. I need my own space.'

Leaning against the counter, she stared at him. 'That's honest, I suppose. Well, here's some news for you. I am just over four weeks pregnant.'

The stool hit the floor as he leapt to his feet. 'Oh, no, you don't. I am not going down that path again.' He about turned and charged to the door where he stopped and turned to stare at her, despair all over his face.

'Finn?' she said as calmly as it was possible to be, which wasn't easy when her heart was breaking out of her chest. 'Talk to me.'

'I believed in you, Kate.'

'Why change your mind?' She was pregnant, not about to slice his heart out of his chest. Or had she just done that?

Finn continued to stare at her as though she were a monster.

She gaped at him. What was going on? It was a shock, she'd accept that. She was still coming to grips with the fact she was carrying a baby, but Finn's reaction was way over the top. 'I can show you the test result if that would make it easier for you to accept.'

His mouth dropped open as disbelief filled his face. 'No, thanks. I am not such a sucker as to run with that.' He turned away, stepped through the door.

Kate's head spun while her chest pounded with pain. She had no idea what this was about. 'Finn, stop,' she begged. 'Why are you being so hurtful?'

He turned back. 'You expect me to believe you?' Sarcasm dripped off his tongue, so thick Kate sagged.

She wasn't getting anywhere. 'You don't believe me? Or you don't want to?'

'Both,' he snapped.

The air left her lungs in a rush. Never had she thought he could be so harsh, so rigid in his reaction to her news. This was a new Finn, not the man she'd come to love. 'You owe me an explanation. I didn't get pregnant by myself.'

'Really?'

A baby was a huge issue to take on board. She got that in loads since learning about her pregnancy yesterday. She was still getting her head around it, but Finn was way out of line here. They were in this together, whether he liked it or not.

'Thanks a lot. For the record, I would never lie to you. I might've taken my time about the scars, but I did not lie to you.' She turned away, unable to look any longer at the man who'd got under her radar and stolen her heart. She'd always known this day would come, but hadn't expected it to be because she was pregnant with his child. And certainly not so hurtful she felt as though her body were falling apart. 'I deserve better than this,' she muttered.

Silence engulfed the room.

She hadn't heard Finn leave so presumed he was still standing in the doorway. Well, he could stand there all he liked. She wasn't going to relent and make it easy for him.

When she could no longer stand the silence she gave up trying to be tough and turned to face him. 'Please go, Finn. Now.' He had somewhere to sleep tonight, and even if he hadn't she would still kick him out.

'I'm on my way, but…' He paused and swallowed hard as though getting himself under control. 'I'm sorry it's come to this.'

'Really?'

'And here I was thinking we were getting on brilliantly, no pressure on each other, accepting we both have issues with our pasts. Idiot.'

Finn was still watching her as though he didn't know what to do next.

'Go. Now.'

Get the hell out of here before I burst into tears or throw something at you.

Thankfully he did.

She spun around and picked up the loaf of bread she'd brought home with the groceries to bang down on the pantry shelf, followed by a box of teabags, a packet of coffee beans, a tin of peaches, eggs, sugar, rice.

'Damn you, Finn Anderson,' she shouted. 'Damn you

for that first kiss, and all the sex that followed, and for being so damned kind and understanding.'

Except he hadn't been that understanding when she'd said she was pregnant. Not at all. She dropped to her knees, her head in her hands, and gave into the tears pouring all over her face. Now she really understood and felt the truth of what she'd done. 'Damn you for stealing my heart.'

CHAPTER TEN

FRIDAY MORNING AND the clinic was flat-out busy. It had been that way since the school pet fair.

Kate wasn't buzzing, hadn't felt at all happy since Finn had walked out on her news. She did try, unsuccessfully, to join in the enthusiastic talk about the success of the day as she swallowed lukewarm coffee. 'I think we've gained quite a few more patients.'

'Like we need to be any busier,' quipped Mark. Then he looked at Peter. 'Sorry, boss. Didn't mean it.'

Peter grunted. 'You have a point though. I am going to advertise for another vet, preferably someone keen on the rural side of things. Gavin's coming back full-time next week but he doesn't want to work with cattle.'

'Can't say I blame him,' Kate muttered, glancing at Finn, who appeared more interested in his coffee than what was going on around him. If only she were able to go over and hug him tight to help remove that sad expression he'd been wearing for days, but nothing was ever as simple as that. Besides, he'd probably leap up and walk out of the room, leaving her with a load of questions she had no answers for.

'Finn, know anyone who might like to join you out in the paddocks?'

Finn finally looked up. 'No one comes to mind, but I'll give it some thought over the day and get back to you.'

'Good.' Peter stood up. 'Guess we're done here so let's get the day under way. Have a good one everybody.'

'If only,' Kate thought as she gathered her notepad and pen, and stood up to go to the treatment room. The only good thing about today was that it was Friday and the weekend lay ahead. Hopefully she'd manage a little more sleep. She'd barely slept a wink since Finn left two weeks ago, and now just one look at him and her heart broke all over again.

He might've thrown her under the bus but she missed him so much. Nothing felt right any more. As if she were treading water while trying to keep up with herself. It was as if she'd been living a lie with Finn yet she still didn't really believe that. He was too tender and caring to be the angry man who'd snapped when she'd told him she was pregnant. She'd spent hours wondering what that was about and had come up with nothing other than maybe it was something Amelia had done that had hurt him badly.

'What's up first?' she asked Di, who was walking beside her.

'I think it's Percy, the rabbit. He's got a swollen foot this time.'

Percy was known to suffer any number of ailments because his owner, a little old lady with nothing else to do but spend all her time with her pet, kept imagining problems.

'A saline solution should see to that.' Kate smiled grimly. If only everything were so easily fixed, but saline solution would do nothing for her heart.

'I think Finn's going out to see Doria's other horses this

morning. That will be hard after having to put the other two down after that accident.'

Why tell her that? She didn't need to know what Finn had on his plate for the day.

'It will be.'

The accident that had led to the second kiss she and Finn had shared. Followed by sensational sex. She didn't call it lovemaking any more. She might've been falling for Finn, but obviously that hadn't been the same for him. Pain hit her. She missed him like she'd never have believed. She'd known she was falling for him, but had had no idea just how deep she'd got. She loved him. That was it in black and white.

'Hey, Di, you got a minute?' Finn called from the other end of the hallway, sending a shiver down Kate's back. 'I need some info on Doria's horses that you've got somewhere.'

Di turned back. 'Sure. It's all in the system but I've also got a file in my desk I can lend you.'

Kate pretended not to notice the way her heart rate increased at the sound of that sexy voice. If this was how she reacted now, then the days and weeks ahead were going to be downright difficult to get through.

But, and her back straightened, she was not going anywhere. This was the job she loved. The people she liked working with were here, and she could get through anything that came her way, even seeing Finn often. They were back to being colleagues, not friendly workmates. She was broken hearted, but she was alive and kicking. She would cope, no matter what. She had to.

Finn had helped her get past the scarring problem and she would not go back to being fearful of what a man might think of her scars. Thanks to Finn, that was over. He had rejected her for reasons unknown but this time she wasn't letting that take over her life. She was still looking ahead, not over her shoulder.

Finn watched Kate slowly walk into the treatment room. She looked as tired as he felt, if not more so. Was she not sleeping either? Or was the pregnancy affecting her already? He didn't know if it was too early for her to start feeling out of sorts yet. Anyway, he was probably looking for an excuse so that he didn't have to face the truth—he'd let Kate down badly. In fact, he'd hurt her terribly.

The instinct to protect his heart had made him walk away without explaining his reaction, a terrible thing to have done when he'd expected honesty from her all the time. She'd trusted him with her truth. He should've done the same.

It isn't too late.

Or it might be. Only one way to find out. First he owed her an apology. A big one. A genuine one. One that let her know he'd be there for their baby no matter what happened between them. Kate deserved the best from him. So did their child.

'Where're you off to first?' Peter was back.

'Got to see Doria's other horses.'

'Can you go out to Johnson's after that? One of the milking goats has mastitis.'

'No problem.' He dumped his mug in the sink and headed away, trying to leave Kate behind, but she followed him with images in his head of her naked body under his, dishing up their dinner, laughing and talking together. Of the shock and pain when he'd refused to hear her out when she'd said she was pregnant.

How could he let her go? Face it. He couldn't. Everything he wanted was right here if he had the guts to go for it. Had the courage to move on and give his heart to her. Would she give him a second chance? He needed to take the risk anyway, beg her to forgive him if he had to. Deep down he knew she wouldn't hurt him. Not deliberately. But she might walk away. Sometimes a person had to take risks. If *he* didn't then he was never going to get over what Amelia did and therefore he wouldn't have a wonderful life with a fabulous woman and that baby growing inside her. Their baby.

So what was he going to do about it? he wondered for the umpteenth time. Kate wouldn't let him back in as easily as he'd wished for. He couldn't blame her. He'd been so quick to react against her news that he'd have a hard time convincing her he'd not do something like that again.

As he pulled into the farmyard where Doria waited for him, he heaved a sigh. At least he had the day to think about everything and hopefully come up with the right answers to all the questions flipping through his head.

'Hello, Kate.' Finn stood on her deck, looking tense and worried.

Which upped the anxiety tightening her as she walked across the yard towards him, determined not to let him get to her. Not until she knew why he was here anyway, and then only if it was about something that would make her happy.

Her heart sank lower than it already was. Whatever had brought Finn here, she doubted it would be anything to get excited about. He'd been so blunt when she'd told him about the baby that there was no way he could've put that behind him and want to move forward with her.

Unfortunately, now he was here it was hard not to rush over and throw herself into his arms and never let go. Seeing him at work every day had only intensified the pain of not being able to relax with him over a meal or drink, and made her more determined that she wasn't going to be made a fool of again.

'Hello, Finn. I didn't expect to see you this weekend.'

'I'm sure you didn't.'

'What's this about?'

'I'd like to talk about us, and the baby.'

So he wasn't about to get down on bended knee and say he loved her. No surprise there. Stepping around him, she said, 'Come inside. It's chilly out here now that autumn's making its presence felt.'

He followed her in without a word, which worried her further. He wasn't a big talker, but she'd have thought he'd want to get whatever he'd come to say off his chest so he could leave again.

Closing the door, she went into the lounge and sat on the sofa.

Finn took the chair opposite.

Looking directly at the man she was trying hard not to show how much she loved, she asked, 'What's up?'

'Kate, I am so sorry for not immediately believing you about the baby.' He stood up and paced to the window and back, sat down again. 'But I do believe you. I did almost immediately after my outburst. It was obvious you were telling the truth by the way you spoke and the stunned look in your eyes when I reacted how I did. I couldn't be more sorry if I tried.'

Once again he'd stunned her. 'I'm six weeks along.' Her eyes were locked on him, as though daring him to trust her. She still didn't think he fully believed her.

'Kate, I truly accept we're having a baby.'

She wasn't rolling over. 'Why didn't you come and talk to me earlier, then?'

'Because I didn't realise that I was stuck in the past and therefore ignoring the fact I was well on the way to finding the future I so dearly want. You've done that for me, Kate.'

She tried to relax, but there was more to come. At the very least, she needed to know what role he thought he'd have in their child's life. 'That's a start, I suppose.' She wasn't being very forgiving, but she had a broken heart to protect. And a baby that needed her.

Finn stood in the middle of the room, watching her. How the hell had he managed to walk away? She was everything he wanted. He loved everything about her. 'Kate, I need to tell you what else happened between Amelia and me.'

'Go on.'

She wasn't making this easy, but then he could hardly blame her after the way he'd reacted about the pregnancy. Deep breath. 'After I found out about the bankruptcy and then Amelia's gambling addiction, I was gutted. Angry. And hurt. I spent a lot of time trying to figure out where to go from there. Amelia had done a number on me and I struggled with that. But I also understood that addiction is not something that goes away because a person wants it to.'

Kate remained quiet. Was that good or bad?

He continued. 'I went to stay with a friend while I got my head around everything. Amelia went home to her parents, who thought I was the guilty party because I should've seen what was going on. They might've had a point. Who knows?'

Again she said nothing, making his heart thump heavily.

'Two weeks after everything blew up in our faces, Amelia came to tell me she was pregnant and suggested we try again.' He stopped. Inhaled again and continued laying his heart out there for Kate to see all the cracks. 'I wasn't going to walk away from my child so I knew I had to work something out. We agreed I'd move in with her at her family's home until I got a job and could pay for a rental property. I got a job within days at a local vet clinic.'

He looked away, staring out of the window for a long moment. This was it. The real crux to everything that had gone down with Kate. 'At the end of my first week some of the staff invited me to the pub as a welcome gesture. I couldn't say no, even though it meant forking out money for a round of drinks I didn't have spare.'

Kate nodded in understanding. 'Fair enough.' She wasn't giving anything away.

Finn watched her, his head and heart filled with sorrow. He wasn't getting anywhere with this. Might as well get it over and done and leave. 'I walked into the pub and there was Amelia, dressed to the nines in clothes I'd never seen before, drinking and chatting up a man at the bar. Drinking while pregnant? That made my blood boil. I went up to her and demanded she come outside to talk to me. Surprisingly, she did, and that's when I learned she was not pregnant, and never had been. It had been a ruse to get me on side so she didn't have to go without anything until she found another, richer man. Which she did within a very short time.'

Kate locked a fierce gaze on him. 'You outright rejected me at the mention of the pregnancy. No matter what happened in the past, I did not deserve that. It's no excuse for accusing me of not telling the truth.'

He deserved that, but it still hurt. 'I'm not making an excuse. I'm explaining. I don't want your sympathy. You deserve the truth. I didn't think I was ready to give my heart away again. But over these past two weeks I've missed you so much I feel I'm continuously breaking into little pieces.'

She sat, her back straight as possible and her head high. 'You think I'd do anything half as bad to you as Amelia did?'

'No, Kate, I don't. Not at all.' Never.

Her face softened.

Was that a good sign? Was this going to work out after all? He waited patiently.

'You've helped me through the rough stuff, too. I feel whole again.'

Wow. Finn risked reaching for her hands, and sighed with relief when she didn't withdraw them. 'You're amazing. You know that?'

Kate blinked. How could she stay mad at Finn? He'd laid everything out for her to see and know what drove him. A small laugh escaped. It felt so good to have her hands held in his. This was Finn, the man she'd inadvertently given her heart to. She didn't want it back. But they weren't out of the woods yet.

'I wasn't up front with you about my problems, Finn, and I regret that. But it also helps me understand why you lashed out when I told you I was pregnant. I can't believe Amelia lied to you about being pregnant.' Talk about a manipulative woman.

'Which is why whenever I came up with a reason to stay with you, I found another to go. I was fighting putting everything behind me because it seemed too risky when really all I had to do was look forward.' His hands tightened around hers. 'Kate, sweetheart, from now on I'm all about getting on with living the life I've always dreamed about. I love you so much, Kate. I really do.'

Wow. Finn loved her. All the tightness around her heart melted in a flash. Dreams really did come true. There was a flutter in her stomach, and a lightness in her head.

Take this slowly, Kate.

True. She was so relieved about what he'd told her that instead of taking it slowly and working through it all she was rushing in without stopping to consider everything. So she slowed everything down by asking, 'How do I know you won't reject me again?'

His eyes widened and he stared at her for a long moment. 'Is that how you see it? No, don't answer that because that's exactly what I did.' His chest rose and fell rapidly. 'It was instinctive to protect myself. I didn't stop to absorb what you said. If I had I wouldn't have said those things. I swear I wasn't rejecting you deliberately, Kate.' His face was full of remorse.

Her heart turned over. She knew what it was like to have her heart broken, so understood where he was coming from.

She hadn't always dealt with her hurt very well either. 'Can you see us working through future problems together?'

'I don't want it any other way. But I can't promise that I won't make mistakes as we go along either.'

'Nor can I. We're normal, I guess.' Did she hold out any longer? He'd not held back in answering her questions. Anyway, what was the point when she knew exactly what she wanted? That was to open her heart to him completely, to be honest and open.

'Finn, I love you. I have done for a while.' The pain of watching him leave the other week had finally been replaced by love and warmth and relief, no more hesitation. 'Damn it, Finn, I love you so much it hurts. In a nice way.'

He was up on his feet and hauling her into his arms, his mouth coming closer and closer until he covered hers with those sensual lips she'd missed. She fell in against him, her hands feeling his warmth as she ran them up and down his back. He kissed her deeply, a kiss filled with promise and love and a future.

Tipping her head back, she stared at the man who'd changed her life for ever in the best way possible. 'Finn,' she whispered, and swallowed. Started over. 'Finn, we've both had trust issues so we understand each other well. I am totally in love with you. I can't imagine living my for ever without you.'

'Back at you.' He drew a deep breath. 'And our child.'

'And our child.' She nodded, her smile getting wider and wider. Then those wonderful lips returned to hers, pressing hard, devouring her with a kiss that was better than any she'd ever experienced with him. That said it all. She loved Finn. He loved her.

He said softly, 'Sweetheart, I can't believe this.'

She tipped her head back and smiled like crazy. 'I can.'

'I'll be pinching myself so often just to remind myself how lucky I am that I'll be black and blue all over. You're the best thing ever to happen to me.' Finn swung her up into his arms and headed for her bedroom. From now on their bedroom.

She'd found the man of her dreams, and she wasn't letting him go.

Monday morning and the usual meeting before the week got properly under way. Kate sat beside Finn in the tearoom, trying hard not to look besotted, and knowing she was failing. There'd been a permanent grin on her face since Finn had told her he loved her. In between packing up Finn's few belongings and shifting them back to her house, where this time his clothes were sharing her wardrobe, they'd spent a lot of the weekend showing just how much they loved each other. Her bed had never had such a workout. Or her body.

'Right, I think that's everything,' Peter said. 'Unless anyone's got something to raise, we'll get on with the line-up of animals booked in this morning.' He was looking at her as if he expected her to say something.

Just as well, because she and Finn did have an announcement to make. 'I have something to say.'

Finn leaned a little closer so his arm was against hers as he gave her a nod. They'd discussed this over breakfast that morning.

'Finn has moved back into my house. This time we're sharing the main bedroom.'

'Woohoo.'

'Awesome.'

'About time.' Peter grinned.

'That's great news, guys.'

Finn held up his hand. 'Wait, there's more.' His arm went round her waist, pulling her closer to his divine body. 'We're getting married in June and you're all invited.'

The congratulations coming from everyone filled the room with noise, and made Kate's heart swell with happiness. This was wonderful. These people had become such a part of her life and now they were sharing her and Finn's excitement. She held up her hand and called above the racket, 'But wait, there's still more to come.'

Slowly everyone quietened, watching her avidly. 'Come on, do tell.'

Kate glanced at Finn. The love in his eyes made her melt on the inside. 'Okay, here it is. We are having a baby in late November. Watch this space. Oh, and this time you're not invited to the event.'

If Kate thought her news would be received quietly with a few lovely comments, she was wrong. The room exploded with laughter and she was being hauled to her feet for hugs from everyone. Finn was clapped on the back by the men and hugged by the women. She caught his eye and winked. Love you, she mouthed.

'Back at you,' he said.

Then Di held up her phone. 'Sorry, everyone, but we have an emergency. A cat versus puppy. Both need attention.'

Warmth spread throughout Kate. Nothing got in the way of helping sick or injured animals. This was her life and she had all she could possibly want. Her hand touched her abdomen, and she smiled. These days it was about the baby and nothing to do with the past. She and Finn had found their futures—together. She couldn't be happier if she tried.

* * * * *

If you enjoyed this story,
check out these other great reads
from Sue MacKay

Healing the Single Dad Surgeon
Paramedic's Fling to Forever
Marriage Reunion with the Island Doc
Resisting the Pregnant Paediatrician

All available now!

MILLS & BOON®

Coming next month

NURSE'S TWIN BABY SURPRISE
Colette Cooper

'I can see you're dressed in scrubs but I can't just let you crack open this man's chest without confirming your identity.'

Glittering sapphire eyes met hers and her breath locked in her throat. He was even more stunning in the flesh than he was on screen...almost impossibly so. She was aware the team around them were continuing with the CPR – compressions were being quickly but steadily counted aloud; monitor alarms still rang out reminding them the patient's vital signs were critically outside of parameters. She knew what was going on around her but for a moment, the centre of her focus were the two deep blue eyes looking back at her, laser like, penetrating, silently assessing. Her determined resolve not to find him attractive wavered. Straightening the front of her uniform, her instinct telling her to look away, she held his gaze.

'Max Templeton,' he replied, one dark eyebrow raised and clearly having completed his appraisal of her, 'cardiothoracic consultant.' Was he trying to supress a grin?

Continue reading

NURSE'S TWIN BABY SURPRISE
Colette Cooper

Available next month
millsandboon.co.uk

COMING SOON!

We really hope you enjoyed reading this book.
If you're looking for more romance
be sure to head to the shops when
new books are available on

Thursday 19th December

MILLS & BOON

Afterglow Books is a trend-led, trope-filled list of books with diverse, authentic and relatable characters, a wide array of voices and representations, plus real world trials and tribulations. Featuring all the tropes you could possibly want (think small-town settings, fake relationships, grumpy vs sunshine, enemies to lovers) and all with a generous dose of spice in every story.

♪ @millsandboonuk
⊚ @millsandboonuk
afterglowbooks.co.uk

#AfterglowBooks

For all the latest book news, exclusive content and giveaways scan the QR code below to sign up to the Afterglow newsletter:

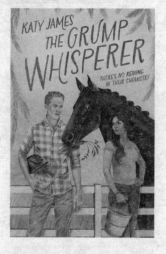

LET'S TALK
Romance

For exclusive extracts, competitions and special offers, find us online:

f MillsandBoon

X @MillsandBoon

◎ @MillsandBoonUK

♪ @MillsandBoonUK

Get in touch on 01413 063 232

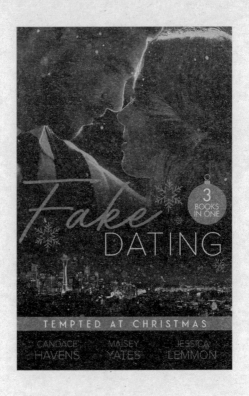